Crimson Moon

CASCADE WOLVES
CRIMSON SERIES

By
M.A. Kastle

M.A. Kastle
PO Box 812
Helendale, Ca 92342

Crimson Moon / M.A. Kastle. -- 1st ed.
Paperback: ISBN 978-1-7359534-2-7
Ebook: ISBN 978-1-7359534-3-4

To everyone that has supported the Cascade Saga, thank you. I hope you enjoy Crimson Moon (what Mr. K refers to as the bridge series) and the Cascade Wolves. This book was fun to write. To those who helped with this book, I give you, my thanks.

Mr. K and the Minions- Love you always.

Books by M.A. Kastle

Cascade Saga Series
Bone Chimes
Dark Awakening

Cascade Wolves – Crimson Series
Crimson Moon

Horror
Tales of Woe (Collection)
A Curse Revisited – The Legend of Noah Blyth (Novella)

CHAPTER ONE

Dr. Clio Hyde gripped the edge of the seat and was thankful for the five-point harness, as rubber squealed and the tires of the med van fought to cling to asphalt. With their breakneck speed, metal clanged, shelves rattled, and the monitor looked like it wanted to take flight. She and Mandy, a paramedic, grumbled their complaints, then whispered prayers they didn't crash.

Clio knew Lieutenant Torin Bouldin, head of the soldiers, didn't care and wasn't listening when he needed to get them to the trauma center as fast as possible. A life was at risk. A human life. Roaring down the two-lane road, he pushed the med van with its off-road tires faster as they headed straight for the center of Trinity. A small city in Northern California, Trinity was named after the three encampments built as prisons for the paranormals, magic-born, and their family members during the late 1800's. Back then, miles of steel walls held thousands of prisoners labeled non-human. Now Trinity was home to humans and non-humans, and was governed by a human, Mayor Taylor Hughes, and Baron Healey Kanin, alpha of the Cascade pack.

"Have you gotten through to the trauma center?" Mandy asked as she clutched the side of the bench to stay seated. At the same time, she kept a hand on the gurney and watched the detective's limp body strain against the restraints holding him. They both looked at him knowing it wasn't going to move—it was locked in place—but another corner at the speed they were travelling might prove to be too much.

As one of the trauma doctors employed at Celestial Medical Center, a non-human hospital specifically for the magic-born, Clio was privy to direct phone numbers, and choosing the closest trauma center she called the attending physician. With the relationship between the magic-born and humans sometimes strained, or they just didn't like one another, he or she might not take Clio seriously. Shaking her head, no, the phone continued to ring, and it was trying her patience.

"Come on pick up," she mumbled as she watched the heart monitor. Clio checked the oxygen, the mask, then the dressing on the wound. She was able to stabilize him, but Detective Watt remained unresponsive since Director of Enforcers, Rutger Kanin, extracted him from his truck and placed him in the med van. "Dammit, answer your phone." It wasn't like she called the information desk. A man's life was at risk, and if they didn't answer, she was going to bust through their doors whether they wanted a werewolf in their facility or not. Clio counted two more rings before a male voice announced. Finally, she had reached Edgewood Regional Medical Center and was speaking with Dr. Greer.

"Doctor Greer, this is Doctor Hyde with Celestial. I'm inbound with a Caucasian male, roughly forty, with a single gunshot wound to the chest."

"Celestial, the non-human hospital. You can't bring a non-human here," he stated flatly.

Here we go. "The victim is Detective Watt with the Organized Paranormal Investigations and he is human," she explained. "He's stable but non-responsive."

"Has he been exposed to the lycanthrope or therianthrope viruses?"

"Negative." She wanted to roll her eyes.

"Is one of yours responsible? I'll call the sheriff's department," he warned.

Like I would call you if it was one of mine. Clio shook her head. "Negative. Detective Watt was working with Director Kanin of the Cascade pack, who is currently investigating an abduction." *Sure he was. He absolutely wasn't going in with guns blazing to save his girlfriend ... fated mate*, she corrected herself. "If you call the OPI they'll confirm Detective Watts' identity, and he was working with Director Kanin." Clio listened to the seconds stretching out. "I advise calling law enforcement, this is an ongoing case," she added, hoping it swayed the doctor.

"ETA?"

"Five minutes."

"Are you equipped with MedTech?" Dr. Greer asked as if he doubted her competence.

"Affirmative," Clio stated. She turned to the monitor, saw their approach of the medical center, and entered the ID of the med van. Their location, Med One, identification numbers, and her classification appeared on the screen. He had to give her clearance; she carried the highest rank a doctor could have.

"I have your pin," Clio confirmed. It was time to see if Mr. Personality was going to say yes or no.

"I see you, Med One. The link is live, go ahead and proceed with the download. Doctor Hyde, have your ID ready."

The call ended, leaving Clio with silence. *Bye to you, too.* She looked at Mandy. "He didn't tell us no."

"No, he didn't. But we have to get there in one piece," Mandy mumbled as she leaned with another sharp turn.

The tires cried out, then skidded, making the van jump, and after fifteen painful seconds Lieutenant Bouldin straightened the vehicle out. Clio let the harness hold her as she sat up and continued entering Detective Watt's present condition and her treatment—the medicated combat gauze to stop the bleeding and fluid to keep his heart beating—into the laptop and the MedTech software. When she finished, she sent it to Edgewood, then she took her badge out of a side pocket of her black BDU pants and clipped it to her form-fitting, black compression shirt. Clio and Mandy had both taken their holsters with their Glock 21, 45 caliber pistols tucked inside, along with their radio equipment and knives, and locked their gear in a safe.

Before cutting Detective Watt's shirt off him, Mandy had taken his badge, holster, gun, and personal items and locked his belongings in a portable safe. Lieutenant Bouldin wore his holster, gun, and radio, refusing to give up his gear, and thankfully he wasn't getting out of the med van, so she didn't care if the humans thought they were playing commando. With a radio, laptop, and navigation all connected to the communication's center at the Enforcer's office, if anything happened to the team and they needed help, it was easy for communications to send the team's location. Knowing her pack was infiltrating a witch's coven, who had killed several werewolves, were responsible for murdering one of their own, holding Director Kanin's mate hostage, and were brazen enough to shoot a human detective, it pushed her patience. They needed to get the detective to the hospital and get back to Butte Springs.

"ETA, in one," Lieutenant Bouldin reported.

Clio looked at Mandy, then down at her black shirt, black BDU pants, combat boots, and the Cascade pack's crest identifying them as werewolves and knew showing up at a human trauma center looking like she was going to war wasn't going to give Dr. Greer the professional doctor vibe she needed. There was nothing she could do about it when they left Foxwood, the estate of Baron Kanin, and had prepared for a fight while they looked for Jordyn Langston, their newly appointed soothsayer and mate to Director Kanin.

A soothsayer. Clio had her doubts if it was real or if the baron had created the position to project the pack's power. Or because he ended Miss Langston's self-induced separation and rogue status and needed to give her something to do. Her doubts didn't matter when the witches believed Miss Langston was the perfect sacrifice to raise their God of War to help them destroy mankind. That's what was waiting for them at Butte Springs, and she had no idea what the team's status was.

With the thought, a chill slid down her spine and her nerves jumped under her skin, feeding her anxiety. A sacrifice. Director Kanin nearly lost control in front of human law enforcement when they found what was left of young Zachery's body and a note—really, a poem—for them to find. It promised the end of Miss Langston's life and her role in the afterlife as the god's lover. The unknown on the mountain was going to drive her insane. *Hurry up.* As if answering her unspoken demand, the med van's tires skidded in front of the double doors of the trauma center and came to a hard stop.

"There's a team approaching with a gurney," Lieutenant Bouldin stated.

"Affirmative," Mandy replied as she stood. "Let's get this going and get the hell out of here."

"Copy." Clio unlatched the harness, walked to the doors, and opened both as a man—early fifties, gray hair, gray eyes, and faded blue scrubs—met her.

"Doctor Greer." His voice, calm and assuring matched his stare.

"Doctor Hyde." Clio felt her voice sounded weak, her name rushed, as if she were stressing out like a rookie. *For god's sake, sound like you've gone to medical school and have been working as a trauma doctor for the last four years.* She hopped out of the med van, turned, and grabbed the edge of the gurney at the same time Mandy did, and they hit the lever releasing the locking mechanism.

Dr. Greer and the others watched Clio and Mandy lift the gurney—they didn't use the lowering mechanism—as if it weighed nothing, then the legs popped, and the wheels hit the concrete. Clio knew they were staring; two women, or two men would have struggled with the gurney and the detective's weight. A little reminder they weren't human and were werewolves. Behind her, another man—younger, maybe late twenties, dressed in scrubs—approached, stopped, then pointed a handheld barcode scanner at her. If she wasn't focused on not looking like a werewolf, she would have made a joke. Instead, she turned enough to see him, then lifted her ID badge. He moved closer, and two beeps sounded.

"Identification confirmed. Doctor Clio Hyde contracted to Celestial Trauma Center, Priority Superior. Active member of the Cascade clan. Enforcer. Lycanthrope. Secondary, *Wight.*"

All that status and she was a *Wight.* The definition of Wight; a person of a specified kind and regarded as unfortunate, or a creature. That's what she was, a creature, an unfortunate creature. A not so pleasant way of defining her as half shapeshifter and half human. The human half not human enough for the human world, and the shapeshifter half not werewolf enough for the magic-born world. The shapeshifter half reminded her Purebloods, old families like the Kanins and Langstons, and the other quarter, half shifter, half magic-born, Illuminates made up the Cascade pack. That too was a show of power and established the baron's status. She was neither. It drove her to prove to the baron, Director Kanin, and Captain Wolt she was as strong and as capable as a Pureblood or an Illuminate.

Why it mattered, Clio didn't know. Yes, she did.

Not all children born to human/shapeshifter couples carried the virus and shapeshifted. If the offspring was going to shapeshift, puberty, hormones, emotions, and changes in the body acted like boosters to accelerate the transition. In her case, her father was a Wight, her *genitor*, the male parent carrying the lycanthrope virus. When she turned sixteen, her parents watched for her to go through her transformation, so when her seventeenth birthday came and went without her wolf coming forward, they accepted she wasn't going to be a werewolf like her father. As time continued to march on and she remained human, she saw the hurt in her father's eyes mixed with relief as if he hadn't wanted her to carry the burden. Then she turned eighteen.

The transition had taken her in the middle of the night, her wolf tearing her human body apart as it reshaped bones, muscles, tendons, and organs in agonizing pain. The first shift can be deadly, the human body fighting against the animal coming forward, and if they fail to fully shift, the primal instincts of the wolf trying to take over the mind can drive them insane. As her screams filled the house, her mother called the baron, and with his help she shifted into her wolf form. To say she was a late bloomer was an understatement and reminded her she was inferior to Purebloods and Illuminates. Wights rarely advanced in the pack and were considered a weaker species. The polar opposite of Wights were Purebloods; they shifted as young as toddlers, and continued to gain power and strength as they matured. It was the same with a magic-born/shapeshifter, Illuminates, they shifted at a young age and their strength and power continued to increase. Not human enough. Not werewolf enough. Damned place to be in.

Dr. Greer examined her work, no doubt judging her skill, scanned the tablet in his hand, and met her gaze. "We have his information. He's stable letting us transfer him here, no need for you to go inside."

"Have it your way." Clio gave him her back and unbuckled the restraints freeing the detective. Taking several steps back, she watched as a flock of people rushed in with their equipment to swarm him.

"This is his gear. Badge, weapon, personal items. I have an inventory list if there are any questions," Mandy explained to the nurse as she handed the portable safe to a woman wearing purple scrubs. "The combo is written on the card, it also has my number, and the number to reach Director Kanin."

The young woman with pale brown eyes stared blankly at the metal box with the pack's crest imprinted on its top. "Do you want it back?"

"Affirmative. You can call me, my number is right there, and I can come by and get it, or someone can take it to Celestial. It's up to you," Mandy replied.

"Fine. Expect it at Celestial." She took the box, the card, and walked away.

"Yes, ma'am," Mandy mumbled.

With rushed orders, the team of multicolored scrubs wheeled Detective Watt into the hospital and disappeared.

Wight. She knew it, lived it, but the word stung. Like being denied entrance into the hospital. Clio watched the double doors slide closed, and told herself she was damn good at her job. She saved lives just like they did. Magic-born, Pureblood, Illuminate, Wight, or human. So why did she have a complex? Clio knew the answer, and it ate at her. As a trained enforcer, she pulled duty as the Kanin family's doctor and backup when needed, but nothing took away from not being one of them. She was pulling double duty now, enforcer and doctor, and was headed to Butte Springs.

"Load up, we're leaving," Lieutenant Bouldin ordered.

"Nice people," Mandy joked with tension in her voice. "I live for dealing with humans."

"Right. I bet they have a great bedside manner." Clio lifted the gurney at the same time as Mandy, and they rolled it on the tracks to lock it in place.

The Highguard, the elite and powerful of the magic-born, shared the Pureblood and Illuminate's opinions and saw all Wights as lesser. Among Wights there was an unspoken line drawn between those born and those infected. It didn't matter if the Highguard granted the transition, which they rarely did, or they were infected against their will, they were a lower class of Wight. Maybe it made those born with the virus feel closer to the Illuminates, she didn't know, and it didn't matter to her.

After the Crimson Years, the war between magic-born and humans, and the destruction of the encampments, a government funded agency called Patriot Angels worked to create antidotes for the lycanthrope and therianthropy viruses. She knew a handful of infected shapeshifters who survived the Patriot Angels' experiments, and one of them was Aydian. He served in the Army, had an exemplary military career, then was deemed unfit for service, medically retired, and turned over to PA, who wasted no time in infecting him with the lycanthrope virus.

After infecting him PA's doctors injected him with NH01. The intent behind the vaccine was to decrease the potency of the lycanthrope and therianthrope viruses. They wanted to eliminate the viruses' effects on the body and to reduce the overall strength of the shapeshifter and eradicate their heightened senses. The shapeshifter wouldn't grow stronger, making their animals weaker, and it would take their healing, regenerative capabilities, and immortality from them. If NH01 proved successful, they would require every shapeshifter, Pureblood, Illuminate, and Wight to have the injection. Weaker meant manageable. With magic-born and shapeshifters living among humans, they needed security, something proving to the population they remained in power, at the top of the food chain, and they controlled the weak. PA was also responsible for White 47, a synthetic silver, and Cobalt 27, a synthetic cobalt used as weapons against the Fae, shapeshifters, and other magic-born. Even with their weapons, the humans' downfall was not believing in magic and then giving the entire paranormal community name tags like lycans, therians, and non-human, to make them less lethal. Human. Non-human. The great divide.

Despite their best efforts and years of testing NH01 was an epic failure. Aydian's senses were as heightened as hers, if not that of an Illuminate's. He was strong and disciplined while he was in the Army, and became a strong, powerful werewolf who was at Butte Springs working side by side with

Director Kanin and Captain of Enforcers, Ansel Wolt. He didn't have an issue being a Wight. That also bugged Clio.

She lingered for a second, taking one last look at the trauma center, her thoughts clinging to Dr. Greer's expression as he examined the compress, then climbed into the med van, Mandy behind her.

"We're buckled in. Try not to kill us," Clio ordered.

"We can't die, Doc." Lieutenant Bouldin smashed the accelerator. The diesel engine roared, making the tires squeal and he peeled away from the hospital. On the open road, he gunned the med van and headed back to Butte Springs.

"Base, Med One is en route," Mandy reported.

"Copy," Blix responded. "Relaying your position."

"Copy." Mandy gripped the edge of her seat as the van leaned into a corner.

The reception they received at the medical center, the speed the lieutenant was traveling, and what they were going to find at Butte Springs maxed her anxiety, its claws digging into her. She fully understood Lieutenant Bouldin's need. As head of the soldiers, he hadn't wanted to drive them to the hospital ... no, he wanted to be there with Director Kanin, the enforcers, his soldiers, and in the middle of the action. He wanted to be there to be side by side with his people and take back one of their own.

And there were witches to kill.

CHAPTER TWO

Absolute insanity.

Ansel felt the energy spill out from the woods and slither toward them, its feel like quick bites of evil while the night pressed down on them. As the chanting heightened to frenzied cries and howls, his wolf growled in warning, its urgency flowing through him and making his heart pound. He checked his surroundings, found Rutger, and watched the director's body tense as he stared at the thicket of trees where the noise was coming from. Ansel couldn't comprehend how Rutger was keeping himself from losing his mind, knowing his mate was here somewhere in the midst of the chaos.

"While they're busy chanting, we'll search the cabins. We need confirmation everyone is gathered by the trees," Rutger began. "I don't want anyone at our backs."

"Affirmative," Quinn replied. He took quick glances at the lights and trees, then to the cabins. There was no telling what they were going to find.

"I'll take the left. Ansel, Quinn, Aydian, you're with me. Kia, Charles, Alex, Kellen, take the right," Rutger ordered.

"What are we going to do when we confront them?" Kia asked. Her black-lined eyes narrowed as she drew imaginary circles on the butt of her gun with her fingertip.

"Dart them," Rutger answered.

"Was hoping the darts were a joke. And when we get to the chanting crowd and they turn their madness on us, what are we supposed to do? Ask them to stop, it hurts our feelings?" Aydian asked, his sarcasm blatant. "They're witches." His eyes darkened to blue steel, seeming to try to pierce the darkness hanging between him and the witches.

"Dart them," Rutger repeated with a growl in his words.

"Why? They murdered Zachery, cut him apart," Kellen argued. "They have one of ours. Each one of them deserves to be torn apart."

"A bullet is too kind," Aydian added as he looked at his dart gun.

Rutger growled a low sound, getting their attention. "They do, every one of them. We. Are. Not. The. Law. And the law is on its way. You're going to dart as many as you can." Rutger took his dart pistol, made sure it was loaded, shook his head, and met the gazes of the enforcers and soldiers. "We're going to the left. You're going to the right. Now move."

Ansel eyed the enforcers as they split up and started toward the cabins while the edges of the single-lane, dirt road faded and blended in with the dried grasses, clover, and small rocks. When night swallowed them and distorted their forms, he took his position behind Rutger and headed in the direction of the closest building. Anxiety radiated and adding to the uneasy feel, a male voice could be heard over the witch's chanting, as if he were inciting their excitement.

They approached the first cabin, its rickety door hanging free from the frame, weather beaten siding swinging in a breeze that carried the sweet, like syrup, scents of herbs and flowers. Ansel didn't know if he was going to be able to handle the smell of tea ever again after being at Butte Springs.

He inhaled the bitter scent of burnt wood, the dull fragrance of lavender, sweet chamomile, and werewolf. A female werewolf. Pack. Jordyn had been there. He entered behind Rutger, dart gun drawn, and felt ridiculous, as if someone was playing a joke on him. Using his senses, which had failed him more than once when he dealt with the witches, he searched the open room.

"She was here," Rutger growled, his eyes blazing gold.

"Affirmative. Her scent is hours old," Ansel replied softly. "The room is empty."

He watched Rutger search then stop at a stone slab. Looking like an altar that would have taken several men, if not a crane to move, he approached it and shuddered when he saw ropes, dark stains, and evidence someone had been tied down. Smears of oil shone in the sliver of light from the full moon beside pottery smelling of Wolf's bane. They sedated her.

"I can smell her," Rutger whispered. He touched the altar, running his fingers through the glistening oil, and brought them to his nose. "Over whatever the hell they used on her, I can smell her."

"First cabin, cleared," Kia reported.

"Second cabin, cleared," Aydian reported.

"Affirmative," Ansel responded into the mic. "She isn't here. We need to move on."

"Affirmative." Rutger turned, his gold eyes blazing through the dark, his shoulders thickening with his wolf.

"We'll find her," Ansel assured. He stood at the door while Rutger stalked out of the room. They needed to find her. To save her and to save Rutger.

Weeks before Jordyn's kidnapping, there were security details for Rutger's brother's upcoming wedding, which had turned into a publicity nightmare. Additional security was needed for the arriving leaders of factions, and for the dignitaries from the Highguard. With representatives coming from the ruling council of all magic-born, it proved Baron Kanin and the Cascade pack were worthy of their attention and held eminence with the Highguard. Everything needed to be perfect. Then a serial killer began leaving bodies on Cascade territory, and the human task force of Organized Paranormal Investigations requested help from Rutger. His attention was split between the wedding, the murders, and dealing with the OPI.

In the middle of it all, the older sister of the bride and Rutger's ex-girlfriend, Jordyn Langston, arrived in town. She left Trinity three years earlier without a word to anyone, moved to Butterfly Valley where her photography was displayed in a gallery, and dated a human. When people found out she had chosen a human over Rutger, the Second to the Alpha, rumors flew, his emotions spiraled, and his pride crashed and burned. Jordyn's return to Trinity prompted the baron, without Rutger's knowledge, to have a shadow watch her and two soldiers follow her, until she became their soothsayer. With the shadow and soldiers standing down, her life in Butterfly Valley coming to an end, the witches moved in and kidnapped her. Rutger had been helpless to stop them.

"Director, you're needed," Charles reported.

"Did you find her?" Rutger asked. He left a neglected cabin, the wood floors bowing like they wanted to give up, and marched toward another one.

"Negative. You need to see this," Charles urged.

"Negative. Continue the search." Rutger ripped the door off a cabin and peered inside.

"It's urgent," Aydian insisted.

Ansel met Rutger's angry glare. "It's Aydian." The enforcer dealt with Post Traumatic Stress Disorder from being infected with the lycanthrope virus, then experimented on for three years by the doctors of PA. If he thought Rutger needed to see something, he had a good reason.

"Fuck," Rutger mumbled.

"Location?" Ansel left the cabin with Rutger beside him.

"Fourth shack on the left," Kia reported.

Through brush and limbs, the moon cast white spiderweb shadows on the rocky ground. The unusually cool, June night continued to slip into the lower temps and promised to take them to the low forties while the treetops swayed in the chilled breeze. Above them, a dull melody played between pieces of silence when the chanting paused. Ansel stopped and looking up saw bones—human and animal—dangling from limbs, their shapes catching shards of light then vanishing into the dark. He started to tell Rutger when he saw he had been left behind. Running to catch up, he followed him, and they closed in on the cabin and caught the distinct scent of death. The bone chimes were forgotten when he recognized there was a body, he paused, bodies inside. *Do not be Jordyn.*

"Is this the last cabin?" Rutger asked as he approached.

"Affirmative. You need to go inside. She isn't here, but you have to see to understand what they did to her," Charles explained. "We need Doctor Hyde."

Rutger looked at the cabin, then at Aydian, who nodded his head, his darkened eyes holding a wild edge. "Fine. Kellen, find out where Med One is."

"Sir," Kellen replied.

Ansel stepped inside, holstered his dart gun, covered his nose and mouth with his hand, and walked through the dark room. Kia waited at a door, her eyes reflecting whatever she had witnessed, and when they were close, she opened it for them, letting a bank of stench escape. Ansel coughed, trying to get the sharp taste of spoiled food, rotting corpses, and Wolf's bane out of his mouth. The combined strength of the odors sucked the oxygen from the air, making it thick and hard to breathe. Remaining behind Rutger, they stalked down the narrow plank stairs to the dirt ground, and into a room bathed in a sallow glow from yellow lights. Ansel cringed as rage and hate coiled inside him from the abuse of one of his kith and kin.

"I'll kill them," Rutger growled.

Jordyn's clothes, jeans and one of Rutger's T-shirts, stained with blood, and several crimson-stained zip ties sat next to the bars of a cell. Draped over a makeshift bed was a dirty, green, wool blanket, its ends sitting in the fine dust of the floor, and there were plates of meat scattered across the dirt. They both stopped when they saw the blackened skin of arms, legs, and patches of hair wired to a frame in the shape of a cross.

"What the hell is that thing?" Ansel asked.

"I don't know. I don't want to know."

"They locked her in here for days," he mumbled in disbelief.

"The meat on the plates is from a werewolf. I bet they used Zachery. She would have recognized him," Rutger growled. "She would have felt him."

After the wedding, the baron made Jordyn the sooth-sayer for the pack. What it meant, Ansel didn't understand, but it did explain the baron's need to protect her. As a result of her return and new status, Rutger reclaimed his birthright as Second to the Alpha, and they were announced as One-Flesh and fated mates. Ansel had his doubts, as did the entire pack, but standing in the room staring at the remains proved someone thought they knew what she was.

"They're getting crazy," Kia reported, her voice breaking.

Ansel clicked the mic at his collar. "On our way."

Rutger hesitated, his body tight with tension, then took lead. Leaving the room and cell behind them, they exited the cabin and joined the waiting group. Thankful for fresh air, Ansel inhaled and exhaled, but couldn't get rid of the stench clinging to his BDUs.

"Med One is en route," Charles reported.

"Copy. I want teams of two. You'll go in from the west, south, and north sides to surround them," Rutger ordered.

Ansel froze when a female scream cut the air at the same time power surged from the clearing like an electrical shockwave. Insanity. "Shit."

Rutger twisted around, roared, and took off, his werewolf speed propelling him in the direction of Jordyn's screams and the clearing. Absolute chaos.

"Pair up and take your points." Ansel clicked the mic. "Remember, you're darting them. No hand to hand, no shifting, no hard ammo."

No one replied as they dispersed into the wood's shadows, leaving him to follow Rutger.

Clio gripped the seat, gave Mandy a sideways glance, and saw her knuckles were white from holding on. Lieutenant Boulder hit the dirt road, skidded the tires, and pushed the med van faster. She wanted to point out they weren't going to be any use to anyone if they crashed.

"I wish I knew what we were going to find," Clio said as she raised her voice over the sound of gravel hitting the sides of the van.

"Me too. There's been no word from communications. It's either no news is good news or they're in trouble." Mandy adjusted her earpiece and risked letting go of the seat to check her radio.

"Was thinking the same thing." Clio wore her tactical belt, drop down holster, gun, and radio, and felt like she wasn't doing anything. The tires kicked up rocks, sending them flying into the van and the woods.

"Med One, downloading their location to your nav," Blix reported. "Standby for orders."

"Copy," Lieutenant Bouldin replied. Seconds ticked by as silence stretched out. "ETA, fifteen minutes. Be advised, the baron is at the location and requesting Doctor Hyde ASAP. You've been instructed to have tranquilizers at the ready."

"Clarify." Was she going to give someone a shot or did she need to have a tranq gun ready? Was it for a werewolf, maybe Miss Langston, or a human, one of the witches?

"Tranq gun for the director and the soothsayer," Blix answered instead of the lieutenant.

This was ridiculous. "The director?"

"Affirmative."

Clio and Mandy looked at each other, their previous thoughts becoming a reality. The team was in trouble. "We'll use the rifle for multiple shots, and 3cc darts."

"Yes, ma'am," Mandy replied.

"ETA in eight minutes," Lieutenant Bouldin informed them.

"I'm not taking any chances, I want the cage," Clio ordered. She hated thinking she needed it, but the baron advised tranqs for the director and the soothsayer. She understood Miss Langston, she had been held prisoner and her condition was unknown. But the director, the strongest in the pack? Miss Langston's life must be at risk and Director Kanin was doing what an overprotective wolf would do if his mate was threatened. Lose control. Bestial. Bloodlust.

"Five." A low growl ran through the word.

The lieutenant's anger for having been ordered to drive them to the hospital reared its head. Yes, saving the detective's life was important and added to the overall relationship the pack had with human law enforcement. Still, compared to fighting side by side with his soldiers, the enforcers, and saving the director's life and the life of a pack mate, it was insignificant.

Clio and Mandy lifted two doors, waited through the van jumping the road, and at the same time slid the gurney inside. She reached up, pulled a lever, and a White 47 cage unfolded as it lowered to the metal floor of the med van. Leaving it loose in case she had to transport it, she turned her attention to a door. The lock clicked, she took a gas-based rifle and handed it to Mandy, then a second one from the rack. The dart rifles weren't secure with a code because by themselves they were harmless. She took her badge, waved it front of a small refrigerator door, entered her number code, and heard the lock disengage. Inside sat a variety of bottles and vials of sedatives, painkillers, BioThropy, and syn sanguine solution that were protected in shatter proof containers. *Good thing*, she thought as she waited for the corner to end. At the bottom, she pulled the drawer open, and reached for six preloaded darts.

"We're here. Get your guns, Doctor," Lieutenant Bouldin ordered.

Clio handed Mandy six darts. "If you need all six, we're in trouble."

"I hate this." Mandy loaded the weapon and secured it over her shoulder.

"Agreed," Clio replied as she loaded the gun. She was a part time enforcer, full time doctor, and was heading out with a rifle full of tranqs. Her target ... one of her own.

Clio set the rifle on the cage, stepped around it, opened another drawer, and snatched a backpack. It held the same supplies as she used on the detective, plus treatment specific to shapeshifters. BioThropy, to stop the spread of silver in the circulatory system, and syn sanguine fluid, to replace the loss of red blood cells and hemoglobin while increasing the platelet count. Shoving her arms through the straps, she grabbed the rifle, prayed she wouldn't have to use it, and reached for the door.

Before she touched the handle, Lieutenant Bouldin opened them, letting the night's fresh air filter into the sterile inside. "Locked and loaded?"

"Affirmative, sir," Mandy replied. She stepped out, rifle ready, and exhaled when needles of power landed on her. "There's some serious shit going down."

Clio stepped into the night and directly into a wash of magic that skated over her, causing her to pause. She didn't usually feel the effects of magic or power—she blamed her human side—unless it was the baron, and he was projecting his authority. Director Kanin's power warned her, but it wasn't the same. Not being sensitive to their magic and the strength making them an alpha made her ultra aware of her actions. She needed to remember to act submissive around the baron, his family, and those with rank within the pack. This was different. It was thick and felt sinister as it lashed out like it was searching for something. Someone. And she knew who it was. The soothsayer. When screams, yells, and cries streaked in the air and a dozen orders flooded her earpiece, she raised the rifle. *What the hell is going on?*

"Doctor Hyde, now," Baron Kanin ordered into her ear. A growl held his voice, his concern overriding his authority.

Clio looked at Mandy, then the lieutenant, and asked, "Location?"

"Ansel is coming for you," Baron Kanin replied.

She started in the direction of light, a dim glow from a cluster of trees, deciding walking was better than waiting, and tried using her senses. There were werewolves everywhere, and another force, like magic, ebbed around the shapeshifter's essences. Clio needed to know if she was right, and if the lieutenant and Mandy sensed more than she did.

"Are you feeling the magic?"

"Affirmative," Lieutenant Bouldin answered. "Evil. It has to be the witches."

"Same here. The enforcers and soldiers are everywhere." Mandy replied.

Clio's doubt with her senses eased as she marched around enforcer vehicles sitting off to each side of the dirt road while others were parked wherever they stopped and looked abandoned. Not a good sign. They had been in a rush.

"Doctor Hyde, this way." With the sight of Dr. Hyde, Mandy, and Torin, Ansel's anxiety eased. He skidded to a stop, waited for them to follow, then headed in the direction he had come from.

"What are we looking at?" Clio asked.

"Miss Langston has been injured. Director Kanin isn't taking it well. Prepare to tranquillize the director and treat Miss Langston for multiple lacerations." He wasn't going to go into more detail. The baron would protect Rutger, Jordyn, and the pack from human law enforcement and their judgments when everything was exposed. And it would be exposed. The night was a cluster of problems.

"Multiple lacerations?" Clio asked as she took a mental trip through her backpack.

"Affirmative. Also, starvation and dehydration. She's unresponsive." Ansel paused, listened to the commotion in the woods, used his senses to track the enforcers and soldiers, then started walking. He couldn't sense the witches, the magic giving them cover and allowing them to escape. He hated it.

"Why hasn't she shifted?" Even unresponsive, Miss Langston was a Pureblood, and should have been able to shift and heal her wounds. Especially with Director Kanin's assistance.

"Prolonged exposure to Wolf's bane. She's paralyzed." Ansel heard Dr. Hyde inhale as he kept his emotions locked down, not wanting the others to feed off him, the magic was enough. The image of Jordyn's arms and throat bleeding freely sat in front of him the same way Rutger's desperation and dread clung to him. Jordyn was fighting for her life as Rutger held her in his arms.

"How long are you talking?" Clio asked. Her five feet four inches, with med pack and rifle, struggled to keep pace with Captain Wolt's six feet four inches, long stride, and his easy gait over the rough terrain. Clio assumed the day the director found the letter and Zachery's mutilated body was when Miss Langston had been kidnapped. Obviously, she was wrong.

"Four days. We don't know what else happened. Because they're witches, it's clear they were combining other plants, and some kind of magic was involved, to what extent no one knows," he explained. Ansel stopped, grabbed the rifle from Dr. Hyde, tucked it into his shoulder, and took his stance.

Clio gasped, shocked by Captain Wolt's speed and precision, and stopped beside him. His set jaw, narrowed eyes, and stance were that of someone who was comfortable holding a gun and pointing it at their target. She was going to ask what happened when the director's roar, rough with pain, made her freeze. Made them all freeze. It took her seconds to search the scene and comprehend what was happening. Miss Langston's body was wrapped in a white sheet that had been turned to varying shades of scarlet, crimson, and pink. Then she saw the slash across her throat as it bled freely. Her arms had been flayed and were bleeding, her skin ashen and gleaming with a sheen of sweat. Clio couldn't tell if Miss Langston was breathing or if her heart was beating. There was no missing the fact that Miss Langston was dying.

Director Kanin's knees sank into the soft dirt, his black BDU pants beige with dust, and his top glittering with blood. Clio stepped back, putting Captain Wolt in front of her, and Mandy beside her, not wanting to get caught between the armed enforcers. The director's body thickened, his face losing the edges of its human shape, and the hazy gold veil of his wolf's beast hovered over him. He was losing the battle with his beast and was going to go Bestial. Tranquilizing him might slow the progression, but what would happen when the tranquilizers wore off? *To stop him, we should use real ammo.* Damn, she hated thinking that way, but he would survive.

"Give her to me," Baron Kanin ordered, his voice targeting the director.

Director Kanin growled his answer, a low threat, and hugged Miss Langston's limp form to his body, leaving crimson smears on his cheeks and lips. Clio's heart felt like bands were wrapping around it and had started squeezing at the sight. She needed to get to Miss Langston before she bled out and they lost her to true death.

"I need to get to her," Clio pleaded into the mic. "Let me help."

"Negative," Baron Kanin replied sharply. "She's trying to shift."

The radio cut off, and Clio shook her head in disbelief. She was standing ten feet away from them, medical bag in hand, and was told to stand down. With a perfect view of the scene, she knew Miss Langston wasn't trying to shift ... they all knew she wasn't trying to shift. She wasn't freaking moving. Clio looked at Captain Wolt's back, his muscles tight under his body armor, his stance solid, and the rifle trained on Director Kanin. The Director of Enforcers.

"She's dying. She isn't trying to shift," Clio whispered as she took a step closer to Captain Wolt. "I have to get to her before it's too late."

"Stand down, Doctor Hyde," Ansel warned. Despite watching Rutger drowning in sorrow and losing himself to the beast while his mate bled to death in his arms, Ansel would obey the baron's order and stop Dr. Hyde. Fear and the unyielding pressure from magic intensified his emotions, making it harder to stand by and watch when the pack might lose two lives this night.

Fated mates. It was a curse.

"Give her to me. I will help her, son, please," Baron Kanin pleaded. "You're running out of time."

"Mine," Rutger thundered. His lips drew back to expose his lengthening canines, while the bones of his face moved under his skin like snakes, tightening his flesh as his wolf emerged. "She. Is. Mine."

Ansel sucked in a breath as the magic holding the air and concealing the witches tore apart as if someone had taken a knife to it, and the shreds, as if they had a life of their own, fell to the ground and died. With the spell hiding the witches from the enforcers and soldiers broken, they hit his senses and told him where they had scattered.

"Find them," he ordered into the mic. "Find all of them." He knew Jordyn destroyed the spell, but how she did it he didn't understand.

"Affirmative," Kia replied. Her rushed reply was followed by enforcers and soldiers as they began their search.

"Son, give her to me." Baron Kanin reached for Miss Langston's unmoving body, and when he touched her, it caused her arm to fall to the ground.

The carvings had stopped bleeding, leaving muscle and tendons exposed. Clio's instincts screamed Miss Langston was gone. When the magic fell and the air returned to normal, she died. To convince herself she was wrong, Clio searched for Miss Langston's heartbeat but couldn't find it in the mix of werewolves. She had to be wrong. There was no way Miss Langston died right in front of her after the baron ordered her to stand down.

Director Kanin roared, its exhausted sound carrying pain and sorrow. His gold eyes met Baron Kanin's as he stood and gently handed Miss Langston over. After the baron eased her to the ground, he cut the saturated bindings to reveal jagged lacerations surrounded by blackening bruises, dying flesh, and symbols riddling her bare body. Clio focused on the wet streaks glittering on her cheeks and her half-open copper eyes staring at nothing. Dead. She cried knowing she was going to die in the arms of her mate.

Clio's heart sank as she stood by and watched someone, Pureblood Jordyn Langston, and Second to the Alpha's mate, die a true death. She didn't do anything to help her. Was stopped from helping. She felt sick as bile teased her throat, and inhaling, she was unable to get enough oxygen. Fighting against the feeling of failure, she clenched her hands in fists.

In front of them with his wolf twisting into a beast, Rutger's roar coiled with his fury and primal torment; his eyes glowed gold and stared at nothing and everything.

"Now," Baron Kanin roared.

Ansel sighted on Rutger and pulled the trigger. It wasn't the same as a gun, it let you know you shot with a blast of air. The first dart hit him in the left arm, the second in the right arm, the third in the right thigh, the fourth in the left thigh. He would have liked to hit him in the stomach, greater impact, but Rutger was still wearing his body armor. With the fifth dart sticking out from the side of his throat, Rutger dropped to his knees, his arms loose at his sides, a growl leaving his parted lips.

"Enough," Clio ordered as unshed tears burned her eyes. Five darts were excessive, and she couldn't take watching Captain Wolt continue to shoot the director.

Ansel hesitated with the sixth shot, then ignoring Dr. Hyde, the next dart went deeper into Rutger's neck. Only then did he hand the empty rifle to her, and leaving her and her complaints, he stood guard over Rutger. It needed to be done. He wasn't going to lose Rutger or Jordyn. In the distance, sirens blared and the distinct sound of a helicopter closed in. The damn calvary had arrived. Beside him, Rutger knelt in dirt, pine needles, and leaves, his arms at his sides, his breathing coming in harsh gulps of air, as if he couldn't breathe. His emotions radiated from him like a building storm. The tranqs weren't going to last long. Having done their job, and he couldn't handle seeing them move with his pulse, Ansel grabbed the two darts from Rutger's neck, pulled them free, then removed the ones in his arms.

"Son, listen to her heartbeat," Baron Kanin began. "Listen and take solace."

Rutger's entire body shuddered as his hands hit the ground, stopping him from falling and landing on his face. Jordyn's wolf form lay in front of him, her dark coat a contrast to the crimson-stained sheet.

"Mine," Rutger whispered as he reached for her.

"Yes, she is yours," Baron Kanin assured. Keeping his eyes on the director, he ordered, "Doctor Hyde, get the cage and put Jordyn inside. I'll transport Rutger and meet you at Celestial."

"Are you sure you want to take the risk?" Clio asked. Normally she wouldn't question her alpha, except this was a definite exception to the rule.

"Affirmative. Cage Jordyn."

"Sir," Clio replied. She pushed away what she had witnessed, Miss Langston dead, the guilt riding her because she failed to help her. Dead one minute and alive the next, it couldn't be real, it wasn't real. None of it felt real. Clio watched the wolf breathing, didn't believe it, and headed to the med van.

CHAPTER THREE

Ansel merged to the turn lane, slowed, and turning right drove between the statues depicting the Norse goddess Eir, of mercy and healing, and the serpent entwined staff depicting the Greek god Asclepius, to enter Celestial's parking lot. Behind him, the baron and baroness drove their SUV, and behind them were the baron's sentinels, Sousa and Troy. The caravan a show of Cascade's status and sovereignty.

It had been over two weeks since they rescued Jordyn and Rutger had nearly gone Bestial. *Bestial,* the definition of the magic powering the symbiotic relationship between the human spirit and the wolf spirit becoming corrupted, and like poison saturating the shifter's body, warping its mind, and destroying the balance between the two. Ansel never imagined it was real. Never thought he would witness its force corrupt someone, much less Rutger. All because death had cradled his mate and tempted to take her to the ether. The resting place of the truly dead. Had Rutger lost himself, his animal form would have turned into a humanoid covered in fur with a wolf's head, standing over eight feet tall on hind legs, with muscled arms thicker than its human counterpart, claws with the dexterity of human hands, and a wide chest. It resembled a creature from myth. A monster with insatiable bloodlust.

To prove he was in control of himself, his wolf, and Bestial wasn't a threat, Rutger preformed multiple stress tests. He shifted from human to wolf form without losing control of his wolf, exercised in both forms, and attended counseling sessions with Dr. Carrion. To test his emotional strength, he visited with Jordyn, and then had to leave her without being agitated or confrontational.

Like today, Ansel thought. He didn't know how Rutger was going to react when he left Celestial while Jordyn remained behind.

With the combination of the wedding between Tanner, the baron's third son, and Bailey, Lord Langston's daughter and Jordyn's sister, the kidnapping, witches, and the murder of several werewolves, Cascade had become headline news. Everywhere. Reporters had been at the courthouse, Celestial, at the gate of Foxwood, and Rutger's house trying to get information. As Rutger prepared to be discharged, Ansel worried who would be waiting at the hospital.

"Base, Celestial is secure," he reported. Mildly surprised with the lack reporters, his anxiety backed off and stopped attacking his thoughts. He pictured the hospital parking lot overrun with media vans, photographers, and broadcasters, the way it had been for days. There weren't any at the front or at the back. He hoped the attention and the news hounds had jumped to some other tragedy.

Rutger and Jordyn's lives had been put under a microscope, and everything they did scrutinized. Like Rutger's position as Director of Enforcers, and how Jordyn had lied about what she was—werewolf, lycanthrope—to the gallery she worked with and Mr. Myers, her human boyfriend. And a soothsayer, no one knew what it meant but that hadn't stopped the media from going wild and adding whatever colorful addition they wanted. Ansel would have liked to be escorting both Rutger and Jordyn but on Dr. Carrion's recommendation, she was staying at least a week longer. Her therapist wanted her to work through emotional issues associated with Post Traumatic Stress Disorder. One of the subjects Dr. Carrion pointed out was how Jordyn blamed herself for what happened to her, Rutger, and for Zachery's murder.

A topic Jordyn wouldn't discuss with Dr. Carrion, because it was priority one top secret, was that she died, her heart stopped. The baron forced her wolf to obey the moon, and then pulled her animal from her. With her human body too weak to shapeshift, and her human mind open and impressionable, the baron incited his magic and drove his power into her wolf's essence. Jordyn's wolf obeyed the power of the full moon, and with the baron's magic, she shifted, and her life was returned to her. The witnesses swore on their lives to keep it a secret, and those who thought they knew were told they were wrong, like Dr. Hyde. The baron went as far as to tell her she didn't know what she was talking about because her senses weren't as developed as a Pureblood's or Illuminate's. It was harsh, especially when Dr. Hyde had a hard time accepting she was a Wight.

"Base, the Kanin family is secure," Ansel reported.

"Copy. Advising Doctor Hyde," Mandy replied.

With the two vehicles following, Ansel drove around the light, pewter stone and concrete twenty-five-thousand-square-foot building, its green windows gleaming emerald in July's early morning sun. They didn't stop at the guest and patient entrances, or the emergency entrance, and passing three med vans they headed toward the back. He paused as the gate rattled across its rail, and when it cleared the two lanes, he drove over the steel, pulled up, and made sure Sousa was following. With the attention they had been getting, the baron decided it would be safer if they picked Rutger up at the secluded security entrance.

Ansel turned his truck around and backed into a space on the right side of the double doors while Sousa, mirroring him, did the same thing and parked on the left. Between them, the baron backed up and stopped in front of the doors. Getting out of his SUV, the baron's thick-muscled build matched his authority and power, while his gray, button-up shirt, jeans, and boots gave a relaxed look. Baroness Kanin with her classy style of pale pink, fitted blouse, beige slacks, slip on loafers, and thin frame was the exact opposite of the baron. Werewolves aged slower than humans, and Purebloods aged even slower; the baron and baroness were over three hundred years old, their age never showing. The tragedy aged them like years never had. They looked older, both wore the creases of worry on their faces and tension in their shoulders. They had faced losing their eldest son, his mate, and their kith and kin.

As they approached the set of doors, they opened, and four hospital security guards stepped out. One on the left and one on the right to hold the doors, while the other two flanked Rutger and Dr. Hyde. When he was outside, Rutger squinted and shuddered as if trying to shed the hospital from his skin. Ansel waited by his truck, not wanting to get in the way of the baron and baroness, while wanting to grip his brother's shoulders to make sure he was real.

"Son," Baron Kanin greeted. His dark hair was styled away from his angular face, his coffee brown eyes held an edge of gold, while his shirt, open at the collar, exposed his tattoo of the Pureblood Kanin ancestry.

"Good afternoon, Baron Kanin," Clio greeted. When Dr. Carrion advised her she would be escorting Director Kanin to the secured entrance her nerves had hit an all-time high, which she didn't think was possible. Why wasn't Dr. Carrion escorting his patient?

"Doctor Hyde. How's Jordyn?" he asked.

"She's well. The director was able to visit with her today, and they talked. She shows improvements every day," Clio explained.

She faced grieving families, car accident victims, and consoled the waiting family members and on a good day she was happy to patch them up and send them on their way. The director and Miss Langston were different. Clio wasn't equipped to help them. Dr. Carrion oversaw their care, and hadn't let the director see Miss Langston until he felt they were ready. When they were allowed visitation, Miss Langston wore her yellow, cotton tunic, matching baggy pants, and thick socks, while the director wore a white T-shirt, loose sweats, and slippers. They looked beaten, sleep deprived, depleted of energy, and their pain scarred their faces. Clio, Dr. Carrion, and two of his assistants observed the meeting, making sure neither lost control nor had an emotional breakdown. She didn't think they were violent, especially Miss Langston—she didn't meet your eyes when she spoke to you. Instead, she stared at the floor or to the side with a faraway, dazed look. The traits of a submissive. And Rutger, he stared at Miss Langston.

"You're sure Jordyn isn't ready?" Baron Kanin asked. Rutger, wearing a worn T-shirt, cotton pants, and worn-out running shoes, turned toward her, making strands of his dark brown hair with amber highlights fall forward.

"Negative. Doctor Carrion wants to see her for another week, for her emotional wellbeing," Clio answered, and reminded herself when she was at Celestial she wasn't an enforcer.

"I understand," Baron Kanin replied. Taking Rutger by the arm, he urged him toward the car. "Come, son, let's go home."

"My bag," Rutger mumbled. His foot dragged as he stepped to the side, looked around aimlessly, and his dull eyes landed on the baron.

"I put it in the car." Ansel wished there was something there telling him Rutger was inside.

"Has Lord Langston been here to visit with Jordyn?" Baron Kanin asked. He let go of the director when the baroness gently held his forearm in her small hands.

"Affirmative." Clio cringed when the director didn't oppose the hold, as he would have before. "They've had a couple of meetings. He talks about her photography, his work, Bailey, and Tanner. She doesn't respond, and when he asks her directly, she nods or shrugs her shoulders. She was verbal today with Director Kanin. Isn't that right, Director?" Clio asked.

Miss Langston wasn't just dealing with the emotional repercussions of having been kidnapped. She returned to Trinity, faced her failed relationship with Director Kanin, was made the pack's soothsayer, became One-Flesh with the director, lost her place with the gallery—who had gotten a court order to keep her from entering the building—and her human ex-boyfriend was causing problems. He had tried to see her on multiple occasions. Average height, angular, thin face, dismal blue eyes, with his styled, sandy blond hair, and overflowing with self-importance was the polar opposite of the director. He had worn a crisp, white button-up, tie, suit jacket, slacks, loafers, and looked every bit of the professor he was when he demanded to see Miss Langston. Clio looked at the director. His rich, coffee-colored eyes, dark mahogany hair, muscled body, and authority had Clio wondering what Miss Langston had seen in the human. Maybe it was what she didn't see. Herself. The pack.

"Yeah," Rutger answered absently. He inhaled, looked at the hospital, his eyes glassing over, then exhaled.

Ansel watched the interaction between the three of them and thought about the report the baron had given him to read to better understand the situation. And to respond accordingly if something happened. Dr. Carrion diagnosed Jordyn with Post Traumatic Stress Disorder with social isolation, severe anxiety, flashbacks, fear, emotional detachment, and depression. He had diagnosed Rutger with PTSD, stating agitation, irritability, hypervigilance, and avoidance of the trauma.

The baron ordered the doctor to retract the medical records, stating the Second to the Alpha, Director of Enforcers, and fated mate to the pack's soothsayer wasn't going to have paperwork confirming a negative emotional diagnosis. The Highguard could use it to take Rutger's birthright, position as director, and the Sacred Writ of Rutger and Jordyn's joining of One-Flesh. The information could also be used to take the baron's title and the pack from him using the canon, vote of no confidence and weakness. *It proves how ruthless and fucked up the Highguard is, and solidifies the reason the Cascade pack keeps a low profile.* He nearly laughed with the thought. The witches plunged the pack into the media, human law enforcement, and it was a matter of time before the Highguard sent someone from the Prosecution Administration.

They were living on borrowed time.

"Son, let's go home." Baroness Kanin urged Rutger to the backdoor of the SUV. He paused for a heartbeat, and Ansel prayed he did something resembling the old Rutger. He didn't. He dutifully followed the baroness, and when she opened the door he ducked inside, sat back, and stared forward.

As a precaution, Clio didn't think the director cared, she waited for the baroness to shut the door, making it harder for him hear them. "It's going to take time. He responded to the physical stress and emotional strain from Miss Langston's kidnapping, her injuries, and believing she was going to die, and having nearly lost himself to the beast. Like Doctor Carrion explained, once Director Kanin realized she was all right, he began feeling each emotion, and Doctor Carrion helped him understand them one at a time and how to deal with them. Seeing her and being able to talk to her lessened the effects of the event. Having said that, since he had shown signs of going Bestial, Doctor Carrion would like you to keep a diary of Director Kanin's behavior."

"Of course. Thank you, Doctor Hyde," Baroness Kanin offered with unshed tears in her eyes. "We need to get him home." She lightly touched the baron's sleeve, gave him a shielded gaze, and walked to the passenger side door.

Leaning into the car, Ansel said, "I'll be by to see you." Rutger turned slightly and nodded, his usually intense eyes dull and blank. "Take care, brother." He waited for a response, but Rutger continued staring at something, which wasn't Ansel, without saying anything. Closing the door, he walked back to the baron. "Let me know when you're ready."

"I will," Baron answered. "What is Jordyn doing to keep her here?"

"Doctor Carrion believes she is sleeping in wolf form to feel protected. Doing this will do one of two things; one, she won't shift into her human form because it means she is vulnerable to attack, or two, once she shifts and remains in human form, she won't shift back to her wolf form. She believes being a werewolf is the reason Mr. Platt kidnapped her. She is also dealing with the emotional distress of losing her place at the gallery, which was her lively hood, and those who were her friends have turned their backs on her because she's a werewolf. Doctor Carrion wants her to sleep in human form, face the changes in her life, and express how she feels about them." Clio waited for the onslaught of questions and saw the baron stare at her like she was from another planet.

"She is here with us, that's what's important," Baron Kanin finally replied.

Clio wasn't so sure. If Miss Langston wasn't a Pureblood, her insistence to disregard her wolf wouldn't be detrimental to her life and health. In Clio's opinion, Miss Langston needed to go home where she would feel comfortable, without living under a microscope, and eventually she would accept her wolf and life in Trinity. She could understand Dr. Carrion's concern, though. No one knew how a person was going to react, the mind was a tricky bitch.

"Hopefully with the director leaving it will be an incentive for her to want to complete the tasks so she can also go home. I know she wants to, but she has to work for it. Doctor Carrion isn't going to let her have her way simply because she demands it, and I agree with him." Sure she did, because she was a therapist. Not.

Clio wasn't her therapist, wasn't a therapist at all; her specialty was emergency medicine. She was playing the middleman because Baron Kanin wanted to talk to someone from the pack and not a Deviant, a human with supernatural traits. Being the head doctor for the future med room at Foxwood, an enforcer, and having a working relationship with Captain Wolt, meant it was up to her. Plus, the Chief of Staff ordered her, citing the same reasons. It didn't help her nerves as Baron Kanin stared at her with burnt gold eyes of the Kanin family, exuding all the authority of an alpha.

"I understand. Thank you, Doctor Hyde." Baron Kanin gave her his back, took three steps to the car, got in, and sat behind the steering wheel.

Clio held her breath as she watched Captain Wolt pull away, followed by the baron, and lastly the sentinels, the trio driving out of the concertina wire topped fenced area of the hospital. With them on their way, she turned, and released the breath she had been holding. She'd done her job, or at least part of it. Walking through the open doors, into a narrow hallway, the guards falling in behind her, she groaned when her cell phone rang. Clio snagged it from her pocket, and seeing the number wanted to ignore it. Maybe she hadn't done her job.

"Captain Wolt, what can I do for you?"

"You did well. Standing up to the baron and keeping your shit together isn't easy," Ansel offered in a casual, friendly tone. Listening to Dr. Hyde explain what was going on with Jordyn, then answering the baron's questions made his respect for her triple. First her attention to Rutger and Jordyn at Butte Springs was exemplary, then the continuation throughout their treatment proved she cared about the pack.

"Because I'm a Wight?" She marched down the hall, took a left into the break room—the guards continuing without her—and finding a chair, she sat down. The conversation she had with the baron, that her senses weren't like the others and she hadn't sensed Miss Langston's death, blared in her head. Despite the shot of fury, Clio was too stressed and too tired to be angry and offended by Captain Wolt. It didn't stop her from giving him her default retort. Her shift was over in a couple of hours and she wanted to go home, where silence and a tequila neat were waiting for her.

Ansel's frustration sat in his exaggerated inhale and ex-hale and he hoped she heard him. "Negative, Doctor. Because there is a court case coming and both Director Kanin and Miss Langston will have to testify so justice is served, and in order for either of them to do so, they have to be of sound mind. The baron has made you and Doctor Carrion responsible for making sure they pass the state re-quired evaluations. And because Baron Kanin was staring you down as his oldest son, Second to the Alpha, sat in the car as if his brain has taken a vacation. And because his daughter-in-law is locked up and you hold the damn keys, that's why."

His clipped words cut into her, making her rub the back of her neck with regret, then she slid her palm down the leg of her scrub pants. "Captain Wolt, I'm sorry, it's been a long day." *I have a giant complex.*

"No apology, necessary." Ansel hit the button on the screen of his laptop, ending the call. Dr. Hyde had serious baggage about being a Wight, and thinking she wasn't good enough, and he wasn't going anywhere near it. He had his own shit. His job. Rutger.

Ansel stopped, checked to make sure the baron and sen-tinels were behind him, waited for several cars to pass, then pulled out to the main road and started toward Foxwood. He couldn't stop himself from thinking there was something about Dr. Hyde he liked. He knew her when she was an active enforcer, had partnered with her a couple of times, but the time he had spent at the hospital talking to her, depending on her, he felt they had become closer. Each time they spoke he stared into her baby blue eyes with streaks of honey, that held a sliver of a challenge, and interest stabbed him. Maybe it was the way her eyes stayed the same color when she shifted into her wolf form. It could also be her strength, her tenacity. Why she continued reminding everyone she was a Wight, he had no idea. Ansel was lying to himself. He did know why, he accepted her for who she was. Not what she was.

Clio hit the big, red button, placed her phone carefully on the table, because she would smash it otherwise, and sat back. "Way to be an idiot," she mumbled.

Captain Wolt must be under a lot of stress after taking over the enforcers, standing in for Director Kanin, and being the first person Baron Kanin called. Yet, he took the time to call me, and complimented me on a job well done, and I accuse him of thinking I'm incapable of doing said job. She saw his brown eyes marked by bronze, narrow on Director Kanin as if wishing there was something he could do to help. She shook her head. His compliment meant more to her than she wanted to admit, and rather than accept it, she told herself he had ulterior motives. He was lying to her. He couldn't possibly be interested in a Wight. She was an idiot.

"Doctor Hyde to the emergency room. Doctor Hyde, report to the emergency room."

Thankful for reality, Clio grabbed her cell, shoved it in a pocket, and opened the door to meet Dr. Kolt. "I was on my way. What are we looking at?"

"Med Two brought in two boys," Dr. Kolt reported. His six-foot height didn't intimidate her five feet four inches, like Captain Wolt's six foot four inches. Their strides were well matched as they both turned and headed up the hall.

"What's the problem?"

"They were jumping from trestle to trestle when they missed. They fell about twenty feet and sustained broken bones, lacerations, and concussions," he replied.

"Trestle?"

"Trestle bridge. In this case it's a railroad bridge. When the train was crossing the bridge, they jumped." Dr. Kolt gave her a brown, nearly black look that said youth was wasted on the young.

"Magic-born type?" Clio quickened her pace and mentally prepared herself for the energy of the ER. If it was a witch, a Fae, or anything besides a shapeshifter those injuries were potentially life threatening.

"Shifters. I've set their broken bones to heal properly, the lacerations have been cleaned and covered with treated bandages, and once they shift their concussions and injuries will heal. If they aren't already, the boys are teenagers, football players, healthy, and will heal quick," Dr. Kolt explained, his deep voice holding his doctor tone.

"Then why am I needed?" Clio slowed her pace, eventually coming to a stop.

Dr. Kolt walked ahead of her, stopped, and faced her. "One is a werewolf from Cascade, the other is a therian from a clowder, I can't remember the name. Both parents are saying it's the other kid's fault." He looked annoyed, which for an elf of the Seelie court and high privilege, it was probably his resting bitch face.

"Of course they are," Clio mumbled. "Granite Peak?"

"Correct," Dr. Kolt answered. "Do you know them?"

"I know Cascade has a friendly relationship with them. I also know they're bobcats and are difficult to deal with on a good day. It doesn't explain why I need to be there. Are they ready to be discharged?" Clio knew what this was and wanted to remind everyone she was a doctor not a hostage negotiator, or a mediator. Rather, she was the hostage.

"Yes, we're ready to discharge them. The parents won't

let us and won't leave until someone from the Cascade pack talks to them." His heavy gaze held his frustration; the scowl he was trying to keep from creasing his face caused winkles fanning out from his brown eyes. His hands were in the pockets of his crisp, white lab coat like the action was going to help his patience. "I figured you were the best choice since you've been dealing with Baron Kanin."

Right. Clio wasn't going to take their orders and listen as they bickered back and forth. She took her cell and dialed communications, explained to Mandy what was going on, and that she needed two enforcers, cautionary.

"You think you need enforcers?" Dr. Kolt asked. He started walking, making him slant his head to look at her with narrowed eyes. "Won't their presence contradict the statement Celestial stands for? I mean, you're inviting Cascade's police force, which resembles a military unit, into this hospital. It's supposed to serve as neutral ground and sanctuary for the wounded and defenseless."

With Miss Langston in the building, safe and secure, it didn't ease the nervous feeling of having an argument in the ER. "Celestial is a safe haven when treated as such. Cascade pack owns this hospital, and their presence will be a show of force and remind the clowder exactly whose territory they're on. The key, Doctor Kolt, is I have part of the baron's kith admitted here, and will use force first, I'm not taking chances with outsiders. Plus, parents can act crazy when it comes to their kids. No matter how rotten they are or what problems they create, like this, the truth seems to escape the parents. Add in two different factions and the authority of Cascade and you have problems," Clio replied. Everything had the potential of becoming a political nightmare, and Cascade had had enough.

They turned left and started down the hallway, the voices

of angry parents drifting toward them. Before they reached the ER, she heard arguing, two females doing most of the yelling. *Great. Moms.*

"Dr. Hyde," Tony greeted with a grin. "Morning."

"Morning," she replied absently. She watched the med van driver for a second as he headed for the paramedic's lounge and shook her head.

Dr. Kolt pushed the doors open, making them swing back and giving her time to pass. They met four of the hospital's guards and a wall of magic from shifters trying to prove their strength. Two guards wearing pale blue polo shirts with Celestial's crest, beige tactical pants, and shoulder holsters, stood beside a bed while the second pair stood beside the other. The parents created enough of a commotion someone called the guards, and they felt they needed to stay. Closing the distance, Clio recognized the familiar feel of werewolves but not the clowder; they felt feline enough she knew they were cats, but it ended there.

If she had been a Pureblood or an Illuminate, she would have sensed their animal and logged their scent. As a Wight, she would have had to ask, then explain it was for the report, not because she lacked the ability. It would take seconds for disdain to cross their faces when they realized what she was. Her mind shoved her insecurities down—like Captain Wolt hanging up on her cooled her anger—and she concentrated on the boys. Clio didn't have to ask what kind of magic-born they were or where they were from, the forms had been filled out. Granit Peak clowder was the closest; being four hours from Trinity, it bordered Cascade's territory. The boy had traveled to Trinity to hang out with the other. Simple.

"This is your son's fault! He's from here, mine isn't," the shorter of the two women argued. "Who jumps from bridges?"

"Why is your son here?" the taller woman demanded. She squared her shoulders and stood straighter as if showcasing her height. "On Cascade territory?"

They were standing beside the beds like they had been told to go to their perspective corners by a ref. The taller woman with her hands on the white sheet, the shorter woman with her hand resting on her son's shoulder. Both boys were wearing pale green gowns, bandages, casts, and embarrassment.

"Excuse me," Clio tried. They ignored her as they were ignoring the guards keeping them from touching each other, at the same time their husbands had taken a step back. Since she was the head doctor for the ER, she wasn't going to be rude until she was forced to. "Hello, I'm Doctor Hyde, head of the ER."

"Mason and Grace Corelli, and their son, Brent. He's seventeen," Dr. Kolt explained over the accusations. He flipped a page, then stated, "The clowder family is Ted and Marcy Dooley, and their son, Kyle, same age as Brent."

"Your son called my son," Mrs. Dooley answered. If she noticed Mrs. Corelli's height and the intention behind her actions, she ignored it well. She wore a loose, floral blouse, capris, and tennis shoes. Her copper red hair sat at her shoulders, and she glared at the other mom with amber/yellow eyes of a bobcat.

"A phone call forced him to Trinity and to jump from a bridge beam?" Mrs. Corelli asked. She chuckled and mocked, "Must be a submissive."

Clio shook her head. There was going to be a fight unless she stopped them. "Excuse me," she said slightly louder. They gave her an impatient glance. *Right.*

As if on cue, the double doors swung open and two

enforcers entered the ER wearing black on black BDUs, with Cascade's crest, tactical belts, drop down holsters, and combat boots. They wore their authority like body armor, and with their hands on the butt of their pistols, everyone including the couple other patients stopped what they were doing to watch.

"Enforcer Kia, Enforcer Aydian, thank you for responding," Clio greeted.

When she advised Mandy the enforcers would be cautionary, a presence, she expected to see Luca or Skylar—women usually appeared less threatening—hell, maybe Luke or Quinn, as they were patient. Under no circumstance, did she expect to see Kia, the woman was sharp and fierce, or Aydian. In the Wight world, she was a higher class then Aydian, having been born a werewolf rather than infected. It bugged her he didn't care, but then she didn't think he cared about anything except getting the job done. Aydian's lack of empathy and Army discipline was the reason Director Kanin used him for dangerous jobs. Like when they stormed the coven's mountain hideout. Both enforcers nodded in response, they're eyes taking in the scene while they gauged the parents. Neither stepped forward to take charge but rather let Clio handle it and remained a presence.

"You called enforcers on us?" Mrs. Dooley asked. Her eyes held a level of fear that erased any signs of cat.

"Affirmative," Clio stated. *I have your attention now.*

The enforcers served as Cascade's law enforcement, responding to calls, patrolling pack property, and making themselves visible throughout Trinity. After Miss Langston's kidnapping, the baron ordered the enforcers to increase their patrols, heighten security at Foxwood, the baron's estate, the Summit, their meeting grounds, and at the director's house. The inner workings of the pack shifted from casual and friendly, to strict, borderline military. Clio knew it was only a matter of time—maybe when Director Kanin resumed his duties, or when Miss Langston was discharged—before it would become stricter and the rules inflexible. Mrs. Dooley's response and the fear drifting from her was proof of the force the enforcers had become.

"You are in Celestial, a hospital in the Cascade territory and owned by the Cascade pack. If you hadn't noticed during your tirade, there are other patients being treated. Your son is not the only one. You are causing a disturbance, and my guards aren't going to deal with it. Hence, enforcers," Clio explained and raised her hand to stop the woman from interrupting. "I have been informed by Doctor Kolt your son has been treated, his bones set to heal properly, and his lacerations are cleaned and bandaged. You can either take him back to your territory and have him seen by your local physician or take him home where he can rest. I suggest you wait seventy-two hours before he shifts to make sure the bones have started to mend. Or you can continue to argue, and I'll have the enforcers escort you and your family, who you are embarrassing, out of this hospital and then out of town."

"Escort them out," Mrs. Corelli demanded. Her face was pinched with her anger while her brown eyes held a level of arrogance, and her hands were on her hips as if to punctuate her status.

Clio met Mrs. Corelli's glare. "Enforcer Kia, I want a formal complaint filed against Grace Corelli for disturbing the peace, intimidating a visitor, delaying a discharge of an underaged patient, and trying to incite violence on neutral ground. I will give a written statement," Clio advised. She turned to the Dooley family. "What will it be?"

"My apologies, Doctor Hyde. We don't want any trouble. We'll take Kyle home," Mr. Dooley offered.

"Very well. Would you like Enforcer Aydian to escort you to your car?" Clio asked.

Mr. Dooley looked at Aydian, whose blue eyes resembled stones, his military background showing itself in his short, blond hair cut close to his head, his square shoulders, muscled build from living in the gym, and his hard expression promising pain. "N-No, th-thank you. We'll b-be fine," he stammered.

"I called for a couple of wheelchairs, they should be here in a second," Dr. Kolt advised. He kept an eye on Aydian like the enforcer would open fire on the lot of them.

"Doctor Hyde, I have to object to the complaint on my wife," Mr. Corelli started. "There's no reason to have something like a misunderstanding permanently in her record."

"You should have objected to her behavior." Clio let that sit between them, then met Mr. Corelli's irritated gaze with her own. "A misunderstanding? You mean how the four of you started blaming each other? The boys are friends, don't corrupt their friendship with your skewed beliefs."

"I don't think you're in a position to tell us how to raise our son," Mrs. Corelli countered.

"I'm not telling you how to raise him. Mrs. Corelli, you think you're better than they are, your attitude is offensive to them and goes against the beliefs of Baron Kanin and the Cascade pack. If you don't want a report filed, you'll abide by the rules," Clio explained. "And have some manners."

"I'm good, Mom. Can we go home?" Brent asked. He adjusted his position, lifting the cast around his ankle and calf several inches off the cotton sheet, then lowering it.

"Take your son home, Mrs. Corelli," Clio urged as politely

as possible. To her side, Aydian and Kia took several steps in opposite directions, allowing two nurses to push wheelchairs between them. "Help Brent and Kyle into the chairs, then to their cars. Aydian and Kia will escort you." She changed her mind. There was no way she was trusting either set of parents to not start arguing in the parking lot.

"Yes, Doctor," Cruz answered. His muddy brown eyes, bronze skin, and black hair were distinct contrasts to his stark white scrub top and royal blue pants.

Cruz Lattner was a perfectionist, a werewolf belonging to Cascade, and one of the few domineers—the stronger wolves in the pack—who didn't serve with one of the branches of the pack's enforcement. His humility confused Clio at times, like when she instructed him to do something or when he dealt with a patient. He stopped beside Brent's bed, locked the brake, adjusted the left side, and straightened to his six-foot height.

"Are you ready?"

"Wait. My leg hurts and my head feels fuzzy."

"It's going to hurt, you broke bones, and hit your head. On rocks. By tonight the pain should be less. If it isn't, to be cautious, have your physician check to make sure your leg is healing properly," Clio advised. "Remember how that feels the next time you feel the need to jump from trestles."

"Yes, ma'am." Brent gave her a half smile, like he was already planning on going back, he couldn't let the trestle beat him. Lifting his leg, he put his right arm over Cruz's broad shoulders.

"On three. One. Two. Three." Cruz lifted the teenage boy as if he were a small child and not a football player and gently lowered him to the chair.

Dr. Kolt moved in, and holding the cast placed it in the bracket to keep it from shifting while he was wheeled out of the hospital. "You're all set."

"That goes for you, too." Clio turned her attention to Kyle and Rayette as she finished with the wheelchair.

"Ma'am." Kyle wasn't looking at Clio, he was gazing at Rayette, a grin curving his lips and making the bandage taped to his temple scrunch into his hairline.

She smiled back with her green eyes gleaming behind blonde lashes, her pointed ears covered by flaxen curls, and stole his teenage heart.

Clio couldn't stop herself from laughing. Everyone loved Rayette. The petite, elven woman belonged to the Seelie court of the Shasta-Trinity National forest, was an empath, and a beautiful woman.

"I see Kyle is feeling better."

"Son, close your mouth, she's out of your league," Mr. Dooley teased.

Mrs. Dooley shrugged her shoulders, her face neutral as if her son making eyes at the nurse was normal, and took the plastic bag with Kyle's clothing and belongings. "Thank you, Doctor Hyde, for not making this worse than we tried to make it."

"You're welcome," Clio replied. "Enforcer Aydian will escort you."

"Yes, Doctor Hyde, thank you," Mr. Corelli said. "I hope this resolves the issue with the report."

"Of course," Clio replied. "Enforcer Kia will escort you out."

She wasn't going to make a report ... no, she was going to do a little background check on the Corellis and find out exactly why Mrs. Corelli thought she could act the way she did. It was hard to know every person in the pack when Cascade's population was over one thousand and that number didn't count the klatch—the magic-born who weren't were-wolves, but lived under the umbrella of Baron Kanin's authority. When the families were out of the ER, the hospital, and in the parking lot, Clio's shoulders relaxed.

"Teenagers." Dr. Kolt faced Clio. "At least that's over."

Clio watched the enforcers march behind the families and shook her head. "Thankfully."

"How did it go with Director Kanin?"

"Fine. They're anticipating Miss Langston's discharge," Clio replied.

"Aren't we all." Dr Kolt gave her a sorry not sorry look, then walked away.

Yes, aren't we all, she thought as she headed to her office. With Miss Langston discharged the hospital would return to normal and Clio's duties as go between would come to an end. Hopefully.

CHAPTER FOUR

Ansel sat in a dark brown, leather, wingback chair staring over the large, walnut desk and the bookcases lining the wall. Worn spines with faded titles lined several shelves when newer books with stark lettering ended the row. The baron's late arrival was out of character for him, and left Ansel waiting in the silent office with the baron's authority lingering, staring at the books and the photography of Nearctic Valley. Waiting gave him time to think about the photos—they were Jordyn's—and then about Rutger, his return to work, and his position as Captain of the Enforcers. Baron Kanin put him in charge the night Rutger was admitted to Celestial, and the duties and stress were wearing on him.

When he saw Rutger's wolf veiling his human shoulders, he knew Rutger had been seconds away from losing himself and drowning the wolf in rage to become a half man, half wolf humanoid with bloodlust. He did what he had to and heard the soft pops of the dart gun, then Rutger going to his knees, Dr. Hyde pleading for him to stop, and the sirens of law enforcement. The smells, sounds, and sights of that night were forever scarred into his memory. Like the fear of losing Rutger and Jordyn was embedded in his heart. He was doing his best to show confidence and strength in order to keep up the morale of the enforcers and pack members but knew he was failing. He'd never had people depend on him the way the baron and the pack were. For years it had been him, and some things were hard to change. Ansel inhaled and exhaled to calm his anxiety. It was the past, and Rutger and Jordyn were alive. A part of him hoped the baron was going to tell him Rutger was ready to return. Except hope was a bitch and Rutger wasn't ready.

"Sorry for the delay," Baron Kanin stated as he entered the office. He moved his thick mass with the ease and fluid motion of a trained fighter while his usually tawny eyes held slivers of gold.

"Sir." Ansel stood, shook the baron's hand, felt the buzz of his power, and sat down as he walked around the desk. "How can I be of service?"

"First, Captain Wolt, your loyalty to me, the pack, and Rutger makes me a proud alpha, thank you," Baron Kanin offered.

"My honor." Ansel's heart raced with the raw honesty the baron was giving him.

"I asked you here because I have received the approved plans for the Summit, the security measures for Rutger's house, and diagrams for the new gate. They include cameras and the treehouses along the drive. I would like you to look them over, and if there is anything I've missed, please make a note. Since the construction blueprints have been approved, the demolition workers will be here this afternoon, so I need the office cleared out and communications moved. During the building of the new office, I've purchased a command center, basically a big truck, and once it arrives, that's where communications will be moved."

"Affirmative, sir. I'll talk to Torin about having soldiers help. The Summit and Foxwood will have the same treehouses?" Ansel asked.

The *treehouses* were manufactured trees that would be tucked among the pine, oak, and cedar lining the drive from the gate to the estate, then around the house and building, all equipped with cameras and perches for snipers. As he worked on the treehouses, reports, and keeping track of enforcers, and the day-to-day workings, he kept telling himself Rutger was coming back and it made the days seem shorter, the workload less stressful. But after seeing Rutger sitting in the baron's SUV and detached from the world, it felt like he was never going to return. The thought made the weight of sitting in Rutger's chair and the pressure of overseeing the security of the pack press on his shoulders.

"Affirmative." Baron Kanin hesitated, his eyes darkened, and he sat back.

The baron kept to the canons of the Highguard, the pack, making the decisions no one else wanted to make, and faced the anger from the pack and the division some were hell-bent on creating. Right then, Ansel got the feeling the baron missed talking to his son. His confidant who understood the burdens of the pack, was there to help ease the tension, and made dealing with it easier. It was a partnership. Sitting in front of the man made him feel like a fraud. The baron had taken him in, treated him with respect, then like family. Fraud. Liar. Impostor. There weren't enough words to describe the way he felt as the baron eyed him with his gold gaze, giving him respect he didn't deserve.

"My lawyers have informed me the case against the witches will be a closed court. The attention it has received and Mr. Platt remaining at large has the state feeling the defendants' lives could be in danger." He held up his hand when Ansel tried to interrupt him. "I know how wrong it is. The upside is Rutger and Jordyn aren't expected to testify in front of a courtroom packed with people, the media, or in front of a jury. They'll give their statements to the judge, prosecutor, defense attorneys, my lawyers, and a verdict will be given. And we'll be able to keep Jordyn safe."

"How does Rutger feel about it?" Ansel knew Rutger didn't care who he testified in front of as long as the witches went to prison.

Baron Kanin exhaled. "I don't think he was listening to me. He's worried about Jordyn, nothing else. There is also the chance they will release several witches due to the defense attorney claiming they were Mr. Platt's victims. They were coerced and acted under duress."

"You can't be serious?" Ansel objected. "I didn't see one of them trying to stop Flint from killing Jordyn. I did see all of them chanting and all of them using magic to escape. They weren't innocent when they fired on Detective Watt and his men. No one was coerced."

Baron Kanin raised both his hands. "I agree wholeheartedly. Jordyn wasn't able to positively identify anyone except for Mr. Platt, the men who kidnapped her, and the woman, Andrea, who Mr. Platt murdered. The others being held were involved in the shooting with the OPI detectives, and Detective Watt. There are six of them claiming they weren't involved in the kidnapping or shooting. They were there believing it was a coven and not a cult. Their psychiatrist is claiming they're the victims of physical and psychological damage."

"My ass," Ansel mumbled. He couldn't believe what he was hearing. If it had been a shifter, it would have taken a second for the courts to hand down a death sentence. "I'm assuming you told Rutger. Does Jordyn know?" He couldn't wrap his mind around the idea they were going to release murders. Serial killing witches who stalked Jordyn for months. If they were released, there was going to be revenge and blood.

"I have, and his reaction was the same. I think it's best she doesn't know. At least until she comes home and feels safe." Baron Kanin sat back in his chair. "What did he see? What did they do to her?"

It was Ansel's turn to exhale as the sounds and images of the night filled his head. "He saw Zachery's remains in the cell where they kept her, the altar where they chained her, cut the symbols into her body in preparation for the sacrifice, then Jordyn hanging upside down from a tree, her bleeding body over an altar. The witches were surrounding her, chanting, and waiting for Flint to kill her. It was insane. The evil was thick. They acted like they were in a trance. Flint is a madman with powers." He felt the pressure from their wicked magic as if he was back at Butte Springs.

The baron's brows creased, his eyes burned gold, and anger wafted on the air. "He used to be a madman with powers, now he is just a man. Jordyn broke him as much as he broke her." He closed his eyes as if saying Jordyn was broken out loud gave it meaning, like a confession. Rubbing the back of his neck with his hand, he leaned forward, and rested his elbows on his desk. "Before law enforcement has a chance to find Flint, I think he will go after Jordyn. It's imperative you look at the plans and make sure every detail, every security breach at Rutger's house has been exposed and eliminated."

Ansel hated hearing the emotion in the baron's confession and detested the words 'Flint broke Jordyn'. Dr. Hyde's warning came back. Jordyn would have to prove she was stable emotionally and mentally before they released her. "I'll look at them in my office. The quicker the changes are made the better."

"Agreed. Now about Rutger. Leaving Celestial and being able to walk around freely at home, near his job, his enforcers, a place that's familiar and comfortable has helped bring him around. He's already showing signs of improving." Baron Kanin paused; the look of grief dimmed his eyes, and his shoulders tensed like he didn't believe what he was saying. "I'm praying his absence from the hospital forces Jordyn to follow Doctor Carrion's instructions. They need each other. More so now than ever."

The intimate conversation they were having was way out of Ansel's comfort zone. He was an enforcer, Rutger's captain, a weapons expert, and could tear through an enemy's tactics like he was erasing points from blueprints. He was silent death. It was who he had been trained to be over one hundred twenty years ago. He pushed his past aside, had to, he didn't need the memory.

The feeling of being a fraud gave him the sweet scent of burning cinnamon and pungent aspen that attacked him, the heavy smoke blurring his vision, and burning his eyes. Her cold touch was demanding, possessive, and her fangs felt like the tips of blades pulled from ice as they slid into his flesh. The memory of her soft moans as she held him then drank from him made him want to shudder from disgust. He had been nothing more than an animal kept in captivity. Shoving the memory down, he jerked himself out of his past, and forced the scarred face of the woman who trained him into the oubliette where it festered, until his will weakened, and she clawed her way up like a living nightmare.

"I can be there for Rutger. I understand him. I can't help Jordyn," he admitted. With the memory sitting on his skin like a ceaseless hostile breeze, he wanted to look away from the baron and down at his jeans, boots, the floor. He had been owned like a possession and marked by the woman. He was a fraud.

"You don't have to. By helping Rutger, you're helping

Jordyn." The baron's voice gained its alpha tone—stern, strong, and confident. His tawny eyes narrowed on Ansel as if his mind cleared and he was seeing him for the first time. "I know the responsibly you've shouldered over the last couple of weeks, and unfortunately it doesn't look like there will be a reprieve, at least for another week when they release Jordyn. Do have anyone helping you?"

He didn't. And Ansel didn't have the skills to be CEO, a records keeper, clerk, friend, confidant, and then an enforcer. Rutger held the position of Second to the Alpha, the baron trusted him with pack business, and Director of Enforcers. He oversaw the security for the properties, delegated calls according to who best fit the need, worked with local law enforcement, and was the fated mate to the pack's soothsayer. To say he bore a heavy weight would be an understatement. Captain Wolt kept people organized, trained, and at a distance. Distance being the key.

"Negative, sir. With the increase in patrols and security at Celestial there hasn't been time to stop one person and have them remain at the office."

"I understand. May I suggest Lado? He's meticulous, strong, smart, and will take orders without his pride and wolf getting in his way," Baron Kanin explained.

Lado Reyes, an Illuminate, half elf, half werewolf, and a domineer, was six feet and two inches of muscles with delicate elf characteristics, like his pointed ears and pastel green eyes with hints of brown the color of coffee. The baron was right, Lado wouldn't let his werewolf domineer cloud his judgement, but the man was quiet and self-aware of his elf half. He reminded Ansel of Dr. Hyde, and her attitude about being a Wight. His magic-born background wasn't Lado's only problem. His mom, Caucasian—with porcelain skin, darker green eyes, and strawberry-blonde hair—was part of the Seelie court, while his father—with his dark skin resembling night and deep brown eyes—was a member of Cascade. Lado was an Illuminate and bi-racial in a world that loved to stick people in a box to define them. There was no defining him.

"Is there a reason why you suggested Lado?" Ansel asked. His skepticism about the man and his self-doubt was evident in his question.

"We need him, and he needs this. Lado trains and is an expert in the fields but has watched from the sidelines for far too long. It's time for him to take an active role of enforcer. The director is in my family room staring out a window, his captain is doing the job of two, maybe three, the pack's soothsayer is in the hospital, the pack is living under the scrutiny of the public because of the media's attention, and the enforcers are being run into the ground with patrols. I would move a couple of people over from the soldiers, except they're as stretched with security and the renovations as the enforcers. And I will not expose the slayers and shadows." Baron Kanin sat back with frustration, bringing a groan from him and his leather chair.

The shadows reported directly to the baron, leaving their identities a secret to the pack, enforcers, and soldiers. The slayers weren't as covert. Ansel knew them, trained with them, but the pack didn't; they did fear them and their skills as assassins.

"Understood. I'll have him report to my office," Ansel replied. He would talk to him and find out if Lado was interested. If he wasn't, there was nothing he was going to do to change his mind, besides release him and find someone else. In the Cascade pack, it's mandatory for every person to serve two years as a soldier. Some stayed, promoted to enforcer, but most left to peruse other interests. A month ago, there was no need for extra patrols, security, and twenty-four hour a day monitoring. A month ago, no one had been attacked, murdered, or kidnapped.

"Thank you." Baron Kanin stood, the tension in his shoulders easing. When there was a knock on the door, Ansel knew the meeting was over. "It's Gavin. I'm sending him to the Summit to talk with a group of men to find potential enforcers and soldiers."

"Good luck to him. The kidnapping and murder sent a shock wave through the pack. Everyone senses the changes and fears the consequences. It makes the threat of human's interference real," Ansel explained. An accusation from a human would bring more trouble than it was worth.

"Time will tell what the future brings. Thank you, Ansel. If there is any change in Rutger, I'll let you know, maybe then you can talk to him." Baron Kanin stepped around his desk, gathered several rolls of papers, and handed them to him. "Look the plans over."

"Sir." Ansel took the bundle and headed to the door, turned the lever, and pulled it open. "Gavin."

"Ansel," Gavin greeted as he entered the office.

Resembling his parents, he was a thinner, softer Rutger. Ansel never noticed the differences of strength and certainty between the Third to the Alpha and Rutger. The authority and responsibilities Rutger shouldered made him the man he was, while Gavin hadn't had the same obligations and it showed. That was about to change. Gavin was going to be given more duties, most of them concerning the politics of the pack. He would be a representative facing the public and the leaders of the factions under the baron's rule. Ansel was glad it wasn't him. The door closed silently behind him, cutting their voices off and leaving him alone and in silence. Walking down the hall, his boots made whispers on the marble, while there was the hint of conversations coming from deeper in the house.

"Sousa," Ansel greeted the sentinel.

"Captain." They shared a glance before Sousa opened the right side door, and holding it, Ansel walked outside and into July's heat.

Above him the cloudless, cerulean sky let the high sun pour its fervor down on him. He could smell the sweetness of heated grass and the fragrance of dulcet honeysuckle drifting on the breeze and it eased the fragment of fear from his memory. He ignored the weight of it and approached the Enforcer's office with confidence. He belonged there, with the pack, with the enforcers; they accepted him and gave him a place. No one could take it from him. Once inside, the air conditioner stole the pureness from the air while the voices coming from communications tapped at his thoughts. He would check on them, then head to his office to look over the plans.

"Anything new?" Ansel asked. He stood in the door jamb with the bundle of plans cradled in his left arm. Mandy sat in front of a monitor while Luke and Kellan stood behind her.

"Not really," Mandy replied without looking at him. The others turned to stare back at him, their faces neutral.

Vague answer. "What's going on?" Ansel entered the room, and crowding Kellen and Luke they moved out of the way, leaving him behind Mandy. "What the hell?"

"All right, nothing new. I sent Kia to check on them. This is her report," Mandy explained.

"Kellen, go back up Kia. I don't want her there by herself," Ansel ordered. "If Mr. or Mrs. Oliver refuses to follow orders, call Celestial and have the metal health team respond. I'm not taking any chances."

"Copy, on my way," Kellen responded, and headed out of the room.

"Mandy, let Kia know backup is en route. If this happens again, I want to be notified. And I want an incident report made every time there is a disturbance. Understood?" Why she hadn't told him to begin with irritated him and made his job that much harder.

"Affirmative, Captain," Mandy responded. She looked at him with blue/violet eyes holding her concern and questions.

"I understand the pack and the enforcers are in a state of flux. We will operate like a military team, meaning I expect discipline from the enforcers and the pack. If someone thinks they can behave as the Olivers have been, they're wrong."

"Sir," Mandy replied as she sank in her chair.

"Sir," Luke replied.

"I can't believe Mr. Oliver managed to get drunk," Ansel mumbled under his breath as he headed to his office.

Being a Wight, Mr. Oliver didn't metabolize alcohol the same way a Pureblood or an Illuminate did. Still, it would take gallons of liquor to get him drunk. He wasn't going to judge the man or his wife harshly, when they lost a son to a serial killer who hadn't been apprehended. But their disturbances needed to stop, or humans were going to take notice, and once they did human law enforcement would be forced to step in. The couple wouldn't have the resources or mercy with humans as they have with the pack and Celestial. He walked by Rutger's door and paused. Damn, he missed being able to talk to his friend and hoped Rutger pulled himself together. Continuing down the hall, he opened the door to his office, dropped the bundle of plans on his desk, making papers shift, and a pen hit the tile floor and rolled under his chair.

"It's going to be a great day," he mumbled.

After picking up the pen, he tossed it to the desk, sat down, adjusted his thigh holster and gun, and he set his cell on the desktop. The reports, sitting scattered across the pale pine with several manilla envelopes, reminded him he needed to send them to the baron, while a computer monitor sat silent beside a travel coffee cup, which had been sitting there too long. He needed to remember to take it home. When the baron announced the office would be going through a remodel turned new construction, he easily packed the two pictures, a framed map of Cascade's territory, several books, a stack of maps, and equipment he hadn't put away, into a couple of boxes. The office felt empty, forgotten, and made his dismal mood worse. He needed to be moving, outside, on patrol, anything besides being locked in his office and looking over plans.

Ansel didn't have a choice, Rutger and Jordyn's safety was priority. He straightened the reports and folders, grabbed the first set of plans, and spread it out on his desk. It was the technical drawing of Rutger's property. He rubbed the back of his neck, felt tension, then drew his fingers through his thick, dark auburn hair, pulling its ends free of the collar of his T-shirt. He didn't know how the baron expected to secure the property when the six acres of lakefront land was wide open and a giant security breach. Scrawled at the bottom of the plans were the baron's notes. They would start with the entrance, by creating one farther from the house, then installing a license plate reader, camera, and sensors along the driveway. Along the perimeter there would be cameras and motion detectors, save for the lakefront, the sensors would be closer to the house. Ansel read the improvements to the house and whistled.

All the windows would be replaced by ballistic glass, the doors would be reinforced with steel, and more cameras, palm vein scanners, motion sensors, and LED floodlights that switched to UV lights. It was a military grade security system linked directly to the communications center where an enforcer would monitor the information. In the event an intruder activated the system, it would initiate the cameras and they would begin recording to create a video and transcript, at the same time it had the capability to be live streamed to the baron's office, communications, and accessed by an enforcer from the laptops in their vehicles. The wiring alone was going to be extensive, and the refitting of Cascade vehicles was going to take time. He pictured the new communications room looking like a command center and war room.

At the end of the list and the baron's notes was Rutger's rough signature. He couldn't possibly understand what he was doing to his house, could he? Was fear driving him to modify the beautifully built, custom, two-story log home to the point of making it a prison? Is that where he expected Jordyn to live? Was she going to spend her life locked up and away from the world? As she had been for the last couple of weeks at Celestial.

A chill slid down his spine, dragging glass shards with it, and hit his hips.

No, she couldn't. Magic was changing them, her, and she was going to have to accept the inevitable. Whatever that was going to be. As the baron had said, time would tell.

Ansel shook himself, disengaging him from his thoughts to focus on the plans. He didn't see anything he would change—maybe less, definitely not more—and rolled the paper up. Taking the second roll, he flattened it on the desktop, stared at the Enforcer's office, and whistled at the projected ten thousand square feet of building. Yes, the new communication room was going to be a frontier tech command center with state-of-the art screens, computers, cameras, a digital audio station, and office equipment. It was going to serve two purposes; keep the pack safe and have the proper evidence to give to human law enforcement if they were attacked. Attacked.

He hated to think it was possible. Tearing his gaze from the blueprint to eye the stack of files filled with potential enforcers, their backgrounds in dispatching and computers to work in communications, made him feel buried. If only he could discuss it with Rutger. Minutes ticked by as he stared at the plans he didn't see, his thoughts clinging to worry and adding to his stress. The baron trusted him, and he would do what needed to be done. His thoughts seized when he jumped in his seat as someone knocked on the door.

"Captain," Mandy greeted as she hesitantly peeked around. Her violet, blue eyes landed on the blueprints and rolls of plans. "Kia and Kellen left the Olivers' house and are on their way back. I have a preliminary report. Do you want it now, or do you want to wait until they get back?"

How long had he been sitting there? "Is it urgent?" he asked and sat back. When he said he expected military discipline, it was because the baron ordered it. The pack was going through a transition from human casual, informal professionalism straight to military rigid, and he was the person responsible for making the enforcers follow the order.

"Negative. Mr. Oliver calmed down, and Mrs. Oliver promised he wouldn't leave the house. Kellen told them he would call Celestial and have Mr. Oliver taken in for observation if he did it again." She paused, looked at the rolls of paper, then met his gaze. The shift in mindset, casual to strict, was making everyone unsure of themselves.

"They did good work then. I'll sign the report, and you can add it to theirs."

"Affirmative, sir." Entering the office, she handed him the folder.

Ansel lifted the thin edge, removed the report from inside, glanced over the typed account, shook his head, placed it on the blueprints for the expanded office, and without heavy pressure, scrawled his signature across the bottom. When he was done, he gazed at it for a second, then put his pen down, returned the report to the file, and handed the folder to Mandy. "Thank you."

"Sir." She gripped the folder, hesitated, then headed to the door.

"One thing."

Mandy turned on the ball of her boot and faced him.

"I need Lado Reyes' file ASAP."

"Would you like the file or do you want me to send it to your computer?"

"Computer. The quicker the better," Ansel replied.

Mandy nodded. "Sir."

When the door closed, taking her footsteps, the bolt clicked, and he was by himself. Ansel repeated the process of rubbing his neck, the knots in his muscles, drawing his fingers through his hair, and sat back with an exhale. After he read Lado's file, he would call him, meet with him, then find out what to do with him. With his patience thinning, he rolled up the blueprints for the office and took the plans for the Summit and flattened them on the desk. He didn't know what he was expecting after seeing the first two sets of plans and their extensive increase in security and size, but the

Summit went even further, making him exhale an exaggerated breath. They were going to pave two turn lanes from the main highway into the Summit, lengthen the road by a half mile, and widen it to four lanes instead of two. The modifications would involve the city's planning committee, meaning someone was going to have to deal with them. It wasn't Ansel.

The motive for the shift in the road was the addition of another security gate. By putting it farther from the road, it wouldn't cause traffic to back up to the highway, and the person would have time to go through security protocol while a camera recorded their actions. They planned to plant mature trees along with shrub brush—no one was waiting for saplings—along the fence line to conceal the new treehouses, turrets, and cameras, and the trees would block anyone from trying to see into the Summit. The additions gave extra security to the Summit where the pack gathered at the Conclave, communed with one another, and ran freely without the threat of being seen by humans. It also gave extra protection to their burial grounds where every clansman had been buried. His mind went to Zachery Oliver, his parents, and then the way the baron had welcomed him to the pack.

After Baron Kanin preformed the inclusion ritual, making Ansel kith to the pack, and the celebrations ended, he had walked the sacred burial grounds, taking in its expanse and thanking the gods for giving him a place to belong. Surrounded by aged headstones, some wood with carvings in them stood like sentinels while the feel of the dead and their wolf essences wove through them to thicken the air. It had been ten years since he arrived in Trinity, running from the past haunting him, his mind tired of replaying the faces of the men and women he killed, and drained from being an instrument for a monster. It had taken him a couple of years to weaken the instinct to fight, and the ever-present feeling there was danger around the next corner or an enemy was hunting him.

With the moment of weakness and his past riding his thoughts, it weakened his walls and made him think of his lies. Ansel lied to the baron, the background investigators, the pack's council, Rutger, anyone who asked where he came from and what he did. With years of deception, he was good at it. The purpose of the questions was to assess his worth to the pack, if they could trust him not to betray them, and he lied to them all. *Not lied,* he thought, *just down-played my abilities in combat, tracking, and my understanding of military science. My capabilities as an assassin.*

Stop, it's the past. He may have lied about where he was from—truth, North Dakota—his age—truth, one hundred and forty—however, he wasn't a complete liar ... he told the truth about his parents.

When a fire began eating its way across the plain, scorching the ground and leaving it black and barren, it had taken his parents' lives and left the house he grew up in a pile of ash, as well as the barn and everything they owned. He knew the moment the blaze swallowed his father, had felt it in his soul and his wolf's spirit, then his mother's screams punctuated the feeling of loss. He raced toward the barn to watch the inferno wrap around her thin frame, her long, black hair curling up to her skull. The scent of her burning flesh hit him, as fragments of ash fell from her body, then he watched her crash to the charred ground. In a heartbeat, as if their wolves were drowning in pain, they cried out to him, and their bodies gave into true death, their souls going to the ether and leaving him alone.

Grief engulfed him as if the fire had captured him, and he waited for its scalding claws to take him. When his body felt like he had swallowed embers and was burning from the inside out, he knew the flames had caught him. The heat dried his tears, and he closed his eyes against the wave of the blaze. The smell of burning flesh polluted his nose. He didn't move while his hair singed, his skin blistered, and his heart raced, sending him into shock. Ansel's breath left his smoke choked lungs, and he resigned himself to death, then an arm, like a metal band around his chest, broke his ribs, and he heard whispered curses. One second he was in the middle of hell, then he was thrown into the cellar and the door slammed closed and with its echo in his ears he was cast in darkness and cold.

He didn't know how long it took for the fire to sweep over the thick wood protecting him from its wrath, turned it to embers, and left him exposed. With charred fingers, he grabbed baskets, root vegetables, whatever was near him, and tried using them against the searching flames, heat, and smoke invading the small space. Then his lungs seized, making him cough and choke, the material of his shirt fell from him, and his skin melted from his body, the pain crippling him. He was extremely aware he was trapped, there was nothing he could do to save himself, and the desperation had pushed his sanity to the edge. Gazing up through the burned hole, smoke had dammed the sun from the sky, turned day into night, and he heard the flame's storm crawl over the land as he waited. And waited. He didn't think he slept, or dared close his eyes, he still saw his parents, the flames, and felt their loss as if it had struck him and buried itself in his core.

When she found him, he was lying on the dirt floor,

blisters rippling over his flesh, his open wounds oozing, death gripping his failing body, and his wolf spirit waiting to drift to the ether to join his parents. She came back for him. She had risked her life to snatch him from the blaze and his parents' demise. They had made sure he was alive, their voices sounding as if they were far away as they wrapped his wounds, then carried him out of his dark grave.

She should have left me there, he thought. Days and nights dragged by, one running into the other while he prayed the fire came back and finished what it had started. As he healed, he begged her to let him go, to return him to the fire. Her reply had been a gentle laugh that entered his mind, making him cling to life.

Bronte, with her softly spoken words, convinced him to return to the living, and Ansel, obeying her, shapeshifted and healed his wounds, saving his life. He owed her a debt he would never be able to repay. He didn't care and didn't fight her and couldn't when grief and loss had made him numb, and he had nothing else. There was nothing left. Following the traditions of both his parents, and with his heart torn from his chest, Ansel sifted through ash, trying to find the remains of their bodies. Once he thought he had enough and was confident it was them, he gave them a proper burial and left with the Covey. He hadn't died in the fire ... no, he died the moment he left his parents' land. The world that knew Ansel Wolt ceased to exist. Taking his place at her side, he became Brando and belonged to Bronte and her Covey.

The pack knew Ansel was a Pureblood, a DNA test proved it, and nothing else. His family had been dead for one hundred and twenty years, their DNA never added to the Assembly software. His family and background remained a secret. His lies hid where he was from and why his parents lived in the middle of nowhere, had kept to themselves, and no one questioned them. When they died, it was assumed he did as well, and it freed him from their legacies. The world was a different place a hundred and twenty years ago. Being a Pureblood werewolf from two different backgrounds, American Indian, Mandan, and his mother a Pureblood werewolf from Italy, had made him unpopular. With strong casts from the Fae, his mother served as a priestess to the pack's lord, held council with him, had status with the upper echelon of the synod, and held a title with the Highguard. Ansel heard his mother, her accent curving the stories she told by candlelight, and then his father, who had served as a shaman of his tribe, would tell them tales, reciting the old ways, the magic in the land, and the spirit of the wolf living inside him.

While he was healing, he had fits of delusion, and with tears sliding down his cheeks, told bits of their stories. Drawn by the myths, priestesses, and shamans, Bronte demanded he tell her who he was and what magic he possessed. He obeyed, and understood his magic and legacy was the reason she had taken him in and trained him. Then favored him. She believed he had come from royalty.

Ansel wanted to laugh with the memory as he let go of the plans, the paper rolled up on its own, and he set it next to the others. He wasn't going to add his name to them, it wasn't necessary; the baron obviously wanted another set of eyes, nothing else.

The blueprints for Rutger's house, the Summit, and the office were precise, detailed, and covered every possible threat and then some. On the outside, it would look like the entire pack had gone paranoid and was building a base/compound, not upgrading security. When he returned the bundle to the baron, he would tell him there was nothing

Ansel would add. But before he met with the baron, he had to talk to Lado and find out if the man was up to the job.

He pushed the mouse around, bringing the monitor to life, and saw Mandy sent the file. Clicking on the icon marked L. Reyes, it opened, giving him a report of Lado's life. Lado Reyes, enforcer for three years, nonactive, male, second son to Hank and Glory Reyes, Illuminate, elf, werewolf, a connection to the Seelie court. Ansel knew the relationship with the court would come in handy. He continued reading. Heightened sight, hearing, strength, smell, speed, the usual attributes of a werewolf. Scrolling the page, it listed his training, the classes he passed, the calls he had been part of—all three of them had been welfare checks. The information stopped.

Farther down the page, he found what he was looking for; Fae casts, empath, it explained the welfare checks, and a strong sense of protection. As a werewolf, the instinct to protect one's mate, family, and pack drove the wolf, then add the instincts from his elf half and Lado would have a hard time refusing to obey his natural instincts. There was a note at the bottom of the page, two signatures confirmed the information had been reviewed and no other action needed to be taken. Bracketed in red it stated Lado submitted temporary leave papers and spent two months under the Seelie court's healers.

Interesting. No reason given. Ansel picked up his cell phone, scrolled through his contacts, found Lado, and hit the number.

"Captain Wolt," Lado greeted.

"Lado, I would like to see you in my office," Ansel said in way of a greeting.

"When?" Lado's voice lowered.

"As soon as possible." He heard truck engines and voices as if he was right outside. "Where are you?" He hadn't seen Lado when he arrived at the office, and since he wasn't an active enforcer he would have no reason to be there. Searching the report, he didn't find anything indicating Lado had resigned. He had the wild thought Lado may have gotten a job and forgot to formally notify the baron.

"I'm walking through the office door, Captain. I was helping with the new communications vehicle."

Ansel heard wind through the cell, then Mandy's voice as Lado walked down the hall. "Copy." He ended the call and waited the three seconds it took him to reach the door. "It's open."

The enforcer entered, his black hair cropped close to his skull, leaving his pointed ears exposed. He wore his black BDU top tucked into matching pants, shined, black combat boots, gun, thigh holster, and his eyes narrowed. "Captain Wolt."

Ansel would never have to worry about Lado following the new rules. "Please sit."

Lado sat and met his gaze, his pastel green eyes resembling seafoam dimmed to dirty moss with his emotions. His empath magic reached out from him as if it was threads touching Ansel, the feel like fingertips against him. He wondered if Lado knew what he was doing, or his nerves were getting the better of him. "I see in your file you responded to a welfare check. The report ends, then states you spent two months with the Seelie court. I could contact the court, and I'm sure they would give me an explanation. I doubt it would be the truth. And I would like to know the truth."

Lado's thick chest expanded with his inhale while his eyes swirled with three different shades of green. "The welfare check was for a one thousand year old fairy named Ander, who had been a warrior." He inhaled and exhaled, watched Ansel's reaction, then continued. "He left his faction to come to the US, which is unheard of, and they excommunicated him. He lived as part of the klatch under Cascade, and the Seelie court welcomed him into their fold. He lacked family, and when his time for passing came, he was alone. I wasn't going to leave him, and did what I could. Unfortunately, I left myself open, and when he passed the emotions of a thousand years descended on me, nearly turning my brain to mush and splintering my psyche. My mother found me lying in his living room in a catatonic state and immediately summoned the court to get me. They took me to the healers, where they drew the sentiments from my mind and lessened the impact of Ander's life. No one knew how strong my trait was, and I was instructed to remain and learn how to control the flow of emotions. After the incident, I was put on the inactive list, but have been called to do menial tasks, like helping to back up the communications rig."

The baron must have felt it was better for Lado to stay away from high stress and high emotional situations. The witches would have been both. "I understand. As you know, until Director Kanin's return, I'm in charge of the enforcers." Lado hesitantly nodded. "With the construction of the new Enforcer's office, the Summit, and the director's house beginning, I'm stretched too thin. I'm in need of someone who can keep track of calls, reports, if there's a question about security, and serve as backup."

"What does that have to do with me?" He tilted his head, his eyes brightening.

Ansel wanted to smile and laugh. It had been a rough morning, and a rougher afternoon, and now an over six-foot-tall werewolf with muscled shoulders and pointed ears stared at him with hope in his eyes like he was a kid. How Lado was able to be meek and hulking at the same time was beyond Ansel. "I'm offering you the job."

"Captain Wolt, are you sure?" Lado asked. He sat straighter, making the butt of gun scrape the chair. "I was inactive for an emotional breakdown."

"You were inactive for enduring a thousand years of life. Although, if there is a call and it's challenging you emotionally, you are to back off. No one wants you to get hurt," he replied. *A thousand years of life from a warrior elf* ... The thought sent shards down Ansel's spine and gave him a headache.

"Affirmative, sir. I train twice a week with an elder. I won't make the mistake again."

"You're confident you can control the influence emotions have on you?" Ansel still hadn't answered Lado's question. He knew what it was like to have different traits of magic from each parent. Control had been instilled in him at a young age. Pain taught the hardest lessons.

"Affirmative." By the expression on Lado's face, he noticed Ansel hadn't answered him. "Are you sure?"

"Positive. I wouldn't ask if I wasn't. There's work to be done. The pack can't be seen as weak, we need to stand as a united force, and I want you to be part of that." Ansel sat forward, his elbows on the desk, and saw excitement in Lado's green eyes. "Are you in?"

"Affirmative." Lado smiled.

"Have you been waiting for this?"

"Affirmative."

Ansel smiled. *That was easy.* "Finish your day, then report to me tomorrow."

"Sir." Lado stood, shifted his holster and gun, gave him a tight nod, and left the office.

Ansel waited a couple of minutes, grabbed the bundle of plans, and headed to the house to report to the baron that Lado would in fact be his second.

CHAPTER FIVE

Stopping, Clio waited for the garage door to rise and stared at the perfectly landscaped shrubs, multicolored flowers, oak trees, rose bushes, and the stucco building with river rock at the base, which was her townhouse in the city. When it was clear, she drove the luxury crossover into the garage, then pushed the button silencing the engine. A pop song lingered, its bouncy tune doing nothing to her mood.

At the end of her shift, she headed to the mental health units, checked on Miss Langston, where she watched the woman sit and stare out a window, then checked in with Dr. Carrion. He was sitting behind his desk entering notes into a tablet and told her he had bad news and good news, but neither were unexpected. The good news was Miss Langston was active, talked when spoken to, and understood Director Kanin had been released. The bad news, she shutdown when she found out the director left. It was more complicated than being upset about his absence. She told Dr. Carrion the director abandoned her, his fated mate. As an empath, he felt she was hiding something from him, and while he didn't think it was detrimental to her improvement, it might be the reason she felt abandoned.

To ease her anxiety of abandonment, he promised to have Director Kanin visit, if and only if, Miss Langston slept in human form and followed a schedule; wake up, make her bed, bathe, dress, eat breakfast, and go outside for exercise. Miss Langston nodded, seemingly dismissing him as she gave him her back and took her seat by the window to stare at nothing. The same place she was when Clio saw her. Pureblood Jordyn Langston had once been one of the most striking and strong women in the pack, then she left. Her absence turned her into a legend of mystery, heartbroken romance, speculation, and was a shining example of what it would be like if you dared rogue status. When Miss Langston came back for her sister's wedding, the woman was even more stunning, and her power felt like it encased her, proving she was a powerful Pureblood.

Days after the wedding's festivities ended, witches reduced her to a shell of who she had been. It was painful to watch. Clio listened to Dr. Carrion explain there was no way to understand exactly what was going through Miss Langston's mind when he didn't know what it meant to have a fated mate. He asked Clio if she believed in fated mates, soothsayers, and if she agreed with the direction Baron Kanin was taking the pack and the klatch. He stated if the baron succeeded, others would follow, and what would happen to the pack's relationship with humans, like him? As a Deviant, would he be accepted as a human or as a non-human?

She wasn't sure and didn't know how to get the answers. She could have told him he was better off trusting a non-human, maybe throw in there she knew how he felt, she was a Wight. There was a large population of humans, called Deviants, with empath, psychic, divination, energy medicine, and precognition abilities employed at Celestial. The human hospitals didn't believe in or trust their traits, making it difficult for them to get jobs in the healthcare industry. Their industries being fortune telling, living as a freak, or hiding their true selves.

Clio skirted the question—she wasn't going to be quoted—and recited something she read from Greek mythology when she was researching fated mates. Dr. Carrion's flat stare told her he wasn't stupid and wasn't buying it, but he let the conversation die. As soon as she could, she made her escape and drove home. To the townhouse in the city. She wasn't the only Wight choosing to live in what was considered downtown and among humans. Purebloods craved the wilds of open spaces without people, their senses being sharp and always giving them information. Illuminates lived in housing developments, sometimes exclusive to magic-born, satisfying both their magic-born half and their shapeshifter half.

Choosing the townhouse had been easy because she was confident no one would break in when they knew she was a shapeshifter and part of the Cascade pack. Most of her neighbors regarded her with quick glances, and when face to face, polite greetings, but it wasn't warm and friendly. She didn't care. She went to work, sometimes pulling a double shift, and if she worked the graveyard shift, she slept most the day, and didn't talk to them. Living downtown put her in walking distance to restaurants, shops, and stores, and the townhouse meant she didn't have to mow the lawn, trim the trees, or worry about the landscaping, the association did it for her. Clio was able to lock her door and walk away.

With no new news, she decided there was no reason to report to the baron. The director left, Miss Langston was upset, a natural response, and Dr. Carrion felt he was making progress. Clio checked her cell, saw there were no messages, let the breath she'd been holding go, and tossing the phone into her bag grabbed the straps, and got out of the car. After heading up the stairs, she opened the door to the hall, met a wave of clean air scented with warm brown sugar with hints of spiced cranberry and cinnamon, and as it swept over her, it pulled her inside. At Celestial she spent her shift in a sterile environment with the smells of magic-born, cleaning solution, and antiseptic hanging thick in the air and clinging to her clothing and hair. The cozy feel of her own space with warm scents was a welcoming relief that eased the stress from the day and washed Celestial from her.

Clio set her bag on the table, dug her cell out, and made her way through the open living room. In her bedroom she pulled the scrub top off, tossed it in a basket, kicked out of her shoes, then stripped out of her pants and socks and dropped them in the basket. Heading to the bathroom, she unhooked her bra, and taking it off, set it on the counter, then freed her strawberry blonde hair from the tight braid, and drew it up in a messy bun. Free from her work clothes, she grabbed a pair of knit shorts, a loose tank top, and in comfortable clothes, walked out to the living room where sunset's gold glow tinted with violet, and smears of rosewood flooded through the large picture window. It cast a medley of shades on the cream walls, antique cherry flooring, graphite couch with its soft throw pillows, matching oversized chair, the brown maple coffee table, and her vintage, red Aubusson rug. This was her space, a piece of the world no one could take from her ... or so she hoped. She hesitated by the window. On the second floor of the house, she gazed at the neighborhood, the people walking their pets, and the peace with which they lived.

A million questions sat in her head, ranging from the director and Miss Langston, if their relationship and being fated mates was real, if Miss Langston being the pack's soothsayer was real, and if there were going to be more changes in the pack. The loudest question, she couldn't stop it if she tried, demanding an answer was if there were going to be other fated mates. Clio wasn't a social kind of person despite living downtown in a townhouse, rarely talked to anyone outside of the pack, and hadn't had a date in six months. The last person to ask her out, she met him while standing in line at the store, had been a therian from the Granite Peak area, Stephen something. They'd gone out to dinner, pleasant enough, then a movie at which time the hospital called her—there had been a car accident—so she left him watching the romantic comedy by himself. The next day, she apologized, was interrupted, and he explained he couldn't deal with her work calling her all the time.

"It's not all the time," she mumbled.

The sun descended behind the mountain peaks, rooftops, and trees, taking its summer glow and letting twilight and its cool colors of indigo, violet, and plum stain the sky. Clio checked the time on her cell—it was close to seven—then for messages and found none. That's what she liked to see. Leaving the window, she padded into the kitchen and took a small tumbler from the dish rack, tequila from the marble counter, and poured two fingers. She wasn't opposed to wine, beer, or other liquor, but tequila had been a drink she shared with her grandpa. Med school had been especially difficult; not everyone was thrilled with having magic-born in attendance, and were less impressed when they found out she was a werewolf. When she visited her grandpa, he would hand her a glass and say, 'Let it loose, girl. Get yourself right.' She would spend the next hour rattling away, barely paying attention to her drink, then she would stop, take a sip and sit back, her mind clear of the mess. They would share a comfortable silence until her grandma would bring them snacks.

Simpler times. Clio sipped the clear liquor, her memories of visiting her grandparents playing, and caught the notes of oak, and relished the sea salt and citrus flavors.

She wasn't ready to eat dinner, and the thought of doing anything but sitting on her couch was beyond her. With glass and cell in hand, Clio left the kitchen, and sat on the couch, her feet under her. Yes, just a moment to relax. Placing her cell on the coffee table, she sat back, took another sip, and the conversation with Captain Wolt and his hang up drained from her, as did the near fight in the ER, and the stress of being the middleman between the hospital and the pack. Twilight's hues drowned under the ebbing night and the streetlights lit up one by one, creating hazy halos below them.

It was easy for Clio to get caught up in the silence, peace, and relaxing until her buzzing cell jerked her out of wonderland, as it micro bounced on the tabletop. The muted room lit up from the screen while it showed her a familiar number and face. Captain Wolt. Her heart plummeted to the bottom of her stomach when their earlier conversation reared its ugly head. What did he want? What had happened? He should be off work. Setting her glass down, she picked up the rectangle of trouble.

"Doctor Hyde."

"It's Captain Wolt, sorry to call so late. I understand Doctor Carrion has granted the director the opportunity to visit Miss Langston tomorrow. I don't have the time of the appointment," Ansel explained.

He wasn't wasting time with small talk, not after hanging up on her. Standing at the rail of his deck, barefooted, his jeans slung low on his hips, and shirtless, he had pulled his dark auburn hair back, tied at his neck, and held a cold beer. The condensation from the bottle slipped over the curve of the glass to his hand and quickly dried in July's evening heat. Ansel had zero desire to call Dr. Hyde, he would have rather talked to the baron, except the baron and baroness closed the doors and were having a sit down with Rutger and Gavin. He tried calling Dr. Carrion only to get this voicemail, leaving him with no choice. Dr. Hyde always answered her cell.

"You aren't going to hang up on me, are you?" she asked with a grin. Clio had no idea why she thought it was funny. Might be the call wasn't an emergency, night was sitting at the window, and she was comfy cozy on the couch.

Is she teasing me? If she is, I like it. "Negative," Ansel replied, keeping it professional. He enjoyed hanging up on her, although he wouldn't have if he knew he was going to have to call her the same damn day.

"Good to know. You could call Doctor Carrion directly," Clio responded and rolled her eyes. Why was she a go between?

"I did. He isn't answering his phone." After taking a sip of his beer, Ansel set the bottle on the rail, wiped his hand on his jeans, and turning around leaned against the edge.

He returned the blueprints to the baron, answered a couple of questions about security, and reported he had spoken to Lado, who would report to Ansel in the morning. With his tasks complete, the baron dismissed him, letting him head back to the office where he helped move furniture, computers, and boxes to a moving truck that would take everything to a storage unit. No one wanted to touch Rutger's office, leaving the job of packing to him. Rutger's desk had been orderly and a mess at the same time, and he packed it up as quickly as possible and tried not to take notice of the personal items Rutger kept. Like the photographs of him and

Jordyn together. It almost broke him thinking Rutger nearly lost his life and his mate. When he finished, and he was happy it was over, he added the boxes and furniture to the waiting truck.

The afternoon had progressed slowly, everyone's mood solemn as they removed traces of their pasts and packed it in the moving trucks. Then there was the final walk through to confirm the building was empty. With memories playing, his footsteps echoed in the abandoned hallways as he walked through the shell of the building and out of a part of his life. The Enforcer's office had been his second real home, a safe place where he was surrounded by enforcers, soldiers, his pack who cared unconditionally and expected nothing in return for their loyalty. It gave him a sense of belonging to a family. After a hundred years of being alone, who knew the need wouldn't die with his parents, and he would continue to crave the refuge a family offered.

"Mmm," Clio replied. "I see."

In attempt to reach out to the human world and to improve human and magic-born relations, Dr. Carrion was one of over a dozen Deviants employed at Celestial. The man was a phenomenal therapist, but he wasn't a werewolf, part of Cascade, or the magic-born population. If he didn't feel like answering an afterhours phone call, he didn't. Clio's cell was attached to her, she might as well have it implanted in her skull.

"I'm driving the director and need a time so I can schedule my appointments around the visit."

The baron and baroness, along with a group of enforcers and soldiers, gathered to watch as an inspector gave the construction workers clearance to begin demolition. Once the walls came down, it had taken them several hours to reduce the old building to rubble. Construction on the office officially began, as did the retrofitting and installation of security measures at the Summit. The baron had intended to work on Rutger's house but Rutger said no, refusing to let anyone on his property until he gave permission. The baron asked Ansel to talk to him about the house and suggested the drive to Celestial would be the perfect time. With construction happening and the coming weeks keeping Ansel busy, he didn't have time to track down Dr. Carrion.

She exhaled, mentally went through her day, and was sure she was free at three. "Captain Wolt, I'll meet you at the security entrance at three. FYI, Doctor Carrion won't be there, he has other appointments, so if the director or the baron have questions, they'll have to wait."

"Copy. Thank you for answering my call," he replied as he turned to see his yard.

Four floodlights with amber bulbs clicked on to create a soft glow bright enough a human would be able to see deep into the woods. For him, the amber lights weren't harsh and didn't hinder his enhanced werewolf vision. Amid cattails, water weeds, and horsetail reeds, geese squawked, flapped their wings, and splashed in the pond. When a couple of ducks flew in and landed, the four stared at each other until a round of squawking from the geese drove the ducks to the far side and among taller cattails.

"Is that geese?" Clio asked and sipped her tequila. Why was she keeping Captain Wolt on the phone?

"Affirmative. They're in the pond yelling at a couple of ducks." Ansel looked at his land and took a drink of his beer. "I think it's a turf war."

His place wasn't the six acres of lakefront with a dock and a massive log house like Rutger's, rather eight acres of wooded land with the pond and a creek running through. It was secluded, a mile off the main road, and you couldn't see the two-story cabin through the oak, pine, and cedar trees shrouding the front of the house. He had cleared brush, saplings, and trimmed several mature trees in the backyard to have views of the mountains, a path to the pond, and a place to set up targets and practice archery. The redwood deck ran the length of the house and stretched out twenty feet, making you feel like you were sitting in the woods. There was a table—where his plate and an empty beer bottle sat—chairs, a grill, and several Adirondacks while in the yard was a firepit and benches. With a life in Trinity and with the Cascade pack, the house offered a feel of protection from outsiders and a place to find peace. *Like today*, he thought.

Clio laughed and mumbled, "A foul turf war."

Ansel listened to her giggle and grasped why he was drawn to her. Clio had an innocence about her that gave her a vulnerability while at the same time she possessed a strength. There weren't shadows in her eyes or a darkness. She didn't live with the sins of her past. He felt he was betraying her by talking to her and didn't deserve to hear her laugh.

"You're at home, not at work?" she asked. Usually the enforcers, like Captain Wolt, were off work at five and did not work from home. Baron Kanin wanted them to have their own time, and if they were going to work, they were going to be paid.

"Affirmative, it's been a long day. I'm getting my appointments straight for tomorrow. If you're interested in leaving your townhouse in the city, for the wilds of the woods, I have great views of the mountains and then there's the geese." *What the hell did I say? What the hell am I thinking?* There was a reason he didn't date. His life wasn't wholly his own.

Friends, family, and people he loved were weapons to be used against him. Ansel trusted the pack to protect one another and knew the enforcers, soldiers, slayers, and shadows would find and eliminate all threats against them. He didn't want the extremists from his past finding him and using someone he loved, because they would hunt them down, and while he watched they would torture them, believing they were punishing all involved and cleansing the world of evil. He had observed and had taken part in the torture, the blood, and the lost lives as they demanded information or prolonged the victim's death. It didn't stop until the victim's screams ended with the last beat of their heart and the witness, their target had gone insane.

Ansel inhaled and exhaled, felt the weight of the tattoo on his side, and saw the blank eyes staring at him, crimson staining their faces, and hearing the weak voices begging for mercy. Bringing someone into his life was a mistake and put the person's life at risk. He liked Clio, Dr. Hyde, and wasn't going to make her a target when Celestial needed her, the pack needed her, and he wasn't going to be responsible for destroying the innocence in her eyes. She loved her job—answering his call was proof—she spent time with her family, extended family, and her friends. She had everything he didn't.

Clio tried to stop giggling but couldn't. Had Captain Ansel Wolt, golden boy enforcer, Director Kanin's right-hand man and his BFF, and a silent strength just ask her if she wanted to go to his house? For an emergency room doctor, getting stunned and not knowing what to do or say wasn't cool ... it was bad, really bad. She could face car accidents, gunshot wounds, and broken bodies, but not Captain Wolt. Staring at his wolf's eyes was like velvet on the skin. *Yes, please, I'll be there in a minute.* Clio wasn't going to indulge in a fantasy. She reminded herself she was a Wight, and he was a Pureblood, and one of the strongest domineers in the pack. The notion of seeing Captain Wolt outside of work and on a personal level crashed and burned.

"No, thank you. I prefer the lovely sounds of sirens and car engines. I'll see you at three." She didn't enjoy them. They blocked the noises coming from her neighbors.

"Copy. Goodnight, Doctor Hyde." Ansel hit the end button, and took a drink of his beer. He didn't have to worry about backpedaling and recanting his offer when the good doctor didn't want to have anything to do with him. Her rejection, nice as it was, was proof he didn't need anyone in his life, and he had no idea how to ask a woman out. He finished his beer, set the bottle on the railing, felt summer's warm breeze on his skin, and stared at the geese, the ducks, and the curtain of night.

Back to business. He didn't even try to change her mind, meaning he hadn't been serious. He pointed out she lived downtown, among humans, and was giving her a hard time. That's all it was. Clio set her cell on the table, held her glass, and sat back on the soft cushions. The night spilled through the window, darkening the living room and creating shadows throughout the space. She sipped the cool liquor, inhaled the spice from the candle, and went over their conversation.

"He has geese and a pond." Clio thought she knew Ansel, Captain of Enforcers, but clearly, she did not. She expected him to have a gun range and a gym to explain his build, ability to fight, and expertise with weapons. Not a pond and geese. Her imagination created a wooded backyard, a pond with grasses along its edges, Ansel standing on his deck, out of uniform. And he would say her name, Clio, with his low voice tangled with his wolf.

"You're hopeless," Clio mumbled. "And lonely. Very lonely." What would a Pureblood with status in the pack want with a Wight who lives among humans? Nothing, that's what.

Her cell buzzed. Her heart sank as the screen lit up, the number and screen blaring in the dark room. "Doctor Hyde."

"Why do I have Captain Wolt of the enforcers calling me?" Dr. Carrion demanded.

"Good evening, Doctor Carrion. He is escorting the director and needed a time so he could schedule his other appointments." *God forbid you call him yourself.*

"Why is he bringing Director Kanin?" he questioned. "I expected Baron Kanin, or even the baroness to accompany the director." He sipped something, and she heard the glass clink on the table. "Family is important for the healing process."

"Rutger and Ansel are like brothers," she replied. *More like thick as thieves.* "I'm assuming the baron feels it would be better for Rutger and Ansel to have time together." No doubt this was a way for the baron to get the director back in the office and resuming his duties. Clio was out of protocol by referring to Ansel and Rutger by their names and not their titles, but she didn't care. Dr. Carrion didn't know about the restrictions happening in the pack. Plus, it was late, and she was tired.

"You told Captain Wolt to use the security entrance, yes? I don't want unnecessary attention with the director's visits. The patients are beginning to calm down with his absence," he explained.

The first few nights Rutger hadn't controlled his power as his desperation and need to see his mate drove him. Since he's an alpha and powerful, it caused the weaker magic-born to live in a state of constant submission. Clio knew Rutger was strong, he was Second to the Alpha, but what she felt when he was in his secured room—more like a prison cell— was incredible and made chills skate down her spine.

"Affirmative. I told him to use the security entrance. I also told him to be there at three, to give Miss Langston a chance to eat and cleanup."

"I'm not available at three."

"I am." Clio took a sip and debated hanging up on the irritated man. The thought brought a smile to her face despite Dr. Carrion's attitude.

"Then I'll see you tomorrow," he replied and hung up.

"Goodnight, Doctor," Clio said to no one. She held her cell, felt exhaustion pulling on her, and with early morning dangling her alarm clock, coffee, and Captain Wolt's visit in front of her, she held her glass and headed to bed. Both the captain and Dr. Carrion had ruined any appetite she might have had.

CHAPTER SIX

Ansel shifted in his seat, adjusted his holster and his pistol, and fought to ignore the weight of his dream. Premonition. Dream. Remembering his parents and how she saved his life provoked the memory, that's all it was.

His button-up shirt—with Cascade's crest on the left side and his name on the right—jeans, tactical belt, and boots felt heavy. Like he was pretending to be someone he wasn't. He tried telling himself, for the hundredth time, it was a dream, nothing more, brought on in a moment of weakness from stress and exhaustion. The heaviest weight was the baron depending on him to take Rutger's place, and letting his defenses down, his past swept in and played in the graveyard of his mind. Then there was asking Dr. Hyde if she wanted to see the views of the mountains and geese from his deck with him. Stupid. It had been a spur-of-the-moment decision and not like him. He didn't make those kinds of mistakes. Weakness. He was getting complacent, and it was going to get him killed.

The dream was a warning he needed to tighten his defenses.

When the nightmare spit him out of its maw, he was sweaty, his muscles felt like rebar, and his mind raced with the life he had led and her face. He tried to relax, telling himself it wasn't real, and he needed sleep. It didn't work. The feeling of danger made his body hum with anxiety, and digging in to him, it made it impossible for him to remain in bed. He gave up and went for a run, ate breakfast, showered and dressed, and was parked in front of communications at six o'clock, minutes before the construction crew arrived. Hitting the keys of his terminal as if they had wronged him, he barely noticed the morning sun challenging the AC as its heat warmed the cab. He hammered a key and brought up the call log from the night before. Enforcers worked two shifts; seven a.m. to five p.m., and the second, five to midnight, at which time communications shut down. Since implementing modifications, a third shift, midnight to seven, was added in order for communications to be monitored twenty-four hours a day. He stared at the truck/motorhome and didn't like the mobile unit, the construction site, the chaos they created, and the feeling of not being in control. Scrolling down the page, he found nothing of significance, and satisfied nothing happened and no one was at risk, he switched screens and checked to see if anyone had signed on.

When an enforcer signed into their terminal as active, it placed them on the roster and gave Ansel a list of names. He compared the active enforcers to another list making sure everyone was accounted for. In the event an enforcer was unable to work a substitute was called, the names and reasons added to the report. A report which he was required to sign and turn into the baron. There were rules which stated details of their work and punishment if the rules weren't followed. Ansel didn't know of anyone who had been given a warning, let alone had been punished. He looked at communications again and didn't like it. Then again, he didn't like anything that morning.

The damn premonition was eating him alive.

Dream.

It had been forty years since he fled her command and left the Covey. After his escape, he lived as a fugitive on the run and as a rogue lived in hiding. He went from town to town, state to state, never staying anywhere long enough for people to know him or for her to find him and unleash her revenge. Those years of running and looking over his shoulder were long, lonely, and heartbreaking. They made him feel like an outcast. He was a Pureblood werewolf and needed a pack, a family, a mate. When he found Trinity and Cascade, his instincts told him he belonged. Then, when they accepted him, he risked everything by staying. Living in Trinity for the last decade made him feel like he had a family, was a vital part of the pack, and was free of her threats.

Despite feeling confident in the pack and protected in the pacific northwest, he didn't allow himself to get involved with a woman and have a mate. Ansel didn't have lovers, and the last time he risked being intimate with a woman he had been in Alaska. That had been a mistake. He didn't have close friends, save for Rutger, didn't go out, and wasn't social. He went to work, then went home.

He thought of Rutger and their relationship and a twinge of guilt struck at him. Their friendship was becoming inappropriate and a risk with Jordyn involved. He wouldn't put Rutger or his mate in danger. As a precaution, he would have to distance himself from his friend, someone he considered a brother, and damn, he hated the thought, especially when the baron and Rutger were depending on him. With the dream clinging to him, he didn't have a choice.

Did he think the dream meant she was closing in on him? Not possible. She stayed in the Midwest and traveled to the East Coast with the Covey. More than once he heard her say she hated the west, complaining the people were uncontrolled and adventurous, the land wild, and they lacked the refinement of the east.

He didn't believe what he was saying. He trusted his instincts, they had kept him alive for one hundred and twenty years, and his were telling him there was danger headed his way. Whether it was her or something else, he didn't know. Movement made him look up from the terminal, and he watched Mandy descend the steps of the motorhome and head straight to him. Ansel clicked out of the screens, leaving the home screen, killed the engine, and got out of his truck.

"Mandy," he greeted.

"Good morning, Captain Wolt. I cleared an area for you inside," she explained. She wore the enforcer's uniform, and pulled her strawberry blonde hair back in a braid. Her face was free of makeup, bringing attention to her blue-violet eyes.

"Thank you. Are you on the third shift?" He didn't think she was, he hoped she wasn't, he liked having her work with him.

Before she answered, a grinding noise had them turning to see a bulldozer push what remained of the office's foundation to a pile of rubble. Behind it, workers capped pipes and protected electrical wires, and an engineer team pointed and looked at tablets. Ansel had no idea what the hell was going on or how they were going to make the new one-thousand-square-foot underground facility with cells and interrogation rooms a reality. Protected by several security points and access granted to the baron, Rutger, and Lieutenant Bouldin, there would also be a specific team of guards. The Cascade's underground prison was going to be a pale comparison to the Highguard's Crystal Palace in a

Siberian tundra. One mile underground and hundreds of acres of footage, it held every kind of magic-born, creatures of myth, and those who had gone insane.

"Negative, I came in early. This is a cluster." She faced him. "The baron would like to see you as soon as possible. Per the baron, I've cleared your schedule from two to five." Mandy took a step toward the white and gray hulk of communications.

Three hours? Ansel followed her to the stairs and stopped. "Thank you. I'm going to see the baron."

"Sir." Mandy took one last look at the site, then disappeared into the vehicle.

Ansel walked around the side of the house to the full view of the construction site and thought it looked like a bomb had gone off. Machinery roared, tore up the ground, while men and women all wearing safety vests carried tools and talked on radios. Advance Construction was magic-born owned and employed magic-born and Deviants. The people working on the office, Summit, and eventually Rutger's house, were all magic-born. No one was going to have Deviants—basically humans—know the inner secrets of the office, or question why Rutger would have UV lights, among others, as floodlights. The Cloaked, vampires, demons, ghouls, and the like were magic-born living in secret, their features, habits, and magic infinitely different and unaccepted by humans.

"Captain," Sousa greeted.

"The baron is expecting me."

Sousa nodded as he held the handle and pulled the heavy, walnut door with its frosted glass center depicting wolves and wrought iron accents. Opening with a whisper, it let a wall of cool air scented with fresh flowers flow into the early morning and over Ansel. He walked inside, going through the familiar foyer, passing the formal greeting room, dining room, the stairs, and the framed photography decorating the cream walls. He heard the baroness' calm voice, her words soothing as if she was speaking to a child, then he heard Rutger. Ansel stopped at the office door, closed his eyes, listened to Rutger's rough growl, and sensed the distance in them. He knocked three times. The talking in the family room stopped at the same time the baron opened the door.

"Ansel." Baron Kanin walked around his desk and sat down. His tawny gaze looked tired, his shoulders tense under his royal blue, button-up shirt, the open collar exposing the edges of his tattoo.

"You wanted to see me?" Ansel asked.

Every Pureblood family in the Cascade pack wore a crest, their depiction of a wolf, and runes of their ancestors. The men wore theirs tattooed on their chests, while the women had theirs on their backs. Ansel, a Pureblood, didn't have one. It had been stripped from him ... he didn't have a family, or a legacy to pass on. He did have a tattoo. After his shower, he stood in front of the steam-dusted mirror, turned, lifted his left arm, and stared at the black and red ink.

"Yes. Thank you for taking care of Rutger's appointment," Baron Kanin said as he sat back.

"You're welcome."

"We explained to Gavin what happened to Rutger and Jordyn, and will explain it to Tanner and Bailey when they return from the coast. Tanner called to tell me they saw the media coverage, and I've advised them not to contact the Langstons to discuss the situation."

"How did Rutger respond?" Ansel asked.

"Better than I expected. In fact, I think he's ready to go

back to work." Baron Kanin's enthusiasm and hope carried in his voice. "When you're finished at Celestial, please take him to his house."

It explained the three hours. "I'll talk to him and bring him up to speed."

"I need to start the renovations," Baron Kanin stressed. "I don't want Jordyn to go home and get comfortable only to have to leave while they work."

"I'll talk to him," Ansel assured. The dream continued to eat at his attention, and sitting with the baron made him feel like he was a trader to the pack. Guilt waged war on the walls protecting him from his past and made him feel he wasn't the person to fight through Rutger's thoughts and convince him having strangers invade his house was a solid plan.

"Thank you."

"Is there anything else?" Ansel needed to think about something, anything, and get to communications and check in with the workers at the Summit.

"I'll be expecting a report on Rutger's visit."

"Affirmative, sir."

Baron Kanin dismissed him as he leaned forward, took a stack of papers, and began reading.

Ansel left the office, closed the door behind him, and paused before heading down the hall. Coming from the family room, he recognized Rutger, the baroness, and the third, Gavin. They were talking casually, their voices carrying along with the smells of bacon, eggs, and fresh brewed coffee. A family united to help heal one of their own. After his parents died, he believed the Covey was his family, his brothers and sisters, and Bronte a strength by his side. The claws of the dream gouged his flesh and it roared to life with his acknowledgement of her name. He promised himself he would never say her name out loud or in his head, he didn't want to give it life or a passage into the present. The Covey, her, the life he left, he needed all of them to remain buried in the dark years of his past.

Ansel shoved his regret to the side, and collecting himself, walked down the hall to the double doors where Sadie stood her post. Two months ago, four sentinels, in plain clothes, stood the standard shift, six a.m. to six p.m., and served the baron and baroness. Their numbers increased to twelve, their shift going to ten hours a day, and their uniform changing to white polo shirts with the Cascade's crest, their name, beige tactical pants, shoulder holster, and they carried a Glock 19 in 9 mm. The enforcers carried a Glock 21, 45 caliber; their task was to stop anyone from getting into the house. If the attackers breached the entrance, the sentinels would guard the baron and baroness, making it close quarters which would unitize the smaller pistol.

"Captain," Sadie greeted as she opened the door.

Across from them, the rumble of diesel engines, the tracks of the excavator clanging, and the screech from the bulldozer as its bucket scraped rocks blasted. Clouds of dust hung in the air around the machinery, their edges fading as the breeze caught them and pulled. The thick, green grass, honeysuckle clinging to the columns of the massive stone porch were frosted in fawn. The construction was going to turn everything within four hundred yards to beige, including his truck. Ansel nodded, stepping out of the house, and she quickly closed the door behind him.

He watched the construction as he took the stairs, then made a left, and walked toward communications. The air cleared, taking the pungent smells of diesel and oil, and bought the fresh scents of pine trees, untouched soil, a ranch in the distance, and freshly watered flowers. On the first step he opened the door, crested the last stair, and made his way inside the hulking vehicle. To the right and along the left side sat a desk, computer, and chair while on the right was an identical setup. On the left was a conference-style area with a center table, peppered with outlets, and four metal chairs. The right side wall held four screens. Under them was a narrow shelf, as if it had sprouted out of the wall like the desks, and another table running the length of the area. On the other side of the conference area, two chairs and swinging tables with equipment that looked like it belonged in a lab. The overhead storage, drawers, and available space held the entirety of their old communications.

"What's with the lab instruments?" Ansel asked. There were three microscopes wrapped in plastic, beakers, a burner, and others he couldn't guess what they were.

"A mini forensics lab. It's a trial run to see if it's necessary." Mandy looked at the assortment, her eyes darkening, and Ansel knew what she was thinking. When was it going to end? How did they get to a place where the pack needed a forensics lab? "Captain, your desk is the one on the left. When the director returns, he'll have the right side," she explained. She turned in the chair, giving him her back, and stared at the screens mounted on the wall. "You'll have a semblance of privacy from the common area."

"Thank you. Forensics needs people," Ansel started as he leaned on the table's edge to see the screens.

One was showing the front of the baron's house, the other gave him a real time of the messages sent between enforcers, and the other displayed calls. It was the best of the best and appeared to be slightly paranoid. Like having a forensics lab. Staring at the screens and the information each contained, he felt like he was watching a military TV show and they were preparing for the apocalypse.

"Affirmative. Doctor Emily Radford, Craig Budig, and Eric Harris have backgrounds in forensics science. Doctor Radford works for the DOJ, and Mr. Budig and Mr. Harris have worked with her."

"Are they magic-born or Deviant?" There was no way the baron would have humans at Foxwood.

"They're part of Cascade. I didn't know who they were either. Apparently, they travel." Mandy stopped, acted like she was listening to someone. "Copy." Her voice changed from causal to stern and riding over the beeps and sounds of the computers. "Go ahead, Summit."

"What's happening?" Ansel asked.

She hit several buttons and typed what Ansel guessed was a command to whoever she was talking to. "They're going to test the cameras at the Summit. If they pass, they'll test the license plate reader, palm vein scanner, and the keypad. Once each measure is cleared, the Summit will be one step closer to being finished."

"I wish the office was that simple," Ansel mumbled.

"Agreed." Mandy faced the screens, her fingers gliding over the keys on the keyboard.

In a blink, they saw Pine Street, trucks and work vans parked along the sides of the road while workers looked at the camera, to their tablets, and back to the camera. Ansel scanned the scene and saw two vehicles belonging to Paradise County deputies, and trucks with Cascade's crests on their sides. *Good.* He hadn't checked the roster since leaving the meeting with the baron and would have to make sure everyone was accounted for. A crystal-clear view of the Summit was on the screen with men working on an open black box with more wires than Ansel ever wanted to be in charge of. The screen blinked and split into six small boxes, each with a different part of the parking lot.

"Main parking lot camera check," a male voice reported.

"Affirmative. Clear. The screen split into six," Mandy responded.

"Just what we wanted. It works," a different man replied. "Sending the confirmation report."

"Copy." Mandy turned slightly in her seat to face Ansel. "He'll send the report to his engineer and technician and they'll send it to the baron."

"Perfect."

"Everything you see here can be accessed by your computer. Enter your name and code and it'll bring up the information. If you need to go over the roster, you can access it as well," Mandy explained.

"Copy." Ansel watched for a few seconds longer, the cameras scanning the different sections of the Summit, except one. "Have the cameras on the west side been installed?"

"Negative. The baron is waiting."

"Did he give a reason?" Ansel checked the time. *Eight.* He had several hours before he took Rutger to Celestial, which left him confirming the roster, hand delivering it to the baron, and talking about the cameras.

"The memo is on your desk. Sir, may I speak freely?" Mandy asked as she faced him. Her violet-blue eyes narrowed on him as her face took on a forced neutral mask.

Right then Ansel hated the new policies. "Affirmative. What is it, Mandy?"

"There's enough reports and memos being passed around to blanket the planet. Is it part of the *new* policies? Waste?" she asked.

"Negative. I think it's a side effect of the chaos. I'll talk to the baron about having all memos and reports delivered electronically. It's not like we don't have a minicomputer in our pocket." That stopped his hand delivery. "When communications is up and running it has to reduce some of the burden."

"Affirmative, sir." Happy with his reply, she went to her keyboard and the men reporting on the security equipment.

Ansel left her and the screens, walked the short distance to his desk, pulled the chair out, and sat down. Two files with his name written across the top sat next to the keyboard and the black screen of the computer. Opening the first one he saw the baron's handwriting scrawled across a copy of the diagram for the west side of the Summit. He sat back in the chair and read the baron was going to put in a road, not paved, barely cleared of brush, to keep it camouflaged. If you didn't know it was there you wouldn't see it.

"Where will it go?" he mumbled.

"Sir, did you say something?" Mandy leaned backward to peek around a wall, her braid hanging free.

"Nothing." He glanced at her and went back to the diagram.

The dirt road would be six miles from Pine Street, three hundred yards from the Conclave, and would run parallel for ten miles to come out on a side street, Rivers Edge. The road was in an industrial area that covered several blocks and was home to warehouses, abandoned and occupied, three trucking companies, and a meat packing plant. The small plant was used to process local ranch animals, steers, hogs, sheep, deer and elk during hunting season, it made it rarely used. He was sure the dirt road would exit to the parking lot of a warehouse. *For what?* He made a mental note to do a drive by to check the property, and to make sure he was right. If he was and the road ended at a warehouse, he would speak to the baron. For security reasons, he needed to know who owned the property.

Ansel clicked the mouse. The computer screen lit up, showing the Cascade's crest in the background and a dozen icons. He found the one for the web, and double clicking, it took him five seconds to confirm the warehouse had been purchased by a silent client. Infinity Knights, a company who specialized in restoration had been put in charge of the lot, and permits had been submitted to the county for construction. The loan was funded by Cascade Mutual, Lord Langston's banking firm. He had no reason to inquire about the silent owner. He knew who it was. Now he understood why Rutger was frustrated when the baron worked in the background and didn't tell him his plans. The road and property had security issues, meaning Ansel would need the plans of both. He clicked his way back to the home screen, clicked the icon for the director's files, and brought up the roster. On a separate screen he typed his password, brought up the active enforcers, logged each of them into the roster, signed off on the report, and emailed it to the baron. Easy.

Before taking Rutger to Celestial then his house, hopefully, he would talk to the baron about the Summit and get plans for the road. With several more clicks he signed out of the director's files, back onto the web, and found a search engine where his fingers hovered over the keys. If anyone saw what he was searching, or checked his searches, it might create questions. Doubts. No matter what he worked on, the damn dream was in every thought.

His past surrounded him, his nerves latching onto threats that would make the dirt road a security problem and leave them vulnerable. The lack of precautions would allow a predator to stalk them, assassinate them, and no one would know. They might, there was going to be cameras and sensors, so communications could watch the ambush followed by the assassinations in full HD color. The road exited to a building on a public road, the pack would have no control over the coming and going of the industrial area. Enforcers wouldn't be responsible ... yes, they would patrol, basically driving by, but the sheriff's department would be in charge. He liked things in order and under control. His mind raced, leaving him not knowing where to begin with the security weaknesses of Rivers Edge.

"Damn," he whispered.

If he was going to be able to work and get something accomplished, he had to know. Ansel typed his request, recent deaths, kidnappings, and unsolved murders of magic-born, into the search bar and hit enter. The page refreshed with articles, obituary pages, and how to contact Paradise County's sheriff's department in case of emergency. He chose an article from the local newspaper and scanned it for details, if they mentioned a weapon, and if a suspect had been named. It would be obvious, and newsworthy, if the victim had been murdered with a sword, odd poison, a dagger. He found nothing. Repeating the search, he entered Cottonwood and Rocky Point counties, both bordering Paradise. It gave him information on multiple cities, towns, and rural areas. Nothing.

Ten minutes rolled into twenty and he found nothing matching what he was looking for. If she was leading the Covey his way, like he believed his instincts were telling him, there would have been a trail of magic-born bodies. Each one with a distinct wound displaying a specific weapon. He saw three delicate feathers in front of a sword, its tip pointed to the sky carved into the Cobalt 27 or White 47 blades, rounds, and arrow tips. If she kept to the old ways. The feathers and sword, she loved, branded them as kindred. A Covey.

The Covey. The black and red ink on his left side reminded him day after day of the atrocities he executed in her name, and the vow he made to her. The vow he broke.

Ansel inhaled and exhaled with the nothing looking back at him. As if her whispered voice rode the wind, it was in his head and infecting his instincts. He was making himself crazy. Giving up, he deleted his searches, and tried convincing himself the dream was brought on by stress and the fear of losing the years of peace and the pack he had been given. Deep down, he knew hiding wouldn't last forever. He lived in peace longer than he anticipated and was desperate to keep it.

The door opened, letting in the roars from machinery, yells trying to override them, and light dust. Leaning back, Ansel saw Lado's large frame not just enter the vehicle but make the space appear small. "There's chairs by the table, I'll be there in a minute."

"Sir." Lado turned and headed to the conference area.

Ansel stared at Cascade's crest displayed on the screen, his attention split between his job and his past. *No*, he corrected himself, *his pack. His dead past.*

Sitting on a chair that made her look smaller than she was, a young witch with big, brown eyes streaked with red looked at her mom, Clio, then her hand. Wearing a pink scrub top, her ID badge clipped to a pocket, black bottoms, and shoes, Clio observed a medical student, Suzy, push blue gel out of thick, white tube and onto the right hand and arm of the girl, who winced.

"The burn smells faintly of lavender and sage," Clio began. "Those plants can't give you a chemical burn." She watched the girl's eyes and the thoughts swirling in her eight-year-old mind.

Witches' weaknesses were comparable to humans, leaving them susceptible to injuries like burns, illnesses, and diseases. The power of the Esme, the Lapis Lazuli coven's mistress provided them with heightened magic and combined with the overall power of the coven it strengthened them and elevated their magic, power, and mortality. It was the reason they remained close and lived in communes. Using a holistic approach, they depended on nature, herbs, metals, and energy from the land to infuse their magic and then transform it into chants, spells, and charms. They also had a healing building in the middle of the Esme's garden—it was surrounded by trees, flowers, herbs, shrubs, had skylights in the roof so the sun and moon were visible.

Clio had heard about it in passing or overheard a conversation; she didn't fully understand what they did. It was one of two reasons she was surprised when Pearl Ashby, Ava Jade's mother, brought her to the ER. The other reason, she would bet money, involved the pack. The Lapis Lazuli coven made it extremely clear they were distancing themselves from Cascade. In a written letter to Baron Kanin, the Esme stated they didn't want to cause any distress and conflict and stressed their relationship with the pack was a priority. She understood their reservations after a black magic coven kidnaped Miss Langston and tried killing her. Mrs. Ashby had to know Miss Langston was a patient at the hospital and was currently residing.

"Do you know what kind of chemicals you used?" Clio asked.

"It wasn't a chemical," Ava Jade answered. Her small voice sounded defeated, like she realized she was going to have to tell the truth.

"No, what was it?" Clio's sense of smell was better than a human's—it was the reason she picked up the lavender and sage—but she couldn't get passed the smell of burned skin. If she had been an Illuminate or a Pureblood, she would have been able to. *Keep reminding yourself.*

"I was smudging." Ava Jade looked down as Suzy wrapped gauze around her hand, between her fingers, and her wrist. "Kelly said my aura was unkept."

Clio looked at Mrs. Ashby for an explanation. "Kelly is the same age as Ava Jade. They're friends. She sees the world through colors. She'll become a strong clairvoyant once she has been trained."

Right. "What did you do?" Clio had to know what happened, more out of curiosity than a medical reason.

"It wasn't working. I couldn't feel a difference. I used a spell, the sage exploded, and the burning leaves landed on my arm." Ava Jade met her mother's gaze.

"It's all right. Next time Kelly says your aura is unkept, we will fix it together. You can't use a spell with fire," Mrs. Ashby chided. She met Clio's questioning stare; she didn't know sage could explode and leave a chemical burn behind. "As a phoenix, Ava Jade has the ability to manipulate fire. She had already increased the fire's combustion, then when she cast the spell, she turned the oils in the sage into an accelerant. It exploded."

"I see. That's one for books, Ava Jade." Clio was reminded of the differences between human children and the magic-born.

Trinity had one of the most advanced human burn units in the state, and treated people from around the nation. Celestial had its own—two to be exact … one for magic-born like witches, and one for shapeshifters whose body was capable of regenerating. Ava Jade's magic revolved around fire, she would never live without it, and her burn was going to heal.

"Do you want me to send you home with ointment and bandages?" Clio asked. She didn't know why they were there.

"No, thank you. I'll seek treatment from the Esme's son, he's a doctor."

Is that so? "What's his name?" Clio asked, hopeful she could get in contact with him and get him to visit the hospital. She would love to have a witch in residence. Of course, he would have to pass a background investigation, and the Esme, Baron Kanin, and the hospital board would have to authorize the contract. She could get it done.

"Doctor William Baines. He has just returned from working abroad," Mrs. Ashby answered.

"I'm sure it's nice to have him back and the coven feeling complete." Clio nearly let her thoughts of having him work at the hospital, and the knowledge he must have gathered from traveling, override the unease Mrs. Ashby clearly wanted her to sense. Her nervousness rolled from her like a weak electric wave while her demand for attention threaded through. She wasn't in the ER for Ava Jade's sake.

"How does it feel?" Suzy asked.

"Good. It doesn't sting anymore," Ava Jade answered.

"Excellent." Suzy faced Clio. "Is there anything else, Doctor?"

"Would you get Ava Jade's paperwork in order?"

"Yes, Doctor." Suzy gave them a bright smile and left them alone.

"I'm curious as to why you're here when Doctor Baines is available to you." And Mrs. Ashby could have treated the burns at home, they were healers. Clio sensed there was more going on and the woman was wanting to have her say.

Mrs. Ashby hesitated, looked around the ER, seeming to eye the werewolves from the Cascade pack, back at Ava Jade, and then Clio. "I have to be honest, I wanted to test your reception, Doctor Hyde. I know you were there when they found the soothsayer, and witnessed the cruelties committed against her. I want you to know we are all saddened by what happened to her. She has the empathy of the coven."

There it was. Not a simple ER visit, if there was such a thing. "The coven, and I use the term *coven* loosely, has been disbanded, and those responsible are in jail. I don't hold you or the Lapis Lazuli accountable. Furthermore, Celestial is neutral ground, a safe place for the magic-born to receive treatment or sanctuary," Clio explained. If one of the witches from Butte Springs walked through the ER's doors, the oath she had taken, and the vow of Celestial would require her to treat the patient and give them shelter. It didn't mean she wouldn't have guards watching them like the serial killers they were. "Why did you choose Celestial? You could have requested a meeting with Baron Kanin."

"Cascade projects unity without weakness, and it protects their own, making it a strong pack. One of their kith, a young male, was murdered, their soothsayer tortured, their Second nearly lost his mate, and Baron Kanin's actions as well as the integrity of the pack have been questioned in the media. Those wounds cut deep, can become infected, and take time to heal. The pack reflects the baron's belief, his willingness to forgive, and his understanding. I came to you because you are an authority here, an enforcer, and are personally overseeing the soothsayer's care. Your soothsayer is defenseless, and to protect her you could have prohibited us entrance, denied care, or disrespected us simply because we are witches. It would have meant Baron Kanin sees us the same way, as his adversaries, not part of the klatch," Mrs. Ashby explained.

She knew Clio was an enforcer and had been at Butte Springs. *Interesting*. She didn't know anything about the director nearly losing himself. She was there as a test. "I assure you, you are not an adversary."

"You've proven this by treating my daughter while your soothsayer is in residence. I couldn't have asked for a better example of trust." Mrs. Ashby placed her hand on Ava Jade's head. "I'll pass your courtesy onto the Esme. This will ease the tension within the coven, we are grateful."

"I'm pleased to have been of service. If you need anything, please call," Clio offered. Because she needed someone else calling her. "And you, young lady, be careful."

"Thank you," Mrs. Ashby replied with a gentle smile. "Are you ready to go?"

"Yes." Ava Jade hopped off the chair, and standing, held her right hand in her left and close to her body.

"Suzy will meet you in the waiting room with the paperwork." Clio watched them leave the ER, their conversation replaying and the idea she was considering calling Dr. Baines. What would the baron say? She had no idea. Checking the time, she saw it was after two, which meant the countdown to dealing with Captain Wolt had started. She shook her head, the sound of her name on his lips, and the sight of him in his backyard, out of uniform plaguing her. *Get a grip*. She headed to her office.

"Doctor Hyde."

With her name she stopped and faced Tony, a paramedic and the med van driver who delivered the two boys. His sapphire eyes held her and added to his uniform of blue polo, with Cascade and Celestial's crests on the left side, his name on the right, dark blue BDU pants, and boots. "What can I do for you?"

"Mrs. Adam's advised me to talk to you," he replied.

"What about?" Clio didn't have a clue and didn't have time to chit chat.

"I'm on the rotation of drivers. I would like to be priority." His eyes gauged her and his auburn hair with blond streaks grazed his collar when he turned his head. He smiled at a passing nurse, who smiled back as her cheeks reddened.

Clio wanted to roll her eyes. "I'm not sure why she told you to talk to me. I don't have anything to do with the drivers," Clio explained. She was going to have a talk with Mrs. Adams.

"I stated I wanted to be assigned to your calls," Tony replied with a grin.

He knew he was good looking and knew how to use his assets, and it almost had her smiling at him. "Why my calls? I'm not on the rotation."

"No, but you take calls. And they're the best. I heard about the detective you transferred to the trauma center."

Lieutenant Bouldin hated it. "It wasn't a call." She shook her head. An adrenaline junkie. "I get you like the fast pace—"

"And driving fast," he interrupted. "Besides that, I'm good at what I do."

She was sure he was. Intense. Confident. Capable. "You're going to show up for work every day and wait around until I have a call? Which rarely happens."

"I will remain on the rotation." Tony shifted his stance, his blue eyes softening.

Puppy eyes. Or in his case, fox eyes. Clio groaned. She would deal with one driver, one attitude, and would explain things one time. She didn't have anything to lose. "Fine. Tell Mrs. Adams to email me and I'll confirm."

"Thank you, Doctor Hyde. You won't regret this." He gave her a smile of victory, held her gaze for a second, and left her in the hall.

"I better not," she mumbled as she continued to her office.

When Captain Wolt arrived, she would have to greet him at the security doors, and she wondered if the casual conversation and friendly atmosphere between them would continue or would the captain wear his professional cold front? She didn't know. Clio ran her ID through the scanner, listened to the lock slide, and opened the door. Photos of the Cascade mountains and paintings of the area lined the soft white walls while pale pine doors added another level of softness not found in the main part of the hospital. Clio stopped at the door, her name on the plate, and swiped her ID card through the reader and entered the number code. When the lock slid, she opened the door, entered her private haven, and sitting behind the desk she took the phone and dialed communications. She could have sent a message to Mandy, except Clio considered her call part work from Celestial and part enforcer.

"Enforcer headquarters, Mandy speaking."

"Enforcer headquarters?" Clio asked. That was new.

"Affirmative. Don't get me started. What can I do for you, Doc?"

Clio laughed. At least at the hospital she dodged the changes taking place. Her mind went back to Captain Wolt and the nonchalant way he asked her if she wanted to go to his house. His house with a pond. Maybe he wanted someone he could shed his cold front and relax around. *It isn't you*, her mind warned.

"I need you to run a name for me."

"Go ahead."

Clio could hear Mandy hitting the keys to bring up the Assembly software, a database of all magic-born in the world. Complied by the Highguard it contained DNA, fingerprints, genus, magic traits, faction, and location. Human law enforcement used a similar version containing both human and magic-born, they called Citizen Base.

"Pearl Ashby, she's part of the Lapis Lazuli."

"Not only part of the coven, one of the circle. The Esme considers her second in command," Mandy explained. "Why do you want to know about her?"

Her heart leapt to her throat. She passed the test and hopefully helped ease the tension between the coven and the pack. Hopefully. Wouldn't want to make things worse. "She came to the ER, her daughter burned herself. I think I should talk to the baron about this."

"Affirmative. I'm emailing a copy of the file to you. When I have a date and time, I'll message you. Be advised with the construction going on, he may request a report. In person meetings aren't taking place."

"Copy," Clio replied as she slipped into her enforcer mode.

"Doctor Hyde, I have to tell you something," Mandy mumbled.

"What? And why do I get the feeling it's bad?" Clio sat back in her chair and prepared herself for bad news, as her imagination went wild.

"You've been removed from the active enforcers. There will be an official letter sent to you stating Baron Kanin's reasons. I thought you would want to know immediately."

Her heart went from her throat to her feet and a chill raced over her skin. He couldn't have told her in person. "Removed. Why?"

"I'm not at liberty to say. But know what you've done for the baron and the director hasn't gone unnoticed," Mandy explained.

"Really? Is my removal supposed to be a reward? I call bullshit," Clio fumed.

"I'm sorry, Doc."

Clio inhaled and exhaled; it wasn't Mandy's fault. "I'm sorry. Thanks for letting me know."

"Sure thing." Mandy hung up and the phone clicked.

Clio set the handset down, disbelief racing through her, and felt as if the baron had pulled the carpet out from underneath her. Was he punishing her? He'd taken the enforcers from her. She had earned her place. What didn't she do? What did she do? Clio didn't fucking know.

Focus. She would ask the baron when she met with him. If she met with him. Things were getting out of control. Shoving her anger down, she thought about the witches and could imagine the tension weaving through the coven from the uncertainty of not knowing if the pack was going to blame them, cut them from the klatch, or retaliate.

"He removed me," she whispered. Her cell chimed, jerked her back to reality, and lit up with a message. Clio opened the screen, and after reading the message, stood, left her office, and headed for other side of the hospital.

The good captain was early.

Clio entered a number, and holding her cell to her ear she waited.

"Doctor Carrion."

"Director Kanin is here. Is Jordyn ready to see him?" she asked. Clio marched passed the nurse's station, a waiting area, and several rooms, her footsteps giving away her anger.

"Yes, Miss Langton is waiting."

"Thank you." Clio hit end and shoved the cell in a side pocket.

Stopping at another door, she slid her ID card, the lock disengaged, the door opened, and she was in the hallway headed toward the security entrance, and the double reinforced steel doors looming in front of her. They used the back entrance for special situations like the director seeing his mate, the baron and baroness, and the Kanin family, an elder, or a magic-born with status. In the time she had been working at Celestial, no one had ever needed to use it. Those were different days. Another swipe of her card and she opened the left side and met July's heat that radiated off the concrete and steel while the bright sun glared down on her making her squint her eyes.

"Director Kanin, Captain Wolt," she greeted as pleasantly as possible, and held the door open.

"Doctor Hyde," the director greeted in return.

He walked inside, his eyes gleaming gold for a breath before turning to their natural brown. His hair had been cut and combed away from his face, he was clean shaven, his black T-shirt, with the edges of his tattoo under the collar, fit snug around his chest and biceps, and his jeans ended in a pair of worn boots. The thick, black band around his left bicep flexed, making the intricate images of wolves and runes move.

"Doctor Hyde." Ansel walked by her, not meeting her gaze, and despite keeping his focus on Rutger and his pending visit with his mate, Ansel caught spice from cinnamon under the stringent smells of disinfectant, cleaning solution, and the sterile environment. *Don't go there.*

As time passed, the dream's power hadn't let go of him like he prayed it would. He finally bullied it to a corner where it waited for him to give in while he tried to concentrate on work. He met with the baron, asked about the plans for the road, resuming installation of the security cameras, and the timetable for the office. His questions were answered with vague replies then the baron *told him* what he and Rutger were going to talk about on the drive to Celestial.

Much to the baron's dislike, they didn't speak. Ansel tried with small talk and when Rutger remained silent, he jumped straight to the upgrades on his house. Rutger responded with no, no one was going to go into his house until he did. When was that going to be? After the visit with Jordyn. Those were his last words. In the years he spent within the pack, he never felt disconnected. When they sat in the cab, the computer chiming with alerts and the sound of tires on asphalt, it felt like he wasn't part of Cascade. The fear of her finding him, his lies, and Rutger's silence coiled into a ball of self-doubt.

Clio wondered if Captain Wolt knew she had been removed from the active list, and if he did would he say anything to her, the way Mandy had? Probably not. With his cold front, he was clearly on duty and had no intention of initiating small talk.

"Director, how are you today?" she asked as she started down the hall.

"Fine. How are you?" he asked in return.

Auto response. Maybe he wasn't doing as well as it appeared. "Doing well, thanks."

When Dr. Hyde took the lead, Ansel fell back, staying behind Rutger, and watched his shoulders tense as Dr. Hyde made an attempt at conversation. She didn't lack manners, her tone was congenial—the conversation light, not serious—was professional, and her timing skilled. If he was bored, Rutger didn't show it. Just as Dr. Hyde was proficient, Rutger was used to talking to dignitaries, lord and ladies of the pack, and acting as an ambassador in a highly political environment. He wouldn't say or do anything to embarrass Cascade or his family and wouldn't offend Dr. Hyde.

Silence wove between them, making Ansel think Rutger was done listening and wasn't going to respond. Then, when he answered her question with a question, Ansel couldn't stop himself from smiling at the piece of the old Rutger. Dr. Hyde continued to lead them deeper into the hospital, like they were taking backroads and were evading the law, while keeping her pleasant demeanor toward Rutger. She did not acknowledge him, no, she wore a cold front like a shield that separated her from him. Ansel figured she was driving home her rejection and making sure he wouldn't ask again. She could drive the rejection like a nail into the coffin because that's where the question was. Dead and buried. Asking her over to his place had been a mistake. Huge. Deadly mistake. The dream was a warning his past could find him, and he needed to keep his distance.

Clio felt their presence, their wolves, and power, but zeroed in on Captain Wolt's strength, and scent, and it added to her anger. Doing her best to ignore him, she continued down another hall. The hospital was sectioned into four different buildings. The emergency room, main surgical unit, and burn ward, the second was a non-emergency clinic, the third was for physical rehabilitation, and the fourth was the inpatient psychiatric facility. The buildings were connected by a series of hallways and elevators, all guarded by cameras, security door scanners, guards, and more halls which allowed staff to go from one building to another without interfering with patients or visitors. She guided the men down another hallway to a set of elevators, and pushing the correct button, stood in front of the men in silence. The tension coming from Captain Wolt was thick enough to cut with a knife, and while the tension was substantial and thickened the air, it was the director's increasing detachment, like a black void, worrying her.

A chime sounded, the doors opened, and she held the left side while they entered. Taking her place in front of their brooding presences, the doors closed with a whisper. Clio pushed the button for long-term patients, and it gently began its rise. She never noticed the size of the elevator, the muted instrumental music, or the amount of time—seconds that felt like hours—it took to reach the floor. The men, their size, and their power made the space, which was large enough to accommodate a hospital bed and staff, feel tight. Another chime and the doors slid open. She released a breath, stepped out, and held the door for the director and the captain.

Ansel waited for Dr. Hyde to lead them. He returned to his post behind Rutger as they walked across tile flooring until carpet silenced their steps, and they entered a waiting room. Tinted windows let gentle sunshine in, brightening the space and adding softness to what could be a harsh environment. A variety of greenery decorated the windows and soaked up the light, while rows of chairs with light blue cushions and tables with magazines were sprinkled between. The tension tightening Rutger's shoulders eased under his black T-shirt, making Ansel's anxiety less, by a slim margin.

Clio approached the desk where a man and woman—both wearing civilian business clothing, the attempt to put visitors at ease not lost on her—sat in front of monitors. "Director Kanin is here to see Miss Langston."

"I'll need to see his identification," the woman said

without looking up from her screen. She picked up the phone's handset, entered a series of numbers, and waited. "Yes, Doctor Carrion." Placing it back into the cradle, she turned her attention to Clio. "If Doctor Carrion has time, he wants to speak with Director Kanin after the visit. He'll message you when they're finished, and you are to escort the director and captain to the security entrance."

The day she was having, and Dr. Carrion was going to give her orders? Clio wanted to roll her eyes. "Of course." She stepped away from the desk. "Director Kanin."

"Your ID," the woman insisted.

"Second to the Alpha is an ID," Director Kanin stated. He narrowed his gold gaze on the woman, while the intensity in his voice and the harshness in his words had her shrinking back.

Clio tried to remain professional by covering her smile with a frown, as the director's gaze had both receptionists cringing and their gazes dropping to their keyboards. Both were members of the klatch, the magic-born living under the baron's rule, and part of the Seelie court. They held themselves above others and tested the pack's authority whenever possible. Today, Director Kanin was in no mood to be politically correct or to humor the woman.

"M-My apologies, s-sir. It w-will be one m-minute," she stammered.

"I'll leave you then," Clio started. "Please let me know when you have concluded your visit."

"Affirmative."

Dr. Hyde didn't give Ansel a sideways glance as she left Rutger at the reception desk then marched down the hall, her tight braid moving with her as she disappeared. Was this a second nail into the *I'm not coming over to see your geese* coffin? Why did it bother him when he knew it wasn't going to work anyway? His past was haunting him. Damn, he hated rejection. That's all it was, rejection. And he might have hurt their once relaxed relationship by having asked her.

To his right a pale door opened, revealing a man wearing a white, button-up shirt, blue and gray tie, navy blue slacks, and loafers. Over the weeks, Ansel learned there were differences between the medical part of the hospital and the mental health area. Staff on the medical side wore scrubs, were talkative, the ER, waiting rooms, and nurse's stations busy with people coming and going while the mental health area was conserved, dress was business casual, and the room, like the one they were in, was quiet.

"Director Kanin, please come this way." With a pleasant smile on his face and his back to the door, he held it open.

Ansel gripped Rutger's shoulder. "I'll be here."

Rutger's face didn't register recognition someone had spoken to him when he took the first step and then the second. Ansel had no clue what Rutger was feeling, was thinking, or if he was feeling and thinking anything.

"You may wait over there," the woman behind the desk advised.

Ansel met her narrowed gaze as she pointed at the rows of chairs. "Thank you."

Unlike the medical unit, he didn't have to weave around other visitors, find an empty chair, or worry about privacy; he was the sole person there. He took his cell from a pocket, sat down in the nearest chair, and with a clear view of the door, checked his messages. Lado was keeping him updated about the calls and the status of the enforcers while Mandy informed him of the progress at the Summit and Foxwood. The security had him thinking about Rutger's house and his refusal to have anyone near there. He understood a part of

Rutger's hesitation; just weeks ago had been the first time in three years they had been together, and her scent was there. She was there, not physically, but emotionally. If anyone opened the door, her essence, the scent of them together, would leave the same way she had. Maybe after his visit with Jordyn he would change his mind. Maybe.

Phone calls, whispered chatter, and staff coming and going was the only entertainment as he waited. Ansel checked his cell; it had been fifteen minutes, and there were two more messages from Lado. A representative from the Seelie court reported one of their guards spotted someone trespassing on their land. Situated in the Shasta-Trinity forest, hikers, campers, and the curious stumbled onto their property. Some had read about or heard the legends of Mount Shasta, the cave going eleven miles beneath the mountain to a lost city and wanted to see it for themselves. Any trespassing was accidental and was the reason the Seelie court's representatives worked closely with the park rangers.

The covenant between the Seelie court and the Cascade pack stated the court wasn't allowed to have their own police force. Chancellor Roarke had been allowed to have personal protectors, and guards to patrol the perimeter of their territory, leaving the enforcers to take care of the calls needing law enforcement's presence. The report wasn't a surprise since it was July and tourist traffic was heavy. Thinking it wasn't a serious problem, Ansel advised Lado to keep in contact with the court and if they wanted an enforcer to respond, he needed to send Quinn. He checked the time, another fifteen minutes. Ansel knew Rutger needed the visit, but he had work to do at Foxwood. On the flip side, the longer visit could ease Rutger's worry, and he might allow the upgrades to his house. And if their visit was going well, his mate would put him in the right state of mind, and he would come back to work. He hated himself for his selfishness. Rutger was better at being in charge than he was.

Like a nervous habit, Ansel checked his cell for the millionth time, heard Rutger's low rumble, which had become his normal response to any question, before he saw him. When the door opened, his power flowed into the waiting room, tinged with frustration, and Ansel's hopes for a good visit crashed. Rutger, with Dr. Carrion nipping at his heels, talking a mile a minute and telling him what he needed to do, tried making a swift exit. Ansel was positive Dr. Hyde said Dr. Carrion had appointments during Rutger's visit, then remembered the receptionist saying he might have time. Damn, he wished the doctor would have left Rutger alone.

Ansel took long strides to intervene as Rutger faced the doctor, and nailing his gold glare on him, growled. Stepping between the two men, he blocked the doctor, letting Rutger walk away. "Doctor Carrion."

"Captain Wolt. If you'll excuse me," he started as he stepped to the left, right, then to the left and tried to pass.

Ansel matched him step for step, his six-foot-four-inch height towering over the shorter man, and his muscled body blocking him. "Doctor."

Dr. Carrion looked up at him and exhaled. "You can't stop me. I need to speak with my patient."

"Yes, I can, and he isn't your patient. What were you trying to tell Director Kanin?"

Dr. Carrion took two steps backward, his irritated gaze going to the hallway Rutger was headed toward. "He needs to talk to Miss Langston, not sit in silence for thirty minutes, or on his phone. He was on his phone. *They* need to establish a line of open communication. She needs to feel safe talking to him about what happened to her and have trust he is listening to her. She needs his confidence and needs to know he won't judge her," he expounded with irritation.

"I'll explain it to him." Rutger knew what happened to her. Since she wasn't talking, he might not know how she felt about what happened to her. There was nothing wrong with her coming to terms with it and then explaining herself. If that's what she wanted to do. He didn't think Rutger would ignore Jordyn. Looking over his shoulder, he watched Rutger disappear. "Have a nice afternoon."

Dr. Carrion grunted. "I suppose you'll schedule his next visit?"

"Affirmative. Call me with the date and time. If I'm not available, leave a message on my cell or with Enforcer's headquarters." Ansel stepped back, met the annoyance in the doctor's eyes, and left.

The visit hadn't gone well, Dr. Carrion's frustration an indicator, and Ansel wasn't going to make it worse by calling Dr. Hyde. The Second to the Alpha, Director of Enforcers, escorted by his captain, were perfectly capable of seeing themselves out.

It took a minute for Ansel to catch up with Rutger and fall in step with him. "You've got a huge fan with Doctor Carrion."

"He talks too much." Rutger kept walking. Stalking.

His civilian clothing of a black T-shirt, jeans, and boots should have looked less intimidating, but it wasn't the case. Rutger carried himself with authority and his power surrounding him. The combination sent staff and visitors scurrying out of their way, like the parting of the Red Sea, and running from their path as the two of them marched down the hall. Adding to his presence were the rumors of his stay. That didn't help.

"He said you sat in silence and then you were on your

phone," Ansel stated cautiously.

"Negative." Rutger stopped, shook his head, and growled. "Affirmative. When Jo came home, she was a confident, secure woman with a challenge in her eyes. The woman I fell in love with and have loved, will love forever. One minute my dreams of our lives are coming true, she's the pack's soothsayer, my mate, and we're ... then she's gone." His eyes blazed gold then dimmed as he inhaled and exhaled. "I did what Doctor Carrion said and talked to the side of her face. He's wrong about her. Jo isn't like that, explaining things, talking them to death and making sure her feelings are out for the world to see. She's private, always has been, I know this. I stopped pushing her. Yes, I watched her. I watched the way her chest rose with her breaths. I watched the way her eyes tracked what was happening outside. I watched her lips part. I watched the way she twisted her fingers, and then her features change with her thoughts. I listened to her heartbeat. Her heartbeat proving she's alive. It's all I have." He whispered curses and took a step with less force fueling him.

It was Ansel's turn to shake his head as guilt from clinging to his dream and worrying about himself slapped him. He shoved his thoughts down; there were things on his list he needed to get done. Following Rutger through the hospital, to the security doors, and then outside, the sun met them, its heat flowing over them, taking the air-conditioned chill from the hospital. A mild breeze brought them fresh air that washed the harsh smells and feel from them. Ansel didn't know how Dr. Hyde worked in it day after day.

"You said you talked to the side of her face. Did you tell her there was a chance they'll release the witches?" Ansel asked. The baron said it was better she didn't know, but he doubted Rutger would lie to her. Standing beside the truck's front tire, his question stopped Rutger.

"Affirmative. I wasn't going to lie to her, she's stronger than that, and she would hate me for treating her like she needed protecting." Turning around, he looked at the hospital. "She has to get out of there."

"She will." Ansel raised his hands in a show of don't shoot the messenger. "Why were you on the phone? I could have taken the calls."

"There isn't a *chance* they'll release them," Rutger cursed as he faced Ansel. "While I was staring at the side of her face and listening to her heartbeat to assure myself she's really here, they let them go. They're free."

His heart stopped. "Dammit."

"Not my choice of word but close."

"What did you say?"

"I told the lawyer I thought it was bullshit. Law enforcement can't fucking find Flint, and now his loyal followers are loose. Jo's safety is in question," Rutger explained with a growl. "She's in there detached from the world because they tried killing her."

"The baron needs to know. There has to be something his lawyers can do," Ansel insisted as he got in the truck. "We know they're out there and we'll protect her."

Rutger didn't reply. He sat back, his glare focusing on something on the other side of the windshield, his hands clasped and resting in his lap like he wanted to punch something or didn't know what to do with them. Every once in a while, he caught him flexing his fingers, checking his palms, then clenching them.

When he was a patient at Celestial's metal health ward, Ansel wanted to cringe. It was a prison cell, concrete floor, with a drain in the middle, no windows, and a twenty-five-foot ceiling armed with lights, cameras, and outlets used to fill the room with gas. Rutger's misery and fear for Jordyn's life pushed his wolf, his sanity, and mind to the brink of losing all three. Fighting the prison cell and unable to see his mate, he punched and clawed the walls until he broke his fingers and tore the flesh from his knuckles, leaving crimson stains on the concrete and covering himself in blood. Two warnings were given, then they filled the cell with gas, rendering him unconscious. Only then were they able to treat his self-inflicted wounds. Ansel thought he would sit there in silence as he had on the drive to Celestial when Rutger turned enough to face him.

"I'm not going to my house. I have business at Foxwood." His brown eyes lost the battle with gold, narrowed on Ansel, and told him Rutger hated not being his own man, and warned him not to argue.

"Copy." He wasn't going to question him, he didn't need the hassle, but he needed to say something about the house and the witches being released, and report it to the baron. "Do you want to talk about when you're going to allow the upgrades to your house?" Ansel gave him a sideways glance, then looked at the road.

Rutger waited so long before answering, Ansel was sure he was going to ignore the question. "I'll talk to the baron."

Ansel closed his eyes for a second from the fragility in Rutger's voice. *Yeah, brother, you're being pulled in a million different directions. I'm sorry.* "If you want Jordyn home, she needs to be protected."

"Affirmative," he replied, his low voice tangled with a growl.

"I'll let it go," Ansel promised. *For now*, he thought.

"Ansel," Rutger said his name with his familiar growl in

his voice.

"I'm not going to bother you about it," Ansel started then stopped. "What?"

"I need your help."

"Name it." Ansel held his stone gaze and wanted to get out of the truck.

"I want Jo home." Rutger hesitated, his features sharpening with his thoughts, and Ansel wasn't going to interrupt him. "We're going to kill the witches," he stated flatly.

"What are you talking about?" Ansel asked. He hadn't shaken free from the dream, the weight of it sitting on his shoulders and in his mind. His past was death. The assassinations of those he killed came roaring back. Hot on its tail and making his heart race was vengeance and the demand of blood for blood.

"Finding them and killing them. I have to protect my mate. The pack." Rutger's eyes burned gold with his determination. "I won't stop until they're all dead."

He knew what it was like to kill for survival, revenge, and on orders, Rutger did not. Yes, he fought for his place as director, but he hadn't murdered anyone, and had been forced to hide from magic-born and human alike. His humanized life didn't allow the viciousness of spilled blood, and the pack didn't need the threat of human law enforcement intervening. Ansel risked a sideways glance at Rutger and saw raw rage in his eyes and tension in his shoulders. His words as he described Jordyn played—he watched her, listened to her. It was all he had. It was going to be brutal and bloody.

"We'll find them. We'll kill them," Ansel promised.

CHAPTER SEVEN

"Get him on the bed before he falls down," Clio ordered. "You said he was shot?"

"Yes." The older male elf with long, blond hair and wide, emerald eyes obeyed and awkwardly helped the nurses lift the slumped body to the bed.

A wave of medical staff surged toward them, squeezing around the elf until he gave up and got out of the way. They continued moving equipment, placing trays of instruments to the side, and readying the machines around the wounded man.

"Everyone, suit up," Clio ordered as she stepped into a white suit, resembling a human biohazard suit. Zipping it up she pulled gloves over her hands with the tight ends stopping two inches over the cuffs and sleeves. "We don't know what he has been shot with," she continued as she went to the side of the bed. The soft face, absent of lines, told her he was young. Like in his twenties young.

"He's unconscious, his heart rate is slowing, temperature lowering, eyes dilatated, there's stiffening of the joints," Cruz reported as he set the elf's taut hand on the bed.

Damn. "Cobalt 27," Clio warned them.

"Is he going to be all right?" the elf asked. His eyes showed his worry as he stared at the scene and the staff working on the patient.

"Jamie, please take ..." Clio faced the elf.

"Elder Macario of the Unseelie court."

Right. "And the victim?" Clio asked.

"Daniel, my nephew," Elder Macario answered.

Her mind raced with the implications. First thing was first. "Jamie, please take Elder Macario to visitor room B, and make sure he's comfortable and has privacy," Clio ordered as politely as possible.

"Doctor." Taking the elder's elbow she gently nudged him to follow her. When he turned, she guided him out of the ER and away from the chaos.

Clio focused her attention on Daniel, the nephew of an elder with the Unseelie court. Rayette had started removing what was left his shirt, and once the blood-soaked material was gone it exposed skin that had gone stark white, leaving the circulatory system a road map over his torso. It didn't look like cobalt. Clio searched his chest and didn't find a wound. "Get ready to flip him."

Cruz stepped to the side of the bed, Rayette beside him, as Dr. Kolt took his place next to Clio. "Ready?"

"Affirmative," Cruz replied.

"Flip." Clio and Dr. Kolt lifted the elf, Clio at his lower hips, thigh, and Dr. Kolt at his side and arm while Cruz and Rayette held him and gently lowered him to the mattress.

"There it is," Clio started as she bent down. Under the scarlet veil, black skin curled back from the edges of the hexagon-shaped wound that had begun to cave in on itself. "It isn't acting like cobalt and it's embedded in the shoulder blade."

She was positive it was something else, but what she didn't know. The darkened veins wove under pallid skin, and the smell of rotting flesh wafted from the elf with an undercurrent of a sharp bite. Clio touched the skin around the wound. It sank in, creating a bigger wound and causing gray blood to pool.

"Whatever the projectile is, it's destroying his muscular system faster than it should. It won't take long for his lungs and heart to stop. Start a line of BioThropy, and another line of syn sanguine. Hopefully, it'll stimulate his heart and get his vascular system circulating, and we need his temp to rise." Unsure of what he had been shot with, she hated administering anything that might make Daniel's reaction worse. "Get him on a respirator and heart monitor."

Rayette positioned his head, placed a mask over his face, and when she fit the straps around the back of his head, she hit a button and the machine came to life.

"What are his vitals?" Clio asked.

Checking the cardiac monitor, the screen displaying the elf's temperature, and the ventilator, Cruz replied, "Slowly stabilizing."

That's right. Keep fighting, Daniel. Clio was thankful for his youth and bloodline. She hated losing a patient, the feelings of failure, she hadn't done enough, and didn't know enough dragging her through the mud riddled with razors. But Daniel, if she failed, his connection to the Unseelie court would turn the attack and death into a political nightmare for Baron Kanin.

"He needs surgery and Doctor Arano. The projectile must come out, and I'm not going to start digging. I don't know what kind of cobalt, if is at all, he was shot with. Do you see the shape? A specific round for an elf? It looks like it had barbs and shredded the skin as it went in," Clio stated. What and who would have done this?

"I noticed and agree. Be ready in five, I'm making the call," Dr. Kolt replied. He held a tablet and began typing. "Entering preliminary findings and treatment and downloading it to surgery."

"Copy." Clio's enforcer side was slipping out with her responses and reminded her she was inactive. "Place a medicated mat on his back, then we're wheeling him out." Clio went to the top of the bed and started unplugging monitors then plugging them back into compact mobile units.

Rayette placed a mat over the bleeding, four-inch, hexagon-shaped wound circled by blackened skin, and an audible hiss sounded. They looked at each other as if to confirm everyone heard it and went back to preparing the bed.

"Clear," Cruz reported.

"Clear," Rayette said.

"We're moving," Clio stated.

With Clio at the head, she pushed while Cruz guided the bed to the left, backed up, and slightly to the right, and they were free to wheel Daniel out of the ER. As they passed the nurses' station, one of them advised there would be a team waiting for them at the elevator. Clio nodded as she and Cruz set a jog and steered the bed down the hallway. At its end, the elevator opened and a team of four emerged, ready to take over.

"Doctor Arano has received the report and is prepped and waiting," a male advised.

"Affirmative." Clio stopped with Cruz beside her.

Two took control of the bed, one checked the monitors, then quickly entered what he saw into a tablet, and the last barked orders as he guided them into the elevator. Her part was over, and it was up to the doctor and the surgical staff. Clio stared at the steel doors as they slid closed, her reflection mirrored in them, her body buzzing with the remnants of adrenalin and the rush. "He better live," she mumbled. She didn't want to tell Elder Macario his young nephew had lost his life.

"Doctor Arano works specifically with the Fae and is educated in weapons. Plus, the kid is young, he should be fine," Cruz replied.

Dr. Arano a Pureblood with the Seelie court was the best. Clio turned, and met his brown eyes and the certainty in them, and couldn't disagree. "He's in good hands. It's time to figure out what happened?"

They headed back down the hall, Cruz stopping at the nurses' station, while she continued to where Elder Macario was waiting for her. The visitor section was intended to keep prying eyes off those inside and respected those with status. Like an elder with the Unseelie court. It had been a shooting with a strange gun, strange round, and Cobalt 27, that hadn't been confirmed and was illegal for a civilian to possess. Government and law enforcement agencies were the only organizations allowed to possess White 47 and Cobalt 27 weapons and ammunition.

Adhering to government regulations, the enforcers were state certified, received training, renewed their license once a year, and reported the use of all weapons and their ammunition supply. It was the reason they were authorized to retain the synthetic silver and cobalt. Clio hated thinking it was a murder attempt with possession of illegal weapons, but she didn't think law enforcement shot the elf. She was going to have to call Captain Wolt, who thankfully was in the building. She entered the hygienic room, removed her mask, gloves, and biohazard suit, and threw them away. Then, after sterilizing her shoes and washing her hands, headed to the nurses' station.

"Could you page Captain Wolt? He's at mental health's residential unit."

"Yes, Doctor Hyde," the female nurse replied as she

picked up the handset.

Clio turned and leaned against the counter, as her mind raced with who would want to kill Daniel, someone from the Unseelie court, and the elder's nephew. They could be against the court and the shooting was supposed to make a statement. If the attack was intended to get Baron Kanin's attention, she assumed they would have shot someone from the pack. Like the witches had murdered Zachery before they kidnapped Miss Langston.

"Doctor Hyde," the nurse said, getting Clio's attention, "Captain Wolt and Director Kanin left about thirty minutes ago."

"What?" Clio asked out of disbelief, not because she hadn't heard the nurse.

A swift wave of heat crawled up her neck and into her cheeks as embarrassment and anger scalded her. Left without saying anything to her. *Fucking figures.* What was she? Their pawn? *Negative, an inactive enforcer.* They said jump and she asked how high. It was her fault. They didn't need her, not really. She was a convenience. Yes, she would do whatever the baron asked, and would help Director Kanin and Miss Langston as much as she could. She was finished with Captain Wolt pulling her strings.

"Doctor Carrion estimates about thirty minutes. He's demanding to speak to you, he says he has something to discuss." The worry in her eyes told Clio all she needed to know, and the conversation was going to be about the director's visit with Miss Langston. It hadn't gone well. What was she supposed to do about it? Fix it.

"Tell him I'm in the middle of something," Clio ordered a little too harshly. She left the nurses' station, walked across the hall, and took her cell from a cargo pocket. Clio didn't wait for Mandy to go through her spiel and reported, "Code three."

"Go ahead," Mandy replied as the sound of keys being tapped sounded.

"I have Daniel, Caucasian male, elf, from the Unseelie court, shot once with an unknown projectile. The patient is in surgery. His uncle, Elder Macario is waiting in a visitor's room. Requesting Captain Wolt to respond." She didn't know what condition Director Kanin was in after the visit that clearly hadn't gone well and didn't know if he would be with the captain.

"Is Elder Macario requesting human law enforcement?" Mandy asked.

"As of now, negative," Clio replied. And she wasn't asking, she wasn't an enforcer. *That's petty.*

Elder Macario could have taken his nephew to a human hospital since it was closer to them. They wouldn't have received the elf with open arms, but with his physiology close to a human's they would have treated his wounds, and the hospital would have informed law enforcement of the shooting. Understanding the crime was non-human, the sheriff's department would have passed it onto Organized Paranormal Investigations, the OPI, who Director Kanin had assisted when the witches started their killing spree. Elder Macario chose Celestial for a reason. Like Mrs. Ashby had. Was this their way of showing their support or testing the strength of the pack? Everyone in the territory knew Director Kanin had stepped down while Miss Langston recovered. Clio didn't see it as a weakness, but that didn't mean the factions of the klatch didn't.

"Affirmative. Captain Wolt is en route, Director Kanin assisting. ETA fifteen minutes," Mandy advised.

"Copy." Clio ended the call, shoved her cell back in her

pocket, and headed toward visitor room B.

"Is there an update?" Ansel asked. He wove the truck through traffic, and getting out of the city's outskirts, sped up.

Rutger twisted the screen around to see it and began typing. "Negative. No word confirming he's refusing human law enforcement. Before you get his statement, you'll have to have confirmation, preferably in writing."

"You don't trust him?" Ansel asked. He didn't know many from the Unseelie court. The Seelie court kept its workings private, and the Unseelie court kept their business in a vault. It made the Seelie court look like it advertised.

"He may have an emotional reaction, and I don't want him changing his mind and demanding human law enforcement. It would make us look incompetent and weak. The pack doesn't need the klatch doubting its abilities."

"Affirmative. Do we go through the security entrance or the front?" Ansel asked.

"Front. We make our presence known," Rutger replied. "Would have been better if I had worn my uniform."

"After the way people moved out of your way today, I don't think you wearing a uniform will matter." Ansel gave him sideways glance with his right eyebrow lifted.

He couldn't help enjoying having Rutger with him and talking like they used to. He wished he would have been able to convince him to let the crew into his house to do the renovations. Rutger's laugh, nothing more than a gruff sound, had Ansel smiling despite himself. Passing the statues of Eir and Asclepius, he drove through the parking lot while Rutger entered their location, alerting Mandy they had arrived at Celestial.

"Communications knows we're here," Rutger reported.

"Copy." Ansel parked the truck and killed the engine, his nerves jumping and tension racing across his shoulders.

Where did the sudden stab of anxiety come from? His dream? The past he felt was catching up to him? Rutger's return to semi-normal, and he didn't want to lose their friendship? He looked over at Rutger as he got out of the truck and stared at the hospital. No doubt he was thinking about Jordyn. Ansel met him and they headed to the frosted double doors, with wolves standing at the base of a mountain and another wolf at the top etched in the glass. Opening automatically, they walked into a sitting area where a desk sat with an older woman sitting behind it.

He expected Rutger to take lead, and when he didn't Ansel stepped up. "Captain Wolt to see Doctor Hyde."

The woman, whose name tag read Merieme, wore a headset, and was typing when she looked up from her screen and opened her mouth to answer. Ansel jerked his head up as the speakers repeated his name and ordered him to the ER.

"Doctor Hyde is waiting."

"Thank you." Turning, he saw Rutger was talking on his cell and had walked several feet away to stand by a window.

When Ansel started toward him, Rutger looked over his shoulder and nodded, giving him his answer. Was the ER another emergency? If it had been, he was sure Mandy would have radioed him, and there wouldn't have been an order over the intercom, but you never knew. He headed straight to the ER and Dr. Hyde. And Rutger? Ansel wasn't going to treat him like child. He knew the way and would catch up with him. Still, he didn't need the Director of Enforcers walking around the hospital, Jordyn out of his reach, and Dr.

Carrion finding him to continue his lecture on how Rutger should communicate with his mate. A million scenarios raced through his mind as he marched the halls. When he reached the desk for the ER, his anxiety had tripled, his thoughts were racing, and the images of the dream planted themselves in front of him.

"Captain Wolt to see Doctor Hyde," he told the man as his name sounded. Ansel pointed up and said, "That's me."

"Yes, sir," the man answered. "One minute."

If he was waiting, it wasn't an emergency, at least he had that going for him.

"Captain Wolt, Doctor Hyde is waiting in visitor room B."

"Thank you. Director Kanin is taking a call. Once he's finished, please tell him where I am."

"Yes, sir."

He left the desk with his confidence in the man wavering between he'll tell Rutger where Ansel was, and not telling Rutger anything. Rounding the corner, he saw the double doors to the ER when Cruz saw him and fell in step.

"Doctor Hyde is waiting for you in visitor room B."

"I'm headed there. Do you have more information than what has been reported?" Ansel asked and kept walking while a knot began raveling in his stomach. Taking a left, away from the ER, he entered the hall lined with rooms where doctors were able to have private conversations with the patient, visitors, or family members.

"Negative. Doctor Hyde has been with the elder and no one else has been allowed into the room. Daniel came in with an odd-shaped piece of Cobalt 27 in his back. He's currently in surgery," Cruz explained.

Odd-shaped piece of cobalt. "Thank you," Ansel replied, cutting off each word.

His dream flared to life, its weight adding to the knot that had been coiling. Reaching out, it tightened and began squeezing the air from his lungs. He marched to the door marked Visitor Room B and grabbed the handle. Behind him, Cruz's presence disappeared as the nurse headed in a different direction. Ansel opened the door and walked into a square room with beige walls, a floral border, padded brown and light blue chairs, a matching couch, end tables with magazines, and a TV in the corner. Above him, warm lighting tried to convince you that you weren't in a hospital in a nondescript room where good news and bad news had been explained.

Dr. Hyde was sitting in a chair, her face serious, and leaning forward her elbows rested on her pastel pink scrub pants. Across from her with his back to Ansel, a man wearing a red T-shirt with a forest scene on the back, charcoal hiking pants, and hiking boots was talking to her. His thick blond nearly white hair was pulled back and held at the base of his neck, leaving his pointed ears, a sign of his Pureblood line, exposed. Ansel didn't have to see his ears to sense the elf's magic and the age it held from his ancestors. As he closed the distance, Dr. Hyde looked away from the elf to watch him approach. Her blue eyes with hints of honey glittered under the lighting, and her strawberry blonde hair held more red. By the look in her narrowed gaze she wasn't completely happy to see him.

"Captain Wolt, thank you for coming *back*," Clio stated, wanting him to hear her frustration. Then he nailed his cinnamon gaze tinged with bronze on her as if his wolf was looking at her and trying to pin her down. Clio's stomach twisted when she stood to meet him ... no, to move and get her thoughts under control. "This is Elder Macario of the Vale, member of the Unseelie court, elder and High

Privilege."

Elder and High Privilege of the Unseelie court, Elder Macario was a man of authority. He might have a close connection with their chancellor, was powerful, and validated the threat of a political move. The threads of his magic reached out, their ends feathering the air around them while his face held confidence, and his worry.

Ansel slid his enforcer's mask on, and met the elf's bright emerald eyes. "Captain Wolt with Cascade's Enforcers."

Elder Macario stood, straightening to his six-foot-one-inch height. "Greetings, Captain." Dark patches and spots riddled the T-shirt, and the front and sides of his pants.

"Do you need a change of clothes?" Ansel asked. If any of the contaminated blood were to soak through, it would absorb into the skin, putting Elder Macario at risk of being poisoned.

"No, thank you. Any pain educed from having my nephew's blood on my clothing is my penance for not protecting him." His emerald eyes darkened to nearly black at the same time his power turned cold.

Strict tradition. Ansel wanted to ask how Elder Macario was supposed to protect his nephew but didn't, he wouldn't be disrespectful. The elder was old, powerful, and expected to sense the intruder and prevent any harm coming to him or his nephew. Someone got passed him. His stomach clenched with the thought.

"Understood. What is the victim's full name?"

"Daniel Ragas of the Low Valley," the elf answered.

"Thank you. I'm going to record this conversation for evidence purposes." Ansel held his cell as he recited the date, his name, position with the enforcers, where the interview was taking place, and the witness. Elder Macario had willfully traveled to Celestial, Cascade pack's property, seeking medical treatment, that's why he added Dr. Clio Hyde as his witness. "I understand Daniel Ragas of the Low Valley was shot with what is suspected to be Cobalt 27. The shooting is a crime, possession of the weapon and ammunition is a crime, as well as trespassing on your territory with the intent to commit a crime. You are within your permissible rights under the covenant with the Cascade pack to contact human law enforcement and have them conduct the investigation," Ansel explained. It was enforcer's version of a contract and waiver in one.

"I'm aware of my rights and relinquish the need for human law enforcement. It's the reason I brought him here, without calling for an ambulance, or having a representative and another family member with me. Daniel is my nephew. He has employment in the human world, and if this were to become news, it would hinder his job. If they didn't fire him," Elder Macario answered.

The media coverage over the last couple of weeks didn't help the relationship between humans and the magic-born. It did call attention to the differences between them. "Let it be stated Elder Macario of the Unseelie court, elder and High Privilege willfully declines the requirement of human law enforcement. He authorizes the Cascade pack's enforcers to initiate an investigation into the shooting of Daniel Ragas." Ansel paused, met the glare with worry at its edges, and prayed he didn't make a mistake. "You stated the victim is your nephew. What are his parents' names?"

"Daniel Ragas of the Low Valley is the eldest son to Adriaan and Iris Ragas *av fjellene*," Elder Macario replied as he inclined his head.

Damn. With the elf's first words, Ansel recognized the accent being Scandinavian. He never would have guessed

Elder Macario was from Northern Europe and kept the old world traditions. Elder Macario wasn't *just* an elder and High Privilege he was part of the chancellor's court, his inner circle. He brought his nephew, who was being sculpted to take his place within the court, to Celestial, instead of taking him to the chancellor's trusted healer. A new generation in the Unseelie court. Ansel had to handle the case with expertise and care while keeping to the court's traditions. He couldn't miss a piece of evidence or offend the elder. He wished Rutger was here.

"Daniel of the Low Valley, eldest son to Adriann and Iris Ragas." Ansel inhaled and exhaled. He needed to sit down as the knot in his middle unraveled, revealing hooks that latched onto his insides. "Please, have a seat. The interview will begin."

"Thank you." Elder Macario sat down, folded his hands, and rested them near his waist. If the blood had soaked through and was affecting him, he didn't give any indication.

"Who owns the property?"

"I do. Daniel and his wife were at my house."

"Before he was shot, what were you doing?" Ansel asked.

"We had planned on hiking near Shasta. While we walked down the drive, we discussed different trails. Then there were the flowers." He paused, gathered himself, and continued. "We mediate in the woods and draw peace from the earth."

Explained the human hiking clothes. "Where were you when Daniel was shot?"

"Part way down the drive there's a garden thick with lavender, violets, white poppies, and peonies. They symbolize peace, and we often tend them and have conversation there. This particular day we were studying the wild daises ... I say wild because we didn't plant them," Elder Macario answered.

"How often is often?" Ansel watched the elder consider his question as if he was thinking about how to answer. Was he going to tell the truth or lie? An elder wouldn't lie to an enforcer.

"As I stated, Daniel works in the human world and his job leaves him with little time. Usually a couple times a week, until the daises. We've been watching them for three weeks." Elder Macario met Ansel's gaze like he should have a suspect and maybe a public execution. Daniel's family had the potential of becoming a problem.

"Does Daniel have enemies, anyone who would want to hurt him?" Ansel checked his cell—there were a couple of messages from Lado—then checked the time, his thoughts splitting between the investigation and Rutger. *What's taking him so long?*

"I'll stress, Daniel is highly regarded. And no. I asked him on the drive here, and he insisted he doesn't have enemies and was positive no one would want to hurt him. I can't imagine anyone hiding like a coward and shooting him in the back with cobalt." Elder Macario spit the word cobalt as if it burned his lips. "If it was someone from the court, they would have faced him. We have etiquettes concerning disagreements among our own."

Ansel believed those in the high court would abide by the rules, it didn't mean there wasn't a lower member, magic-born, or human who wouldn't have a problem breaking them. "You said he works with humans. Could there be disagreements with someone at his place of work?"

"No. He is a viticulturist for a local winery," Elder Macario answered. "They are very distinguished, it's the reason I worry about his employment."

"Did you see anything suspicious, odd, different? Were

there any sounds you didn't recognize?"

"Sound." Elder Macario closed his eyes, his face emotionless, and Ansel and Dr. Hyde shared a look of concern.

"There was a whisper. A chant. As if he was praying."

Ansel's insides went cold. *Not possible.* His dream flared to life, took on weight, and sat on his shoulders. He felt her coming for him. "You didn't pay attention to it, the prayer?" He was glad his voice held, and he sounded like himself.

"No, there were others at the house. Daniel's wife, my wife, they were sitting in the backyard. I assumed it was them," Elder Macario answered. "I heard it and failed."

"You weren't expecting someone to open fire on you. Did you recognize whether it was male of female?"

"Male. He had an accent."

"Did you recognize it?"

"No." He twisted his hands then placed them on his thighs.

"Did you hear the weapon?" Ansel asked. He knew the answer and didn't want Elder Macario to confirm his thoughts.

"No."

"I saw the wound. You're sure there was no noise?" Clio interrupted. There was no way a weapon, which was able to shoot the piece of cobalt shaped like a hexagon with barbs, didn't make noise.

"I didn't hear anything. Daniel was standing in the center of the garden talking about the daises, there was a whisper, then he was on the ground," Elder Macario stressed, his composer faltering.

The shooter had both men in his sights, and targeted Daniel, not the elder. What motive would the shooter have? What made Daniel the target?

"The shooter could have shot either one of you and chose

Daniel. Could this be about you? You're a man with power and status."

"What are you insinuating?" he asked in return. His eyes darkened and narrowed on Ansel. "I was the target?"

"I have to ask. Every possibility has to be addressed," Ansel explained.

"My apologies. This is unnerving."

"I understand. Do you know anyone who would want to harm you?"

"No. My wife and I live very peaceful lives."

Before Ansel had a chance to ask another question, there was soft rapping on the door. All three of them looked at it, then at each other.

"Excuse me." Standing, Clio walked over and opened the door enough to see who was on the other side, but not enough the person could see Elder Macario or Captain Wolt. "Yes."

"The patient is out of surgery, he's stable, and has been moved to the intensive care unit. Doctor Arano asked if Captain Wolt wanted the round, although there's nothing round about it," Henry explained as he held up the evidence.

"Absolutely." Clio took the plastic bag, with the biohazard symbol on the front, and felt its weight. She still couldn't believe the weapon didn't sound like a cannon. "Thank you, I'll pass it on to the captain."

"Yes, Doctor." Henry stepped back and out of the way as the director walked around him.

"Director Kanin." He hadn't been with Captain Wolt and she assumed the director had stayed at Foxwood. Clio didn't hide her surprise as hot embarrassment for not showing respect to the Second to the Alpha heated her cheeks. Opening the door wider, she stepped aside. "Captain Wolt is inside."

"Doctor Hyde." If he noticed her lack of respect, he didn't let it bother him as he walked into the room. Director Kanin's authority wrapped around him, his confidence filled his eyes, his shoulders were straight, and he looked strong. Something changed.

Ansel stood as Rutger entered the room. "The attendant at the desk was supposed to notify me."

"I told them not to, I know my way around. What information do you have?" he asked. His mahogany eyes glimmered with gold for a breath. His wolf stayed near the surface as if waiting for Rutger to lose control and give into the beast.

"Elder Macario is an elder and High Privilege with the Unseelie court. While they were examining a flowerbed, his nephew was shot with what we suspect is Cobalt 27." Ansel then turned to Elder Macario. "Have there been any threats against you, your family, or the court?"

"No. Like I said, we're rather boring," he replied. Elder Macario stood and faced Rutger. "Director Kanin, *velsignelser til deg og din familie.* You have our sympathies and are in our librettos as we lift them high."

The nuance of his accent reminded him of his mom and the way the simplest of words turned into something grand. The elder was keeping to a traditional greeting and Ansel caught the word family and understood the intent. Elder Macario was passing his blessing onto Rutger, Jordyn, and the family.

"Thank you, Elder Macario. I am sorry for the misfortune that has come upon you and your kinsfolk. I understand Doctor Hyde has news of your nephew." Director Kanin turned his attention to Clio, and she saw life had returned to his eyes. Except it wasn't for the love of life, it was in the shape of a furious, dark wolf on the hunt.

"Yes. The doctor removed the projectile, Daniel is stable, and they're taking him to ICU," Clio explained. "Henry brought this." She lifted the bag and started to hand it to Director Kanin.

"I'm not the enforcer in charge," Director Kanin stated. "Captain Wolt is taking lead."

Ansel was almost surprised with the sternness of Rutger's voice, his confidence, and the way he slipped into the role of director. He wasn't the same man who had been in the truck with him, a brooding silence, detached, full of rage, and was planning on going on a witch hunt. Ansel assumed the shift in mood was because of the phone call. Who called him, he had no idea. Maybe it was enough, he would approach the conversation about the security additions. Maybe. Taking the bag from Dr. Hyde, he began opening it and caught her blue gaze as if they were thinking the same thing about Rutger.

"Wait, Captain." Clio swiped her thigh, dug into a cargo pocket, and pulled out a pair of gloves. "While we think it's Cobalt 27 and harmless to you, it's unusual, pointed, barbed, and I don't need you getting poisoned."

"Affirmative, Doctor," Ansel replied with the corner of his mouth curved in a half grin.

He handed Rutger the bag, tugged the gloves on, then taking it back, turned it over in his hands. The two-inch-long shaft with its sharpened point, making it easier to puncture flesh, was a silver/blue hexagon. It glittered in the light despite the clear plastic and felt made from cobalt. Real cobalt. Not the synthetic. Their boldness was astounding, and it was turning his nerves into electricity under his skin.

"It feels real. It's heavy and dense like the element, not

synthetic, and there's an engraving on it," Ansel mumbled the last part.

"Can you see what it is?" Director Kanin asked.

He didn't have to. Ansel's anxiety spiked as he prepared to see a familiar brand. He hesitantly took the hexagon out, making sure the point and the barbs didn't pierce the glove, held it up to see the engraving better, and his insides began caving in on themselves. Three feathers, one on the left and one on the right were slightly lower while the third, in the middle, stood straight and hid the hilt of a sword, its blade pointing to the sky. Feeling like a fraud, dwelling on his parents, his association with the Covey, and the dream all started making sense. The engraving was proof.

"Was Mr. Ragas poisoned?" Rutger asked. Ansel's gaze shifted to him and his question.

"Let me check with Doctor Arano," Clio replied and stepped away from the men.

"I'll take it to Doctor Radford, she's in charge of forensics. Maybe she can analyze it and get a clear picture of the carving. Then we can do a search and see if we can find a match," Ansel stated. They weren't going to find anything.

"You've never seen anything like it before?" Rutger asked. His eyes darkened as they narrowed on the hexagon.

"Not like this," Ansel lied. Sorta lied.

He had never seen anything like the hexagon with its sharpened end, like an arrow, the carved barbs, their tips ready to cling to flesh and then a person's insides. He knew the symbol. That's what it was, because its image was tattooed on his left side over his ribs. Where it had been for over a hundred and twenty years. To keep it from being seen, he never went without a shirt, even in the gym, unless he was alone. The sight of the symbol had him going over the years he spent as part of Cascade, and if anyone, like

Rutger, had caught a glimpse of the ink. With fear and anxiety trying to dominate his attention, and a confession bubbling in his mouth, he concentrated on Rutger, his best friend, and wasn't going to give into panic. Ansel needed to confirm it was the Covey.

"Before you give it to forensics, take several pictures with your cell. We'll take the chance and download the images and run a search," Rutger advised. "If forensics comes back with something better, we'll repeat the search. If they don't, we'll have started somewhere. The shape and engraving are a calling card. Someone wanted us to have this."

It's their signature and a warning. "Affirmative." Ansel wasn't capable of saying anything else.

Clio ended her call and closed in on the three men who had become silent. "Doctor Arano says there is no indication of a poison. But will take blood tests to confirm."

Director Kanin nodded while Captain Wolt made a note, and Elder Macario exhaled with relief. Clio knew the director had been struggling, the way he looked when he arrived a couple of hours earlier, she didn't think he was with them, as in the real world. The glassy-eyed distance took him inside his head where he had been for weeks. It made the shift in his demeaner unsettling. When she met with Dr. Carrion, she was going to ask him how the visit went, as if she didn't have an idea after he demanded to speak with her.

"Is it possible for me to see my nephew? Or at least talk to the doctor? I need to call his mother and his wife," Elder Macario asked.

"My apologies, sir." Clio was caught up in the case she wouldn't be a part of, Captain Wolt, the director's newfound sanity, and forgot Elder Macario might want to talk to the doctor. She faced Captain Wolt and the director. "Is there anything else I can do?"

"Negative, Doctor Hyde. Thank you for your assistance," Ansel replied. "If Director Kanin doesn't have any further questions, we'll leave."

Without answering him, Rutger nodded his reply, then faced the elf. "May your nephew heal, Elder."

"Thank you, Director, as well as your mate and the pack's soothsayer." Elder Macario bowed slightly.

Rutger remained silent as he headed for the door, his square shoulders tense, his unease leaking from his pores. Once away from the commotion of the hospital, Ansel took his place beside Rutger.

"Do you think we'll get a hit from the search?" Ansel asked. *No*

He was trying to get Rutger to talk, the calm director who had followed customs between factions, kept the mood professional, and exuded the confidence and authority of the Kanin family, had shutdown. He was not the same person. Guilt fired through him. Maybe Rutger sensed his lie, his fear, and knew Ansel was hiding something. *Something*. He was hiding everything and lying as he went. He knew who shot Elder Macario's nephew, knew what the symbol carved into the cobalt meant, and knew who had done the engraving.

Ansel was wrong. He didn't know exactly who had pulled the trigger. There were forty years of change separating what he knew and the truth. She didn't change. Still, he didn't know why the nephew had been the target. Could someone have ordered the elf's assassination? The Covey was a group of assassins. Was it a fight between factions? He didn't know. She didn't harm anyone unless it benefited her. Soulless, selfish creature. It struck him like someone hit him with a truck. He had to maintain his distance from people. He wasn't going to turn his kith and kin into cannon fodder because his past was closing in on him.

He needed to stick to the facts and not assume she was closing in on *him*. After that many years, that many kills, there was bound to be copycats trying to make a name for themselves. If she had found him, and he was convinced there was no way that could have happened, she would have faced him, not endanger herself or the Covey by getting attention from a failed assassination attempt. Admitting anything would be putting the investigation at risk, the pack at risk, the Unseelie court at risk, pointing it in a wrong direction, and exposing his life of lies in a useless babbling confession. It wouldn't help anyone. It absolutely wouldn't help him find her.

"Did the elder decline human law enforcement?" Rutger asked.

"Affirmative. I recorded the conversation and will download it, and have a transcript made to add to the case file. I'll have a copy sent to Elder Macario to sign. Do you want a copy?" In front of them the double doors slid open, letting fresh air sweep over them and inch into the sterilized hospital.

"Affirmative. I've never known the Unseelie court to ask for our assistance. Besides minor requests and the gathering once a year to discuss policy, it's been years since they have had any communication with Cascade." Rutger stopped beside Ansel's truck, the setting sun's amber hue turning his eyes brighter.

"Things have changed since then. The territory has to be talking about the construction on Foxwood and security modifications to the Summit. The pack is gathering its numbers and fortifying its walls. From the outside it looks like the baron is getting ready for a war." Before he thought it was paranoid and excessive, now he saw the alterations as a gift. If she was out there, he hoped the massing of soldiers and the building of their fortress was enough to keep her from striking Foxwood.

"Or nearly losing the pack's soothsayer and Second to the Alpha turned the baron into a paranoid recluse who is hiding behind his walls." Rutger faced the hospital. "Right now, this case is *attempted* murder. If that changes and it turns out it was a provoked attack due to a rift between factions, the court has made us witnesses. If it's an unprovoked attack and we fail to apprehend the shooter, it casts doubt in their minds about the enforcers and the baron's authority. Push comes to shove, the court demands human law enforcement because we're inept, and the case, seemingly hidden from the authorities, gets a new audience. Cascade will answer to law enforcement and questioned why it wasn't brought to their attention. We'll be investigated, again, possibly charged with obstruction of justice and trying to cover up a crime. And that's not considering what will happen to the court. The pack can't take anymore negativity among the factions and the magic-born, and definitely not in the media."

"You think they requested us to test the baron, our abilities. Our strength," Ansel added.

Rutger stared at the hospital, then at Ansel. "I'm positive they don't want humans in their business. But like you said, Cascade is fortifying their defenses, at the same time, my continued absence has to play a part of why they chose Celestial. There has to be others within the Unseelie court, and the klatch wanting to know my status, if the pack remains united, and when Jo will be released. The pack's united power is fractured. It would be a dammed thing if someone challenged me."

He met Ansel's gaze over the hood of truck, and Ansel would bet money Rutger wanted a challenge, wanted to burn the grief and fear from his body by inflicting pain on someone else. Then ... something Rutger said hit a nerve and broke his carefully laid out facts she hadn't come for him. The media. His face, along with others, had been all over the news for weeks. The case gained national attention. It was a romance—boy saves girl from evil with supernatural help from his clan. Ansel's strength drained from him and the fear returned.

"You look like you saw a ghost. What are you thinking, Ansel?"

He stilled, like he might fade into the air while he resembled a predator who had sighted his prey. He never used to do that. Rutger was six feet four inches of solid muscle, confidence, authority, and moved like he controlled everything around him, and he owned wherever he was. That person wasn't standing in front of Ansel. Rutger had become a ghost. With his eerie stillness, Ansel felt like he was looking into his soul. *You aren't going to like what you see, brother.*

"This case is a couple of hours old, and it already has more unanswered questions than it should. Elder Macario has no idea who it could be, the nephew can't talk, and that isn't taking political motivation into consideration." He didn't lie, but he didn't answer the question.

"Agreed. While we let the family deal with what has happened, we'll start with forensics and searching the Assembly database."

They continued staring at each other over the hood of the truck. Ansel knew there was nothing in the database. The Covey operated like phantoms—unseen, clean, and silent. The same way he and Rutger were going to work when they hunted the witches and took their revenge. He knew what they were going to do, and they were going to get away with it because he was good at it. It had been his job. He wouldn't have announced his presence by shooting the elf—not just an elf, but a damned elder's nephew—and leaving evidence behind. Why they did, Ansel had no idea. It could be her. It wasn't her. The symbol mocked him while his guilt and fear were tearing him apart.

"Copy." Having to get out from under Rutger's stare, he walked to the door, opened it, and got inside before his will cracked, and the lies he kept spilled out.

CHAPTER EIGHT

Gold, scarlet, and violet bit at the sky and tried to break through the glass to stain the furniture in her living room. Clio glanced at the window, not noticing the setting sun because her thoughts were in a hundred different directions, and back at her laptop. Grabbing the glass of tequila, she brought it to her lips, sipped the cool liquor, then set the glass on the table and began typing.

Mandy sent her Mrs. Ashby's file, then messaged her stating the baron wasn't going to meet her in person and requested a written report. Which was fine. She didn't really want to go to Foxwood. Not only did she hope Mrs. Ashby was sincere and truthful about what she had said, she also hoped she had done the pack a service by eliminating tension between the Lapis Lazuli coven and Cascade. Despite Trinity being a large city with bedroom communities reaching toward the edges of the territory, and ranches extending through the valley, it held onto a small-town feel. They did not need trouble with the factions under the baron's rule and their dissatisfaction reaching the other factions and outland territories.

The pack was reeling from the kidnapping and death of one their own and was trying to come to terms with the changes. First the military strictness then the construction of the Enforcer's office, and the Summit. The chaos left them open for judgements and challenges. She cursed as she opened the file on Mrs. Ashby and started reading. After a ten-year engagement, Pearl Dove married Conrad Ashby, an equally powerful witch, and they had two children—the youngest daughter Ava Jade, and older son Grayson, who were both in training with their scribes. They were fifteen years happily married and both served as part of the Esme's circle. Clio didn't learn anything that would lead her to think Mrs. Ashby was being dishonest. She did wonder how you spent ten years engaged to someone when her relationships didn't last a week. An entire date. An hour.

Clio checked her cell ... no messages, no missed calls, nothing. She closed the file and opened the format for the report, then stared at the screen like it might talk to her and write the report without her. While she made her rounds, the doctor on duty assured her Daniel was going to be fine, he was healing and had been moved out of ICU. She sighed in relief and left Celestial with less stress. She had no idea what the repercussions were going to be, why someone had shot Daniel, and who was next ... if there was going to be a next. Was it an isolated incident? A misunderstanding? It would have to be pretty severe. Was it between factions? She wanted to call Captain Wolt and ask, then stopped herself. Not only had she been taken off the active list, but he had kept their conversation at the hospital professional and curt, killing any attempt at friendly.

While he questioned the elder, she admitted to herself, she liked being beside him, being part of the investigation, and enjoyed his attention. Then watching his somber cinnamon eyes analyze every detail as he listened. He was self-possessed, determined, and wore confidence like a second skin. She wanted to be part of his world, as if his assurance would rub off on her, and that included the investigation. Sadly, as an inactive enforcer she wasn't privy to information about the case. Cooling her anger was the email she received from Baron Kanin's office stating he had formally taken her off the active enforcer roster and put her 'on call' as the head doctor for the enforcers, slayers, shadows, and soldiers.

He went on to state she had been given total control over the new med room being built. No stress. It was an incredible promotion and opportunity, and the idea of having the med room made her feel alive with excitement. It didn't heal the pain of having been removed. The break from Celestial gave her a sense she was someone besides Dr. Hyde and go between. Like she wasn't a Wight trying to outdo herself and prove to the entire damn world she was just as good as an Illuminate or a Pureblood. Damn default setting. When in doubt, please remind yourself you're a Wight.

"It's stress and exhaustion talking," she mumbled to herself.

Captain Wolt calling her out then hanging up on her made her smile. At least she possessed one moment of friendship between them, and the thought made her cringe. It wasn't friendship. Acquaintances maybe. Comrades in arms, she had been an enforcer. Yes, she admitted liking the enforcer, she knew him, she didn't know the man behind the black T-shirt and gun. Never saw him anywhere except Celestial and Foxwood, and never saw him with anyone, male or female. Save for Director Kanin. Those two. Serious bro love there.

"He has geese," Clio told the laptop screen. That was the extent of her knowledge. What did he eat? Drink? What were his hobbies? "Working out." The black tee wrapped around his muscled chest told of the hours he spent in the gym.

She wasn't friends with Captain Wolt and didn't need his friendship or his attention when she had enough on her plate to last her a lifetime. Especially when they started building the med room, she would have to devote time to making it efficient and perfect. She saved her report, sent it to communications to have Mandy pass it along to the baron, opened the internet browser, typed soothsayer into the search bar, and waited for the results. Yes, she had gone by to check on Miss Langston after talking to Daniel's doctor.

Clio sipped her drink as the page loaded with a million options. Okie dokie. The changes, the strict rules, the security measures being put into place, and the new Enforcer's office being built from the ground up, started with one person. Jordyn Langston. Soothsayer. Did Clio really believe there was such a thing? She was a werewolf who had treated a witch's daughter, so it was possible. Did she believe the director and the soothsayer were fated mates? No. That was bullshit. How would you know if you were fated? Director Kanin and Miss Langston broke off their relationship, didn't speak for three years, each dated someone else, and suddenly she comes back and they're mated. No. It was a fairy tale.

And she knew she wasn't the only person to have doubts about the direction the baron was taking them. The Lapis Lazuli coven and Unseelie court, however, not only seemed to believe it but respected the turn the pack had taken. Or it was their way of not wanting to disagree with the baron after Butte Springs and the murders. They could be testing the pack's resolve, or biding their time, and when they had the evidence they needed, they would reveal the truth of their feelings. The rumors about bringing the traditions of the dark ages back caused anyone who feared getting unwanted attention from humans to second guess the baron and anyone who supported him. Hesitating before she clicked on a link promising to take her to the definition of soothsayer,

Clio knew she would do what she always did and research fated mates. If she couldn't find what she was looking for on the internet and countless sites, she would find books—old books, tomes, a scroll, anything to help her understand. She looked at her cell and the blank screen. It was an unusually quiet night, and the lack of action was unsettling. She rubbed the back of her neck, groaned, and questioned, did she want a busy night or the quiet?

"Quiet."

She clicked another site, scrolled down, and found nothing sounding like Miss Langston. Click. Click. Click. Another site and a box popped up asking if she was over eighteen. Clio wasn't sure if she wanted to risk a virus by clicking yes, but she had to know. A second question asked her for her email, which she didn't give to them, and a third asked if she was non-human or human. Human, of course. The page went black for a second, then a picture of Miss Langston appeared on the screen.

"Dear god." The evening sun cast a gold hue against the front of the gallery, almost highlighting Miss Langston. Her raven hair was straight, her dark eyes made darker with eyeliner, and she wore a silver top covered by a waist-length, black leather jacket, jeans, and red high heels. Clio had to admit she was beautiful.

"Because she's a Pureblood." And the doubt of being a Wight reared its head. She pushed the feeling aside and started reading.

Miss Langston was a Pureblood from the Langston family, the article mentioned her parents, her boyfriend, the baron and baroness, the Director of Enforcers, and the Cascade clan. It detailed the murders, kidnapping, the coven of witches and the preceding investigation. The article went on to give a short retelling of her life in Butterfly Valley and her return to Trinity. At the bottom there was a description of a real soothsayer, a person supposed to foresee the future, a prophet, seer, oracle, the list when on until it stated it wasn't a lycan photographer from Trinity with boyfriend problems. If anyone could prove otherwise, the owner of the website invited them to explain their side.

"No, thank you," Clio whispered.

While it didn't answer her question, the article—like one you would find in a gossip magazine—would remove curiosity from the average person, human. Scrolling back up to Miss Langston's photo, her features were sharp and soft at the same time and matched her confidence and elegance. Fast forward, and Miss Langston was sitting in a rocking chair, blanket over her legs, staring out the window, her raven hair pulled back in a loose ponytail, her T-shirt covered by a zip-up hoodie and hung on thin shoulders, and her cotton pants had been trying to swallow her. She lost weight, muscle, and worst of all her confidence. Because of her human half, Clio got away with skipping meals, not hitting the gym to burn energy, and she didn't have the physical need to be with the pack. She could go for a month before the nagging feeling she was missing something started.

Shapeshifters were pack animals and depended on the physical touch of their mates, the connection to the entire pack, and the power from the alpha. Miss Langston hadn't been with the pack in a month, wasn't with her mate, and hadn't seen the baron, her alpha. Her wolf was suffering. Dr. Carrion was a Deviant, Clio reminded herself, and wasn't always ready to believe the inner details of shapeshifters. He had assured her Director Kanin's visit, despite his sitting in silence and not talking to her, had gone well enough he expected to discharge Miss Langston within a week. Couldn't be soon enough.

Clio hadn't learned anything and didn't think she was going to when the sites ranged from pagan religions, cults, how to start a cult, and personally owned websites giving you their take on the subject. The truth, whether Miss Langston was a soothsayer or a symbol of what the baron wanted would come out when Miss Langston went home, and her life started. She left the site, clicked out of the browser, stared at screen and the background, then the forgotten half of sandwich and stray chips sitting on a paper plate beside her laptop. She really needed to fix herself an actual meal and eat it without sitting in front of her work.

Her cell chimed and lit with a picture. Her mom. Taking her phone, she replied with the same thing she said every night and ended the message with I love you. Done. She was done. Clio left the stool, the bar height table, laptop, and grabbing the plate and her glass, she walked over to the sink. She drank the remaining tequila, felt its warmth as it slid down her throat, set the glass in the sink next to the one from the night before, threw the paper plate and chips in the trash, then headed to her room. She would start her search all over again in the morning.

Minutes ticked by, creating hours, and strung them together as Ansel stared at the ceiling fan above his bed, the rotating blades catching the moon's light and slicing through cast shadows on the walls. He kicked the covers off, letting the gentle breeze from the open windows and from above flow over his bare chest and legs, his left arm under his head, his hair pinned under it, his right across his stomach and rising and falling with his breaths his fingers touched the sheet underneath him. The early morning air carried the scent of the woods, and a calming he wished would take him away.

The weight of the projectile, the prayer, and the wounded elf riddled his thoughts while her face sat in his head, and when he closed his eyes, her glare held him in its vile grasp. Sometime during his stare down with the ceiling fan and its constant rotation around its guts, he had, against his will, fallen asleep. Ansel woke with a jerk, the feeling of the nightmare on his skin like thick oil he was never going to wash off and the sweat-soaked sheet beneath him.

The sun replaced the moon, and with every muscle in his body feeling like rebar he swung his legs over the side his feet, landing on the carpet. He hung his head, feeling his back aching from tension, and the thundering voices pounding against his skull. He needed to make sure it was her and if it was, he needed to find out why she was there. A forty year grudge was hard to believe. Grudge, he owed a blood debt.

After a shower, coffee, and food, he sat in the idling truck, the screen blinking with updates, and despite it being early morning, the air conditioner hummed, its cool air keeping the sun's heat from invading the cab. The warehouse sat to his left, looked abandoned, the parking lot a mess of broken asphalt, dead trees, dried grass, crumbling concrete borders, and old realtor signs. Studying the building, he noticed the windows along the roof line and doors were intact, the roof-top looked secure, and the siding solid while a faded name scarred the front, making it difficult to tell what company it had been years ago.

Ansel put the truck in gear, slowly left the shoulder of the street, and turning, drove over a speed bump wearing dull yellow paint and headed toward the rear of the building. Pallets of material sat forgotten, the black plastic covering flapping in the breeze, the tattered edges caught in piles of leaves, trash, and dirt. An old truck, parked as if it had been a quick deployment, sat at the back, grocery bags clung to the tires, the back bumper, and leaves and pine needles were scattered on its windshield. He pulled behind it, the curved windows on either side of the center rear window were smudged and he noted the license plate, the old school blue with yellow letters and numbers, and using his cell took a quick picture. The vehicle would have been considered a classic if it wasn't forgotten, but right then it was scrap metal. Ansel continued and found what he was looking for, the mouth of the dirt road. There was a gate, nothing special, wasn't going to keep anyone out when you could jump over it, then for the first time, he saw the chain link fencing hidden by overgrown vegetation, shrubs, and trees, following the perimeter of the property.

Nothing special. Was more of an afterthought. Like the warehouse was having an identity crisis and didn't know if it was going to look abandoned or a work in progress. Even the truck added a touch of someone forgetting they were there. He didn't believe it. Yeah, there was something going on. Why he hadn't been told, he didn't know. Maybe it was above his paygrade, and maybe he was supposed to be busy with an attempted murder case, his past coming back to haunt him and hunting witches. If Rutger was capable of pulling himself together long enough to focus.

With the details of the warehouse doing their best to take his mind off her and what she was going to do next, Ansel slowly approached the entrance of Foxwood. Workers huddled around utility trucks, loaders, tools, and pallets of material. Foxwood's entrance stood wide open, soldiers flanking each side, while several men and women started dismantling the ornate wrought iron gates. The familiar swinging gate was being replaced with one weighing three times as much, was studier, and followed a rail. It would be activated by a palm vein scanner, unique code, or controlled by communications. Ansel drove past the commotion, down the mile-long drive peppered with more trucks and workers as they began installing motion detectors, cameras, and breaking ground for the treehouses. Closer to the mansion he wove through construction equipment, saw Rutger's truck parked in the same place it had been in for over a month, and the mass of weeds growing beneath. He was sure with Rutger's need for revenge and his interest in the case he would have been waiting for him at communications. Ansel didn't see him.

He thought about the conversation—if a couple of words from him could be considered an actual conversation—concerning the security upgrades to his house, and hoped Rutger would have gone home and prepared it for the crew. That didn't happen, and he wasn't in sight, but it didn't mean he wasn't inside. He parked, the massive truck and trailer taking a good chunk of land and nearly dwarfing the mansion. The baron's three-car garage attached to the opposite end of the house was going to look small next to the new professional garage they planned on building. All maintenance to the vehicles belonging to Cascade would be transferred over to in-house, taking the work from several garages in Trinity. The loss of business was going to offend some people. The baron wasn't going to cut them off, and had offered several magic-born the opportunity to work for Cascade. The baron was building a stronghold and creating an empire. Ansel couldn't wait for the construction to be completed and for things to settle down, get back to normal, and he could get back to work.

If I'm around. Shuddering with the thought and how real it was becoming, the night, the lack of sleep, and seeing her face every time he closed his eyes weighed on him. And added to his guilt. Between midnight and four in the morning while the fan made its rotation, and exhaustion and denial played in his head, he convinced himself it wasn't her and he was going to solve the case and close the door on his past for the last time. Then sunrise hit him, he saw Rutger staring at him, questions in his hard gaze, and his senses returned, erasing his delusions and killing his false hope.

Ansel turned the key and the truck's rumble fell silent. Out of his truck, the grating, yelling, and machinery churned behind him as he headed toward the six steps of the trailer. Before he reached the door handle, a soft vibration spread over his chest. He took his phone from the pocket of the enforcer's uniform of a BDU shirt that he didn't normally wear, saw a familiar number, and his heart pounded.

Distance. "Captain Wolt."

"It's Doctor Hyde."

He saw her bright azar eyes, pictured her staring at him the way she had, like she was memorizing his face, when he was at Celestial. "How can I help you?" Ansel asked as he turned around and headed back to his truck. Getting in, he sat behind the wheel, communications in front of him, and the noise from the chaos beside him muted.

"I wanted to give you an update on Daniel."

"How is he?" Ansel stared at the decals advertising different companies, from the manufacture of the unit, the electronics, the tires, and ordered himself to keep it professional. He did not need to lose himself to a life he would never possess, never know. And he didn't want a repeat of the night before.

"Doing well. Doctor Arano is confident he'll be able to go home in a couple of days. Considering the projectile used and it being cobalt, I'm surprised he wasn't hurt worse. It looked dangerous and unusual." Clio's voice waivered, and she checked herself, not wanting to sound like she was baiting him for information, which she was. Reminding herself she was interested in the case and not wanting to hear the low rumble of wolf and man coming from him. Cause you don't know him, and he doesn't want to know you.

"That's good news," he replied. When he realized he sounded like an unfeeling ass, relief flooded him. Ansel checked Daniel's health off his list of worries and moved onto the next one.

Clio paused with the lack of care in his voice. "Thought you might want to know."

"Affirmative, thank you. Is there anything else?"

"Negative. One second, how is Director Kanin?" Clio wanted to immediately explain the reason behind her question. The director had acted like his normal self—calm, controlled, confident—but then there was the rage in his eyes like his wolf was staring at her. The weight made her flinch and want to stand down from him. With his cold front sending ice through the phone, she wasn't going to defend herself to Captain Good Mood. She would have wasted her breath and made a fool out of herself at the same time.

"Director Kanin is doing well." *Sure he was.* The cab of the truck started to close in on him while the cell felt like it weighed a hundred pounds. "If there's nothing else, I have appointments."

Right. "Affirmative." Clio hit the red circle, ending the call, and calmly set her cell on the desk.

She wasn't sure if affirmative was a correct response, and she didn't care. He had taken unfriendly, business-like, and professional, which she of all people understood, coated them in ice and threw them at her. Direct hit. And it hurt. She hated that part the worst and it was embarrassing. A tempting offer to checkout his view of the mountains, and she went straight to 'oh my gosh he might like me'. A Wight. *Yep, remind yourself of that.* Not the fact you rejected him, don't know him, he doesn't associate with anyone, let alone you, and is investigating an attempted murder.

Ansel looked at the screen like it might explain what happened and where her instant anger came from. He kept it business, didn't say anything wrong as he clearly stated he had appointments, which he did, and wondered what could have set her off? As if he had to have someone spell it out for him. They needed to hit him upside his head with it. She hadn't spent years on the run, never having a home, protecting herself from threats, and had never known what it was like to be used and hunted. No, Dr. Hyde lived her life free from fear, humiliation, and pain, and her demons didn't taunt her. Being innocence, she expected to be able to talk to anyone. She wasn't worried that talking to him made him a target.

Fear, shame, death, and lies were his life.

Disgrace crept over him and he shoved it aside. Despite his best efforts, Dr. Hyde had distracted him, and dammit, he forgot to ask if Daniel was able to answer questions. If Rutger was going to be part of the investigation and they went back to Celestial to question Daniel, they would no doubt see Dr. Hyde, meaning he was going to have to act like nothing happened. *Sure.* It didn't change what he had to do ... he couldn't, wouldn't put her in danger. That's where he was right then, believing the Covey was responsible and they were playing a game he didn't understand. And until he got a grip on what was happening, everyone he came into contact with was a potential victim. He left his truck, straightened his shoulders, shoved his doubts as far back as he could, took the stairs, and entered the center of communications. To his right, Mandy sat at the desk, her fingers going over the keyboard, her eyes on the monitors.

"Anything happening?"

"Negative, sir. All peace and quiet," she replied without looking at him. "Well, as quiet as it can get with all that."

"It's pretty bad," he mumbled. "Did Doctor Radford have anything for me on the Ragas' case?"

"Affirmative, the file is on table, and the projectile is locked in the safe. She said she's going to be at Celestial if you wanted to talk to her," Mandy answered. "They moved forensics there to be closer to research."

Ansel looked where the equipment used to be, was thankful it wasn't in communications any longer, grabbed the file marked with Cascade's crest, forensics, Ragas' case and stomped the short distance to his desk. The humming computers, beeps, fans, and the air conditioner were the only noises between himself and Mandy. There was the deafening level of his thoughts like they were trying to turn his brain to mush and blow his ear drums out. Sitting down, he bumped the edge, and the motion brought the computer to life and the screen lit up with Cascade's crest. *I'm going to find who shot Daniel*, he promised the crest as if it was the baron sitting in front of him. He flipped the file open, skimmed the first page detailing what tests were ran, turned it over, and froze. A clear image of three feathers and a sword that might as well have been poster-sized sat in front of him. He needed to stop anyone from seeing the picture.

"Who else has seen the file?" he demanded loud enough people outside might have heard him.

"No one, sir. Doctor Radford finished late last night and had the file sent over." Mandy leaned back in her chair to see him around counters and walls.

Their eyes met, hers ladened with exhaustion, his darkened by his secrets, and Ansel wanted to wince. They were being worked into the ground, literally if the outside was any indication. "Any word on the director?" he asked, trying to cover his panic at seeing the symbol larger than life and as a piece of evidence. It felt like the barrel of a gun had been pointed at him. Keep it a secret and add another lie to his mounting betrayal. Negative. He would keep it out in plain sight, and act like he didn't know what it was. He was working an investigation, nothing more.

"Negative, sir."

"Thanks."

Going back to the picture, his heart pounded in his chest like it wanted to escape and leave him behind to face the consequences by himself. He forced his focus to the case and began reading the report. The projectile, while hexagon in shape, its tip razor sharp, the barbs on its sides hooked to cause damage, wasn't cobalt or the synthetic Cobalt 27. *What?* He continued reading until he found kyanite crystal. Was it harmless? According to Dr. Radford while it effected the Fae the same way as cobalt, their bodies naturally fought against infection, stopping the poison from becoming worse. Good news. Daniel wasn't in danger from any residual effects from the crystal being inside his body. Ansel nearly stopped reading, it was the information he was hoping to have, then he spotted familiar words and his eyes roamed the page. The kyanite, blue/silver was a potential danger to shapeshifters, at risk species included American Indian shapeshifters, the others didn't matter. Ansel's heart stopped.

The next paragraph caused his lungs to abandon him. Advise added information; according to the *crystal age*, kyanite crystals are extremely spiritual and are used for healing among the human population and select magic-born. He couldn't read fast enough. While according to myth, and this part made his skin turn cold and his blood freeze in his veins, kyanite crystals were used in ritual killings of those belonging to a holy order. Like his mother. This was directed at him. She revealed her presence in his territory by harming an innocent with a weapon designed for him. He heard her say his name with her throaty sound, Brando, Italian origin, meaning *firebrand, sword*. Her sword. She had saved him from fire's wrath and always enjoyed telling him fire had brought them together. She was ice to his flame. The thought made his stomach churn. She notched her arrow and letting it go it struck its target. He could feel the arrowhead in his chest and every breath drew it deeper.

How did he keep the report from the baron and Rutger? He didn't. Couldn't. Where did he start looking for her? What the hell was he thinking? She knew where he was, and he was an enforcer. The Covey had been watching the elder, no doubt his house, who he talked to, his day-to-day movements. He failed. Dr. Hyde. Rutger. Lado. Hell, all of the enforcers. The pack. He knew how her mind worked and how she processed information. Thankfully, he had been strict with who he interacted with, except Dr. Hyde and inviting her over to see the mountains and geese. Like they were his pets. They kinda were. She knew about Clio, his attention toward her, and would be jealous of the doctor. Her unscarred skin, easy laugh, family, and relationship with him. There was no relationship, but she wouldn't care. Once rage took over truth and lies didn't matter.

Revenge mattered. Death mattered.

Ansel gathered the shreds of his mind and tried piecing them together enough he could form a complete thought. He wanted a minute of clarity to think. The first thing he needed to do was get a copy of the report to Dr. Hyde. The information about the kyanite would prove to be useful in the future, and he would give the projectile to the research lab where the techs would break down the crystal. His priority was conducting a thorough investigation, meaning he needed to call Elder Macario to confirm it was all right to examine the scene where his nephew had been shot, and from there he might get an idea where the shooter had been. With his thoughts doing circles around what he learned, the Covey, the absence of Rutger and human law enforcement, he was feeling lost and alone.

Exactly like she wanted him.

With her on his mind, he wasn't focused. The proof being he didn't go straight to the scene after talking to Elder Macario at the hospital when he started the investigation. He could have questioned the elder's wife and his nephew's wife, but his mind had stalled. Rutger would have told him what to do, human law enforcement would have told him what he couldn't do. Easy. The directions his mind raced had nothing to do with the pack. It was her. Protecting himself. That was a hard habit to break. If they were in town and targeting the Unseelie court or using them to get to him. Why use them? She knew where he was. The kyanite was proof she wanted to get his attention. It didn't change his mistakes or his inadequate investigative work. A sloppy oversight because he was thinking about himself. Ansel looked at the stack of paperwork sitting in front of him and was amazed how Rutger would have had it done and moved on to the next task.

One thing at a time. Reaching up, he took a manilla envelop from the stack, set it on top of Dr. Radford's report, and opened it to the face page. It contained the transcripts from the interview giving him the victim's name, his phone number, address, and the reporting party's information. He scanned the page, found the number he needed, and entered the digits into his cell phone. Ansel inhaled, exhaled, pressed the green circle, and waited.

"Hello," Elder Macario greeted, his stern voice lacking the uncertainty and worry it held the day before.

"Good morning, Elder Macario. This is Captain Wolt. Is it possible for me to see the scene where Daniel was shot?" With pen in hand, he added to a 'to do' list, checked it, and put the pen down.

"Yes, my wife and I will be here all day. Daniel's wife will be here as well if you need to speak with her."

"Affirmative, thank you."

"I believe I gave you my address. I'm afraid I wasn't completely myself yesterday," Elder Macario offered.

"Understandable. Yes, you gave it to me. I will see you in a little over an hour," Ansel answered. He had access to the Assembly and would have been able to search for the elder's information. The Highguard 's people oversaw the data collected and what was added to the records, but if they felt the info was of a sensitive nature, they withheld it. The Assembly could be unreliable.

"See you then, Captain."

Ansel heard the phone click and checked to make sure Elder Macario had hung up. With the call ended, he looked at his list, which should keep Lado busy until he returned from seeing the elder. He delegated Lado the task of check-ing and then finalizing the roster and sending it to the baron. Not having to go through the roster freed Ansel from having to spend time on it or waiting for everyone to sign onto their consoles. Lado's other tasks were the usual, keeping Ansel updated on the construction, the security upgrades, if there were calls, and if Rutger left Foxwood. He stressed the im-portance of notifying him if there was a call that appeared abnormal. The list would keep the enforcer busy in commu-nications and he would stay at Foxwood where he would be safe.

When Ansel returned, he needed to convince Rutger the construction team had to begin the upgrades on his house. It was imperative they started the renovations before Jordyn was discharged from Celestial. He couldn't imagine the stress it would cause if she was forced to leave while people were coming and going. She needed to feel the house was her safe place. He also wanted assurance Rutger and Jordyn were protected from Bronte and the Covey. Checking the list one last time, he left the paper on the keyboard, stood, then went to the conference center.

"Send a copy of Doctor Radford's report to Doctor Hyde and tell her to forward it to research if Doctor Radford hadn't already. If Doctor Radford has additional information, let me know ASAP. I'm headed to Elder Macario's residence to check the scene."

"Copy," Mandy replied without looking at him. "I'm en-tering it into the log to keep track of you. If the baron needs you or the director."

"Has anything come back from the Assembly on the im-age?" He was a liar.

"Negative. I'll keep watch for it."

"Copy. Lado is due in half an hour. I left a list of things for him to do on my desk."

"I'll tell him." She turned in her chair. "Is he going to be your second in command?"

"Affirmative. While I'm standing in for the director." Ansel wasn't sure if he was reassuring Mandy or himself.

When Rutger returned, he was going back to being the captain—nothing more, nothing less. Unless the Covey exposed him, then he might not be captain or an enforcer, or part of Cascade. Rogue. Liar. Assassin. Cold-blooded killer. He ignored the raging thoughts and focused on getting out to Elder Macario's house.

"I'll add him to your alerts." Mandy faced her bank of screens and started typing.

"Copy. I'll be back." Ansel watched the action on the screens for a minute longer, seeing who was active and who wasn't, then headed outside.

A roar of engines from trucks, machinery, and a bank of dust met him as the tires and tracks chewed through land as they cleared the ground for the garage and parking lot. The engineers were studying their tablets, plans, and talking to one another over the hole in the ground where the underground facility was going to be. Ansel already thought of it as their dungeon. He quickly checked the front of the house and saw Rutger's truck hadn't moved. *Good.*

He paused, debated meeting with the baron to tell him Lado was working and was the contact while he was out of the office. He wanted the baron to tell him what was going on at the warehouse on Rivers Edge. That would take time he didn't have. Damn, he couldn't wait for the office to be completed and for Rutger to return. Things needed to get back to normal. One last look at Rutger's truck and he prayed he stayed put until Ansel retuned.

With the chaos behind him, he got behind the wheel of his truck, started the engine, and backed up. Quinn pulled in front of him, gave him a half wave, then parked. Years ago, Rutger created *his* team, a specialized force, the few he trusted unconditionally, and served as examples to the rest of the enforcers. People considered the team elite, as they stuck together and were close to Rutger and Ansel. Those men and women were the first to arrive. Guilt simmered in Ansel's stomach, churning his coffee into acid that mixed with his lies. As he struggled to think past the guilt, Kellen pulled in, one of the team, gave a half wave, and Ansel turned left and started out of Foxwood. The mile-long drive, cluttered with trucks of all kinds, backhoes, and a hydraulic jackhammer, sat still while they guided a crane to the shoulder. The crane would lift the treehouses, then lower them into their locations.

Part of him felt like he was escaping Foxwood, the disarray, the baron, and Rutger, while the other part of him knew he was working the case and was going to find who shot Daniel. Then he was going to end his affiliation with the Covey for good. And there wouldn't be any witnesses, just as she had trained him.

Forty-five minutes later, Ansel was following the road and its curves like a winding river to the Shasta-Trinity National Forest. Tall pine and oak shrouded the two-lane road then opened to grass fields where cows lingered. Skirting the forest, he continued north toward the Unseelie court's region, and felt the magic of the area vibrating in the air. With a past spanning thousands of years and rooted in legends and mythology of a medieval time, the Seelie and Unseelie courts outwardly remained true to their canons and from an outside appearance were wary of one another. The Seelie court professed they used white magic, versus the Unseelie court who used black magic and were evil. Their chancellors acknowledged the contention between their kith and kin but that didn't always hold true to the declarations of the past. The two courts bordered one another, and having adapted to modern times, they communed together, and several had married one another. Absolutely normal.

It made him question their professed evil and if they were being honest. Baron Kanin would never allow anyone living under his rule to do anything that would bring human law enforcement into their private matters or get attention from the human world. He had heard rumors of the Unseelie court and the tactics they utilized, but did it make them manipulators of the dark arts? Negative. They allowed their past and rumors to wrap the court in mystery and used it to intimidate and keep the shroud of ambiguity. Like the Cascade pack, the klatch, and other factions, the Seelie and Unseelie courts lived mostly humanized lives.

The pastures ended and the woods thickened with trees and outstretched limbs ladened with emerald leaves and pine needles. Ansel made a left, and leaving the main road, the magic grew stronger, sharper. Maybe the rumors were true. His senses told him he was on Unseelie land, its intensity making him shiver, but there was another power, a slight in magic causing him to pause, and reminded him there was more to his past than her vengeance. He could handle them. He would do what he had been doing for a hundred and twenty years, he would ignore them. If they didn't find out about her and use her to force him into their fold or to expose him.

To distract himself from his personal problems, he checked the navigation, drove five more miles, and saw a sign with the chancellor's crest that reminded him what was at stake. Making a right onto a paved driveway, he followed the narrow lane to a circle drive where a cluster of dogwoods, their large green leaves and white blooms hanging from its limbs, dwarfed a variety of roses and irises. An elder with the Unseelie court was fond of his flowers. That was absolutely evil. Ansel would have laughed except the tension tightening his muscles stopped him, as did his imagination feeding him the Covey, and an elder elf powerful enough to start a feud with Cascade. He stopped when the walkway to the single-story, cedar-sided house, complete with shutters, sat on his right. There was an investigation to work, and he was going to his job.

CHAPTER NINE

Before killing the engine, he checked the screen for alerts, saw nothing the others couldn't handle, and by the looks Mandy and Lado were doing just that. Then he checked his cell for messages from Lado. Nothing. He was free to do his investigation. Getting out of the truck, he walked around the front, and toward the single door, painted red, with a wreath made from grape vines and decorated with some kind of flower he didn't know the name of. Which wasn't a surprise. He raised his hand to knock when it opened, a sweep of cinnamon-scented air drifted out, struck him as if it had been a fist, and a clear view of the backyard through large windows sat before him.

Elder Macario stepped into his view and blocking him for a second, held the door. His blond hair highlighted by white was back and away from his face, his sapient, green eyes leveled on him, and Ansel felt guilt rise up from his belly to invade every cell. He did what he had done all morning when it raised its ugly head and shoved it down. The memory cinnamon had brought on was tougher to fight forcing him to gather what control he could.

"Good morning, Elder Macario."

"Captain Wolt," Elder Macario started. "Would you like to see the scene or talk with Isa, Daniel's wife?"

Wife. More guilt tumbled through him, tangled around

his confidence, and squeezed. If Daniel had died it would have been a different visit if Ansel had been involved at all. "I need to check the scene."

"Certainly." Elder Macario stepped out, closed the door behind him, and took the lead.

Ansel followed the elder, his steps purposeful as he made his way around the front of his truck and down the drive. To their right a flower garden—shaded by pine, oak, and cedar trees—was bright with dozens of colors, while clusters of ferns added greenery. As if there needed to be more. When they had walked for several minutes, were close to the end of the drive, Elder Macario stopped, the tip of his loafers touching dirt.

"I was standing right here. Daniel had walked down the slope to see the daisies. No one planted them there and there they are." Elder Macario turned his head to look at Ansel.

He felt like he should say something about the daisies but for the life of him, words escaped him. They were daisies. Without responding, Ansel started down the embankment, his boots slipping in the fallen leaves, dried grass too weak to break through the foliage, at the same time he tried not crush the other flowers. Picking a path around the cluster of plants, he trekked deeper through the bed, then faced the elder, took a step, then another.

"Right there. Daniel was standing right where you are."

"Copy," he mumbled.

Someone shot the elf in the back. *Coward.* The shooter had been close to the house. A bad sign. Before he saw the blood peppering petals and the ground, a currant of iron drifted up through the heavy floral scent. Ansel bent down, drew a breath, held it, tasted the different flavors, then let it out. He picked up Daniel's scent, his blood, the varied flowers, and damp dirt. Nothing unusual. Nothing giving away the shooter's genetics. *They had walked close to the entrance of the drive*, Ansel thought as he turned to face the road, but they didn't cross the property line. Because they knew who and what they were targeting. He didn't like the trees sitting between himself and the highway, and liked the trees across from the property even less. Scanning the forest, he searched for a possible avenue giving the shooter a clear shot. His boots scraped dirt, two inches to the right, and the woods opened to a line clear of trees and limbs. He looked down at his boots and saw the impressions of Daniel's prints beside his, the blood splatter, and farther out his handprints. Ansel let a slow breath out as he looked back up at the massive cedar tree where the shooter had been. A clear shot. An easy shot.

"I know I asked you this yesterday, but you might remember something today, any detail counts. Did you hear anything, a car engine, someone across the street, rustling of brush?" Ansel asked.

"Just the whispered prayer. I heard it all night, it wouldn't leave me." Elder Macario looked across the road at the line of trees. "It came from there, didn't it?"

"Affirmative." If the elder heard it from across the road, it was on purpose. "Is your hearing sensitive? Heightened?"

Elder Macario met his gaze and held it as he trained his features erasing any emotion. "Yes. More so when I'm on my property. Why?"

"The shooter may have wanted you to hear it. Did you sense anyone, and another magic-born, their power?" Ansel asked.

"I don't think so." Elder Macario's eyes darkened. "There was a tremor I didn't recognize."

"That's good. Could you tell what kind of magic-born it came from?"

"No." He shook his head. "It was indistinct."

She had that kind of power. "After Daniel was shot, did you hear anything?"

"No, I was shocked, and I didn't pay attention," Elder Macario explained, his practiced mask cracking and making his face pinched with frustration and regret.

"That's understandable, sir."

"They didn't have to worry about me seeing them. When Daniel collapsed, I drug him out of there, got my car, and drove him to Celestial. I didn't think about what would happen if they approached the house where my wife and Isa were." He closed his eyes for several seconds before opening them. "I fear I failed."

"You did what you thought was best. They didn't cross the property line. How often have you and Daniel been checking the flowerbed?" Ansel asked as he mounted the embankment.

"Three weeks. We didn't plant the daises, they're wild. With the changes happening, we were watching for a sign," Elder Macario answered. "Maybe whoever is responsible used the daises to get us out here."

Changes happening? With the pack? Or the Unseelie court? It was definitely the pack and Jordyn, their soothsayer. Who was in the same hospital as Daniel. Ansel stored the detail. "I'm confident they were watching you, but they didn't target you. It brings me back to why they shot Daniel. He didn't know anyone who would want to harm him?"

"No. I've asked Isa, my wife, his parents, and we couldn't come up with anyone. What do you think about the flowers?"

"I don't know anything about flowers, sir, and think the flowers are just flowers. But you stated you were watching for a sign. What kind?"

"While all flowers are gifts, and have a beautiful bloom, the daises can be evasive. A poison wrapped in a humble box." He watched Ansel with narrowed eyes. "Like mistletoe it can choke the weaker floras around them."

"And the sign?" Ansel pushed. He hated playing twenty questions.

"Your soothsayer was attacked."

There it was. "Go on."

"I do not want to speak about a subject that might offend."

"You believe the daises are a sign. What you have to say about them is relevant," Ansel assured.

"She was attacked by a magic-born. One of our own. Like the daisy attacks its own by devouring their energy. Feeding off those around it. I believe there is a poison among us." Elder Macario took his heavy gaze from Ansel, looked at the flowerbed, then back to him. "But I have been known for being melodramatic. I will have to consult the others. The medical staff at Celestial has treated Daniel and his family with the highest regard. The court appreciates the expertise and kindness showed."

Devouring. Feeding. He stopped from physically shuddering as the memory of her teeth withdrew from his flesh. It wasn't about him. It was about the pack. He would have to tell the baron. Ansel understood the logic behind what the elder said, it would appear to be a sign and there was a poison among them. Was it the witches? They had been released and Flint was free. Was it her? The elder had heard the prayer which was a violation of the rules. Defying her spoken word. It was comparable to breaking the

Highguard's canons, both ended in a death sentence. And it exposed their oath, position, and alerted the target. Like the hexagon and its carvings, he was the only person who would believe the elder had heard a prayer. The string of words promising devotion and the end to an evil drifted through his mind under his actual thoughts and questions. Did she know him?

"May I speak with Isa now?" Ansel asked.

"Yes." Elder Macario looked across the road to the trees. "The land holds its secrets, but only for a time." Then at the area where Daniel had stood, and giving both his back, started toward the house.

Neither of them said anything, letting silence fill the minutes, when the elder opened the front door, stepped to the side, and waited for Ansel to pass. The cinnamon-tinted air washed over him, bringing his memories to the surface and making his skin crawl. He shoved them back as best he could and trying for normal gazed at the house. A common house from the outside, an Unseelie elder residence on the inside. There were masks, faces of elves, their pointed ears sharp, their eyes painted with vibrant colors decorated the cream painted walls. Textiles with runes and the moon's phase hung on two walls, a window separating them, half-way down a couch cut off the view. Sitting on the couch were two women, one older, gray hair up in a tight bun exposing her pointed ears, her pale teal eyes, and her hands in her lap resting on a white tunic. The second woman—younger, brown hair held back in a braid, pointed ears exposed, her chestnut eyes streaked with red, her cheeks redder from having wiped tears away. She twisted her hands in her lap and over her knit skirt. Pureblood elders with the court. If he screwed this up, he wouldn't have to worry about the baron or Rutger finding out about the Covey and his past.

Isa inhaled, wiped tears from her eyes with a tissue, then stared at him as if she had a dozen questions for him. He was thankful Daniel lived, was doing exceptionally well, Dr. Hyde's words not his, so he wouldn't be lying when he told her not to worry. Although, Ansel doubted the tears were for fear her husband's life was in danger. If Elder Macario shared his theory about the daisies being a sign, then she had to be thinking the assassin would return to finish the job. It wasn't going to happen. The Covey made its point.

"Isa, this is Captain Wolt with Cascade's enforcers. He needs to ask you some questions," Elder Macario said in a tone like he was speaking to a child.

In response, she nodded her head, wiped more tears, and twisted the tissue instead of her hands. "Pleased to meet you, Captain Wolt," she squeaked out.

"First, do you have questions for me?" Ansel asked.

"Do you think he'll come back?" The words rushed from her. "I mean, her ... I mean, he didn't—" She didn't finish the sentence.

"Negative. They didn't cross the property line, because they know your safe here. If they had any intention of coming back, they would have already. My presence proves Cascade and the enforcers are involved and will do everything we can to keep you safe and find out who did this. Elder Macario, do you have access to guards?" Ansel took his eyes from Isa, who had visibly relaxed, to the elder.

"Yes. I wasn't going to post the court's guards when we asked Cascade for help. I have no intention of offending Baron Kanin by not trusting him," he replied.

"Understood. If you would like Cascade to send soldiers, it can be arranged," Ansel offered.

"I think a team of the court's guards and Cascade's

soldiers will serve as a statement that the court and the pack are working together, and will give Isa the protection she is seeking," Elder Macario suggested.

"Agreed. I'll make the call." Turning his attention back to Isa, he asked, "Did you hear anything before or after the shooting? A vehicle? Someone on the property? Anything out of place?"

Isa considered his question, or questions, and sat silent for so long Ansel thought she was going to stare at him rather than answer him. Her eyes widened, were damp with new tears, and the entire time, Elder Macario and his wife stared at him as if their glares were going to bore holes through him.

"Someone was on the property?" she whispered as tears slipped down her cheeks. She shuttered and looked at the elder's wife.

"Isa, he said they didn't cross the property line, because they understand our power. I believe he's asking if you saw someone. If you didn't, there was no one here," the woman responded. Like the elder, she used a voice suited to calm an upset child. She turned her teal gaze to Ansel. "I am Nolelia, Macario's wife. I didn't see anyone. We were outside and I was watching the hummingbirds feed from the sage. I would have seen them, if not sensed them."

"Ma'am. What do you mean sense them?" Ansel asked.

"The garden and I have a synergistic relationship. Our magic is plant based. If there had been an intruder intending on harming us, the garden would have warned me," she explained.

Of course it would have. That's why the shooter remained across the street and hadn't crossed the property line. Ansel didn't know enough about elves, the courts, or their magic, and it was obvious. They were more powerful than they acted and that was a problem. He would have to look at the covenant they signed with the baron and if it detailed their magic. And while his gut feeling told him the Covey had made their point, and she was planning her revenge on Ansel, there was a possibility Daniel's magic may have been the reason he was the target.

"Thank you, ma'am. I'll request four soldiers, two at the entrance, and two who will monitor the road." He met the elder's gaze to have it drill into him, like the elder knew what Ansel was thinking. "With the drive and road covered, it leaves you free to place your guards where you are most comfortable. Maybe at the door to the house." He turned his attention to Isa and tried for confidence. "Would that make you feel more secure?"

"I think so," Isa mumbled. Taking the other woman's hands, she said, "I want Daniel home."

"Yes, dear. He will be home soon," Nolelia assured as she patted the Isa's hands.

"I'll take my leave then." Ansel turned, thought about running to the exit to get out of the house, and started toward the door. Freedom.

"Thank you for being understanding, Captain," Elder Macario offered as he opened the door.

Ansel stepped outside, thankful for the fresh air, the fragrance coming from the flowers, and away from Isa's despair. "Yes, Elder Macario."

"You look as if you have a suspect in mind," he stated plainly.

The man was observant. Ansel's anxiety spiked, then gave him her face, the way she sighted her rifle, and the whispered words of the prayer. He flipped flopped between knowing it was the Covey and hoping to hell it wasn't. It could have been an enemy of the court targeting someone they considered important, maybe a warning for the elder, and it wasn't about Ansel at all. Because there was another group using the Covey's symbol that was carved on a crystal.

"I'm not going to get ahead of myself. I do have a place to start. I'm confident you're safe," he answered. His voice held his assurance even as it went up in flames. "Do you know anything about kyanite crystals?"

"They're more symbolic than anything. We don't possess them, their association with death is against our beliefs. Why do you ask?"

"The projectile was kyanite. Where would one obtain them?"

"Any mystic shop. Like oils, crystals are used for multitude of things."

"Thank you for your corporation," Ansel said.

"If there is anything we can do, please ask." Elder Macario nodded and stepped back into the house.

Ansel gave a slight nod in response, turned to his truck, walked around the front and getting in started the engine. He searched the area with his senses, felt the buzz of magic, its reach threading through the plants, and the residents in the house. He hadn't known about their magic. The shooter had and kept his distance. It was easy for Ansel to think the shooting was directed at the Unseelie court, and it wasn't about him and his past. The prayer stopped him from believing his delusions. Putting the truck into gear, he headed toward the road, and when he was at the end of the drive, he crossed and parked on the shoulder. He left his truck and walked over brush, fallen trees, saplings, rocks, while checking his surroundings, the distance to the flowerbed with rogue daisies, then stopped.

At the time of the shooting, the sun would have been at the shooter's back, and on Daniel. Ansel grimaced at the clear path to the yard. It was painful to look at. He could picture Daniel talking about what wild daises meant as the sun filtered through tree limbs its bright beams like targeting lasers on the elf. Why Daniel? If it was the Covey, why hit the Unseelie court? Ansel stepped back and looking up checked the height the shooter would have had to jump to get the protectory right, and have the damn hexagon hit its target. With a wobbly step backward, his heel hit a rock and stopped him. Carved into the bark and down to the skin of the tree were three feathers in front of a sword its tip pointed to the sky.

The Covey.

The shooter had time to carve the symbol, stalk the elves, learn about their magic, and confirm the shot. Absently, Ansel scratched his left side, could feel the tattoo, making him feel like an animal she owned. When modern times gave him the option of having it removed, he thought about a life without it. Would it cleanse his soul? Negative. That was impossible. Would it magically terminate his tie to her? Negative. It did remind him of his place, the risk the Covey was to his life, and why he didn't have a mate and would never have one.

Guilt simmered in his stomach and rising teased his throat with bile and began burning a hole in his esophagus. He forced himself to swallow, then with shaking hands, took his cell from a pocket and snapped four pictures. See, gathering evidence. *For my own trial.* He took another couple of pictures; one confirming the distance between the tree and the flowerbed, another of the house, the road, and then the tree itself. They had stalked the elves and watched the house. Seeing Isa's eyes filled with tears and the need to find the

Covey feeding his anxiety, his thoughts zeroed in on protecting the pack. With cell in hand, he called communications.

"Captain Wolt," Mandy greeted.

"From my location can you find out who owns the property? If it helps, it's directly across from Elder Macario's residence," Ansel reported. He stared at the woods, the mountains, and felt a tremor work through him. Someone magic-born owned it and knew he was there.

"Affirmative, standby."

While he waited, he went back to the tree, glanced at the symbol, checked for disturbances, then used his senses to search the area. He found animals, the magic holding the land, and nothing else. Any disruptions in the dirt, pine needles, and brush looked like they had been corrupted by the wildlife. Inhaling, he tried to find a scent he recognized, something solid to confirm it was her and the Covey. There was nothing, as if it had been wiped clean, and he made a note.

"Captain Wolt, it's owned by a corporation. I sent you the report. If you want me to dig deeper it'll take me a while," Mandy explained.

"Is the corporation based in California?"

He didn't have to scale the tree to check if the shooter left evidence behind. The void where there should have been a scent told him all he needed to know, and with his enhanced werewolf sight, he could see there wasn't clothing caught in bark, hair, or anything suggesting someone had been there. The absence of a presence, scent, or a trail of power bothered him.

"Affirmative. The land has changed hands four times in the past eighty years. In the last two years there have been several sanctions filed to keep it from being developed."

Not unusual when it backed up to Forest Service land. "Could you find out who the prior owners were?" During the time when immortals kept their life spans a secret, they used different techniques to keep humans from exposing them. There was magic holding the land and that didn't happen overnight. It took years for the land to accept the magic and years for the owner to amass that kind of power.

"Affirmative. It might take me some time," Mandy advised.

"Copy." Ansel ended the call. Frustrated there wasn't a scent or evidence to identify the shooter, and marched out of the woods and to his truck.

On the way back to Foxwood he had plenty of time to go over his evidence, the carving in the tree, the prayer, the stalking. The Covey. Where was he going to start looking for her and her band of assassins? Nothing was adding up. It was the Covey. Why did they hit Daniel? She knew Ansel would be the person investigating. It wasn't news he had taken over when Rutger officially went on leave until further notice. The entire damn territory was aware. Hell, the Highguard knew and that meant the world knew. Did it make the enforcers look weak? Negative. Did it make the pack look weak? Negative. Did it make them appear shaken and unsure? Affirmative. Like the new construction.

Some serious shit went down, and both Rutger and Jordyn deserved time to heal physically and emotionally. Again, everyone, the entire territory felt the same way. The territory wasn't the Covey. He gripped the steering wheel, his knuckles turning white, tension racing across his shoulders and down into his wrists. Any questions about the warehouse, road from the Summit, the securities risks, and what the baron was planning was lost in the cluster of his mind. If the baron wanted him to know about the warehouse, he would have told him. He didn't. So, it wasn't his problem. Yet.

One thing at a time, he reminded himself. When he was back at Foxwood, he was going to call every hotel/motel in the area then bug Rutger about the upgrades to his house. Then he was going to try to steal some free time in order to start his search for her.

Clio sat back in her chair, her elbows resting on the arm rests, the computer screen glaring at her, and the email she carefully constructed causing needles of doubt to enter her confidence.

She was an emergency room doctor, and would oversee the newly constructed state-of-the-art medical facility at Foxwood. And from what she understood the Enforcer's office, garage, and security upgrades were going at warp speed and would be done in a couple of months if not sooner. She was going to have her proposal for the med room ready, and she needed to have someone she could trust to help her. Not only trust, but they needed to know about the magic-born and were willing to expand their medical knowledge to myths, legends, ancient writings in old tomes, basically any history relating to the magic-born, believable or not. That's why she wrote the email.

Clio exhaled as she read the string of words again. She wasn't recruiting for Celestial. The hospital didn't have a problem recruiting employees. Any magic-born and Deviant in a fifty-mile radius wanted to work at Celestial. From medical staff, housekeeping, maintenance, and grounds keeping, people saw the hospital as a place to be themselves while helping others. Because it was a sanctuary for the magic-born. She said those very words to Pearl Ashby, the Esme's second of the circle. She went back to staring at the screen, the words blurring as her attention went one direction and her thoughts went another.

If she didn't ask, she would never find out, and she wasn't capable of living with would have, could have, should have. Especially if it meant saving peoples' lives. Clio re-read the email; everything was spelled correctly, punctuated, and ended with her name and information. How crazy was she for contacting the Esme's son, Dr. Baines, about a job at Celestial? Very. She hit send.

"Well, that's done," she mumbled to the office.

Like it or not. Clio half expected the room to explain in great detail how the baron was going to question her about having communications with a witch and then offering him a job at Celestial, Cascade property, and hopefully Foxwood, his estate. His home. It was true the pack didn't blame the Lapis Lazuli coven for Miss Langston's kidnapping, or Zachery's death, but the slightest reference to witches created tension so thick you could cut it with a chainsaw. Or two. The baron had Rutger. Rutger had Ansel. Ansel had Lado, at the moment. She needed a BFF, a golden boy ... Dr. Baines to be exact. Sure, when she started explaining herself to the baron using that strategy, he would stare at her like she had grown a second head. Then with gold eyes holding power and authority he would demand an actual explanation. Perfect.

The knock on the door made her shift her eyes from the screen to the pale wood standing between her and ... Dr. Carrion. Suppressing a groan, she clicked out of her work email, stood, and walked to the door. "Doctor Carrion. How can I help you?"

He slipped past her and sat down in a chair in front of her desk. "I've decided to discharge Miss Langston."

Do come in. "That seems abrupt," she replied. Clio made her way around the desk, moved her white lab coat out of the way, and sat down. "Has she completed her exercises? Sleeping in human form? Eating? Responding to interaction?"

"If she were anyone else, I would err on the side of caution and wait another week, but she grows increasingly disinterested. To answer your question, yes, she speaks when spoken to, is eating regularly, is taking care of her hygiene by herself, without being reminded ... having said that last part, she refuses to wear anything but that oversized sweatshirt and the lounge pants." He stopped, took a breath, his frustration clear in the lines creasing his face, and his tone. "I sense desolation, overwhelming grief, and if I have to look into her dead eyes while she is smiling at me for one more day, I'm going to have to be admitted," he finished.

"I sympathize with you, Doctor Carrion. I was serious when I said werewolves need their pack. Maybe she is better off with her mate. Are you going to require her to continue therapy?"

Dr. Carrion looked defeated. Besides his naturally occurring human arrogance, the sharp edge of animosity over his own kind defining him as a Deviant, he was a good man who treated his patients with the upmost care. Miss Langston was damaging his confidence and he didn't know how to help her.

"Yes, I'll see if we make any progress. If not, I feel as if I have failed." He sat back, his narrowed eyes on her.

"You haven't failed. Miss Langston's situation is unique, as much as her emotions are." Clio wasn't sure she was telling the truth, and wasn't sure she believed Miss Langston was a soothsayer and how it might have changed the woman. "I'll contact the baron and tell him. If you could write a summary of her care, they will help as much as they can," she explained. Hopefully, Director Kanin was able to care for her.

"I will," he said as he stood. "Thank you, Doctor Hyde."

Clio gave him a smile and waited for him to close the door behind him before reaching for the handset, then dialed Foxwood's private number. "This is Doctor Hyde, may I speak with Baron Kanin?"

"May I inquire what the call is about?" Sadie asked.

"Miss Langston," she replied.

"Please hold."

As Clio waited, she drew circles on a pad of paper, her mind going between being Dr. Carrion's cheerleader, the go between, and Captain Wolt. She was going to have to call him next, what fun that was going to be, and she pushed the tip of the pen into the paper.

"Doctor Hyde, how is Jordyn?" Baron Kanin asked.

"Doctor Carrion has informed me Miss Langston is ready to be discharged." Clio waited for the baron's questions, the need to speak with Dr. Carrion, were they sure Miss Langston was ready.

"Excellent. When will be a good time?"

No questions. All right. "Anytime. How is Director Kanin? Will he be picking her up?"

"Yes, Rutger will be there, I'm anticipating an hour."

"Excellent. Please, tell him to use the security entrance," Clio advised.

"Of course. Thank you, Doctor Hyde."

"You're welcome, Baron." She contemplated pushing further and requesting an audience with him to discuss Dr.

Baines when the line went dead. "Baron?" Silence. She turned the handset over and stared at it like a voice would come through the tiny holes and talk to her. Shaking her head, she pressed the switch hook, listened for the dial tone, then entered the number for Dr. Carrion's office.

"It's Doctor Hyde. Please advise Doctor Carrion that Director Kanin is on his way to pick up Miss Langston. ETA, one hour," Clio relayed to the receptionist.

He repeated what she had told him then hung up.

Was she going to call Captain Wolt? Negative. She notified the baron, and he would notify the director. Anyway, Captain Good Mood was working on an attempted murder investigation, at the same time the construction and security upgrades were going full steam ahead. *He might be stressed,* she told herself, *which would explain his rough tone and sharp responses.* She had a job, stress, but she didn't take it out on people. Like she cared. She did not care. Clio looked at her cell phone. *Let it go.* She grabbed the cell off the desk, shoved it in a pocket, and headed to Miss Langston's room.

Hallway after hallway led her to the extended wing, and through the back of the hospital where non-employees weren't allowed. Clio said hello in passing, her focus trying to remain on Dr. Carrion, the baron, the director, Miss Langston. Not the attempted murder on an influential person from the Unseelie court. The longer she obsessed over it, the more she thought it didn't make sense. Yeah, because she was the investigator. She wasn't even an enforcer. She was a doctor and finding a solution was her job, it was in her blood, she couldn't stop what she was. Clio entered the waiting area and headed toward the desk where the male from the day before was sitting.

"Miss Langston is expected to be discharged."

"Yes, I have her papers. You can go back, she's waiting in her room," he replied.

"Thank you." Clio left the desk, and walking to the door, the lock disengaged, allowing her to pull it open.

The walls of the hall were decorated with paintings of landscapes, cottages, spring scenes that hung beside snow-covered mountains and cabins, the carpet silencing her footsteps was a soft beige. It was supposed to exude calm and peace, but it looked creepy and purposeful. She was sure no one noticed the hall or the pictures, their minds in different places. Clio continued and passing rooms, offices, visitor rooms, then at the end it branched off into two hallways, the suites where long-term patients stayed. Miss Langston was the only patient in the long-term care wing and the emptiness let silence hang. She stood in front of the door, her dead eyes. Not dead. Carrying the weight of her demons. Clio thought of Captain Wolt. Was that why she obsessed over him? She saw the darkness sitting in his cinnamon depths. His past. What happened to him? Wasn't her problem. Miss Langston's file had been removed, and a tag ordering the room to be cleaned sat in its place. Lightly rapping, she waited for a second, and opened the door.

Long-term care rooms resembled studio apartments, minus the kitchen. To the left was a queen size bed, with a pale blue comforter, a nightstand with lamp, to the right was a sitting area, couch, chair, coffee table, and more lamps. Placed by the door was one suitcase, a new looking travel bag, and a zip-up hoodie had been draped over the suitcase. Miss Langston was sitting in a rocking chair, a blanket over her legs despite July's sunshine beaming through the window and warming the small area. She was wearing the oversized gray sweatshirt Dr. Carrion hated, and loose gray pants, both resembled the utilitarian sweats found at Fox-wood. The only thing missing was Cascade's crest. At least she matched. Then Clio saw she was wearing Hawaiian print flipflops that looked right out of the store new, like the travel bag. She thought the shoes were strange considering the sweats. Miss Langston clearly didn't care.

After the kidnapping, Baron Kanin had a team go to Butterfly Valley and pack up Miss Langston's house, then had everything she owned stored in the pack's private storage. She owned nothing but the clothing she brought with her when she returned for her sister's wedding. Her look was the exact opposite of the woman Clio had seen at the wedding wearing jewelry depicting her family's Pureblood legacy, bridesmaid's dress, and heels. She couldn't stop herself from staring at Miss Langston's back, her black hair in a loose braid a nurse had to have helped her with, and her sunken shoulders under the mass of cotton material. To say she felt sorry for the woman was an understatement.

"I can feel you and your pity," she whispered without turning to see her.

"My apologies, Miss Langston." Clio inhaled and exhaled as Miss Langston stood, and holding the throw in one hand, faced her. How a person could look defeated and exude authority and otherworldly power she didn't know.

"No need for apologies, Doctor Hyde."

"You're being discharged. Are you ready to get out of here?"

"Yes." Her haunted cocoa brown eyes held slivers of copper as she stared at Clio. The power coming from her drifted out like the wind had caught its threads and was twisting it in the air.

"Excellent. Director Kanin will be here to pick you up," Clio explained. *Keep calm*. She felt like looking down at the rug and boring holes through it and into the tile floor beneath as Miss Langston kept her gaze on her.

The conversation with Dr. Carrion and his feeling of failure came back to her. It wasn't from Miss Langston's detachment from life; there was the detachment, then there was her raw power. As an empath, Dr. Carrion would feel her magic and the power of her wolf. And if the soothsayer was real, and she held the Collective of the pack, its past and the spirits of their dead, what had he felt? Miss Langston's magic was tangible and forced Clio to admit, she needed to consider soothsayers were real, and Miss Langston was indeed one of them, and just maybe so were fated mates. She wasn't sold and wasn't prepared to believe the last part. Still, she couldn't refute the magic and power seething in front of her as proof. Clio risked turning away from Miss Langston when someone knocked on the door. It silently opened, revealing Dr. Carrion and a nurse.

"Would you take Miss Langston's bags to the security entrance?" Dr. Carrion asked the nurse. She nodded, gave Miss Langston a half bow, then grabbed her bags and left the room. Dr. Carrion faced the two women. "I'm sad to see you leave, Miss Langston. I would have liked to have helped you."

Miss Langston gave him a sheepish smile, Clio couldn't believe she pulled off, and replied, "I wouldn't be going home if it wasn't for your help, Doctor Carrion. Thank you."

"I'll take that." He chuckled. "Your appointments have been set up and you'll receive a reminder the day before. Now you're free to leave."

"I'll be escorting her." Clio watched Dr. Carrion watch Miss Langston, and a sliver of jealousy burned her middle. What the hell was she doing? A whirlwind of mystery had formed around Miss Langston, from her three years in

Butterfly Valley, Baron Kanin's announcement of her being a soothsayer, fated mate to the Second to the Alpha, and the kidnapping hadn't helped. Despite the oversized clothing, plain appearance, even with her jet-black hair and cocoa eyes, she was a shining star in a dark night. "Director Kanin should be here shortly."

Miss Langston approached Dr. Carrion, shifted the throw over her forearm, and took Dr. Carrion's hand in hers. "Thank you again. I appreciate your time and your help."

"My pleasure," he replied softly.

He actually lowered his head and smiled. Clio's confidence took a direct hit that sent shockwaves to her pride. After giving him an elegant nod, as the Pureblood she was, she walked to the door, opened it, and disappeared. Clio didn't say anything to Dr. Carrion, she couldn't without her voice giving away her jealousy and frustration. She followed Miss Langston, and catching up with her halfway down the hall, they walked in silence save for the slapping noises of her flipflops on skin and tile.

Patients, doctors, nurses, hospital employees all stopped, lowered their heads in respect, then stared as the Second to the Alpha of the Cascade pack's mate and their soothsayer, with her head held high, walked by them. Miss Langston smiled, nodded back, and gave soft replies as they passed the nurses' stations, offices, exam rooms, short-term rooms, and to the back where silence moved in.

"You'll be able to resume your photography," Clio said to break the silence.

"Yes." She didn't look at Clio, didn't pause.

"Director Kanin's house has beautiful views." The two-story log cabin, which she could fit six townhouses in, sat on Nakoma Lake, its deck stretched out from the mountain and was built on stilts to give you the feeling you were suspended. If you wanted to be closer, you could go down to the lake and sit on the dock with your feet in the water. "You'll be able to enjoy the sunsets and the lake." *Views of the mountains*. It made her think of Captain Good Mood, his geese, and his cold front. She wanted to know what he thought of Miss Langston and Director Kanin and needed to stop doing that. Clio wondered if Captain Good Mood would stare at Miss Langston like Dr. Carrion had. She needed to stop that, too.

"Yes, they are beautiful," she replied.

Auto answer. Miss Langston said the correct words, replied when necessary, showed interest, and it was all a lie. Her eyes were focused on what was happening in her head and closed off from the world as she stared at nothing. Clio understood Dr. Carrion's frustration.

"Here we are." Clio swiped her card, entered her code, and opened the door, the guards who had fallen in behind them remained in the hall. Summer's heat swept inside, taking the harsh, sterile smells from her for a minute, then they battled back and the soft scent of fresh air dissipated.

"Doctor Hyde," Director Kanin greeted. He was wearing a plain blue T-shirt, a button-up over it, jeans, and his worn boots. Not meeting her gaze, his eyes rolled gold as he stared at Miss Langston like she was the only person in the world.

Fated mates. Right. And if Captain Wolt stared at you that same way? *Stop.* "Director Kanin," she replied to say something to cover the lightning bolt of jealousy shooting through her. Clio felt the buzz of magic as it wove between them and that made her feel like she had walked in on an intimate moment. She had to get away from them. "Here are Miss Langston's bags, and if either of you need anything, don't hesitate to call."

"Thank you for your kindness," Miss Langston commented as she met Clio's gaze.

Clio hesitated and stared at the swirling copper and black of her eyes as if they were mocking her doubt. "You're welcome."

Director Kanin took both bags then stopped. "How is Daniel?"

"Doing well, he should be able to go home very soon," she replied.

"Good to hear." He walked to the truck, placed Miss Langston's bags inside, then walked back and gently held her by the elbow. "Jo, are you ready?"

"Yes," she replied with a smile.

The same one she wore whenever someone talked to her. The difference between Miss Langston talking to staff and talking to the director was her cocoa eyes blazed copper, proving there was life there. Its spark had been temporality snuffed but it was coming back, and the director was part of that. Fated mates. Clio was starting to change her mind. Or she wanted to believe it could be true and there was a mate out there for her. Either one was going to get her in trouble.

The jagged edges of jealousy came roaring back. The blue streaked with brown were her human color and her wolf's eyes, and she aged quicker than a Pureblood. She couldn't stop herself from thinking Captain Wolt's cold front was because she was a Wight, and he was a Pureblood. Jordyn Langston was the shining example of what a Pureblood whose family had status in the pack as elders, had to offer. Poise. Confidence. Perfect features. The respect of the pack. And gleaming wolf eyes.

"Again, if you need anything ..." Clio watched the director, his height and build a stark contrast to Miss Langston's petite frame, tuck her to his side, lead her to the truck, and helped her inside.

"Thank you, Doctor," he replied as he rounded the backend.

Clio's cell buzzed in her pocket and she appreciated the distraction. As the director backed out of the parking spot, she turned and headed back inside.

"Doctor Hyde." She walked toward her office intending on getting back to her normal routine now that Miss Langston had been discharged.

"It's Captain Wolt. Have you checked your email?" Ansel asked.

"Negative. I've been working. I have this job," Clio replied, a smidge too harshly. Yeah, she could do cold business. Especially with jealousy's strings tying knots around her mood.

Ignore her. "I had the forensics file on the Ragas case sent to you. Interesting information. After you're finished reading it, I would appreciate it if you would forward it to research." He made her mad, and she wasn't going back to friendly conversation. That was fine with him. Part of him hated it, and part of him knew he didn't have a choice. Not when he was being watched.

"Affirmative." Clio stormed through the hospital, pissed off he thought he could call and start telling her what to do. "Anything else?"

He winced with her tone. Her anger traveled to his console and was trying to set it on fire. "How is Miss Langston?" Ansel needed to talk to Rutger.

"Discharged." That's right, one word answer.

"Dammit. When?" Ansel increased his speed, like it was going to shave days off his time and not seconds.

"About five minutes ago. Director Kanin picked her up."

How the hell did Captain Good Mood not know where his BFF was?

"Copy." Ansel hit the end button on his console and couldn't get to Foxwood quick enough.

"Hello? No fucking way." Clio looked at the screen to see the background picture of her standing beside her parents. Why did everyone feel it was okay to hang up on her? *I'm a glorified door mat with a complex, hello default setting.*

"Doctor Hyde to the ER. Doctor Hyde to the ER," the male voice ordered over the intercom.

Clio shoved the cell in a pocket, changed directions, and headed toward the ER. Where she was respected because this was her world.

CHAPTER TEN

Ansel stopped the truck, killed the engine, and getting out headed straight toward the house. He didn't pay attention to the enforcer's vehicles, who was there and who wasn't. The lot was a mess of equipment, trucks, vans, the growling of engines, people, and they were everywhere. Ansel's world felt like it was closing in on him knowing they were all potential victims. Rutger's truck was parked where it had been when he left, the weeds unfazed by his coming and going. Taking the steps, Ansel stopped in front of Abigail.

"I need to see Director Kanin."

"They're expecting you," she replied.

Expected. They know I'm responsible for the shooting. Guilt sat like concrete in his stomach. He should have kept the crystal and the forensics report a secret ... not a secret, just out of sight until he had something solid to go on, at least it would have delayed the inevitable. While he watched Abigail open the door, his thoughts chased the lies he had told, the betrayal they weren't going to forgive him for, and the family he was going to lose. He stepped inside and to the left and waited.

"Both the baron and the director are in the baron's office." Abigail gave him a questioning smile, stepped outside, and closed the door behind her.

Ansel remained where he was, standing there like an idiot

and feeling like he didn't belong. As if one of the sentinels should escort him to the office like he was a common visitor and not the Captain of Enforcers. Inhaling, he started down the silent hall, the elegant marble under his feet, the pale pearl walls decorated with Cascade's past surrounding him, and the expensive furniture reminding him what he had come from. Nothing. They gave him what he had. Yes, he worked for it, fought for it, held his position, proved himself reliable, honest, and an asset to the pack. Ansel stood at the door, heard soft voices in the family room, and recognized their scents. Jordyn. The baroness. With his head bowed, he raised his hand, knocked a couple of times, and waited. The tension in his shoulders was going to cripple him.

Rutger opened the door, motioned to a chair, and said, "Have a seat."

"Thank you," he mumbled as he entered the office. The baron sat behind the desk, the collar of his button-up shirt open, his elbows resting on the top pulled his sleeves, and slivers of burnt gold colored his brown eyes.

"I've read the forensics report. The kyanite crystal is a new development, not because it's a danger to shapeshifters, but the civilian uses, and the myth behind it. It makes it readily available." He took a page, and lifting it, seemed to be reading. "The assassin knew it wouldn't kill Daniel. I find it interesting the kyanite crystals were used in ritual killings of those belonging to a holy order. They've exposed their weapon and now we can find a way to counter its effects. Like Rutger pointed out, I believe it's a calling card. They think one of us should know what it means," Baron Kanin explained.

Ansel swallowed the lump in his throat and the guilt it was made from. "Agreed. I went to see Elder Macario, he reported he and Daniel had been studying wild daises for a couple of weeks and were looking at them at the time of the shooting. The elder mentioned they hadn't been planted and wondered if it was a sign of the changes coming. He used the analogy stating the daisies were a threat among their own. He believes there is a poison in the territory."

"He told you this?" Baron Kanin asked.

"Affirmative, then said he was known to be melodramatic, and he was going to consult others. Where Daniel was standing in the flowerbed there's a clear shot from across the street. I believe either of them could have been the intended target," Ansel explained. "The flowerbed sits down an embankment, and that's where Daniel was."

"They were being watched?" Rutger asked.

"Affirmative. The same marking etched in the projectile was carved in a tree. I took photos of the scene, and will download them. I had Mandy do a background check into the owners of the property." Ansel feared his voice was going to give out on him. He needed to keep it together.

"Good. Have you forwarded the report to research?" Baron Kanin asked.

"I sent it to Doctor Hyde, to make her aware of the crystals, and if there are other victims, she has something rather than nothing. I advised her to forward it to research if Doctor Radford hadn't already," Ansel answered. "I haven't heard confirmation she received the email." She has this job.

"She helped with Jordyn's discharge, I'm sure she has been busy. Did Elder Macario say anything else?" Baron Kanin asked.

"He believes he heard someone praying before the shot was fired. Male with an accent. There's at least eighty yards between the tree, where I believe the shooter was, and where Daniel was standing in the flowerbed. He confirmed he has enhanced hearing, but I also believe the shooter wanted him to hear what was being said, or at least know he was there. Due to Isa, Daniel's wife, staying with the elder, I've requested two soldiers be placed at the driveway entrance and two more to monitor the road. They will have the court's guards around the house. A show of united strength will deter a repeat attack and Isa is pretty shaken." Ansel knew he was digging his own grave. He needed time to find her, without anyone else getting hurt.

"Do you think he's telling the truth? Due to the shock and fear of an attempted assassination, he might be wrong. It could have been his imagination." Baron Kanin held Ansel's gaze and waited for him to answer. "And if he believes there is a poison, he could be trying to sway the court against the pack."

"I didn't sense any animosity from him or felt he lied."

The baron's eyes narrowed, and stabbing through him touched his soul. If he said he believed the elder heard the prayer, it would give away information he knew to be fact. It meant he knew who was behind the shooting. If he said he didn't believe the elder, it would be saying the elder was potentially lying to an enforcer because he was a hysterical mess or trying to go against the pack. What Ansel admitted would change the direction of the case. It would change the baron's opinion of him. Then they would ask him why he thought the elder was telling the truth. *I know the prayer. I've said the prayer, hundreds of times.* Would be the wrong answer. He didn't know where to start looking for her and didn't have the time even if he did. With his heart in his throat, he wasn't going to add another lie. He was going to answer their questions, accept their doubt, and do his best to find her and make her pay.

"I believe Elder Macario is telling the truth, he also hasn't made assumptions or has tried to create an elaborate story since the investigation started. The family has been upfront, and they exposed their magic and their heightened abilities."

"Noted. If you believe him then that's all I need. Do we have any idea what kind of groups, besides religious, say prayers? Especially before an attempted assassination?" Baron Kanin sat back in his chair, his brown eyes carrying his thoughts.

"I can start a search—"

Rutger cut him off before he had a chance to finish his answer. "Negative. With Jo here, I'm not going anywhere. I can do the search."

The baron eyed Rutger, the gold and dark brown playing in his stare while he contemplated his son. Was it doubt in Rutger's abilities? Or the calmness in which he volunteered after learning the witches had been released? Or they both knew Ansel was guilty and was waiting for him to stand up and admit he knew who it was and doing a search was a waste of time and not necessary?

Ansel was going to have a heart attack when Baron Kanin finally said, "I agree. Rutger will do the search. It leaves you free to work."

"I'll start this evening." Rutger sat back in his chair, his eyes locked on the baron.

How Rutger was staying calm when he vowed to kill the released witches Ansel didn't know. Then again, Ansel was sure he was losing his mind to anxiety and guilt, and maybe Rutger was also losing his mind and Ansel couldn't tell.

"Then I'll check with Doctor Hyde about the file," Ansel stated.

"Good. How is Lado working out?" Baron Kanin asked.

Tension was gripping him despite feeling like he had

dodged a bullet. "Fine. I gave him a list of things needing to be done while I was at the elder's house. He checked in a couple of times with updates."

"Excellent. Rutger, do you have any questions?"

Rutger shifted enough he met Ansel's gaze. "Do you think it's a lone shooter or more than one? It appears they have multiple sets of eyes if they stalked the elder for weeks. It would have taken one person double the time, plus getting the weapon prepped and the carving in the tree."

"I hadn't thought about that. It could be more than one. They easily move around and aren't concerned with time," Ansel answered. "If one person was spotted watching the elder it would have alerted them, more than one and no one noticed. There are hikers coming and going in that area." It had him thinking about the earlier call from the Seelie court and the hiker spotted on their property. Except the guard reported a trespasser not a hiker. He would ask Lado about the call.

"You believe they won't go back to the elder's place and finish what they started?" Rutger's forearms rested on the chair's sides, his left leg crossed his right knee, and his T-shirt pulled with his muscles. His eyes were dark, questioning, and held the nightmare he was trying to survive.

"With the soldiers and court's guards, I'm positive they won't go back, and they left evidence. It's one thing hitting an unguarded man, it's another challenging the Cascade pack's authority as well as the Unseelie court. If they meant to make a statement, they have. For us, and they would have no way of knowing, it would mean losing the investigation to human law enforcement and it would create more attention. I think this group likes to operate under law enforcement's radar."

"It is a potential threat to shapeshifters. We don't know the full effects kyanite crystals will have on us. If the projectile and the elf are a message, do you think they'll target someone else?" Baron Kanin asked.

"It's hard to say when we don't know why Daniel was shot. It could be a warning to the Unseelie court, to the pack, or the territory. If they do target someone else, I'll assume it'll be someone from the pack, maybe, and it's a big maybe, from the klatch, they have our attention. Might be trying to flush one of us out," Ansel answered. *Yeah, like me.* It was a matter of time before they came for him. He felt his time with the pack and living in Trinity slipping through his fingers.

"Keep us updated, and if you need Rutger, don't hesitate to call him." Baron Kanin took a glass of water from the desk, the slice of lemon sinking to the bottom to be buried by ice.

Ansel focused on the reason he needed to speak with Rutger. "They released Jordyn, are you ready to work on the upgrades to your house?"

"Affirmative. After this I'm going there to get a few of her things. She'll stay here while the work is being done." Rutger's demeanor changed and he sat straighter, his shoulders tensed, and his chest looked like steel beams had wrapped around it. The baron had two men on the verge of falling apart in his office.

"Let me know when you're ready. I'll help anyway I can." Ansel stood, nervous energy pulsing in his muscles, and he couldn't get out of there fast enough. "I'll be in communications and checking in with Lado."

"Copy." Rutger stayed where he was, as they both waited for him to leave.

Taking the hint, he left the office, heard the faint whispers of Jordyn and the baroness, and headed to the double doors. It was imperative he find her and stop them from harming anyone else. Standing on the front porch, he looked at the construction site, his thoughts racing and his guilt building then headed to communications. He hadn't lied but he hadn't told the truth. His instincts told him to go back inside and explain the entire situation. They deserved to know the truth. His future with the pack depended on his honesty. Damn he felt like a coward. Ansel shoved it down. He would find them and prove to the baron and Rutger he was a man of his word.

"Sir, have you heard from Lado?" Mandy asked.

He stopped short of his desk and faced her. "Negative." He checked his cell to see the last time the enforcer had checked in. "Last update was two hours ago. You don't know where he is?"

"Negative. A human reported they saw a lycan in animal form." She brought up a screen. "A huge wolf was running down the side of the road when it disappeared into the woods. Since the reporting party was human, Lado insisted on talking to them, and left to check it out. Thirty minutes later, he reported he was at the scene, the reporting party wasn't present, and he didn't find the wolf. There was no communication, so I contacted him figuring he would have a report and return to base." She turned to a screen and started typing. "Let me check. GPS put his truck at the out-skirts of Cascade territory where it stayed for two hours when it moved. I'm getting his current location."

"A human called the enforcers about a lycan in animal form?" Ansel asked. "Because they saw a huge wolf running down the side of the road." It didn't make sense and had his instincts roaring with a warning. "Did they give you a name?"

"Negative. They hung up." Mandy stopped talking,

inhaled, and exhaled, and her fearful gaze narrowed on him. "Oh god, I let him go without backup."

They had Lado. "We don't know that for sure. Where is he?" He wanted to believe it wasn't them, Lado had checked a call, simple, and was returning to base. So he didn't check in, it wasn't like every enforcer gave Mandy a minute by minute report on what they were doing. Ansel took three long strides and stood beside her.

"I let him go."

"He's a trained enforcer. Where is he?"

"I'm checking. This thing has been acting up all damn day," she fumed.

"Try his cell," Ansel ordered.

"Copy." Mandy tapped keys, a second later the enforcer's cell rang, and rang, and a gentle voice told them to leave a message.

"Has he ever ignored a call?" Ansel asked, knowing the answer.

"Negative." She ended the call and went back to typing. "Something is wrong. Is it the case? The person who shot the elf?" she asked without facing him.

"I hope not but I am investigating them." *Liar.* Maybe they wanted Ansel out in the open. "Where is he?"

"Foxwood."

"Say again," Ansel demanded.

"He's along the drive. Maybe he didn't hear his cell."" Mandy replied and started to say something else.

Ansel didn't hear her, his ears buzzed, his imagination raced, and his body tensed with the truth. It was them. "Where?" he ordered with frustration.

"In front of treehouse two. He isn't moving. Do you want backup?"

"Affirmative. Have Luke and Quinn follow," he ordered as

he turned from the monitors, Mandy's clicking keys, and he left communications.

Starting his truck, the screen came alive with beeps, chimes, and lines of information at the same time Quinn and Luke both got in their trucks and waited for him to take lead. He didn't know what he was going to do if they harmed Lado. Confess? Search for her? How did he get past the gates, the workers, and the soldiers? And why would they let him go?

Gods, let him be all right. Maybe he hadn't heard his cell. Right. Ansel backed up, turned around, started out of Fox-wood, and toward Lado. With communications behind him and the scenery a blur, a million possibilities flooded his crowded mind and attacked him by screaming louder than his sane thoughts. He was going to lose his mind to insanity, stress, and guilt and that was before he found out Lado's condition. In the rearview mirror he saw the two trucks keep-ing up with him then returning his attention back to the road he slammed on the brakes, swerved onto the opposite shoulder barley missing Lado's truck, and skidded to a stop. Luke and Quinn stopped several yards back and got out of their vehicles.

Ansel gripped the steering wheel, his knuckles turning white, his fingers aching, and he wanted to rest his forehead, slick with sweat, on his hands. He couldn't. He might have missed the back end of Lado's truck but had to swerve to miss the crane parked on the shoulder making him look ir-responsible and inadequate, and he shouldn't be in charge of the investigation. His attention was split ... no, shattered. Killing the engine, he gathered himself, he had a job to do, and getting out made his way to Lado. He refused to meet Quinn or Luke's gazes, there was no way he wanted to see the questions and the doubt in their eyes, it would crush what resolve he had. Walking along the side of the truck, the front end was off the road and concealed by shrubs, while tree limbs rested against the driver's side door.

He slipped down the slope, and getting his footing used his forearm to shove brush and limbs out of his way enough he made room to open the door. Ansel tugged the door back, making metal groan, and a wave of heated iron and rot drifted out as the pained moans coming from Lado sounded. His head rested on the steering wheel, his arms loose at his sides, and his skin glittered where blood had leaked from his ear to make a trail down to his neck and the collar of his BDU shirt. Sticking out from his shoulder, arm, and side were silver/blue crystals while around them blood soaked the material and it had started to stiffen as it dried. They resembled the same type of crystal as the projectile, and where it might not have harmed the elf, it was poisoning Lado and his wolf, and there was something else. With the smell of rotting flesh weighing in the air, Ansel pushed Lado's thick body back to the seat, revealing two more crystals sticking out from his neck. The blackened skin shriveled up around the wounds, loosened, and the dead flesh fell to his legs. Lado turned his head, his bloodshot eyes weeping scarlet, and staring at Ansel, his lips moved with silent words.

"Don't move. I'm getting you help," Ansel assured as he took his cell from his pocket and dialed. "No one comes any closer," he ordered. He waited as it rang, the shrill sound louder than an explosion. "Doctor Hyde, do not question me. I need you and a med van at Foxwood, ASAP."

Dr. Hyde instantly started with a hundred questions and Ansel closed his eyes, gave what answers he could, and ignoring the others chose silence over excuses. Her interrogation continued, he told her there was another problem he didn't know what it was, maybe poison, he rambled then detailed the condition of the wounds he could see. He felt his words sounded rushed, and he wasn't making sense. Dr. Hyde's orders were like a current coming from her, then she was running, and he heard an engine in the background.

"Captain Wolt, are you there?" Clio nearly yelled into the cell. She hit the button on the screen and the call switched from her cell to the computer and filled the cab of the med van. "Ansel?"

"I'm here. It's Lado, he's an Illuminate, elf, werewolf ... there are hundreds of them." Taken back by the sight, Ansel gripped the door as scarlet seeped from Lado's eyes, nose, and mouth. The crystals were going to destroying him.

Lado closed his eyes when the blood increased, his swollen eyelids barely closing, while purple and garnet smeared his face, neck, skull, and clothing. Blood leaked from his nose to his mouth where his parted lips allowed more to dribble down his chin to his throat. His hands looked broken, his fingers crooked, and Ansel was positive his elbow was pointed in the wrong direction. How the hell had he made it back to Foxwood? Riddling his torso, thighs, calves, and the straight areas of his arms were more spikes. No. That was wrong. Spikes were clunky, thick, pain by brute force. He was looking at needles, the size of nails, slender, the heads thicker than the body and flat as if you could use a hammer to drive them home. They were elegant spines of blue and silver shimmering in the early afternoon sunshine, the backdrop of wet scarlet on his black BDU pants highlighting them. It was as if someone had dusted him with glitter. Ansel saw the Covey hold him down while she drove the spines into his joints and body then they broke his arm, hands, and fingers so he couldn't take them out. Why hadn't he shifted?

"Hundreds of what?" She wanted to reach through the console and jerk his attention back to her. "Talk to me, Captain Wolt."

A low moan saturated with pain brought Ansel out of the haze. "Needles. Spines. Kyanite crystals. Did you read the forensics report?" He had to keep it together.

"Negative." She should have read the report, but his instance irritated her and now she was paying the price of walking into a situation blind because she had an attitude. She hated going in blind.

Dammit all to hell. Ansel had to start at the beginning. "The projectile Daniel was shot with was a kyanite crystal. The crystals are not as harmful to the Fae, their bodies will eventually fight the effects. They are a threat to shapeshifters, the extent unknown. Lado is an Illuminate, werewolf, and elf. There are hundreds of them, all over him. Each wound is bleeding, the blood is black, and his skin is rotting," Ansel tried explaining everything at once and felt he explained nothing at all. "He's bleeding out of his eyes, ears, nose, mouth, the crystals are acting like silver. I think he's been poisoned, unknown type. He's bleeding out."

She sucked in a breath. DIC, disseminated intravascular coagulation, the proteins that control blood clotting became overactive and he was in danger of bleeding out. Clio refused to let her worry sound in her voice. "We're going to save him," she assured. She mumbled a string of curse words as Tony, her personal paramedic and driver, made a corner that nearly sent them skidding. "Stay with him. ETA twenty minutes. And Captain, do not touch him under any circumstances. Got it?" she ordered. Clio hoped to hell he got it. "Tell. Me. You. Got. It."

"Got it," Ansel mumbled on auto.

"Do you know who is responsible?" she asked. She said the words as quickly as possible to keep his attention. "Do you need backup?"

Nothing.

"Do you need backup?" she demanded. "Captain Wolt."

"I'm at Foxwood," he replied as if it explained everything.

His voice drifted and the line cut off, leaving her with the tires eating asphalt as they raced along the two-lane road, then the outskirts of Trinity. She was racing to Foxwood where something unnerved Captain Wolt, the silent strength Director Kanin relied on, and it had her heart beating against her sternum, and her pulse in her ears with the thought. She knew she had to smooth things over with him, they worked together and they couldn't go on the way they were. Too late for that.

Clio took her tablet, typed Lado Reyes into the search bar, and a second later his medical history came up on the screen. Illuminate, werewolf, elf, Captain Wolt told her as much, empath, and had been put on the enforcer's inactive list. If she wanted a reason why, she would have to contact the Seelie court. All right. Next was the date he resumed light duty, and scrolling down to the information section, it added the details Ansel had told her. The kyanite crystal, his condition, because she had no idea what the hell was going on besides DIC, what the crystals were doing, and hit enter. Celestial immediately returned, confirming they received the report and was preparing an operating room. The surgeons would be briefed with her information and the forensics report. She typed, update pending, and set the tablet in the console.

"He didn't sound like he got it," Tony said from the driver's seat, his deep voice making the words rumble between them. The ends of his hair skated over the collar of his polo shirt as he checked traffic, the road ahead, and cars behind him. He gave her a quick sideways glance, the confirmation he thought Captain Wolt was in trouble in his eyes, and went back to the road. "He isn't locked down. Something got to him."

"You're right. He sounded upset. It gives me a bad feeling," Clio responded.

If Captain Good Mood, mister I'm always cool, calm, and collected, was losing control it had to be really bad. *Hundreds of them. Needles. Spines. Nails.* She didn't know. Just like she didn't know what the hell was happening. The question repeated itself like it was on a loop in her head. The answer remained the same, she didn't have a clue. Or who. Or why. Clio watched the monitor for updates and told herself she had to keep her thoughts straight and focused.

Once the road opened and traffic thinned to nothing, Tony pushed the med van faster, while communications tracked their progress. His tawny eyes narrowed, his shoulders relaxed under his polo, his hands holding the steering wheel as if he wasn't driving like a race car driver. She saw through his façade, Tony Reed, paramedic, one of ten Pureblood red foxes living as part of the klatch, sensed the distress and loss in Captain Wolt's voice. Clio sensed it too, but it wasn't the same. Yeah, she had to do something. She didn't like it, and knew she was going to have to face the baron and his questions, and the director's infamous interrogation. Not to mention it was Miss Langston's first day home and there was a potential threat at Foxwood. She was a doctor first, and while it might be betraying Captain Wolt's trust, she had to do something. She didn't know what kind of trouble he was in and she needed to protect the baron, baroness, the director and Miss Langston.

Clio entered the private number on the screen and waited. "Director Kanin, priority." The line went silent. No one was going to ask her what the call was about. There was no wordless melody to irritate you, no credit card offers, no vacation bargains, no please hold for the next available operator, just dead silence.

"Director Kanin."

"Priority Two, Code Black. Possible Priority Thirteen."

Priority Two meant a pack member was being threatened and needs backup. Code Black meant a pack member wasn't capable to mentally or physically able to handle the situation. Priority Thirteen, she hated the possibility, the damn number explained itself, overrode all other priorities, and meant a magic-born was threatening violence, had lost control of themselves and their animal, and the life of innocents were in danger. Something spooked Captain Wolt—maybe it was DIC and Lado's condition—and he had driven to Foxwood, or Captain Wolt was losing control over his wolf. It wouldn't be the first time one of the pack had let their animal rule over them in a highly emotional situation.

Before she arrived at Butte Springs, Baron Kanin reported a Priority Thirteen and a Code Black for Director Kanin, and he had been tranquilized when his beast shadowed his body. He would have gone Bestial. Did she think Captain Wolt was going Bestial? Negative. The exact opposite if he felt responsible for Lado. If she was wrong, she would deal with the repercussions, if she was right, and she hoped she wasn't, they would take Captain Wolt into custody. Since there wasn't an Enforcer's office, he would be placed in a containment room at Celestial. As the director had been.

"Where?" Director Kanin's gruff voice demanded.

"Foxwood, location unknown. Enforcer Lado is in trouble.

Med Two is en route," Clio explained. "No confirmation on backup." Doubt tied a noose around her neck and tightened. Was she betraying Captain Wolt?

"Copy." The line went dead.

Clio looked at the screen. "Shit." She switched screens wanting to see the action log and was denied. Nothing. The screen was blank. Going to their location, she watched the woods close in on the road, and wondered if he was going to bring backup. "Shit."

"You had to. His safety and the enforcer's life are priority." Tony turned the wheel, the tires skidded on asphalt, the med van leaned into the turn, then righted when the road straightened. "ETA two minutes."

Two minutes of hell.

Ansel was sure his heart stopped, the blood in his veins drained through him like he was a sieve, and his lungs were frozen clumps in his chest while he stared at Lado's body. He had stopped himself a hundred times from touching the enforcer, the needles that moved with his labored breaths, and worked to keep Lado's faint heartbeat in his head. When he heard tires humming on the road, a vehicle's engine, and felt magic-born, he knew he was dreaming. Oxygen deprivation would do that.

His senses searched and found a werewolf, pack, specifically, Dr. Hyde, and relief washed over him, making his legs feel like jelly. Her presence made the last twenty minutes, feeling like an eternity, fall from his shoulders, only to be replaced with a new dread. Dr. Hyde. He called her without hesitation. If they were watching him the same way they watched Daniel, they would see her and know there was something between them. Dr. Hyde would become their next victim. Ansel would be brought to his knees if he saw Clio's innocent eyes marred by scarlet as she bled out, then the needles scarring her porcelain skin to slowly kill her. Feeling Clio's life drain from her would destroy him while it would serve as part of the plan to end him.

Tony drove Med Two through Foxwood's gate and immediately slowed when Captain Wolt's truck, parked on the shoulder, its driver's side door open, came into view. On the opposite side of the road there was a truck nose first in a ditch, its front hidden by brush. Behind it were two others, with Cascade's crest on their sides, and Clio recognized the enforcers, Luke and Quinn. Director Kanin slowed his vehicle, pulled it to the same side as Captain Wolt's, and parked. She didn't wait, she slung a med bag over her shoulder, grabbed a second bag containing plasma, and an antifibrinolytic drug to prevent further blood loss, and headed to the wreaked truck.

"Captain Wolt," she said softly as she approached. "It's Doctor Hyde."

Ansel slowly turned to see her, the red duffles, and a paramedic behind her. A spike of jealousy burned through him with the male's closeness to her, and it added to the out of control feeling he was fighting. "Doctor Hyde," he mumbled.

"Let me see him." Clio watched the cinnamon drown under a sharp bronze, his wolf rising for an instant then fade to his natural color. Taking his upper arm, she held it. "I need to see Lado."

"Affirmative." Ansel looked at her hand on his arm, and back to Dr. Hyde to meet her worried gaze. *Please don't touch me.* "He's been missing for a couple of hours. It must have taken all of his strength to drive here."

"Not sure why he didn't drive to Celestial," Clio wondered out aloud.

"I don't know." He had no idea why Lado would risk his

life to get to Foxwood when help was at Celestial. Why hadn't he called for a med van or backup? Because he wasn't going to put another enforcer's life at risk and wouldn't endanger anyone from the hospital. Ansel would have done the same thing.

"He's going to be all right. We're going to take care of him." With gentle reassurance, Clio squeezed Captain Wolt's arm, felt his muscles tense under her palm, and letting go of him, her fingers trailed down.

She hated leaving him feeling desperate and sad as he stepped out of the triangle of the truck and driver's door to give her room. There was heartbreak inside him, she felt it, and like a living thing it was surrounding him. She did, however, feel relief with the director's presence. *He will make sure the captain is taken care of,* she told herself. She wasn't betraying him by having called the director. She followed protocol and she secured his safety. So why was guilt flooding her middle? And why did Clio feel the need to touch him and be the person to console him? She wanted to ease his pain and take the shadows from his eyes. Stop. It was stress ... and she was losing her mind.

"Is there something I can do?" Ansel questioned.

He met Rutger's gold gaze, backed down, and stepped back from Dr. Hyde, her feel, and Lado. This wasn't a fight he wanted to have, and he didn't want to clash with Rutger when he needed his help, and he wouldn't question Rutger's authority while *his* enforcers were present. They would know the case involved him. They wouldn't know how or why and that didn't matter, he put one of his own at risk. Despite her touch, her comfort, Dr. Hyde thought he was a threat and called the Director of Enforcers. When the paramedic stepped closer to her, and they shared murmured words, his body wanted to stop, and shutdown from the guilt coursing through him.

"Let her do her job," Rutger advised firmly with a gentle edge. He pointed to his truck and motioned him in the direction.

Ansel obeyed then watched more enforcers park their trucks and cars along the drive, creating a perimeter while others blocked the gate and entrance into Foxwood. The area had been sealed off. Their priority the baron and baroness' safety, and Jordyn was on the premises.

Clio examined Lado, saw he was in full DIC which would threaten his organs and brain function, and there were hundreds of nails, crystals. His skin was pasty, glossy with sweat, and he was going in and out of consciousness. She left Tony with Lado and going to the passenger side climbed inside the truck. Taking a pair of gloves from the bag, she pulled them on, then working with efficient ease, she took surgical scissors, cut the material from the sleeves of Lado's BDU top, large enough to work freely and for the catheter, its pad, and the tubbing, without the material pulling on it and causing more pain. His ashen skin tore like tissue paper from the slightest touch, and she did not need to make it worse. Taking an air syringe from the bag, she removed the cap and stuck the tip to the center of Lado's chest and shoved the end. She disposed of the cylinder in a biohazard bag, grabbed another one and repeated the process. Lado's body jerked, he moaned, and satisfied, she took her gloves off, put them in the same bag, and replaced them with a new pair.

Clicking the mic clipped to her scrub top she asked, "Are we clear?"

"Affirmative," Tony responded. "Transmitting engaged, streaming to Celestial."

"Copy. Lado Reyes has multiple nail-type objects

imbedded in his body, is in active DIC, bleeding from his ears, eyes, nose, and mouth. A line of BioThropy has been administered to slow the progression of the kyanite crystals, one of san sanguine to slow the bleeding, and plasma expanders to restore vascular volume. I've hit him with two cylinders of adrenaline to get his heart beating." Searching Lado's body, she found a nail with its end close to the surface, took a pair of surgical scissors from the bag, and cut around the protruding crystal, then extracted it from his side. It made a hissing sound, the skin turned gray, and the wound started bleeding and oozing thick, yellow liquid. Lado's back arched off the seat, his eyes opened to stare at nothing, and a brittle cry left him. "Removing the nails is too dangerous. I don't know how the crystals are effecting him."

The word nails made his skin crawl. From his place beside Rutger's truck, Ansel listened to Dr. Hyde relay her actions to Celestial and wanted to apologize for his cold front. Why? He would be putting her life at risk. When the paramedic brought the gurney and they removed Lado from the truck, Ansel's eyes roamed over the unmoving body, and the blood glittering on his enforcer's uniform. He didn't deserve a pack. A family. He didn't deserve to talk to Dr. Hyde let alone have her as a friend. Lover. He couldn't stop from watching her in her T-shirt that hugged her curves and black scrub pants as she worked to stabilize Lado for transport. The chance for him to apologize or have her as anything other than an acquaintance was going to be taken away from him.

Weakened and feeling helpless, he let his mind chase trails better off left alone. He would never know her touch, hear her laugh, breathe in Clio's scent. He would never feel her in his bed. He spent his life hiding from his enemy and was going to lose everything anyway. A life wasted. He looked at Clio with new eyes and saw her strength, loyalty to the pack, to him. He didn't know why he was having intimate thoughts about her and didn't care. She hadn't hesitated, hadn't questioned him as an enforcer, and hadn't accused him. Notifying Rutger was following protocol and there was nothing he could do about it except to tell Rutger the truth. Was he capable of the truth? He had been hiding for so long, he didn't know any other way. He knew his mind was being torn apart by panic, fear, and loss as it hit his heart. The inferno of emotions forced him to admit it wasn't the attack on the elf, Lado, or the needles. Selfish bastard.

The countdown to his death had started.

"Is he going to be all right?" Ansel asked.

"The bleeding has stopped. When we get him to Celestial, they'll be able to diagnose the crystal's effects, counter its advance, and remove them. Lado is strong," Clio answered.

"The nails could have been poisoned. She might have used something exotic, odd, something you wouldn't expect," Ansel explained. She took pride in making people suffer by her hand.

Exotic? Odd? Who the hell are these people? She? Clio stopped, faced Captain Wolt, his bronze eyes staring blanky at Lado. "She?" Why was jealousy invading her thoughts? Maybe it was the way he said *she*, with an intimate softness that excluded her. He was wrong, he didn't know who she was, he was worried about Lado. Plus, this *she* didn't care if there was another she.

"Sorry, I didn't mean you wouldn't check. I just was trying to help." Ansel ignored her emphasis on his use of the word she, hated he had given away a piece of the puzzle, and didn't know why he cared when he had nothing else left to hide.

Yes, he did. He didn't want Clio to know what he had

done, who she had been to him, and the way she had betrayed him. From the pack, he had nothing, and knew it wouldn't do any good to cover his tracks, defend himself, or deny his past. In a matter of time, it would be exposed, and he would endure his punishment and it would end with his death. What would Clio think of him then? The once strong and loyal Captain of Enforcers was really a fraud, an assassin, a coward. She would hate him. She would look on him knowing it was his fault innocent lives were put at risk. She worked to heal people and he worked to destroy them. He wanted a drink. Maybe drink until he was numb then pray death took him.

"I understand." Clio evaluated Captain Wolt and didn't believe he was losing himself to his beast, his eyes were their signature cinnamon, and he wasn't crumbling under the stress of finding Lado.

She didn't have any other choice, even when her instincts were telling her he was hiding something. She gave Director Kanin a shielded look, and saw the same doubt in his gaze. What the hell was wrong with Captain Wolt? Then she turned her attention to Lado.

"Doctor Hyde, surgery is anticipating our arrival," Tony reported.

"Copy. Let's go."

Clio adjusted the bags on her shoulder, gripped the metal handle, and began pushing the gurney. Taking the opposite end, Tony guided them to the med van where he opened the back doors.

"On three. One. Two. Three." They both lifted the man and the gurney into the van, its wheels fitting into the rail, then Tony shoved hard and slammed it into the locks. The jerking motion brought a soft moan from Lado, and he fell silent. "Ready?" Tony asked.

"Affirmative," Clio answered, getting in behind Lado. "Let's get him to Celestial."

"Med Two, incoming, ETA twenty minutes," Tony reported.

Celestial responded, reporting there was a team ready to meet them and an operating room had been prepped. Ansel should have been relieved, but he wasn't.

"Director Kanin, who will notify his parents?" Clio asked. She did not want to be the one to talk to Lado's parents. She hated that part.

"I'm having an enforcer do it now. Lado was responding to a call, and we will follow protocol as this was a work incident. They targeted an enforcer. I've ordered Kia and Owen to meet you at the hospital, and they will remain there as Lado's security and show we protect our own," Director Kanin explained.

"I reported Captain Wolt. What are you going to do, Director Kanin?" Clio asked. This was not the time, but she needed to know what was going to happen to Captain Wolt.

"He is in control of his faculties and hasn't displayed signs of losing control or harming an innocent. You made the report when you didn't have all of the facts, Doctor Hyde."

Embarrassment scalded her cheeks, and her pride took a direct hit. "So you're going to ignore it." A Priority Two, a Code Black, with a possible Priority Thirteen—she hadn't acted irrationally, she was protecting her pack and the Kanin family.

"Negative. I may not understand the grounds for the report, but I will take it under consideration," he replied. "It's time for you to go."

"Copy." Clio felt like she had been dismissed, her opinion cast to the side, and the feeling of inadequacy rushed back with a vengeance.

Her default setting screamed like a siren, and she could hear the baron tell her she didn't know what she was talking about. Because she wasn't as good as a Pureblood. Forget the fact she was a doctor. Director Kanin slammed the doors closed and hit the left side, signaling Tony they were ready to leave. Fighting to slough the humiliation and incompetence from her shoulders and soul, she took her seat near the cab of the med van.

"I can't secure him, so you can't drive like a bat out of hell," Clio warned.

"I'll do my best." Tony grinned as he put the van into gear and took off as if he had rockets.

Ansel watched Dr. Hyde and the med van turn around, maneuver around enforcer vehicles, then head out of Foxwood. What happened? He wanted to ask Rutger who loomed next to him, the director's power flowing out from him like a tidal wave that made Ansel's wolf nervous and his skin crawl. Then he thought about getting in his truck and driving home where she would find him and get on with whatever she had planned for him. Despite the reprieve death was beginning to be, he didn't think his legs were going to work, but he couldn't stay where he was and he couldn't stay at Foxwood, not when this was his fault.

"I need to go with them."

"Negative. Lado's parents will meet the med van at the hospital, and you do not need to be there." Rutger faced him with gold eyes, his broad chest stretching his gray T-shirt with the pack's crest over his heart, tight across his torso. Then, he looked at the road, Lado's truck, and lastly at Quinn and Luke. "We need to talk."

"I went to Elder Macario's house, questioned him, came back here, met with you and the baron, then went to communications. Mandy asked if I knew where Lado was, I said no, it had been two hours since he last checked in, that's when she tried calling him, no answer, then checked his location with GPS. He was on Foxwood. I had Quinn and Luke follow as backup, found Lado, called Celestial, you can check communications' records. Here we are," Ansel explained. He wanted to run away, far away, before they found a cell to lock him in.

"Luke, drive Lado's truck back to the office. Quinn, you follow him," Rutger ordered.

"The driver's side seat is covered in tainted blood," Ansel warned.

"Luke, you'll have to cover the seat. Do not let his blood touch you, I have no idea what it will do, and don't let anyone near the truck. I want it processed by forensics."

"Affirmative, sir," Luke responded.

Both enforcers followed orders, Quinn getting into his truck, and Luke taking a tarp from his truck covered the seat. Within seconds they were headed toward communications, and the baron who would have questions.

"Doctor Hyde reported a Priority Two, Code Black, with a possible Priority Thirteen. She thought you were losing your mind and your wolf to the beast. She does not jump to conclusions, and that means you gave her a reason to make the call. Want to explain why this rocked you?" Rutger asked.

Ansel rested his right hand on the butt of his gun, his left on his tactical belt, stared at the ground, his boots, and tried to think of something to say. He could go straight lie and Rutger would catch it and it would make him look guiltier. If that was possible. There was always a half truth, which was better than the truth. He could give it a shot. "It was Lado's first day as an active enforcer and this happened. They broke his fingers, hands, and arms, then filled him with nails. He endured the pain and drove back to Foxwood for a reason. He knows who they are. He knows their identity. He isn't safe," Ansel replied. It was more truth than lie.

"You said *she*. How do you know it's a female?" Rutger asked.

"It was a figure of speech. I smelled an order I didn't recognize, saw Lado's skin, assumed it was poison and told Doctor Hyde." Ansel was going to gush the truth everywhere and it wasn't going to be pretty. "What are you going to do?"

"Right now, nothing. Go home and wait for me," Rutger ordered.

"Why?" Ansel asked automatically. He wished he could have taken the word back as soon as he said it. He was in no place to question anyone, let alone Rutger.

"I found the witches." Rutger's eyes blazed gold then dimmed as he gave Ansel his back and walked to his truck.

Right.

CHAPTER ELEVEN

At the double sliding doors of the emergency room, Tony slammed on the brakes, making the med van skid to a stop. Clio braced her feet to stay in her seat at the same time she gripped the gurney and Lado, attempting to stop him from sliding and hitting the doors of the van.

"Nice, a crash landing," Clio grated.

"I didn't crash," Tony argued with a grin. "A team is headed our way."

"Copy."

During the drive, Lado's vitals were automatically trans- mitted to the waiting surgical team, leaving Clio to enter the last treatment of BioThropy and the second time she had to shock Lado's heart, into the laptop. She had lost him twice, and twice was able to bring him back. It must be the poison Captain Wolt mentioned. He had stopped bleeding, and mumbled words instead of making low sounds. His status gave her confidence he was going to survive.

Tony opened the back of the van as a half dozen people wearing hoods and biohazard suits crowded behind him. "Ready?"

"Affirmative," Clio replied as she stood. She hopped out of the van, grabbed the gurney, unlatched it and rolled it out, the front legs lowering then the back wheels landed on the ground.

"Doctor Hyde," Cruz greeted as he took Clio's place.

"Doctor Hyde," Geraint greeted as he took the left side, his brown eyes gleaming through the clear plastic of his mask. "Tony."

"His heart rate is dropping. Get him to surgery," Dr. Kolt ordered over the commotion.

As the medical team began working on Lado, Clio stepped back and listened to the instructions and watched the cluster of people rush into the hospital. A wave of relief washed over her. Lado was in excellent hands, she was at Celestial, her turf, where she felt strong not weak and not someone Director Kanin disregarded with a wave of his hand. Her reasons for the report weren't unfounded, and she wasn't acting irrationally. It didn't matter what she told herself, his words cut deeper than she liked to admit, and threw her straight at her default setting. Would Director Kanin have disregarded her had she been a Pureblood? The answer was yes, and she knew it, no matter how her inner voice argued. He was Second to the Alpha, which gave him authority over the pack, the Director of Enforcers, and made the decision.

"What did Director Kanin think about the report?" Tony asked. His bright blue eyes held an edge of his fox when they caught the dimming sunlight.

"He said he was taking it under consideration," Clio replied sternly.

A mental lecture and she still wanted to gripe, let frustration taint her words and tell him everything the director had said to her, but stopped herself. The director hit her pride with a bat and that was her problem, her emotional reaction to the situation. She was a professional and wasn't going to air dirty laundry in public, and as much as Clio trusted and respected Tony, he wasn't pack.

"You called out his second in command. His second who

oversees the director's personal team of enforcers who obey every command, without needing authorization from Baron Kanin. The director trusts him more than he trusts anyone, and everyone knows they're like brothers. Director Kanin protects his own, and he is his own, what else did you think would happen?" Tony asked.

Except it wasn't a question, it was an accusation. The tone in the paramedic's voice gave away the shard of jealousy coloring his words. Clio never saw whatever Tony was accusing the director of but could imagine how it looked from the outside. The enforcers were a specialized unit, trained to deal with the thousands in the pack, the klatch, and the human population. Outsiders, like the klatch, weren't allowed to be enforcers, the baron believing they wouldn't protect the pack like pack would. It was the difference between a paid guard who promised to take a bullet when shit hit the fan and a parent who would risk life and limb to protect their child. If the guard failed, they had nothing to lose but a job, whereas if the parent failed, they would lose a piece of themselves.

Clio admitted the eight enforcers close to the director were distinctive, she missed the feeling, and were intimidating especially if you weren't part of the inner circle. The director's personal team. That had changed with everything else, but instead of the team melding back into the roster of enforcers, and serving like everyone else, they had tightened their borders. The invisible line separating the chosen from the others had been solidified with concrete, doused in fuel, and lit on fire to make sure you felt the burn when you got to close.

It was the witches and their invasion into the pack's territory and the failed security. The assault unbalanced Baron

Kanin and made him feel vulnerable. Without hesitation, Clio blamed Miss Langston for the new Enforcer's office, the security upgrades, the military strictness, and had been wrong, at least to a point. How was this new string of attacks going to change them? Cascade and the faction's population had grown, the media attention hadn't helped, to the point of getting attention from everyone. Mostly crazies, but like Tony pointed out, the factions of the klatch had their opinions of what happened behind the gate of Foxwood. Right or wrong.

"Did you hear me?" Tony asked.

"Affirmative. Director Kanin protects his pack, all of his pack, and those of the klatch. If he thought Captain Wolt was a danger to an innocent, he would detain him," she answered. It was the truth.

"You talk like an enforcer," he said casually as he eyed her.

"I used to be." Clio held his gaze.

"One of the few, I'm guessing." Tony smiled, his eyes bright, his stance comfortable. She was sure he fooled everyone with his boyish charm and teasing tone, but she had been an enforcer. He was trying to push her buttons. "I didn't know I was in the presence of Cascade greatness."

Clio readied a retort when she was interrupted. "Doctor Hyde, Mr. Reed, you need to get to decontamination," Commissioner Courter ordered.

"Sir," Clio replied. If Commissioner Courter was giving her orders, something was wrong. Really wrong.

"Afterwards, I need to see the both of you in my office. Immediately." With the last word he marched away from them, his black suit, white button-up, and black shined dress shoes a stark contrast to the biohazard suits, and her own stained scrubs.

"That sounded ominous," Tony mumbled.

"Agreed." Clio watched the sliding doors close on his perfectly trimmed white hair and ramrod straight back.

"Do you think he'll question your report of Captain Wolt?" he asked.

Damn, she called using the laptop in the med van instead of her cell and it made it part of the transcript of the call. Stupid. "Negative. We have a high-ranking person from the Unseelie court and now an enforcer, both attacked by the same person, or persons, and no one is sure if they are safe. The attacks are easy to keep from human law enforcement, but not from the factions. People have questions."

"Like what is the baron doing to stop it?"

"Affirmative," Clio answered.

"Cool, calm, and collected. Thought I was going to rattle your cage and break through your hard exterior." He cocked his head, his grin curving his lips, and laughed.

"Excuse me?" Clio asked. Her thoughts were racing with Captain Wolt, the wounded look in his eyes, the director, the attack, and if someone had targeted the entire Cascade territory. She had no idea what Tony was talking about.

"Never mind. I'm parking the rig so it can be cleaned. Want a ride to the back, then hit decontamination?" Tony headed to the driver's side, then stopped and faced her. "Doc?"

"Yeah. Yes." Clio missed something, damn fox, and wasn't going to ask. When he requested to be put as a priority on her calls, she should have said no ... not only no, but hell no.

Going to the passenger side, she got in, and couldn't shake the feeling she made the right call. Not because she had to be right. Captain Wolt had been put in charge of the enforcers, was in charge of the investigation, which had to be stressful, and then to have Lado their next target, it mocked his ability to do his job and protect the pack. How did Baron Kanin see it? And would the baron replace Captain Wolt? She didn't know. Damn, she wished she was part of the chosen.

An hour later Clio's skin felt raw, she could swear she heard her hair squeak, and she was wearing clean scrubs, smelled of body wash, not poisoned blood, and was making her way through the hospital and administrative offices and to the commissioner's office.

Commissioner Elwood Courter, a Pureblood elf with an ancestry threaded through Norse mythology, had been one of eight the Highguard petitioned to oversee Celestial. His lineage made him powerful and strong enough to stand up to Baron Kanin if the situation demanded. Since the Cascade pack owned the hospital, and members from the pack and klatch sat on the board of directors, the Highguard commanded a person be placed as head who wouldn't be bias toward Cascade. Of the eight the Highguard hand selected, the elders of the territory voted for Elwood Courter. Clio hadn't had the pleasure of speaking with him, he kept to himself, stayed in his office, and with the offices belonging to the board members having their own entrance, no one saw them. The ordered meeting tangled with her fear to create a churning sensation in her stomach she was sure was going to make her double over.

With muffled steps the empty hallway stretched out in front of her, the art hanging on the pale walls replicas of famous painters made it look more administrative than hospital and gave the feeling she was being sent to the principal's office. Making a right, she saw a small waiting area with chairs, a reception desk, and Tony wearing a clean uniform, his auburn hair combed back from his face.

"Fancy meeting you here, Doc," he greeted as he stood, wearing his signature grin.

"Right." Clio didn't have anything else to say.

She hadn't said a word to anyone after leaving the med van, decontamination, or the shower, her thoughts focused on the meeting and the topics the commissioner wanted to discuss. Like her betrayal of Captain Wolt's trust, Director Kanin ignoring her report, the baron having a problem with her behavior, and those weren't even the worst of her thoughts. She hadn't had the chance to sit, it seemed the receptionist was waiting for her, then Tony gave her a sideways glance with sapphire eyes that sparked for a breath.

"Doctor Hyde, Mr. Reed, Commissioner Courter will see you now." With a wave of her thin hand a pale door opened. The woman wore a pastel purple blouse, beige slacks, and heels that completed her professional appearance while her blonde hair with gold highlights sat on her slender shoulders, and her blue nearly white eyes held her lineage. Commissioner Courter brought her with him from Europe, and it was rumored they lived together in a mansion at the edge of Trinity.

Mr. Reed. Clio hadn't heard anyone call Tony, Mr. Reed in the three years he had worked for Celestial. Then again, she had never been sent to the commissioner's office with anyone, let alone by herself. He remained where he stood, allowing her to take lead. It was either he didn't want to go first, or it was ladies first … either way, she didn't want to be first. Clio cringed. She was an emergency room doctor, was the authority on the call, and her job was to protect those who worked for her, like Tony.

"Thank you," Clio said, passing the woman.

"Thanks," Tony mumbled as he followed Clio.

They walked side by side down a short hall when it stopped at a spacious office. Two coffee brown leather chairs sat empty in front of a darker desk the size of a small car. Expensive lamps graced either side, a stack of books, their spines creased and cracked took the left side while a desk top computer dominated the right. Behind Commissioner Courter, a wall of windows let sunlight pour into the office. To her right was a matching leather couch, mini bar, deep green plants basking in the light of the sun, and a bookcase. To the left, bookcases framed a small sitting area, more formal, and the mini bar had been replaced with filing cabinets. She could stick a half dozen of her offices in the space. It paid to be the commissioner.

"Doctor Hyde, Mr. Reed, please have a seat," Commissioner Courter insisted, his gray eyes resembling gunmetal narrowed on them.

"Sir." Clio took the seat to the left, tried to sense anything from the sound of his voice and his facial expressions, and found nothing giving away the reason they were there.

"Sir," Tony replied as he took his seat beside Clio.

Placing his arms on the desk, he steepled his long fingers and met Clio's gaze. "I have received inquiries from the Unseelie court concerning Daniel's care and his safety."

It wasn't a question, rather a statement, and it had her instantly angry. "His care has been exceptional and his safety a priority. Rest assured, neither will be an issue because Doctor Arano is releasing him," Clio explained at the same time she defended the staff.

"I understand. They fear the person responsible will attempt to harm Daniel again, as there is an Illuminate from the Seelie court, with multiple wounds, in admittance. It can't be a coincidence. With this second attack, they fear Captain Wolt isn't qualified to lead the investigation and are considering human law enforcement."

Bad choice, human law enforcement. "The attack didn't have anything to do with the Seelie court, Lado Reyes is an enforcer with Cascade and was responding to a call. No one is going after the Unseelie court's people, and if they were, they would have by now. This is about Cascade," she argued. Clio knew this how? Because it had something to do with Captain Wolt, she knew that.

"Elder Macario doesn't share your confidence, nor does Mrs. Ragas, Daniel's wife," Commissioner Courter argued.

"Mrs. Ragas is scared and rightly so. The fact remains this isn't about the Unseelie court or the Seelie court," Clio tried and felt she failed.

"Is that your professional opinion as a doctor?" His eyes narrowed, and she felt the years in them weighing on her. "As you are not an enforcer."

"Sir." Clio was sure she was inch tall with the slight reprimand and reminder she had lost her position.

"Mr. Reed, do you share Doctor Hyde's assessment?" Commissioner Courter's voice turned cold, his gray eyes a dull silver, while his authority demanded a confession from them both.

"I'm not in a position to say. I'm a paramedic and I drive the med van. I'm not an enforcer and have nothing to do with the investigation," Tony stated.

"You do have an opinion on the case and how it's effecting the hospital," Commissioner Courter insisted. "The employees."

"Sir." He gave Clio an apologetic look, his blue eyes that glittered in the waiting room went flat. "With Director

Kanin's attention elsewhere, Captain Wolt and the enforcers are making the situation worse. Anyone of us could be attacked."

Clio wanted to throw her hands up in defeat, yell objection, and ask how this was relevant. Why the hell was someone's opinion on a case they had nothing to do with appropriate? He was the med van driver.

"Captain Wolt didn't act like himself today, and his inexperience is a threat to us all," Tony finished.

"Thank you, Mr. Reed, that will be all. You're dismissed," Commissioner Courter said.

"Sir," Tony replied and stood.

Inexperience? Clio wanted to scoff when she felt Tony's eyes on her, and ignored him, she felt low key betrayed. She kept her gaze locked on Commissioner Courter, not that he was better. His gunmetal gray eyes held a shard of agitation he directed at her and her faith in the enforcers. Tony's retreat faded with his distance, allowing silence to sit thick between them and fester until the receptionist confirmed he had left the wing.

Thankfully. She released the breath she had been holding.

"I asked Mr. Reed how he felt because his opinion is shared by others in the klatch and that includes the employees of this hospital and the Deviants. There has to be an assurance of security, confidence they're safety is a priority and the enforcers are actively working to protect the pack and making the same strides to protect the klatch." Commissioner Courter leaned back in his chair, his guise of thinness disappearing under toned muscles as his chest pulled his white, button-up shirt tight. "The public is aware of the construction on Foxwood and the security upgrades at the Summit. It would appear the Kanin's are sitting behind their stronghold while everyone else is left unprotected."

There was no hiding the fortress the baron was building. "I understand. Baron Kanin would be more than happy to give the assurance the enforcers are doing everything within their power to find who is committing these attacks. The safety of those in the territory is a priority." Clio found herself sitting on the edge of her set and leaning forward.

"Your loyalty to Baron Kanin is admirable."

Clio wasn't loyal, she was indebted ... no, grateful, and she would protect them. Her thoughts stalled. Baron Kanin, his family, the pack, they gave her a place and a chance to do what she loved when no one else would. The human world, her mom's world, didn't want to have anything to do with her. Over the last couple of months, the baron, the director, and Captain Wolt showed her how much they depended on her. *You're confusing that with begging for their crumbs*, her default setting hissed. Director Kanin hadn't brushed her off, he was doing his job. He didn't take sides.

"I've been told about the conversation you had with Mrs. Ashby and the treatment of her daughter. I commend you on your ability to keep the integrity of the hospital and conciliate what could have been a political disaster for the Cascade pack. You conduct yourself with competence and a transparency no one may question."

"Thank you, sir," Clio responded. She wasn't sure where the conversation was going, but one thing she had learned through her life was the second part wasn't going to be as nice.

"Having said that, Doctor Hyde, how do you feel about Captain Wolt?" he asked, his gaze narrowing.

Yep. This is where the ax falls.

Ansel parked his truck in front of his house, and with the engine idling stared at nothing while gripping the steering wheel and wondering what the hell was happening to his life.

He was losing it, that's what was happening. She was there and was going to take it away from him piece by piece. His eyes focused on his house, the porch, the trees, his land, the first place he felt like he belonged. And he was going to lose it to a ghost from his past. Where was his investigation? Stalled, he didn't know where to look for her. Ansel grabbed his cell and dialed the number and waited. Lado's body was a mess of dead skin, nails, and blood, he couldn't risk the other enforcers' lives. He brought the roster up on his screen and checked how many enforcers were active.

"Captain Wolt, how may I help you?" Mandy greeted.

"I need the enforcers to partner up, and if there aren't enough, call whoever is off duty," Ansel ordered.

"Standby."

The line went silent, leaving Ansel hoping she was implementing his order.

"The baron and Director Kanin will have to confirm the order. You've been put on limited duty," Mandy explained.

Ansel closed his eyes with regret. "Whatever you have to do. Don't let anyone go to a call without backup," he insisted.

"I won't. I promise. Is there anything else I can do?"

"Where is Director Kanin?"

"He's taking Miss Langston home."

"What?" Ansel sat straighter in his seat and stared at the screen as if it was going to explain Rutger's plan to him.

"I don't know the specifics."

"No, I know that. Thank you." He didn't wait for Mandy to respond before ending the call.

He didn't know why Rutger would take Jordyn back to his house when the upgrades hadn't been installed. Without them, she was defenseless if Flint and the witches the court system released returned. The ones Rutger said he found. He felt like he was being pulled in a million different directions. Daniel, Lado, who was she going to target next? And Rutger had thrown out security and gone off the deep end.

Ansel killed the engine, hesitated for a second as his thoughts raced, gathered his gear, and made his way into his house. After slamming the door behind him, he marched across the open living room to the dining table where he dumped everything. His house, his private space welcomed him in its silence and the mixed scents of his soap, the surrounding woods, and the fading smells of breakfast. He made a circle as he stared at his home as of for the first time. He was going to lose it the same way he had lost his place with the pack.

"Come in." Ansel leaned against the edge of the table and watched Rutger enter the house. "Why did you take Jordyn to your place?"

"It's her home." Rutger's hands rested on his hips. His stance was stiff, as he glared at him with gold eyes.

"She's safer at Foxwood," Ansel argued. He knew it wasn't going to do any good and arguing would make Rutger more adamant.

"She is my mate, and she is at our home." Rutger inhaled and exhaled. "Go change your clothes."

Ansel looked down at his uniform identifying him as Captain of Enforcers and didn't want to lose it. Unbuckling his thigh holster, then his tactical belt, he set his weapon beside his tossed gear.

"Leave your cell."

"Why?" He took it from a pocket and set it on the table.

"It has GPS."

"Give me a minute." Ansel looked at the stuff that had validated his existence for years and left it behind him. Leaving Rutger in his living room, he hit the stairs, made his way down the hall passing bare walls, two closed doors, and at the end walked through the open entrance.

His room opened before him, the walls, bedspread, his modest belongings sitting on his dresser told a visitor nothing about him. The material belongings revealed zero details, hobbies, friends, lovers, just a room someone slept in. After unbuttoning the BDU top, he dropped it on a chair, then pulled his T-shirt over his head and dropped it beside an empty frame. He had planned on putting a picture in it, and didn't, not knowing what picture. It remained empty. He paused to touch the tattoo on his side, a reminder of who was after him, and opened a drawer and took out a gray pullover. He shoved his arms through as he walked back down the hall and the stairs, making sure it covered the tattoo before he entered the living room. Rutger had moved to stand by the door, his back tense under his shirt, his hand teasing where his gun usually sat against his thigh. Like Ansel, they had been conditioned to always be armed, and without their weapons they were naked.

"Do I need a weapon?" Ansel asked, breaking the silence.

"Negative," Rutger replied as he opened the door and walked out. "Let's go."

Ansel exited, locked the door behind him, and stepped down the stairs. "Isn't this Jordyn's car?" Rutger stood beside the sporty, red SUV, his six foot four inches dwarfing the vehicle while his board shoulders and thick build had Ansel wondering how he got inside.

"Affirmative. There's no GPS on it," Rutger replied.

Right. Ansel looked in the backseat and saw a bouquet of dead flowers he recognized from Bailey and Tanner's wedding, and a pair of high-heeled shoes. The day her life stopped. The day the witches ripped it away from her. Beside the remnants was a black duffle bag. She always carried gear and extra clothing.

"Like she might hear my voice on the wind, I would stand on my deck, and beg her to change her mind and come back to me. I wanted her home. I didn't want this," Rutger confessed as he stared at Ansel. "I'm enough of a selfish bastard, I'm glad she's home."

Fated mates. That was a nice way of saying they had been cursed. "The witches were watching her for months. Her connection to the pack was a bonus for them."

"I feel like I trapped her, and now she is in a house that will be turned into a prison, without any of her belongings. She has an oversized sweatshirt she lives in, that's it."

Ansel was going to be Rutger's friend and assure him he hadn't trapped her, and it had been a couple of days since her discharge. She needed time. Then his enforcer side kicked in and the situation unfolded in front of him. "Your truck, cell, and gun are at your house. You're using her as an alibi." They stared at each other over the shiny red roof. The setting sun's warm gold rays sent scattered light through the tree limbs as its warmth faded with its descent.

Rutger's eyes blazed gold as he took his glare from Ansel to look into the backseat where it lingered on her abandoned belongings, then back to Ansel and he opened the driver's door. "Affirmative."

"You can't be serious?" Shaking his head, he got into the

vehicle, the sweet scent of vanilla, dried flowers, and female drifting inside. He couldn't imagine what Rutger was thinking. He wanted to lecture the director about using his mate as an alibi, using her car in a crime, then leaving her at home by herself when the security upgrades hadn't been added and Flint was free. It wouldn't do any good, and he figured he had a better chance of making a brick wall understand.

"Jo is stronger than you think." Rutger started the engine; the soft purr was nearly inaudible comparted to their diesel engines.

Brick wall. "What's the plan?" Ansel asked.

"First, you've been put on limited duty pending the baron's review of Doctor Hyde's report. Quinn is taking your place, and Luke will act as his second. Per your recommendation, until whoever is doing this is caught, all enforcers will have a partner. No one will respond to a call without backup no matter how trivial it may seem. I don't want anyone ambushed." Rutger checked the road, left Ansel's driveway, and headed toward Trinity.

Limited duty. At least he wasn't fired. "A guard from Seelie court called reporting a trespasser. I advised Lado to tell them to keep an eye on them and if an enforcer was necessary to call us. There's a chance they have a description, you should have someone talk to the guard. And I think there should be patrols on the outskirts of town and Cascade properties."

"Ahead of you. I read the report, and the transcripts of the call Lado responded to. There will be enforcers present throughout the territory and the public is urged to call if they see anything that looks suspicious. But if they target an innocent like Daniel again, we won't know until after the attack. The Unseelie and Seelie courts, and to an extent the Lapis Lazuli coven, don't believe in suspicious, they believe in fates and their traits. On the other hand, the factions of shapeshifters are all about suspicious and will keep watch," Rutger explained. "They believe we're all at risk."

"Has the Unseelie court said anything?"

"The chancellor is asking questions about the investigation, and Daniel's wife fears they will try to harm him again. Understandably, Elder Macario is taking the wife's side. Lado's mother is part of the Seelie court and has asked her chancellor for help. His father is pack, and has assured the baron, he trusts our ability. If they decide to consider human law enforcement, they can't, they're bound by a contract. If they try to break the contract, they'll forfeit their leverage giving Cascade the right to reevaluate the covenant between the courts and the pack. The baron doesn't want to use his authority to tighten his hold on the klatch but will if necessary."

Rutger gave Ansel a quick glance with gold flecks floating in his dark eyes and his power flowing around him. "He and I agree the attacks were prompted by availability. Lado responded and was alone, not a specific victim. He's reassuring both parties, offering extra guards, and explaining the measures being taken, and we're doing what we can with the resources available."

"Why not specific victims?" Ansel felt like confessing, then jumping from the moving vehicle.

"The victims are unrelated. Save for the attacks bringing questions from the klatch, which is why I expressed to the baron I think it's an outside faction trying to undermine the pack's authority. If there was a perfect time to hit us and prove we aren't the strength we profess to be, it's now."

Ansel wanted to tell him he was right and wrong. It was an outside threat, but they wanted to destroy Ansel, not the pack, although she would see it as a bonus if the klatch gathered their numbers to take the pack down. He didn't say anything, he stared at the side of Rutger's lean face. He sounded like the director, the man he knew, and his old self. Except for the part he was using his mate.

"What are we going to do tonight?"

"Nothing."

Rutger drove on, leaving the mountains as hints of the city sprouted up along the sides of the road, turned highway while the radio's low volume played a slow song Ansel hadn't heard before. He couldn't believe he was sitting Jordyn's car. It was like a private piece of her life, and while she was trying to heal, they had invaded it and were using her and what innocence she had left. They sat in silence, the tires on the road and the low hum of radio the only noises between them as Trinity's scenes blurred and faded.

"Where are we going?" Ansel asked. The scenery changed from Trinity's businesses and edge of the city to ranch lands, to open road. They were thirty minutes outside of the city, and heading toward Butterfly Valley.

Rutger made a right, drove down a crumbling, one-lane road, the SUV bouncing as he hit potholes and cracks in the asphalt, and continued to drive without answering. When he slowed the car, Ansel saw an old farmhouse, its front porch in need of repair, its roof line sagging in the middle, and the shingles slipping off.

"What is this?"

"A house."

"Explains everything," Ansel mumbled.

Rutger drove around the back of the white two story, the tires crunching leaves, brush, and rocks, parked beside a concrete building half buried in the ground, and turned the key, quieting the engine. "A hundred years ago the house, a guest house, a small sawmill, and that processing cooler were built by the Shaver family." Rutger pointed to the half buried concrete building. "The land includes forty-five acres and has its own water. Nothing has been touched in three years."

"Three years?"

"Affirmative. After I asked Jo to marry me, I bought it. I thought if we had a getaway, a place we could relax and get out from under the eyes of the pack, it might be different. Then Jo left. I came out here a couple of times to work on the inside of the house, something to keep my mind off her absence, then I stopped." Rutger got out of the car.

"No one knows you own this?" Ansel asked.

"Negative. On paper a businessman from the East Coast owns it."

"If someone tries to contact this man?" Ansel stared at the aging buildings, which made him think of the warehouse, then toward the back and the overgrown land.

"They'll have to leave a message with his investment firm," Rutger answered.

"Like father, like son." Ansel met Rutger's narrowed gaze. "You've mastered your father's business practices?"

Rutger smiled, it was a predator's grin of victory, like he had captured his prey. "Affirmative. I'm his Second, and work for him. This is what I wanted to show you."

He started toward the concrete building while taking a ring of keys from his pocket, and choosing one, unlocked one of two paddle locks, chose another, repeated the process, then worked to unlock the two others, making metal grind on metal. Replacing the keys, he pulled open the heavy six-inch-thick door, causing leaves, dried grass, weeds, and twigs to build up as the bottom grated over red dirt. Stale air slowly filtered out as if it wasn't sure it was allowed to escape its flat edge dissipating in the fresh air.

Ansel took a step back, letting fresh air sweep the scents of aged blood, raw meat, entrails, and tanned hides from him. "You haven't been here for three years. When was the last time anyone was here?"

"Forty years."

"It looks like a family homestead. How did you get the place?" Ansel took in the house, the wraparound porch, and the worn-out swing gently swaying in the breeze.

"When the owners died, it was left to a daughter and a son. They moved to Southern California, felt this was a waste of their time, and sold it and everything inside for next to nothing. Why would you want acreage, space, and quiet, when you can have a plot, your neighbor is within arm's each of you, and your city's anthem is sirens." Rutger stepped inside and disappeared into the dark.

Ansel hesitated, knowing all the small talk in the world wasn't going to change why they were there. The processing room stayed at a constant sixty degrees, was soundproof due to being half buried and made from concrete and was built for slaughtering. He looked behind him, didn't hear traffic from the highway, and walked inside. Rutger had turned the lights on, two fluorescent tubes hung from the low ceiling, casting a tired artificial glow on the butcherblock counter, band saw, large porcelain sink, stainless steel hooks, and the row of knives. Nothing had been touched. It transported Ansel years into the past, and for a minute he pictured the house alive with activity, voices from the family drifted, the squeaking from the swing added to the sounds of cattle in the distance and teased his ears. Then she stepped in front of him, her chin glittering scarlet, her eyes blazing with her bloodlust, and she reached out to him with her thin fingers and long nails.

"Ansel." Rutger was looking at him. The light at his back shadowed his face, making the lines fanning out from his eyes deeper.

"What?"

"I was saying, we bring them here, dismember them, then take them to the mine. They'll be buried under tons of gravel and dirt."

"Where's the mine?" he asked on auto. A chill raced down his spine with the mingling of memories and her way of destroying everything she touched.

"A couple of miles. There's a backroad, making it possible to skip the main gate, not that it matters, no one is there at night," Rutger explained.

"How long have you been planning this?" He saw Rutger's truck parked in the same place every day; there were weeds growing under it and beside the tires, it looked like it hadn't moved in months.

"Doctor Carrion said I should concentrate my attention on a hobby, to keep the mind busy." Rutger flicked off the lights, casting them in a forgotten dimness.

"I don't think this is what he meant." Ansel raised an eyebrow and shrugged. "I could be wrong."

"You're wrong." They left the room behind them, and after Rutger locked everything up, they stood beside the SUV in an awkward silence.

"How do you know where they'll be?" Ansel asked, needing to feel the sun's warmth and hoping it chased away the dread.

"I have someone watching them."

"Anyone I know?"

"Negative."

"You've gone completely rogue with this?" He understood why he wasn't the person Rutger depended on, but it didn't stop the hurt or the feeling of being left out from burning through him.

"Affirmative. I won't put Jo or the pack at risk." Rutger kicked at a rock and sent it colliding into the building. "Or you. I shouldn't have showed this to you. You have enough going on."

"Negative. Whatever you need, I'm here," Ansel insisted. If he proved his loyalty to Rutger and Jordyn it might help him when the truth erupted, and it was going to erupt.

Rutger gave him a sideways glance and stilled. "I was hoping you felt that way. Tomorrow night we retrieve them and bring them here."

"We end them." Ansel's eyes blazed bronze with his promise.

CHAPTER TWELVE

Clio sat crossed legged on her couch, a glass of tequila on the side table, and stared out the large picture window as twilight's advance of violet, azure, and pink gripped the evening sky. Tony had asked her on a date, which she declined, and not because she was holding out for Captain Wolt. Like he might see her as something else besides a figure at Celestial. Maybe he did a little ... no, she didn't think Captain Good Mood would see her as anything but a means to an end. Then there was Tony and their conversation.

"Hey, Doc, I wanted to make sure you're all right," he started as he fell in step with her. He had changed out of his uniform and into a white T-shirt with a band's name scrawled across his muscled chest, jeans, and boots. His auburn hair had been combed through with his fingers, leaving the ends to skirt the collar of his shirt.

Clio nearly rolled her eyes. "I'm fine. Everything is fine."

"Right. I said what I felt was the truth. Captain Wolt doesn't know who shot the elf, and now an enforcer has been attacked. If they can assault an enforcer and get away with it, who will be next?" Tony asked and stopped walking. "Captain Wolt has to answer to someone."

Clio faced him. He wasn't giving her his grin, and his blue eyes darkened as they narrowed on her. She tried concealing the edge of anger in her voice at the same time she straightened her shoulders in defiance. "The enforcers are doing the best they can."

"Their best doesn't seem good enough," he scoffed.

"They're trained investigators. Even with the training a real situation is different, and no one has faced rogue witches, death magic, and whoever is behind the new attacks." Clio let condemnation lace her words.

"Defending them, how predictable." If he noticed her disapproval, he easily ignored her.

"Are you jealous of him? Of all the enforcers?" Clio demanded.

"No. You. Are." He turned from her to stare at the woods behind the hospital, inhaled, exhaled, then met her glare. "You aren't one of them. You're one of us."

If she hadn't been shocked into silence by his statement, she would have had a reply ready to shoot back at him. She didn't. It was her turn to inhale and exhale, trying for calmness. She couldn't lose her temper in the parking lot, it would get her in worse trouble. She had to think of something to say and bury her instant fury.

"Listen to me very carefully, I'm not jealous. If I said I didn't miss it, I would be lying. But I have been given an opportunity to do what I love, like Cascade has given you. Captain Wolt is pack and has been my friend for years. I care about him regardless of his position and status." Despite the breakdown of communication, unless he needed something, and the wall of ice he built between them. "They're under a lot of pressure to be perfect, and judging every move doesn't help anyone."

"Dammit." Tony shoved his fingers through his thick hair as he cast his gaze down and looked at the ground, kicked at the loose gravel, then back to Clio. "I'm sorry. I know he's pack, but you are part of us, here. Maybe I am jealous of him and the attention you give him, like when you held his arm trying to comfort him. You don't let anyone in, you keep all of us at arm's length. You're a certified hard-ass. I know I'm not pack and I'm not a doctor, but you could see me as more than the med van driver."

He had stunned her into silence twice in one day.

"Bastard," Clio mumbled with the memory of their conversation.

Damn Tony. She didn't keep everyone at arm's length. She wasn't a hard-ass. She had a career, a job to do, a med room to equip, and needed to keep the respect of her peers. Reaching for her glass, her movement brought a muffling sound from the couch and broke the silence saturating the room. She lifted the drink, sipped, tasted the spice on her lips, set the drink down, and checked her cell. Nothing. If there had been a disciplinary action against her, someone would have told her, right? Affirmative. If Captain Wolt disagreed with the report, would he talk to her about it? Nope.

Clio saw the hurt in his cinnamon eyes as she held his arm, her fingers looking small next to his thick muscles, and felt the warmth of his skin. Then the commissioner's words played through her thoughts slamming into her musings. She explained the report, Lado's condition when she arrived at the scene, the effects of Director Kanin's absence, and her feelings on Captain Wolt. She kept it professional. Maybe too professional it sounded analytical and cold. She couldn't help it, wouldn't change it, and shrugged like someone could see her. As if on cue, her cell lit up and started mini bounces on the tabletop. Reaching for it, she didn't recognize the number, thought about letting it go to voicemail, she'd had a shit day, then snatched the vibrating rectangle. After the day she had there was no telling who it was.

"Doctor Hyde," she greeted.

Breathing. One second. Breathing. Two seconds.

"Hello?"

Click.

"Is someone there?" Clio waited for a second, then looked at the screen to see it had changed to the background picture. *Weird.* She brought up the recent calls, checked the area code, then the rest of the number. Choosing a name from the list, she took her glass, and sat back to resume staring at the last colors dying under night's assault.

"You've reached Cascade communications, this is Mandy speaking how may I help you?"

"It's Doctor Hyde. I have a number I would like you to run," Clio explained.

"Let me have it."

Clio recited each digit, and when she had given Mandy the entire number, she sipped her drink.

"Are you drinking?" Mandy asked.

"Yes, ma'am."

"Lucky. Give me one sec."

The line went silent, leaving Clio listening to nothing except the voices in her head, her default setting, and Tony. She could go on one date, what would it hurt? She needed to get out more anyway. It would prove she wasn't an impenetrable glacier and wasn't consumed by her career. No. No. She was consumed and she would be lying to him. Why the hell was she interested in Captain Good Mood at all when he couldn't stand to be around her?

"It's a burner cell, the area code is out of North Dakota. Sorry, Doc, I couldn't get anything else on it. Do you think it has something to do with the attack on Lado?"

"I don't think they would call one of us, especially me. Most likely it's random or a telemarketer. Might be about the warranty on my car."

Mandy laughed, then stopped. "If you feel you're in danger, I can have soldiers posted outside your place. The baron won't object," she stressed.

"Not necessary, just wanted to cover my bases. What's the status on Captain Wolt? No worries if you can't tell me, I understand," Clio added. She hated being on the outside. Was she jealous?

"Actually, Captain Wolt is on limited duty pending Baron Kanin's review of your report. Quinn is taking charge, and Luke will act as second. Captain Wolt expressed his worry Lado returned to Foxwood because he can identify his attackers, so there are four soldiers at Celestial standing guard. Quinn would like to be notified when Lado regains consciousness so he can ask him if he can give a description. Director Kanin has taken Miss Langston home, making his availability very limited. That sums it up," Mandy replied. "I'll expect to hear from you tomorrow."

"Affirmative," Clio answered on auto as Mandy's reply sank in. "As soon as I receive an update about Lado's condition, I'll let you know."

"Good to go, Doc."

There was an audible click when Mandy ended the call at the same time the background noise stopped and put her back in the silence of her house. Baron Kanin was going to review the report while it appeared Director Kanin had better things to do. Clio didn't blame him for wanting to spend time with his mate, but he could have taken the report seriously. Hell, someone was attacking, not just attacking, but had tortured one of their own. Multiple broken bones, poison, and used kyanite crystals as nails and drove them into his joints and throughout his entire body, and god only knew what else. Director Kanin was off work and at his house while she had single handedly crippled Captain Wolt's authority, leaving Quinn in charge. She hadn't considered the bigger picture, the threat the attacker posed, and leaving the pack to pay the price. Posting four soldiers at Celestial was a start to ease the building concern, still she felt better knowing the hospital employed three dozen guards. She guessed Director Kanin had enforcers making their presence known throughout Trinity, the territory, and the pack's property. Was it going to be enough? She didn't know.

Clio drank the remaining tequila in her glass and stood to get a refill. She would call the baron in the morning and pull the report, at least change the Priority Thirteen. If it wasn't too late.

The sun crept up, its yellow halo cresting the ridge and lighting the dark azure sky, and brought the first hints of warmth. A breeze swept the ends of his brown hair from his shoulders, as it caressed his bare skin, rustled through the treetops, and made the grasses sway until their blades hissed. Closing his eyes, Ansel exhaled a slow breath, quieted his mind, and listening to the wind let its melody carry his thoughts. He saw them going skyward as if in search of the sun and peace the clouds promised when a voice tangled with the curls to deliver her whisper to his ears. Her breath carried a warning, when he felt it on his skin it turned him cold, and he opened his eyes to break the spell the wind had wrapped around him. Like the dream he knew it was a premonition. She was near.

The geese emerged from the thick cattails, and with ripples breaking the still water around them they found a slice of sunlight and stopped. Life was moving forward, the world was turning, and no one was going to stop it for him. He would wait for the baron to make a decision, and then Ansel would play catch up. There was another choice. He vetoed it as soon as he thought of it, it was nothing but trouble. The cost was too high and would expose more than his lies. Standing on the deck, shirtless, his hands on the waist of his shorts, a chilled half cup of coffee sitting on the ledge, he ignored the sunrise and geese. His mind replayed every detail of Lado's wounds, Rutger's need for revenge, and Dr. Hyde's concern when she saw him. Holding his arm where her hand had been, he let himself sink into the memory of her gentle touch and the way her fingers tightened when his muscles flexed and used it to push the warning aside. He knew better.

"It's over without ever having a beginning."

Ansel sipped his coffee, stared at the mountains, and watched the sun's ascension as the day progressed. Without word from Baron Kanin or Rutger, he hadn't gone to work, didn't have a reason, and wouldn't go to Foxwood to be sent home, he wouldn't survive the humiliation. He had gone to the Enforcer's office every day, for years, and without something to do he felt detached, cast out, while the fear and rejection of being a rogue slipped over the honest life he created. He had called every hotel/motel, campground, and realtor in the area and didn't know where she was. She hadn't attacked him, hadn't made any threats, and yet she was taking his life from him. Ansel pushed his fingers through his hair as he growled his anger with the situation, the feel of helplessness, and the downward spiral into darkness he knew his mind and emotions were heading.

No. It isn't over.

He wasn't a quitter. Ansel was going to find her, prove

she was behind the attacks on Daniel and Lado, and then end her and her cruelty, forever. Like he should have years before if he'd had the courage. With his past dead and buried, he would make his confession to the baron and Rutger and hope they forgave him for lying to them and putting the pack in danger. If Baron Kanin withdrew his oath, Ansel would leave Cascade with a clear conscience and no strings attached.

And go where? his mind questioned. Cascade had become his home, the land around him, his territory, and he felt like he belonged. That's the part that hurt. He felt like he belonged, and leaving, no matter how many times he told himself he was capable of moving on, was going to destroy the good left in him.

The shrill ring of his cell phone had him striding into the house and to the table where it sat, the screen bright with a familiar number. "Captain Wolt," Ansel stated out of habit.

"Baron Kanin will see you in an hour," Mandy informed him.

"Copy." Ansel waited for a second, and when the line went silent, he checked to make sure Mandy had hung up.

With the screen clear, he released the breath he had been holding. His heart pounded in his chest like it was trying to crack the cage keeping it locked inside, and his knees weakened. Every stress, worry, and feeling of loss coiled in his middle, its weight like he had swallowed tons of rebar. As he walked back outside, he shoved the cell in his short's pocket, retrieved his mug, and heading inside stopped in the kitchen to set it in the sink. Lingering at the counter, his hands gripped the edge, the butcher block cracking under his grip while the geese squawked. *The geese Dr. Hyde would never see.* He stopped the thought before it further poisoned his already sinking mood.

With his mind racing around the possible topics like Dr. Hyde's report, the Priority Two, Code Black, Priority Thirteen, his involvement with the attacks, and the lack of evidence he had gathered, he dwelled on losing everything. His house. His family. A future. On auto, he made his way upstairs to his room where he began his usual routine of getting ready for work. He wouldn't arrive at Foxwood in civilian clothing, wouldn't look like he had given up and accepted he had lost.

Twenty minutes, which felt like a second later, Ansel was in his truck, the beeping and chimes of notifications coming from the console the only noise while he drove the open road toward what could be the end of his time with Cascade. He didn't know how to get his head out of the pit it was in and the fear from turning the blood in his veins to ice. His worst nightmare was coming true, and she was the reason for it, as he had imagined it would be.

Through Foxwood's gate, the work trucks, men and women, became a blur, then he saw Dr. Hyde. *What the hell?* Taking a double take, he watched her then saw her in the rearview mirror as her pearl white luxury crossover disappeared behind equipment, and the gate. He imagined their conversation as she explained he was losing his mind, he couldn't be trusted, and with her request Dr. Hyde hammered the last nail into his coffin. Damn. There was a part of him, slim as it was, believing in hope, the cruel bitch, that he was going to explain his side and the baron would forgive him. It was his pride lying to him, they needed him, the baron had given him a place because he had proven his worth as a man and a strong werewolf. Ansel's purpose in life was to protect his pack. He had been wrong, very wrong. His heart pounded, his pulse was in his ears, metal bands encased his lungs, and his mind screamed he didn't deserve their kindness when he had lied to them. For years.

Ansel parked his truck in what had become his usual spot, for the moment, killed the engine, and stared at the side of the pack's mobile communications. This was it. He was going to go into the baron's office, listen to him tell him what Dr. Hyde had said, then when it was his turn to talk, Ansel would spill his guts, and beg for mercy. Solid plan. With tension tightening his shoulders, he opened the door and instantly the noise from construction tried drowning out his chaotic thoughts. It wasn't as if he hadn't paid attention to the construction, but seeing the dungeon had been completed, and the second level with offices, gym, and the command center concealed by the walls, he clearly saw it and hadn't paid attention. Trained observer.

Around communications, Rutger's truck was parked in the same place, weeds beside the tires. The sight brought a rough laugh from Ansel and he was glad the construction noise covered the awkward sound. Rutger's truck not only had moved, but he had been making plans and was getting his farmhouse ready to slaughter the witches. Sousa stepped toward the door, opened it, and held it as Ansel started up the stairs.

"Baron Kanin is waiting for you," he reported.

"Thank you." The words pushed from him with force as tension tracked across his shoulders and the bitter bite of humiliation weakened his resolve.

When he stepped inside the entrance, the house's feel wrapped around him, the years he spent there dragging him through the past with its familiarity and holding the once welcoming sensation he had taken for granted. He took a hesitant step, and regret and disappointment replaced the blood in his veins. Abigail cleared her throat, as if telling him he needed to get to the office, so with a false resolve he started down the hall and to the office to get whatever was going to happen over with.

He stood in front of the door, his hand raised to knock when Rutger opened it and held it. "Ansel."

"Rutger," he returned in greeting.

"Come in," Baron Kanin's low rumble filled the room like his power. "Have a seat."

"Sir." Ansel did what he was told and sat down in the dark leather wingback chair while his heart threatened to stop.

Leaning forward, Baron Kanin placed his elbows on the manilla folders in front of him, the movement pulling the white, button-up shirt tight along his shoulders. His tawny gaze marked with his authority held a pointed seriousness. "I'll skip the small talk. Yesterday you reported to Celestial that Lado had been attacked, was wounded, and needed medical help. Is that correct?"

"Affirmative, sir." Ansel needed to keep it together, and had to stop the lump in his throat from choking him.

"As you described Lado's condition, were you in complete control of your wolf?" For a breath, the baron's eyes blazed gold, reminding Ansel he sensed lies.

"Affirmative, sir." The day came back one detail at a time as if it was playing in slow motion. "I was stunned by what happened to him. His arms, hands, and fingers had been broken, there were nails everywhere, he was bleeding out and dying. Despite his wounds and the effects of the crystals, he had the strength to drive back to Foxwood. After the eagerness he showed when I asked him to serve as second, he didn't deserve being attacked. I take full responsibility."

"The only person or persons taking responsibly for the attack will be the assailants. I understand having one of our own assaulted is unsettling and you let your emotions get the better of you, and there's nothing wrong with that. But you are an enforcer, Captain of Enforcers, and a domineer, you're an example of strength and control. After speaking to you, Doctor Hyde became concerned you were losing control over the situation, let alone your emotions and wolf." Baron Kanin stood, stepped around his desk, and walked over to a bookcase.

"The last couple of months have been hard on all of us. First Zach's murder, then Jordyn's kidnapping, the treatment she endured, the release of the witches, Flint remains free, and while we're fighting for normal, there's a new threat." He faced Ansel and Rutger, his eyes holding his age and worry. "They have to be found and stopped."

"I have Quinn and Luke working on it. I believe the patrols and those calling in have served as a warning we aren't going to allow their invasion to continue," Rutger replied.

Ansel hated having Quinn and Luke in charge, and not because he was envious and wanted to be out there searching for her, because she was out there watching them. If she thought either enforcer posed a threat, they would end up like Lado or worse, dead. The sight of the sword's blade going through Dayton's heart blasted in front of him and he forced it back where it belonged.

"Captain Wolt, Doctor Hyde came to see me personally to withdraw the Priority Thirteen as well as add an amendment to her statement." His gaze landed on the folders, giving him a brief reprieve from their weight, then back on him. "She wrote an affidavit stating your training and instincts are vital to the investigation and has confidence in your ability to apprehend the perpetrators. While I agree and am inclined to allow you to resume your duties, I cannot. Commissioner Courter interviewed Doctor Hyde and Mr. Reed, and sent the transcripts to the Unseelie and Seelie courts. They have demanded you be held responsible for your lack in judgement and inadequacies during the investigation. I have emailed Doctor Hyde's report and affidavit to the commissioner as well as the statement explaining the discipline, and I expect it to appease all parties involved. I have decided, you will remain on limited duty through today and tomorrow, and resume your normal duties as Captain of Enforcers, thereafter. You are an important part of the pack and need to be involved in the investigation."

"Affirmative, sir." Ansel's heart had stopped, and his lungs were collapsing in his chest. They didn't accuse him of being part of the Covey, didn't blame him, and he didn't confess.

Baron Kanin walked to his desk and picked up two folders. "Here are the transcripts of the patrols from yesterday and this morning, and the calls received from the klatch. You can read over them and see if there's anything that gets your attention, is out of place, or needs to be investigated."

"Sir." With shaking hands, hoping the baron didn't notice, he took the folders.

"Ansel," Baron Kanin started as he sat behind his desk, the tension in his shoulders relaxing. "Doctor Hyde is a proud woman who works hard, sacrifices her time, and has proven herself invaluable to the pack. Like I said, Commissioner Courter questioned her about her actions and her feelings toward you. When she came here today, she risked her job at Celestial, her position as head of the med room, and her reputation to retract her initial report and clear your name. Not only does she put the pack first, but she genuinely cares about you and your position with the enforcers. When this case is over, you might want to find out if there's more there."

"Sir," Ansel mumbled past the lump in his throat. He did

not need this. Dr. Hyde didn't need him, his problems, his disreputable past, a Pureblood werewolf without a crest. Save the Covey's tattoo. It marked him as a piece of property she used when the mood struck. He felt her fangs in his neck, her hands gripping his arms, her body pressed against his, and his stomach churned. She owned him and was proving her possession.

"She is as driven as you are. You both have concentrated your focus on your careers and have excelled. You might find you have a lot in common," Baron Kanin explained, as a small grin pulled at the corners of his mouth.

After making several noises which weren't words, Ansel finally found the ability to speak. "I don't think we're compatible." *Fated mates*. No, please, no. He already made sure Dr. Hyde hated him, there was no way he was going to change that. Whether he found her or not, he couldn't have anyone in his life. He didn't deserve the happiness.

"Just a thought." Baron Kanin met his gaze and saw the doubt Ansel was trying to hide.

"I'll walk you out," Rutger offered as he stood.

Rescued. "Copy. Sir." Ansel stood, the quick motion moving the chair backwards, bowed, and left the office.

"She might bite," Rutger mused as they walked side by side down the hallway.

"Who?"

"Don't play stupid. Doctor Hyde," Rutger answered.

"If it's me she will. I did not impress her yesterday, obviously," Ansel replied. Or the day before, or the day before, and the day before that.

"We all have shitty days. Plus, she was here of her own free will to change the report. That says something." Rutger stopped talking as Abigail opened the door and held it for them.

Outside, July's sun beat down on the vehicles, the raw ground, and what was left of the grass while machinery roared, orders were being shouted, and nail guns sounded like someone was having a machine gun war. Rutger stepped down the stairs and looked at the fortress being built.

"Where's Jason? Haven't seen him around in a while?" Ansel asked, hoping to change the subject. He did not want to talk about Dr. Hyde, especially after the baron told him they had a lot in common.

Rutger checked the door like he expected to see the sentinel standing there. When he didn't, a brief moment of shock stole over his features then it was gone, and his mask of indifference was back in place. "No idea."

"The baron does what the baron does," Ansel joked.

"Affirmative." Rutger turned slightly to meet Ansel's gaze with a gold glare. "Tonight. I'll pick you up at midnight." Any humor from seconds before was wiped out by dark determination and his wolf's need to hunt.

"Affirmative." It was all he could say without starting a *are you ready for this* lecture, telling him *there will be blood on your hands*, and asking *do you know what the consequences will be if you're caught?* A death sentence delivered by the human court system. Rutger wasn't impulsive and didn't do anything without researching and having a strategy. The witches were no different. Without waiting for Rutger to go into detail or to say anything else, Ansel left him and walked to his truck. He had files to read, a talent from his past to resurrect, and assassinations to get ready for. If she didn't find him first. Which was a possibility.

The folders sat in the passenger seat, silent, while containing the last twenty-four hours of the enforcer's lives and the concerns of the klatch. Ansel gave them a sideways glance, felt like he had dodged a bullet, and leaving the gate to Foxwood behind him, headed in the direction of his house. He was going to confess, it was bubbling inside him like lava, and he was going to free himself of the lies he had told them and pray to all that was holy, Baron Kanin, Rutger, and the pack forgave him. Did he think it was possible? Yes and no. He was going to help Rutger kill the witches, which would prove his loyalty, and his silence would prove he wasn't a traitor, but it wouldn't help him with the pack or the klatch when they saw him as unprofessional, unqualified, and unable to solve a case. They believed in the Director of Enforcers who didn't know where the baron's sentinels were, had taken a vacation to kill witches, and was using his fated mate as an alibi. *The webs we weave.*

The varied chimes and chatter coming from the console filled the cab and tried to take his attention off the night ahead of him and what he was going to have to do. The old feeling of being forced to take a life came roaring back and drove the spike of resentment deep into his soul. *This was different,* he argued. The damn witches had killed one of their own and destroyed a woman's life. They stole her confidence and ripped her security from her. The acts demanded vengeance and they were going to pay with their lives.

CHAPTER THIRTEEN

Clio slid the key card, got the green light, then entered the code and waited for the gate to rattle its way across the two lanes of the private parking. Driving through the employee lot, she couldn't get rid of the image of Captain Wolt's truck when she was leaving Foxwood, then knowing the baron was going to tell him about the report and the changes she had made.

She didn't have a choice, she had to clarify her concerns, the codes and priorities didn't explain anything, even if they assumed, she had more than professional feelings for him. Ice skated down her spine with the admission she cared for Ansel, it made her feel exposed, like she had cut herself open and they could see her insides. The worst part of it she felt like a lost puppy wanting attention and would never get any. Driving down another lane, she saw Tony's four-wheel drive, groaned, and pulled into her parking spot. Hopefully, he left her alone.

Before turning the engine off, Clio checked her terminal, and brought up the roster for the enforcers. The first name on the list was Director Kanin. She thought he hadn't read the report, he had gone home early, and was proven wrong when he questioned her. Of course, he felt responsible for Lado, Captain Wolt, even Tony, and didn't want anyone hurt, and if someone wasn't doing their job, they needed to be removed. She read the line next to his name and saw he was unavailable. Not off duty but unavailable. That was new. Next was Captain Wolt, and he was unavailable as well. Dammit, she hoped by talking with the baron, Captain Wolt would be back at work. Scrolling down, she saw Quinn, Luke, Kia, Kellen, Aydian, Owen, Skylar, and the list went on. They were all active, had been paired up, were being assisted by a dozen soldiers, and were all over the territory.

Clio sat back in her seat while the terminal continued talking and updating the enforcers' locations. They were all over Trinity and the county. This was going to change the pack. She didn't know how much stricter things could get but wouldn't doubt the baron's ability to figure it out. A shadow darkened the passenger side of her car right before Tony leaned down and knocked on the window. Grumbling curse words, she plastered her doctor's smile on her face and rolled the window down.

"Good morning," she greeted.

"Morning. I brought a peace offering." He raised a cardboard container that held two cups of coffee.

Was she going to remain mad at him? No. They worked together, and she wasn't going to have unnecessary tension between them when peoples' lives depended on them. "Thank you." He smiled, his blue eyes glinting in the sunlight, and stepped backward as she rolled the window up, and after turning off the engine, grabbed her bag and got out.

"You have an enforcer's console in your car?" Tony asked as he rounded the backend. "You were one of the chosen."

She laughed. "All enforcers have a terminal. I'm not active, but I'm the doctor for the baron and baroness, and this way communications knows where I'm at," Clio replied. Look at her handling a casual conversation. Who would have thought it?

"Doctor Hyde, the badass. Did you just laugh?" Tony's blue eyes gleamed as streaks of amber swam through them.

"Don't tell anyone," Clio warned. Badass. Hard-ass. Those were not terms of endearment.

"No worries, your secret is safe with me," he said through a laugh. "Wasn't sure what you liked, so went with good'ole plain, black coffee."

She was positive he would keep it a secret. "That's perfect. Thank you, again." Clio adjusted the bag on her shoulder, took a cup from the holder, and sipped. Surprise struck her with the dark roasted notes, smokey sweetness, and lack of acidity. "This is good."

"I'll tell my cousin. He has a bakery and has started roasting his own coffee," Tony explained with pride.

Clio sipped, found she was enjoying the relaxed conversation, the coffee, and company. She hadn't realized the strict rules the pack adopted had changed her, them, and the way they interacted with one another. While everyone was professional, their interaction was sterile, harsh, and cold. She missed the warmth and closeness they once shared, and it saddened her to think it was going to get worse because of the new attacks.

"Your mood changed. What's on your mind, Doc?" Tony asked. Gold sunlight made his blue eyes gleam azure, gave his auburn hair honey highlights, and made his summer tan a deeper shade.

Clio stared at him as if for the first time, noticing the way his broad shoulders filled out his blue polo, and the way his BDU trousers clung to his waist and thighs. She would be lying if she said he wasn't handsome, charming, and his lips and the grin playing on them weren't tempting. But he was those things to someone else. When she saw him, she saw

Tony the paramedic and med van driver, and a friend. Her mind wandered to Captain Wolt and what he would look like out of his uniform while standing on his deck watching the turf war between his geese and ducks. Not that she would ever find out. Clio wanted to beat her head on the hood of her car. She was a professional, successful, and chasing what she couldn't have, and why? No chance of it happening. Career first. Life second. Captain Wolt was out of reach. Tony was standing in front of her, within arm's reach, and if she wanted to find out what he looked like out of his uniform ... well, she could. That scared her and it screamed commitment.

"Doc, you all right?" he asked, his brows drawing in.

"Sorry, lost in thought. I have a packed day and that's if nothing happens," she explained. Lied.

"Yeah, same here." He checked his watch, then met her gaze with his own. "I have a meeting."

"Sounds lovely." A vibration had Clio setting the cup on the hood of her car and pulling her cell from a side pocket. "Doctor Hyde." When she ended the call, she took the cup and started toward the entrance.

Tony was next to her, then ahead of her to slide his key card, his code, and he opened the door. "What's up?"

"Lado is awake."

She left Tony in the hall, rushed to her office where she dumped her bag, left her coffee, and raced toward the critical care unit. The halls felt like they went on for miles and miles, the elevators had slowed to a near crawl, and the doors had multiplied. When Clio reached the critical care unit, she went to the ICU rooms, and almost ran into Dr. Kolt.

"Doctor Hyde."

"How is he?" she asked.

"Like I said, he's conscious. He can't speak, his motor skills are limited, and the trauma from the punctures injured his organs and is worse than expected. Because he's a werewolf, the kyanite crystals have caused damage resembling silver, and the ghoul toxin, where someone finds that I have no idea, continues to destroy his cells and prevents his body from healing. It appears to have reduced his ability to heal. He's on antibiotics, which shouldn't be necessary, and if that isn't enough, his elf half is slowing his recovery. I'm advising his parents he be put in a medically-induced coma and placed in a restoring chamber," Dr. Kolt explained.

Not what she wanted to hear. "Understood. I'll update Baron Kanin on Lado's condition. Is Daniel being discharged?" she asked, the conversation with the commissioner about security and Daniel's safety playing in her head.

"Has been, two hours. He's with his parents and wife," Dr. Kolt answered. "I sent the crystals to research. They're going to try to find out what causes them to affect shapeshifters and how to stop it, and we absolutely need an antitoxin for the ghoul toxin."

She might have used something exotic, odd, something you wouldn't expect. How would you know, Captain Wolt? And who was *she?*

"Hopefully research finds something." A cold wave washed over her with the feeling Captain Wolt lied to her, to them all. She felt betrayed, and her plea to the baron had been a desperate attempt to melt the ice wall Captain Wolt had constructed between them. She was an idiot. She let her feeling dictate how she performed her job. How could anyone take her seriously? *It's your Wight side coming out and the desperation to have him pay attention to you*

Clio flipped the switch on her default setting and looked

through the window, the protective lines of silver, copper, and cobalt making tiny squares in the glass, and watched nurses in Biohazard suits hover around Lado. His pointed ears were close to his skull, a protective mask covered his face while wires and tubes ran to the respirator, his bare chest was marred by bruises and punctures, and plastic pads with more wires ran to a heart monitor and sticking out from his arms were several catheters the clear tubing going to three bags. His usually dark skin was pale but still a stark contrast to the white sheets, equipment encased in white, and the white walls. When he opened his eyes, a soft green like seafoam stared at nothing for several seconds, his lips moved around silent words, his face pinched as if in pain, his fingers twitched, and he closed his eyes.

"You're sure he can't speak?" She needed him to tell them who had done this.

"Yes. He tries but it isn't anything tangible. After watching him and the small movements, I think he's hallucinating. For a werewolf it's bad, for an empath with his history, it's even worse. It's another reason I want him placed in a coma ... I don't want him regaining consciousness, use of his limbs, and harming himself or one of the staff. Again, I have no idea what kyanite crystals and ghoul toxin does to the body or what they're doing to his mind," Dr. Kolt replied.

"Thank you," Clio offered. She looked at Lado one last time, turned, and headed down the hallway toward her office.

She needed to call Baron Kanin to inform him of Lado's condition. Would she tell him her suspicions about Captain Wolt and make another change to the report? Negative. She couldn't change her mind a second time without questions and looking incompetent while the truth remained, he hadn't threatened anyone and hadn't been out of control.

His bronze eyes held her, and Clio understood the look in Captain Wolt's gaze hadn't been fear for Lado's life, while it was there it wasn't the cause, it was fear someone was going to find out his secret. The person responsible. *Her* identity.

Ansel sat back in the patio chair, a beer sitting on the table, a picture sitting next to the bottle, and gazed beyond the pond until his eyes blurred. When he left Foxwood, he had driven through the city, checked the properties the pack owned and found nothing. Then he had gone to the store, completed several errands, and went about his day as if he wasn't facing a night of killing witches that may or may not send them to prison and to their deaths. He wasn't concerned with his life, it was over, he feared for Rutger and if he was convicted Jordyn would lose her mate. It left him considering doing what all people do when they saw the end of their life; put his affairs in order. Sadly it was a testament to his existence, his affairs were always in order.

When he finished putting everything away, he had gone to his room, went to his closet, and retrieving a memory from his past, placed the antique travel trunk on his bed. Lifting the top, the wood and metal groaned while the musty smell of age and a different time drifted to tease Ansel with the years it represented. He exhaled as he let the lid fall back a couple of inches, the hinges stopping it from going farther, and as if waiting for his attention the forgotten weapons gleamed in the sunlight from their foam homes. One on either side of the knives and shortswords were leather handles, Ansel grasped them and lifting, the shelf eased out in silence. Underneath were ten pistols, each one from a favorite decade, and ammunition. The sight took him from his bedroom with modern conveniences to hotel rooms with wood plank flooring, brass beds, thin curtains covering a single window, and the smell of whiskey, horses, and her.

Ansel shuddered as he lifted the shelf out, and placing it beside the first, gazed at the scattered papers and photographs. Through the years, he never kept anything for fear someone would question him where he had gotten them. The guns, swords, and knives were collector items, he convinced himself he could explain, but pieces of history like clothing, watches, furniture, the simplest of things like the first radios, and even his horse's saddles were too much of a risk. He was playing a part and had practiced his speech to sound modern, his use of words the same as others his age. Or the age he was pretending to be.

His attention went back to the papers and photographs, the calligraphy scrawled on the time-stained sheets, and the faces captured in black and white, and sepia staring up at him. He sipped his beer, listened to the geese, and let time drag him back. The sun was setting, its gold, pinks, and honey staining the sky and turning the green grass a shade lighter while the reflection of the mountain ridges rippled in the pond. Setting his beer down, he absently picked up the photograph and met the gaze that had been captured forever.

She sat beside him, her raven hair curled in ringlets ended at her waist, her white eyes streaked with scarlet hidden behind rose-tinted lenses, the scar marring her cheek a shade darker than her skin, and the skirts of her dress brushing his leg and hiding his boot. Her left hand rested on his upper thigh and her right hand sat on her lap while she looked at the camera. At that moment she had been dignified, graceful, and the blood on her hands momentarily wiped clean, as they pretended to be a man and a woman.

A heartbeat of innocence.

"I never loved you," he whispered to the image. He waited for her to respond, could hear her whiskey voice trying to soothe him. Closing his eyes, the picture remained silent, he cleared his throat, and pushed the feelings that had escaped their prison back down.

The butterscotch dyed sun sank behind the mountains, their ridges absorbing the warm glow while ushering twilight's cool shades across the indigo sky. He had several hours before Rutger picked him up. Would they get away with murder? Rutger had the most to lose; his place as Second to the Alpha, position as director, and he would lose his mate, forever, leaving her alone. He didn't know what the repercussions would be if Rutger died, what would happen to Jordyn, and what would happen to the pack? Ansel had nothing to lose when he had spent his entire life making sure he didn't. If he went to prison and then faced the death penalty, her need for revenge would be over. His life would be over. Ended after so many years of surviving. Part of him felt the end and relief washed over him. No more hiding. No more lying. No more running. Peace. He laughed, the sound closer to insanity than he liked, he wasn't going to have peace. People who had done the things he had went straight to hell. Where they burned.

He dropped the photograph on the table, took his beer, and finishing it, set the bottle down. Leaning back in the chair he stared up at the sky and watched night crawl over the expanse, bringing out the stars, and closed his eyes. He suddenly felt the weight of his past merge with his present and it made his muscles tired to the point of dragging him to the ground. His last thought before exhaustion swallowed him was, *I need to close my eyes, just for a minute.*

"Wake up."

Ansel heard someone and felt them shove his shoulder, repeat their demand, and there was a chill in the air.

"Wake up," Rutger ordered.

"I am. I am." Ansel grudgingly opened his eyes to see it was night, the darkness hanging like a thick curtain, and he sat straighter. He had been asleep for hours, wasted hours.

With panic giving him an edgy energy, he searched the table for the photo and didn't find it. What was he going to say if Rutger had found it? Yeah, that's me with the woman who nearly killed Lado, oh and it was taken in the late 1800's, while we were in Iowa. We had been hired to assassinate a magic-born, a Wight, who was using his power to manipulate and scare humans into committing crimes. I cut his throat, and we watched his life drain from him to the floor, while the humans watched, their heartbeats giving away their fear, and their eyes bloodshot from tears. Afterwards, we had sex, and she told me my cruelty was exquisite.

"Looking for something?" Rutger asked.

Ansel wasn't going to be able to help Rutger because his heart was going to explode. "Negative. Nothing. Sorry, I'll change."

"I can't believe you took a nap," Rutger said as he followed Ansel inside.

"I haven't slept the last couple of days. I guess I hit a wall." It wasn't a lie except it wasn't the truth. Taking a trip through his past had a hundred years of pain and fear bringing him to his knees.

"I can understand that." Rutger walked to the front door. "Remember, no cell, no gun. I'll be in the car."

Ansel watched his broad shoulders with the weight of the world on them, and the resolve Rutger was known for keeping them straight as he walked out of the house, the door closing silently behind him. After this night, Rutger would have blood on his hands and no amount of convincing himself he avenged Jordyn and Zachery changed the sliver of humanity's guilt when a life had been taken. Ansel headed upstairs where he changed out of his shorts and T-shirt and into an old pair of jeans, a T-shirt with more holes than he could count, and an old pair of running shoes. He had taken the hint when Rutger wore roughly the same thing. Neither of them were going to keep the clothing.

Thirty minutes into the drive no one had said anything, the pop station playing on the radio was the only noise ... and it was noise. Ansel tapped his foot more out of nervous habit than to the beat of the song he was trying to ignore.

"We're going to stick six people in this vehicle?" Ansel asked. Like cord wood.

"Negative." The pale green light from the dash highlighted Rutger's face and deepened the circles under his eyes, and the wrinkles around his mouth.

Right.

Rutger made a right, taking them out of the city limits, toward the industrial area, and that's when Ansel gazed out the passenger window and saw the warehouse. "Really?"

"Affirmative. It has a military grade security system, complete with cameras. I saw you were here the other day." Rutger drove the sporty SUV into the parking lot and toward the back of the warehouse.

"And the old truck? Is it for decoration?" Ansel couldn't hide the dislike in his voice. Rutger hadn't been honest with him, like he didn't trust him. Wasn't he doing the same thing? Negative. He was protecting his kith and kin.

"It was left here. It's a classic, I might have it worked on or keep it for a project," he replied.

"I get it if the baron had something to do with this, but you?" He couldn't believe Rutger had that kind of pull or money. "If it isn't bad enough, you're using Jordyn as an alibi, you've been distant from the enforcers and the pack, and you did this." Why was he giving Rutger a hard time? Because there was no reason, he needed to make the same mistakes Ansel had.

"Affirmative. I had plenty of time to think while I was a prisoner at Celestial and purchased it soon after being released. The baron required me to sign a contract with the pack because my property borders the Summit. It states if anything happens at the Summit, this serves as a safe place for the pack to gather and as an escape route." Rutger drove to a roll up door, stopped, put the car in park, took a tablet from the center console, and typed a command. A second later the weathered metal ascended, and the car's headlights caught the dents, rust spots, and the aged signs of graffiti.

Ansel was sure Rutger had stayed at Foxwood to heal, and spend time with Jordyn, and to work on their relationship. She was the soothsayer for the pack, and no one knew what it meant, and the emotional chaos of Flint wasn't helping. He clearly hadn't been. When there was clearance, Rutger drove through the opening large enough for a semi, headed to the right where he parked, turned off the headlights, and killed the engine. It left them sitting in complete darkness their wolf eyes had a hard time adjusting to. When he opened the door, Ansel prepared for the interior light to blind him. It didn't come on and he got out of the car.

"What are we doing here?" he asked, his voice echoing.

"Getting the vehicle." Taking the tablet, the screen lit up, and Rutger touched several buttons, making overhead lights come on. "We're sticking six people in that."

It took a second for Ansel's eyes to adjust from darkness

to sudden light, and he saw Rutger was pointing at a gray utility van with Hayden Mines written down its side. "You're using a van from the mine?" Ansel asked.

"Affirmative. If there are guards at the gate, they won't suspect anything when we drive through."

"Besides kidnapping, holding them captive against their will, varied assault charges, not to mention murder charges you'll have grand theft auto added on. Sweet," Ansel mocked. "Go big."

Rutger gave him a sideways glance holding more than mild irritation with his comment at the same time holding a level of knowledge. "I didn't steal it. I have it legally."

"That's a relief. We're saved."

"Funny."

"First the farmhouse and now this." Ansel looked around and saw the inside was being worked on and looked like part of it was going to be offices. Rutger had another life no one knew about. "Your priority should be the upgrades on your house."

"I made some modifications and approval will take some time. Pending that approval, they'll be scheduled," Rutger replied as he walked over to the van.

"I have no idea what kind of modifications you could have made. Your house is about to be a fortress," Ansel said as he followed. "Does the baron know?"

"Get in the van," Rutger ordered, ignoring him.

Ansel found the passenger door unlocked and climbed inside at the same time Rutger got in the driver's side. "I know you've been watching them, but how are we going to apprehend them when we don't have weapons?" He felt naked without his gun, and his truck which identified him as an enforcer for Cascade, which carried the baron's authority.

They didn't have anything.

"We aren't apprehending them, so you can mark kidnapping and holding them against their wills off your list of charges," Rutger replied as he used the tablet to turn off the lights.

"That makes me feel better. Assault and murder it is. Weapons?"

After setting the tablet in the center console, he turned the engine on, and met Ansel's gaze with a gold glare. "A life for a life and we are the weapons."

CHAPTER FOURTEEN

The metal door unrolled behind them, its rusted exterior closing the world off and concealing Jordyn's SUV and the secrets held within. Without lights and life, the warehouse resumed its appearance of forgotten, neglected, weathered, and in the shadows of night it blurred in the taillights. Rutger headed out of the parking lot to the street and away from the industrial area, tension weaving between them making the silence thick and uncomfortable. Driving toward Trinity, Ansel considered asking if he wasn't pushing his luck by being seen in the van despite it being close to one in the morning.

The van itself was a problem, how had he gotten it legally? Who at the mine knew he had it? What if someone reported the witches missing? His mind raced as the lights of the city made his nerves unravel and when he thought he was going to explode Rutger turned off the main highway and stayed to the outskirts of town. Ansel settled in his seat while the questions ate at his patience and tightened the tension in his shoulders. They were headed to a bloodbath.

"I can sense your unease. If you have a question, ask it," Rutger's rumble broke the silence.

"How did you locate them?"

"I told you, I had someone following them," Rutger answered.

"You trust this person?" Ansel questioned. "They could talk to law enforcement."

"He won't. He's been part of Cascade since the beginning. He was in the encampments with the baron and baroness."

"How long have you watched them?"

"Since they gathered. I wanted to be sure they were guilty. I didn't want to believe the system would let serial killers that had been part of a cult out of jail. If they had left town and moved on with their lives, I would have let them go," Rutger explained.

"They didn't leave. They stayed, and they stayed together," Ansel mumbled as he stared at the road snaking out in front of them. He couldn't believe it and he absolutely believed it.

"Affirmative. They don't know where Flint is, so they've been camping where Flint first saw Jo in hopes he finds them. Once they're with Flint, they've made plans to kidnap Jo to prove their loyalty to him." Rutger exhaled like was trying to expel his fury.

"I'm not doubting you, but could your guy be feeding you information you want to hear?" Ansel asked. When did he play devil's advocate?

"Negative. He recorded several of their conversations and sent them to me. There's no remorse for the men they tortured and killed, no remorse for Zachery or for kidnapping Jo. And Flint, they talk about that fucking monster like he's a god."

"That's cult mentality. They think he'll save them." Ansel watched the road and his reservations about killing the witches began dying under the truth. A life for a life. "If they don't know where he is, do you think he'll look for his devoted followers?"

"Negative. With the media's coverage, they've become a liability. I think Flint is so furious about us stopping his plan for world domination, the only thing he's focused on is killing the pendulum," Rutger explained.

"If you believe that, why is Jordyn at home alone?" Ansel asked.

"Because it looks like I'm home. He'll make a move once the witches are reported missing or dead. It'll damage his egotism."

"You're setting a trap for him. First, she's your alibi, and now she's bait. Jordyn needs protection and needs to feel safe. The security upgrades should have been done weeks ago." Ansel could not believe what Rutger was doing, by himself. "Why didn't you tell me?" The look in Rutger's quick glance asked the same questions of Ansel.

"First, I can protect my mate. Second, I stepped down. You're Captain of Enforcers, making you the enforcers leader, and I couldn't risk anyone else."

"What changed?" Ansel asked.

"Like you said, it's a cult mentality, and they believe he's going to save them. They're followers who blindly serve Flint. They're serial killers. The moment they were released they started making plans to kidnap Jo. They will never change, and they don't deserve redemption. They cannot continue. I need help and I trust you," Rutger replied.

Guilt rose up and teased his throat with bile, his stomach churned, and a dull throbbing started at the back of his head, making him want to confess everything. *Lies are making me weak,* he thought as he looked into the night, and knew he had to tell Rutger the truth. It was now or never. Swallowing his fear, he opened his mouth.

"Here." Rutger took the tablet from the center console and handed it to him. "Touch the earth symbol and it will take you to navigation."

Ansel closed his mouth, inhaled his relief and guilt, and working on auto tapped the symbol. "What am I looking for?"

"A red dot. Touch the button for directions and a map will come up."

"You have GPS on your spy?" Ansel asked. At first it appeared Rutger's plan had been stitched together by hope and a prayer, and laced with blind revenge, not with top-of-the-line electronics and GPS.

"Affirmative."

"They're right outside of Butterfly Valley. Jordyn went there?" What the hell was she doing there?

"Affirmative, it borders Cascade. Jo would go there to take photographs and to run in wolf form. The baron believes she was there to feel her territory."

For three years? "ETA in twenty," Ansel reported.

Rutger turned off the highway onto a dirt road, causing the tires to kick up rocks that hit the sides of the van. The headlights cut through the night, casting a glow over red dirt peppered with rocks and the trunks of pine trees lining both sides of the road. The red dot on the tablet grew closer as they drove until they were nearly on top of it.

Ansel touched the map with two fingers, then spread them out to close in on the target. "If this is accurate, they're about seventy-five yards ahead of us."

"It's accurate." Rutger turned the headlights off, let off the gas, and coasted to the right side of the road, the passenger side tires going up the embankment.

"What are we going to do?" After learning what Rutger had been doing the entire time, Ansel had no idea what was going to happen.

"Shift." Taking the tablet, Rutger typed out a message and hit send.

"We're doing this in wolf form?"

"Affirmative. They murdered werewolves, their lives will be taken by werewolves," Rutger replied with a growl threading through his words. In the dark his eyes gleamed gold, and holding a feral edge, he got out of the van. His thick form stood between the door and the cab as he pulled his T-shirt over his head and started on his running shoes.

Sitting on the embankment made the passenger side of the van higher than the driver's, the difference forcing Ansel to climb out to get clear of the door. He stood in the wood-line staring at Rutger as he undressed and exhaling, thought about the Covey's symbol inked in his flesh. If Rutger saw it, it would solidify his guilt, and doom any hope he had to clear his name. Maybe he should let Rutger see it, he could kill Ansel with the witches and leave his remains for the animals. Checking on Rutger, he saw his attention was on the left side of the road and the woods, and he took the opportunity to pull his T-shirt over his head and tossed it into the van. Next were his running shoes, boxers, and jeans.

Completely naked, his body heated, his wolf rose up its essence sealing every fiber of his being as his eyes blurred and changed from human to wolf, cinnamon to bronze. His skin stretched over his shifting muscles and bones, while thick dark brown fur covered his back, front arms, and chest then lightened to tawny down his stomach and hind legs. For a heartbeat, the ether held him in its darkness and sep-arated him from the world then it released him, and he was completely shifted in his wolf form and his senses burst as they searched his surroundings. Ansel stretched, pointed his muzzle to the sky, and analyzed the incoming information.

Rutger stood in wolf form, black running from his ears to his muzzle, then faded out to dark walnut and blending with charcoal down his sides and belly. Ansel met his gold glare, felt his power, and the aggression sweeping around him like his private storm. Rutger nearly lost himself to his wolf turned beast and now as the wolf stood in front of him, he understood the magnitude of Rutger's strength. Raising his head, he went motionless, then loped across the red dirt road and into the woods.

Ansel paused, mentally readied for what was ahead, then trailing behind him kept his dark form in sight as the trees thickened to block the moonlight. They stopped at the edge of a clearing to see red, gold, and yellow flames from a fire climb into the sky and brightened the surrounding area with their glow. A fire to give them comfort and security. In the glow, a man sat on the far side, his auburn hair covered his shoulders and ended in the middle of his chest, while the features of his face were contoured by the blaze, when his eyes gleamed green he had spotted Rutger. The spy. As if he'd been given an order, the man stood, his height putting him over six feet tall, and he began loosening the ties of his smock. The witches preferred clothing. Ansel hated seeing anything resembling the cotton tops and pants after Butte Springs.

With the spy's movement, Rutger stalked to the left, his head low, and Ansel taking the right side flanked the sleeping witches. In wolf form they weren't able to talk to one another, they relied on body language, and the animal's vocalizations of growling, barking, whimpering, and howling. A rough howl drenched in rage shattered the serene silence of early morning and changed safety to tension thick with the promise of death. Before the echoes of Rutger's howl died in the woods, two men sat up, their sleeping bags around their waists, and seeing the wolves, alerted the others. Rutger's anguished wail carrying his wrath and grief sent chills down Ansel's spine while it overshadowed the spy and the witch's yells turned screams.

Rutger targeted the men, his growls resonating in his wake, the brush and ground eaten by his large mass. With the snarls and howls three more people scrambled out of their sleeping bags and tried for cover. When a woman crawled out on her hands and knees, she scrambled away from the fire. One of the men tripped, and catching his balance got to his feet and took off. It took the spy a breath to take chase and leaping, knocked the witch to the ground and tore into his side. The downed witch screamed, the sound muffled by his struggle and his attempt to beat the wolf, who had to weigh three hundred pounds, and failing his cries drowned under the wolf's growls.

The second man saw Rutger stalking toward him and began to kick at the sleeping bag, his fight turned panicked as Rutger closed in on him. Turning to his stomach and his hands and knees, he crawled out of the tangle, got to his feet, stumbled on rocks and brush, and getting his feet under him, started running. Ansel wasn't sure where he thought he was going to go or how far he thought he was going to get when Rutger was faster than him. It took a second for Rutger to knock him to the ground, pin him, and after howling his victory to the sky, clamp his jaws on the man's neck. With rapid jerks of his head, Rutger tore through flesh, and breaking the man's neck decapitated him. Two down. Ansel watched the spy take down a female witch, her begging turned screams piercing his ears as she buried her hands in the wolf's thick fur, her body flaying with her struggle, and her feet slipped on the soft dirt. The wolf covered her with his massive body, his paws keeping her on the ground as he silenced her by taking her throat. Three down.

Rutger targeted his next prey, took the man down, and without flair tore his head from his shoulders. Four down. While Rutger and the spy were finishing with their victims, a woman used the opportunity to low crawl from the fire and the weapons of death. Ansel tracked her, had her erratic heartbeat in his head, her quick breaths making her chest heave, and the need to chase sent energy into his wolf. He let instinct to hunt his prey build inside him until its energy was uncontrollable and started stalking toward her. When she reached the edge of the blaze's halo and night covered her, she stood, her loose cotton pants and smock stained with dirt. Terror sat in her eyes as she watched the wolves tearing the last two witches to pieces. Ansel prowled behind the woman, reaching her as she faced him. She opened her mouth to scream when her magic leeched into the air and over him as if it contained needles, pierced his skin.

The evil, the sights, and smells of Butte Springs roared to life, giving Ansel images of Rutger on his knees, Jordyn's bloody body limp on the ground, and Dr. Hyde's pleas. He growled, snapped his teeth, and lunged at her as she backed up, her bare feet scuffing the loose dirt. His teeth sank into her shoulder, skin tore, bones broke, and warm iron flooded his mouth. The sensation taking him back to the past he tried to forget and the one coming for him, and god he wanted her to fight him. He wanted to unleash his sins, stress, and worry into the female's body. Biting down harder, his wolf's need for blood and death roared in his veins, then her hands gripped his neck, clutched his fur, and he growled with pleasure. Using his weight—he easily outweighed her—he pushed off his hind legs and she landed hard on her back.

Ansel released the bite he had on her shoulder, his teeth unlodging from skin, muscle, and bone, and he put his muzzle a sliver from her face and growled. Her brown eyes were streaked with red, and tears glittered on her cheeks as she began mumbling, chanting, and again the corrupt feel of her magic and the evil it used as power slithered over him. Her right hand, because he broke her left shoulder, came up, and he bit into her wrist before she touched him. Bone crunched in his jaw, her scream echoed in his ears, and letting go of her arm it fell to her side. He was finished with her. Ansel reared back, howled a low, guttural sound stating his revenge, and sank his teeth into her throat. Blood gushed from the wounds and into his mouth, the taste of human tinged with magic coating his tongue, and biting down harder he drove his teeth through her trachea and muscles to crunch her spinal cord. When her body went limp, her heartbeat ceased, and her lungs collapsed with her last breath, Ansel released his bite.

Six down.

He backed up, stared at the dead, then turned to find Rutger staring at him with human eyes set in a human face. His cheeks, neck, and shoulders glittered scarlet, while a darker red smeared his arms and hands. He remained naked, his muscles bunched and exposing the knotwork style of his tattoo—it started at his right shoulder to cover the muscle in black, and curving under his collarbone reached the center of his chest where its edges met the Kanin family's crest of a wolf's head. The right side depicting a wolf with a gold eye, Rutger's wolf and that of his family's, while the left side was a wolf's skull. In the skull's empty eye socket were two interlocked silver rings signifying the commitment he made to Jordyn. When Rutger took his place as alpha of the Cascade pack, the left side would match the right. The wolf would be complete.

It made him think of Dr. Hyde. What did she think of him? Did she care he didn't have a crest, would never have one, he wasn't worthy, and was killing any chance? His tattoo marked him as a criminal. Damn, the symbol of the Covey. When the spy joined them, he had dressed in his smock and cotton pants and had combed through his long hair with his fingers and was staring at him. Ansel had to shapeshift. Taking note of the blood covering, him he hoped it was enough to conceal his secret. Like mist, his human spirit weaved through him, taking his wolf's essence as the ether cradled him for a heartbeat then delivered him into the world in his human form.

Without making a show, he checked his side and saw crimson stained the feathers and sword. "What do we do now?" he asked through an exhale.

"Take the bodies to the mine," Rutger replied, then faced the spy. "Ben, thank you," he started as he took the man's forearm. "The keys are under the top stair. When you start the repairs, let me know."

"The wrongs against your mate and the death of one our own have been avenged, and their evil has been abolished," he stated with a bow. "If you need anything else from me, please call."

"I will."

Ansel and Rutger watched him jog into the darkness of early morning and disappear. "What was that about?"

"The farmhouse. He's a contractor who needs a place to live," Rutger answered as he started walking.

"Why did you show me the house if it had nothing to do with the witches?" Ansel asked. His worry could be from killing the witch, being surrounded by headless, limbless bodies, being naked, exposing the Covey's crest, but he doubted it. His instincts told him Rutger had given him a test, what it was supposed to prove he had no idea.

"I tested your reaction. And you'll help me keep an eye on it and on Ben. He's part of Cascade but had an altercation with another member over a woman. He left Trinity and has been living in the mountains, alone, for years," Rutger replied.

Could it be that easy? Rutger trusted him to keep an eye on Ben and the house? "How did you find him?"

"I was doing a survey at Butte Springs when he found me. I did a background check on him to confirm his identity and what had happened. I talked to him about it, and he said he lived in hiding long enough and the pack needed protecting. And he wanted to live a normal life." Rutger paused in the middle of the dirt road, and facing Ansel silver light of the crescent moon sliced across his crimson-stained face that was tight with his thoughts. "As normal as we're allowed," he ended and trudged to the van.

When Ansel walked into his house, it was nearing five in the morning, the sun was threatening to rise, and he was covered in the blood of witches and mud and smelled of smoke tainted with burned trash. He staggered through the living room, passing the dining room and kitchen, to open the French door and stepped outside. Being at his house, in his yard, and having the soft melody from birds playing above him and the geese squawking in front of him, eased the tension gripping his entire body.

Once they were dressed, they went back, collected the body parts, placed them in the van, burned the sleeping bags and anything else left behind, watched the fire consume the evidence, then put it out, and taking the ashes, buried them. The blood was next, they covered the spilled crimson with animal blood, Rutger got from somewhere, then headed to the mine. Every minute in the van with the bodies helped burn through the adrenaline only to have anxiety—he was sure was going to cause his nerves to explode—try to paralyze him. Everything after the mine was a blur mixed with worry, fear, and making a mental list of things he had to do when he got home.

He stripped out of his clothes, left them in a pile, went back inside and upstairs to his room, and bathroom. His house might not be as grand as Rutger's, but it didn't mean he didn't have his luxuries, like his walk-in shower. No doors and a large window let him see the mountains and valley behind his house. He turned the water on hot, stepped out, and went into his room where he sat naked on the edge of his bed and stared out the window. Minutes ticked by as the sun's gaze touched the peaks and ridges, then reached over the mountains and from the bathroom trendles of steam drifted out carrying the scent of his shampoo and soap to his empty room.

"As normal as we're allowed," he whispered, Rutger's words.

All magic-born had a fundamental understanding of the differences between them and humans and it wasn't just their appearances, it went far deeper and included their way of life. And what their traditions had been before their assimilation into the humans' world. The simplest of things, like being a rogue if you weren't part of a faction, humans would never understand. The situation had his mind reeling out of control with possibilities he didn't think would come to pass, and it all started with Jordyn's return to Trinity. Soothsayer. Fated mates. Her kidnapping and rescue. Rutger risking his life and future to deal the witches their death sentences. Their humanized world was slowly being changed to reflect the ways of the past, their true nature. The pack taking command over their way of life and the baron ruling his territory without human interference.

He was crafting division.

When Baron Kanin found out Ansel had lied about the Covey and was responsible for the attacks, what would be his punishment? Unforgiving like the past? Or politically correct like their present? If he lived. It had been two days since she attacked Lado, meaning she was going to attack another innocent or was waiting for her chance to kill him. Ansel stood, looked at the land stretching out for eternity, then made his way to the bathroom enveloped in steam and needed the hot caress of the shower. Stepping under the spray of water, it soaked his hair, making it flat against his neck and down his back, then the heated cascade rolled over his shoulders, down his stomach, sides, and thighs to tint the river rock bottom a ruddy red.

Today would be the perfect day, Bronte, he thought dryly. *I'm going to be home.*

On the drive to work, Clio had spent the time going over everything she had reported to the baron, his questions, and her answers. She kept it professional, as usual, didn't say anything about Captain Wolt because they were her suspicions and she had zero proof, and she wasn't going to make a report then change it, again.

At her office, the first thing she did was call Mandy, treated it like she was checking in, and learned Captain Wolt was at home, was ordered to stay there but would return to work the next day. She assumed the order was in response to questions from the courts regarding the attack on Daniel and Lado, and the investigation was progressing slowly. And while those details held her attention, she couldn't get Captain Wolt's mystery woman off her mind. *You're not his woman*, Clio reminded herself. Was that jealousy threatening to show its ugly face? Negative, Clio didn't care. The mystery woman was the pinnacle of his fear and the reason for the attacks. Maybe she should call Captain Good Mood and ask. Clio nearly choked on the laugh escaping her.

She scanned her email and didn't see a response from Dr. Baines. How many days had it been? It would be nice if he gave her a yes or a no and didn't act like he was ghosting her. She could use him at Celestial and the med room at Foxwood, the current investigation solidifying her decision. Because Baron Kanin was absolutely going to sign off on having a witch working at his estate when Miss Langston might be there, might be a patient. She hadn't considered Director Kanin. Her mind raced with a speech and endless list of reasons why it was necessary, then she stopped. Planning anything was moot when Dr. Baines hadn't emailed her. Clicking out, she checked her cell, nothing, checked the paperwork on her desk, and groaned. The personnel evaluations could wait, she was not prepared to focus on them, and the soldiers and enforcers paramedic recertifications were going to take ... forever. There was no way she could pull any one of them away from their jobs with the threat of another attack looming and the ongoing investigation.

"Doctor Hyde to the ER. Doctor Hyde to the ER," a female voice ordered.

Clio grabbed her cell phone, shoved it in a side pocket of her scrubs, and headed out of her office. In seconds she was passing the nurses' station, her mind racing with what it could be, and noticed no one was coming for her. Clio raced into the ER, expecting to see nurses, doctors, and a patient or two, and didn't see an emergency. She did see Tony coming around the corner. Spotting her, he skidded to a stop.

"Someone reported an attack and the sheriff's department called us. Do you want to respond?" he asked. His eyes gleamed sapphire while his shoulders filled out his blue polo and his blue cargo pants were tight around his thighs from his stance—half stopped, half waiting to take off to the med van.

"Affirmative."

"Let's roll," he said as he took off.

Clio followed close behind as they made their way in the direction of breakroom where the paramedics waited for a call or after a call they rested. Complete with kitchen, lockers, and showers, it was their home away from home. Passing the door, they continued down the hallway, met a set of double doors, and Tony already had his keycard, unlocked them, pushed them open. They headed toward the med van he considered his, Med Two, and crossed the parking lot. She got in the passenger side as he started the engine and was backing out when she buckled her seat belt.

"Human law enforcement reported the attack?" Clio asked.

If this attack matched the others and the evidence was there, no one needed human law enforcement involved. She didn't want to explain the case, the victims, and how they hadn't reported the crimes. It would put the Unseelie and Seelie court and the baron on the opposite sides of the law. And that wasn't all she was worried about, if there was confirmation it was committed by the same people, she would be forced to take it to the baron along with Captain Wolt's admission he knew the female, and about the toxin. The first report and her haste had her hesitating, she did not want to write a second, when it was basically accusing him of being behind the attacks. That was an accusation where if she was wrong there would be serious repercussions. A shard of ice slid down Clio's spine. She would make that decision when the time came, worrying about it would only ruin her focus.

"Affirmative." When she met his gaze, he smiled. "The victim's info has been entered into the system."

Without replying, Clio brought up the information and began reading. "Female. Cascade. Wight. Drea Owens, seventeen, a minor, was hit from behind and left unconscious. Sounds like a mugging. Or a hate crime." Finding out the victim was Wight it could have been either. She bet on hate crime by someone who didn't tolerate what she was. Different background, hate them. Different opinion, hate them. Different DNA, hate them.

"I thought the same thing but wasn't going to take the chance, and with human law enforcement involved. With your presence it'll prove the pack cares and you know the evidence and can confirm if it's connected to the others," Tony explained.

"True," Clio answered on auto. Her thoughts went back to the Wight, what happened, and doubted the attack had anything to with the case the enforcers were working on.

Tony drove at a respectable speed, since it wasn't an emergency, which saved her from being hurdled down the highway and a Celestial med van getting attention as they sped through the city. At the outskirts, they reached a sub-urb where trees lined the streets beside decorative light poles, the yards were landscaped, the grass green, and the houses well kept. It was an older neighborhood, the houses more ranch style than the popular log cabin look of newer homes. Clio recognized the area and knew most of the resi-dence were either Wights or human. It meant it wasn't looking like a hate crime unless they came in found an easy target, attacked, and left.

"ETA in one," Tony reported as he made a left turn. "And here we are."

Two sheriff department vehicles with their white sides, black hoods, and Paradise's County crests on the doors, were parked along the road. The crowd of eight saw the med van and backed away from the victim and both deputies. Clio recognized the woman with her blonde hair held back in a tight braid and scowl creasing her face as Deputy Harley. A friend and foe to the pack. The deputy wasn't completely convinced the enforcers had the authority to carry weapons, patrol pack property, or respond to calls. As they ap-proached, Clio couldn't help but notice Deputy Harley's stance was giving the impression she wasn't getting the an-swers she wanted. Great. Not the start she needed.

"Do we know who called the sheriff's department and not the enforcers?" Clio asked.

"Negative. Good question though," Tony replied as he pulled to the curb and parked.

Clio got out, went to the side, and opening a door grabbed a medical bag containing the basics. From what she saw as they parked no one was critically injured, and the victim was a werewolf from the pack and magic-born, a minor injury would have healed before they arrived.

Both Tony and Clio approached the scene and the cluster of people. "I'm Doctor Hyde, this is Tony, a paramedic," she announced.

"Doctor Hyde, this is Drea Owens, the victim," Deputy Harley explained. "A neighbor saw her lying on the ground and called us. Once we found out who she was, we called you."

Must have been a human. "Thank you, Deputy Harley." Clio met the girl's gaze when she looked up from her seat on the curb. Her bloodshot brown eyes were glassy and expressed her fear and embarrassment. Her pale skin held a pink tinge from sitting in the sun and she was holding a towel to the back of her head. Clio's first thought was the girl had a concussion.

"You were hit from behind?" she asked as she knelt and opened the med bag.

"Yeah," Drea answered hesitantly.

The question confirmed three things; her hearing was fine, she remembered being hit, and she was telling the truth. Clio's senses weren't as fine-tuned to lies and truths as an Illuminate or a Pureblood's, but Drea wasn't a liar, making it easier for Clio to sense them. Plus, she had Tony who was a Pureblood and would let Clio know if the girl was lying.

"Are you nauseous? Queasy?"

"No."

"Are you seeing double?" Clio asked softly, using her doctor tone.

"No."

"Good. Now let's take a look." She smiled at the girl, who smiled back as she lowered her hand while keeping a death grip on the bunched terry cloth.

Clio pulled on gloves, leaned over, and moved the thick hair to the side to see the injury. Raised pink skin showed signs of bruising, and moving more hair, Clio couldn't see torn skin or other signs of a deeper wound. "Have you shapeshifted?" Wights who hadn't shifted were susceptible to sickness, diseases, and injuries lasted longer, their physiology being basically human. Her information said she was part of Cascade, that could mean she had shapeshifted, or her parents were hoping she was going to. If she had shifted, she was going to heal quickly. If she hadn't, she would be considered late, and the bruises were going to last longer.

The girl looked around, her gaze skating over the deputies and the others watching when her stare landed on a woman, who nodded to her. Mom? "Yes, ma'am."

"Is she your mom?" Clio asked. She watched the girl scan the crowd again like she was looking for someone, then pointed to a woman.

"Yeah, she's right there."

"What's her name?" Weird the woman wasn't fussing over her daughter.

"Barbara Owens," Drea answered.

"Excellent. You're healing but the headache will last for a couple of hours and the bruise blooming will be gone by tonight. Have you told Deputy Harley how this happened?" Clio looked from Drea to the deputy.

"No, ma'am."

"She wouldn't talk until you arrived," Deputy Harley added.

"Drea, do you know who hit you?" Clio pulled her gloves off and put them in a pocket of the med bag.

"Yeah." Drea looked at the ground, twisted the towel in her hands, and drew her knees closer to her chest.

"Want to tell me?" Clio waited for Drea to meet her gaze.

Inhaling, exhaling, she faced Clio. "We were training," she said like it was a confession.

Drea didn't have a concussion. She did, however, have a story. "Explain." Clio dropped her kind doctor tone and inched toward her enforcer's authority.

"I turn eighteen next month and will start my two years with the soldiers. We were practicing self-defense. It's n-no one's f-fault, we were p-practicing, that's all," she stammered.

"It's all right, I understand. So you know who hit you?" Clio pushed.

"We did," a girl answered as she and another girl stepped forward.

"And you two are?" Clio asked.

"Sophia."

"Hannah."

"Are your parents here?" Clio asked.

"No, ma'am," Sophia answered.

"Are the both of you starting your two years?" Clio continued her questioning. Seeing there wasn't anything criminal happening, several people from the crowd left and those standing in the yards returned to their own business.

"Yes, ma'am," they answered in unison.

"I suggest the three of you stop training in the street and scaring your neighbors. They don't need to call law enforcement. The soldiers, who are professionals, will teach you self-defense," Clio lectured. She wasn't going to explain the extent of the training while human law enforcement was present. "And if you want to start early, train with a professional."

"Yes, ma'am."

"Do you understand, Drea?" Clio asked, meeting her gaze.

"I just thought, if I was better ..." Drea began and stopped.

"Why?" Clio closed the med bag and standing helped Drea to her feet.

"I'm a Wight. We all are." As if to back up what Drea said, both girls nodded their heads.

Damn, she knew exactly how they felt, and for second saw her eighteen-year-old self in Drea. "Ladies, if you pay attention to the instructors, do as they say, I mean do everything they say, and work hard, you won't have a problem," Clio explained.

"How do you know?" Hannah countered. "You're a doctor."

"I am a doctor who has served with the enforcers." She shrugged her shoulders. Had, past tense. "I'm also a Wight, and being one isn't an excuse not to succeed." Clio met their gazes.

"You?" Drea asked, her disbelief in her voice.

"Yes, me. I didn't let it stop me and it doesn't define me. Now you're going to tell Deputy Harley and Deputy Elm everything that happened. Then your mom is going to take you three to your house, and you three will explain what happened to Sophia and Hannah's parents." Clio turned her attention to Barbara and said, "My report will go to the enforcers, if you want a copy you may contact communications in twenty-four hours."

"Thank you, Doctor Hyde." Barbara hesitated and eyed Drea for a second. "Doctor Hyde, will this affect Drea's chances to become a soldier?"

"And enforcer," Drea quickly added.

"If the sheriff's department doesn't make a formal report, it won't," Clio answered. She gave Deputy Harley a sideways glance and saw her give a barely there nod. *Good.* "It means you have to stop training in the streets."

"Thank you." Barbara closed the distance between her and Drea at the same time the girls went to her side.

Clio grabbed the med bag and slung it over her shoulder. "Thank you, Deputy Harley."

"No problem."

She met Tony's stare and they headed back to Med Two. Once she put the bag away and was sitting in the passenger seat, Tony started the engine, turned the van around, and they were headed out of the suburb and back to Celestial. She couldn't help but smile as she thought about the girls practicing self-defense.

"Impressive," Tony began, breaking the silence between them and the chatter of the radio and beeps from the console.

"What?" Clio wasn't paying attention to Tony or the drive, she was focused on the girls and how their need to better themselves because they're Wights hit too damn close to home. Is that what she sounded like when her default setting screamed at her? Probably. Did she let it define her? Affirmative, it explained the default setting. She needed to work on ignoring it.

"You not only got one teenager to confess, but three, and they told you why they did it. And Deputy Harley isn't going to make a report and Deputy Elm wasn't surprised."

Clio laughed. "They're pack, it's a little different. No one was hurt, and the deputies understand they're teenagers. Human or non-human, kids are kids."

"Did you really do two years as a soldier?" he asked. His voice changing the mood and the atmosphere between them.

"Affirmative. After it was over, I started medical school, then was promoted to enforcer."

"I guess medical school was too easy?" he joked.

"Something like that." Clio turned to look at him and saw the half grin curving his mouth, his auburn hair grazing the collar of his polo, and thought about his invitation to dinner. Was she saying no because he was a Pureblood, and she wasn't? Or because he was right there. Close enough to touch. Where was Captain Wolt? Out of reach and keeping his secrets from the pack. She didn't need that in her life.

"Why did you become a paramedic?" she asked instead of dwelling on her thoughts.

"Did the always professional Doctor Hyde just ask a personal question?" Tony returned as he glanced at her.

"I have my moments," she responded dryly.

"We all do. I became a paramedic because it allows me to be in medicine and outside of the hospital at the same time. Plus, I get to drive really fast without getting a ticket," he answered.

"I am very aware of how much you love to drive fast," Clio responded.

Tony chuckled in triumph, then let a comfortable silence weave between them. The sounds of the tires, the beeps, and the radio faded as she dove into her thoughts of Captain Wolt, the person responsible for the attacks, how he knew them, and why was he hiding information when it could save someone's life? Did he understand what he could lose? His rank as captain. The pack. His kith and kin. He had to. She knew Captain Wolt wasn't stupid, it was one of the things she admired about him. Maybe she should call him, he was at home. That was stupid. What was she going to say, *Hey the toxin came from a ghoul, where the hell do you get that, and how did you know? And why don't you confess to whatever it is you do know, then I'll feel better. Oh yeah, Tony is flirting with me, would really like it if it was you.* If she was alone, she would have forehead slapped herself.

Director Kanin had to know what his BFF, his brother in arms, Captain Wolt, was doing, hiding, right?

CHAPTER FIFTEEN

Ansel slid the clasp, heard it click, and straightening stood in front of the mirror wearing his uniform. After two days of inactivity the black T-shirt, jeans, boots, and holster felt good and returning to work made him feel useful. He looked at his reflection and flinched when he saw the dark circles under his eyes from not sleeping all night and watching the clock's slow progression and wondering when she was going to come for him. At three in the morning, he was positive he would have given his life if she showed up and started a fight or showed up to face him. Anything. Her absence meant she wasn't done proving she could take his life apart piece by piece. What was she doing? Who would be next? His thoughts latched onto Dr. Hyde and the compassion she should him when she saw Lado's condition. He made her a target.

With frustration nipping at him and images from his life spiraling in front of him, he gave the mirror his back, leaving his haunted reflection behind him, and left his bedroom and headed downstairs. The only impression someone lived in the house and it hadn't been staged to sell was the indentation on the couch from where he had slept. It added to the weight from the night, the last couple of days, the attacks, and the future attacks. There were going to be more, he felt it like he felt her presence when she entered his territory. He was going to the office, communications, he corrected himself, because it wasn't an office, and it was his chance to try and find her. His cell dinged from its place on the table, its shrillness making him jump, and he shook his head with his nervousness. With long strides he was at the table in four steps, the screen displaying communication's number, and for second his heart seized in his chest with the fear they were going to tell him to stay home or worse there was another attack. And it would be worse. She wasn't going to be satisfied with *attacking* those closest to him, the next time she struck she would make a statement by murdering her victim. With his pulse in his ears and his heart sinking to his knees, he grabbed the cell, and read Mandy's message.

That's all.

He stopped at the gate to Foxwood and paused before following the instructions Mandy messaged him. The area was clear of construction equipment, vehicles, workers, and looked as if nothing had changed, save for the difference in the gate. What a difference a couple of days made. He whistled as he lowered the window, stretched his arm out, then flattened his hand on the palm vein reader. In a second it turned green, and he entered his assigned number code. The pad blinked green at the same time the gate rattled and started its trek across the two-lane entrance. Ansel inched the truck forward, and when clear drove over the guide and slowly, to inspect the work that had been done, drove the mile to communications.

The scene at the gate didn't match the activity taking place around the office and garage. There were workers, trucks, cement trucks, and forklifts unloading more lumber and other materials. The office building was closed in as was the garage, and he saw workers through the bay doors as they worked on the lifts inside. With his approach, he was mildly surprised to see his parking spot open, and pulling in, he parked, killed the engine, and suddenly felt like an outsider. A million questions raced through his mind. Did they know his connection to her and the Covey? Were they going to charge him with Lado's attack? Was Lado awake and able to tell them what happened? Did she tell Lado Ansel was the reason she had tortured him?

Mandy came around the corner of communications, waved, then pointed toward the front of the house, or so he assumed. Ansel got out of his truck, slammed the door closed behind him, and met her.

"What's going on?"

"Baron Kanin and the director are waiting for you," she reported, her violet-blue eyes narrowing on him.

"Thank you," he replied, trying to keep his uncertainty from weakening his voice. The shame from having been ordered to stay home and the disciplinary action taken had to have created doubt in the minds of the enforcers about his leadership.

He waited for her to start back, then fell in behind her. When she turned to go to communications, he continued. His heart stopped for what felt like an hour, then slamming in his chest pushed his pulse. Ansel inhaled, exhaled, struggled for calm and plastered a neutral mask on his face. Rutger, the baron, baroness, Quinn, Luke, and Gavin were waiting while watching the construction. They all turned to see him walk up, then went back to watching the commotion.

"Ansel," Baron Kanin greeted.

"Sir." Ansel nodded, then stood beside Rutger. "I can't believe the work they've done."

"Agreed. It's like they're working twenty-four hours a day," Quinn added.

"They are," Baroness Kanin commented. Everyone looked at her as she gave Baron Kanin a narrowed gaze. "Twenty-four hours a day. All night. All day."

"The completion of the Enforcer's office benefits the entire territory," Baron Kanin countered.

"Affirmative, Baron Kanin." She bowed her head. "So you've said multiple times." She eyed him, then turned, and left them.

"You have an investigation to discuss and solve," Baron Kanin said with a growl in his voice. Turning, he followed the baroness into the house."

Clouds blocked the sun, giving the building a gray hue, while a thicker mass was building on the ridge. That's what they needed was a thunderstorm. Ansel watched the rainclouds for another second, then stared forward, not paying attention to the construction but pretending to pay attention. With talk of the investigation, tension wove through his shoulders, tightening as it tracked back and forth.

"Quinn, I'll brief Ansel on the investigation. You and Luke head over to the Summit and oversee the finalizations and when they're complete escort the workers off the property," Rutger ordered.

"Affirmative, sir," Quinn replied.

Rutger waited for them to create distance, then met Ansel's gaze. "We've had a call about a group of magic-born, not from the area, asking questions about the pack. It could be our attackers."

Ansel doubted it. She wouldn't compromise the mission by exposing herself. Still, she had allowed the elder to hear the prayer and left Lado alive, meaning he could identify them. Damn, he wanted to believe she thought she was untouchable.

"Did Quinn question the reporting party?"

"Affirmative, and they gave vague descriptions of the people they talked to, but it's a place to start," Rutger replied.

"Agreed." What the hell was she planning?

Clio eased the crossover over the storm drain between the street and the parking lot, then drove through and picked a place to park. Since it was her day off, she slept in, exercised, and afterwards headed to the coffee place Tony's cousin owned. A good cup of coffee was exactly what she needed. Checking her cell, she saw messages about the med room, junk in her email, and happy she wasn't needed, got out of the car and headed inside.

"Hello, what could I get you?" a young woman with green eyes asked. Her power reached out, a soft hum along her instincts, sensing if Clio was magic-born or human.

Shapeshifter. She wondered if Tony's cousin employed pack members. The girl stared at her, forcing Clio to answer. "Not sure." She should have asked Tony what kind of coffee it was. "Someone had gotten me a cup of plain coffee. Wait, it was roasted here by the owner. I think?"

"She'll have the White Peak blend, and a cherry and chocolate filled pastry," Tony ordered, then faced Clio. "You really did like the coffee."

"Maybe. What are you doing here?" she asked. She lined her blue eyes with soft brown liner to bring out the honey, applied bronze eyeshadow to accentuate her tan, mascara, left her lips their natural pink, and wore her naturally curly hair down. In a loose, white T-shirt, denim capris, and Hawaiian print flip-flops, which reminded her of Miss Langston, she was not the Dr. Hyde from Celestial. This was comfy Clio on her day off.

"Having coffee," he replied as his eyes took her in. His grin was curving his lips and making his sapphire gaze darken as they stared at each other for a second too long.

She broke eye contact, to relieve her nerves, and asked, "How much?"

"Already taken care of, Doc," Tony said, stopping her. "Liv, will you add it to mine?"

"Yes, sir," she answered with a smile.

"Thank you again." Clio met Liv's stare and could swear she felt darts shooting from their green depths. Jealous much? With that she felt a tinge of *that's right* and shut it down. Nothing good would come from thoughts like that.

"I have a table if you would like to join me?" he asked, his usual confidence and flirting weakening under the question, giving it a serious feel. His auburn hair had been combed through with his fingers, creating waves, leaving the ends grazing his black T-shirt that had the graphics of a movie across the cotton hugging his muscled chest and arms, and his jeans slung low on his hips ended in worn boots.

"Well, you did just buy me coffee and chocolate. How can I refuse?" Clio asked, trying to stop her mind from going places it shouldn't.

"Aw, a weakness. It's over here." He waved a hand in the direction of the table and waited for her to pass him.

"What is this?" Clio asked as she hung her purse over the back of the chair and sat down. Beside a half cup of coffee, and what remained of a strawberry danish, were papers, a notebook, a pen, and highlighters, making it look like homework.

"Homework." When he sat down, his six foot plus height and broad shoulders didn't feel as imposing and she wasn't staring at his chest.

"What are you studying, if you don't mind me asking?" She scanned the papers and saw medical terms, then recognized the book.

He looked away from her like he wasn't going to answer the question, and Clio accepted the silence when Liv delivered the coffee and pastry. "Thank you."

When Liv left them alone, he confessed, "I want a job at the medical facility on Foxwood." Then, he looked down at his notebook.

"Foxwood. You said you like being a paramedic, you've claimed Med Two as yours, and you like driving the thing like it's a race car," Clio replied.

"I do, but if there's an opportunity to do more—"

Clio interrupted him and asked, "Is it what you want? This?" And she pointed to the book and notebook. "I was there when you drove breakneck speeds to Foxwood, then witnessed the effectiveness with which you do your job. You live for it like an adrenalin junkie."

He looked away, his eyes skating over the bakery, and back to her. "This is different. I can be a registered nurse and move onto a physician assistant. It's Foxwood, who wouldn't want to work there?" he asked.

She knew of one person. "Negative. Not going to happen. I'm the administrator and it won't happen." Clio met his sapphire challenge with her Wight blue glare.

Tony leaned over the table, bringing his face closer to hers, the seriousness in his narrowed gaze killing the easy going grin he had donned. His fox sat in the swirling blue and amber of his eyes. "Because I'm not Captain Wolt?"

Fuck you, were the first words blazing a path through her mind. Then *fuck him*. Captain Wolt hadn't paid attention to her and he was capable of making her life miserable. One second. Two seconds. She was not going to lose her composure or her tempter in a bakery over coffee and chocolate. "Aw, a weakness." Clio let his words hang between them, and when he sat back, she took her coffee, sipped, was taken back by the richness, and set her cup on the table. She let him stew in his *weakness* for several seconds. "If you gave me half a chance to explain, I would have told you, Foxwood needs med van drivers."

Scarlet crept up his neck to sear his cheeks and azar rolled over his eyes. "I thought ... I mean. Shit, I'm stupid. I'm sorry, Doctor Hyde. Please accept my apology."

"Apology accepted. For the record, I never let my personal life, if I had one, get in the way of what is best for my pack, Celestial, and what will be the medical facility on Foxwood. That includes Cascade's territory and the klatch. If you love being a paramedic and driving like a crazy man, then continue to do it," Clio began. "Don't sacrifice your passion for a position at what will be nothing more than a clinic. Yes, I believe there will be traumas, but very few. And like I said, Foxwood will need a paramedic and a driver."

Her thoughts went straight to Miss Langston. The witches had targeted her because of what they thought she was, and who else was going to do the same? Suddenly, she felt sorry for the woman and covering every security risk felt daunting.

"If I hadn't screwed this up, can I apply for the job?" He met her gaze and gave her his best grin and she couldn't stop from smiling back.

"Affirmative. But I don't want to take you away from your homework," she teased. Clio picked up her pastry and bit into the flaky crust to have a bite of butter, dark chocolate, and cherries. She would have let an appreciative sigh out if Tony wasn't staring at her with a sapphire gaze that held an amber sheen.

He laughed a low rumble that was free and uninhibited. "I think I'll survive." Tony closed his notebook, the textbook, and set them aside. "How's your pastry?"

"Very, very good," Clio replied. "I think I found my new favorite place."

"I realize you won't have dinner with me. Think we could meet here sometime?" He held her gaze, and for the first time let her see he was being sincere, and his grin of confidence hid a man with a shy streak.

"Affirmative." Clio smiled at him and bit into her pastry.

"Don't worry, Doc, your secret is safe with me." Tony smiled, his eyes gleamed like sapphires, and he laughed his low rumble. "I won't tell a soul." He stopped smiling to mimic a key to his lips, then put the key in an invisible pocket.

"You're very funny." Clio laughed, sat back in her seat, and for the first time in a long time felt relaxed and comfortable.

"Have you ever gone rock climbing?" he asked. Picking his cup up, he looked at her over the rim.

"Negative."

"Would you go?"

"Will there be coffee and chocolate?" she replied with a smile.

"Affirmative."

Clio smiled.

At the front of communications in their semiprivate corner, Ansel sat across from Rutger, while folders littered the desktop and the computer screen with the Covey's symbol glared at him.

"If we can get more witnesses, we'll make a map of where they've been seen and maybe determine where they're staying. They can't be in Trinity, someone would have noticed a group of unknown magic-born," Rutger pointed out. "The enforcers would have sensed them."

"I called every motel/hotel and campground, nothing. It doesn't mean they aren't camping, like the witches."

"True. I'll have patrols check the rural areas," Rutger responded.

The longer Ansel stared at the symbol the more it fed his guilt and fear. She was capable of concealing her presence from weaker magic-born, or like those giving vague descriptions, she could confuse one's thoughts. "Who do you have watching?"

"The baron has his shadows deployed, and I have several enforcers monitoring the outskirts. Plus, I've put soldiers in a couple of magic-born owned businesses. I'm hoping they'll need supplies, and expose themselves." Rutger flipped through the folders, checked his cell, then repeated his folder flipping.

"You doing all right?" Ansel asked. It had been seventy-two hours since they dealt with the witches, it was like a fresh wound, and killing wasn't something that went away.

Rutger's head jerked up and he met his gaze. "Affirmative."

"Director, the baron is yelling for you." Mandy stood up from her desk. "He's headed this way."

"What the fuck?" Rutger mumbled as he stood. He marched to the door and flung it open to a darkened sky and a round of thunder that drowned out the machinery.

"Rutger, it's Jordyn," Baron Kanin stated, ignoring the first rain drops. His eyes gleamed gold with his wolf, as his power circled him, carrying his fury.

"What about her?" Rutger asked.

"She told me about the witches," he said in a rush.

"I handled it," Rutger countered.

"You may have dispatched the witches, but you left Flint alive. He has Jordyn," Baron Kanin growled. Lightning streaked across the sky, a deep bellow, as if the storm knew what was happening.

Rutger's black T-shirt was getting peppered with rain drops, while humidity began inching in and the temperature had dropped. If he noticed the weather, he hid it as he stared at the baron with a bewildered look as if the man was speaking another language.

"Flint," he whispered.

Ansel watched them stare at each other as if neither knew what the other was saying and they couldn't comprehend the situation. He knew this and didn't doubt himself. "Do you want backup?" he asked, breaking their trance.

Baron Kanin nailed his gold glare on Ansel as Kellen came around the corner. "Affirmative. Both of you go to Rutger's house. Where is Aydian?"

"Patrols," Kellen answered. "What's going on?"

"Flint is at Rutger's house. He has Jordyn," Ansel answered.

Without another word, Kellen's eyes blazed amber with his wolf then he turned, disappeared behind communications, and Ansel heard a truck start.

"Radio Aydian, explain what's going on, and have him meet us there," Rutger ordered as he snapped out of his shock. "Priority One."

"Copy." Ansel left Rutger and the baron and wanted to yell that using Jordyn as bait had been a bad idea, damn bad idea, damn fool. Getting in his truck, he couldn't start the engine fast enough, and backed up. By the time he was headed away from communications, Rutger and the baron were ahead of him. To cover himself, Ansel wasn't going to use his cell to call Aydian, he was going to make sure communication was on everyone's console and everyone received updates. "Base."

"This is Base," Mandy responded.

"Alert Aydian, he is to respond to Director Kanin's house. Priority One. Miss Langston," Ansel reported.

"Copy." He waited as the silence stretched into seconds that felt like hours while more thick clouds rolled over the mountain ridge to shroud the cerulean sky in gray. "Captain Wolt, Aydian is en route. Do you need further assistance?"

"Negative." Ansel blew through the gate, hit the main road, and losing sight of Rutger cursed. Did Flint have other followers? He didn't know. Damn. He wasn't going to make a mistake by not having enough backup, and if it got the attention of the Covey, he wasn't going to put anyone's life in danger. He was going to need more enforcers. "Base, alert Quinn and Luke."

"Copy. Quinn and Luke are en route," Mandy replied.

Flint. Bronte. What the hell else could go wrong? He took the thought back, he didn't want to know. Weaving through traffic, Ansel struggled to catch up with Rutger, and saw him at Butte Springs losing control over his wolf, going Bestial, and feared the same thing was going to happen if Flint succeeded in hurting Jordyn. Killing her. If Jordyn died, Rutger wasn't far behind. Either he died during the transition into his Bestial form, or the baron was going to have to put him down, like an animal. Ansel whispered another string of curses—he wasn't going to lose his kith—and wanted to roar. If the security upgrades had been completed this never would have happened. She would have been protected. Seeing Rutger ahead of him, he pushed the truck faster, got behind him at the same time Aydian fell behind Ansel. Three speeding Cascade trucks were going to get attention, making him wonder if Rutger was going to call human law enforcement before someone called and reported them.

Rutger took the corner into his driveway, the truck leaning from the speed, and skidded to a stop in front of his house. Ansel slowed as three sheriff deputies turned, followed by two unmarked units.

That was quick. He stopped at the entrance with Kellen behind him, as Aydian parked opposite from him, killed the engine, and got out. Quinn and Luke were next to park their trucks, and joining them they watched Rutger stand at the edge of the woods beside his house, staring at nothing.

"Detective Cliff with the Paradise County homicide. Mr. Kanin, you think Mr. Platt is here?" he asked. His voice, the arrogance it held, and his demeanor told them all he didn't believe them.

"I'm Baron Kanin, and I know he's here. I was on the phone with Miss Langston."

Rutger turned his gaze from the woods to the baron, then the detective. "He's out there."

"They aren't in the house?" Ansel asked.

"Negative," Rutger growled. A shadow of his wolf rose above him, its visible form wrapping around his human body like a vapor molding to him.

"You're sure they aren't in the house? Why would he take her into the woods when there's a damned storm brewing?"

Detective Cliff wiped rain from his forehead as thunder rumbled and lightning blasted through the gray.

Rutger slowly turned his head to face the detective with gold eyes, his skin wearing a sheen from sweat and rain. "Why would he murder people then kidnap her to begin with?"

"Easy, son," Baron Kanin cautioned. "Focus on Jordyn."

"She's out there. I can feel her fear." Rutger's eyes blazed gold, his shoulders heaved with his inhale, and exhaling he growled, "I'm going to kill him."

"Murder is against the law," the detective started.

"No shit," Rutger growled.

"Like kidnapping."

"What are you saying, Detective?" Baron Kanin questioned.

"Well, Detective Cliff?" Rutger pushed.

"Watch yourself, Mr. Kanin, you'll make this situation worse than it needs to be."

"He's a serial killer who tried killing my mate and has come back," Rutger growled. "What have you done about it? Nothing."

"You don't know what he's doing, and I don't know her part in this. I do know you're a suspect in the disappearances of six people. Regardless of what happens here, Mr. Kanin, be warned I'll be questioning you about them," Detective Cliff countered.

Right. After what happened to Jordyn, the detective saw Flint as a human and a victim and saw Rutger as an animal. Ansel had a job to do, and it was making sure there weren't other witches. "Cover the perimeter and make sure it's clear," Ansel ordered. "If there are witches, detain them. By any means."

The detective gave him a sideways glance, telling Ansel he was challenging his authority. Ansel smiled as the four enforcers ignored him and spread out. "Captain of Enforcers Ansel Wolt. This is Cascade property."

"Mine," Rutger growled, getting everyone's attention. The next second, they watched him race into the woods with the baron following close behind.

"Mr. Kanin, stop," the detective ordered. "I order you to stop."

No one was going to be able to stop Rutger, not even the baron, while his fated mate was in danger. Ansel saw the situation spiraling out of control as Detective Cliff barked orders and with three deputies took off after Rutger, leaving the others to watch the driveway. Ansel shadowed Rutger, intending on watching him, and if he started to lose himself to the beast, he would be there to help. Or run interference between him and human law enforcement. Ansel would also be there to protect the baron.

"Report," he ordered over the radio.

"Clear." Kellen.

"Clear." Quinn.

"Clear." Luke.

"Clear." Aydian.

"Move in, hold your positions." His stress level eased a little with the report there were no other witches, unless they were shielding themselves the same way they had at Butte Springs. If they were, they would be dealt with. Like the others.

"Be advised no one is to come or go," Ansel ordered.

He kept his distance as he wove through the woods, the trees above him swaying from the wind, the rain pelting his face as it intensified to soak the grass, shrubs, and pine needles. He kept track of the enforcers' positions while using his senses to search the area for witches. When he felt the evil of their magic, he prepared to detain them anyway possible without getting into trouble with law enforcement. Ansel slowed his run, then stopped when he saw Rutger, the baron, the detective, and deputies had all stopped. Moving to get a better view, he took his position, and his heart seized, his lungs felt deflated, and his pulse sounded in his ears.

"This is not happening," he mumbled. Detective Cliff had been wrong. Very, very wrong.

Flint, with his yellow/white matted hair, bloodied lips, and dirt-stained skin and clothes, held a gun to Jordyn's head, its barrel touching her soaked hair. Rain had caused her eye makeup to run down her pale cheeks, making black lines, her T-shirt was soaked to her thin frame, and her knees had sunk in the up turned sludge. Ansel could smell blood in the air while death gripped the area in its cold claws and Flint's evil intertwined through it all, making the air feel like steel.

Standing in front of her with tension racing across his shoulders, Rutger's fisted hands were at his sides, his stance ready to lunge at Jordyn or Flint. While he looked at his mate on her knees, Detective Cliff wasted no time trying to save the human by convincing Flint to give up the gun. As if watching from above and wanting to add to the misery, the gates opened for the storm, letting thunder crash across the sky, and lightning flashed above them, making it hard for Ansel to hear anything. Like thick ribbons, fog wove from the lake, between trees, and over the July heated ground. He didn't have to hear them when evil leached from where they were and slithered, like a snake, over the distance as if searching for its own. Tangled in its mix was another power, another magic, its feel sharp, strong, and familiar.

Cascade. Pack.

Despite Rutger's wolf taking more of him, Ansel knew it was Jordyn, the pack's soothsayer, and her magic. Leaving his position, he closed in on the group in case Rutger lost control.

"Hold your positions," he ordered over the radio.

No one replied, they weren't supposed to, they would watch and only if it looked like Rutger or the baron were in danger would they break from their positions. Ansel didn't have to order them to do anything else. Stopping beside a pine tree, its limbs protecting him from the worst of the rain, Ansel watched Detective Cliff try to save a serial killer.

"Give me the gun, Mr. Platt."

"No," Flint screamed. "I did it." His eyes were wide with his insanity, his face pitched with fury, and his lips pulled back from his broken teeth. He yelled, only to have thunder steal his words, the rain showering him, and he hit Jordyn on the side of the head with the barrel of the gun.

"Calm down. What did you do?" Detective Cliff asked.

"I killed them. They betrayed me," Flint answered. "Betrayed me. Their savior."

Ansel stilled, not believing what he heard, what Flint said, confessed to. Was it the witches they murdered? Negative. Searching the scene and around the tree where he had carved symbols deep in its flesh, were human body parts half buried in the wet dirt, glistening leaves, and pine needles. Damn, it couldn't be. And if it was, who the hell found them and moved the bodies?

"Mr. Platt, lower the weapon. We can help you," Detective Cliff pleaded.

He doesn't need help, he needs a bullet to the brain, Ansel thought. How was Rutger listening to a detective tell a serial killer he would help him when Jordyn was on her knees with a gun to her head?

Humans.

Division.

They would protect their own.

"No." With the barrel, Flint hit Jordyn harder, making her head snap to the left, and she closed her eyes. When she straightened, he looked down at her and tightened his grip. "My pendulum."

"Mr. Platt, release her," Detective Cliff demanded.

"No. Shut up. No."

Ansel tensed, readying for Rutger to react when magic, thick and possessive, forced his gaze to Jordyn. She was staring at Rutger, her eyes like liquid copper was swirling in them and where there should have been fear in their depths, there wasn't any. There was hate. There was the darkness of revenge. Ansel knew it was truth when Rutger's wolf backed down and his human self gained control. It was Jordyn, his fated mate, and powerful soothsayer. Something was going to happen. He was staring at them, the connection they had, and the power between them when thunder rolled across the sky.

A new torrent of rain relentlessly fell on them to break through his thoughts as the world shifted on its axis and slid into slow motion. In front of him in its gory detail, Flint pulled the trigger, the rain ate the blue/gray smoke from the gun, at the same time Jordyn's eyes closed and she fell to her side, landing in the sodden pine needles, and upturned mud, blood, and human parts. Time snapped back, thrusting him into reality as Rutger rushed to her side, and Flint's body folded in on itself. The honeyed scent of gun powder mixed with the tang from blood, and sweetness of brains saturated the air, robbing the rain from its cleansing power.

It was over.

"Get medical," Detective Cliff ordered over the clashing.

As if sensing the end, the rain slowed to a drizzle, letting the sun break through the thick clouds, its shards hitting the ground around him and intensifying the thick moisture in the air. No one else moved, they stared at the scene as if they couldn't believe what had happened while Ansel stopped himself from leaving his position and rushing forward.

Clicking the mic to the radio he ordered, "Hold your positions. Target is down. I repeat, target is down."

CHAPTER SIXTEEN

"The rain is letting up," Tony said as he held the door open, letting Clio walk through first.

"Thank you." When she was outside of the bakery, she was thankful the thunderstorm was passing, the sun was trying to beat back the clouds, and the rain had turned to a gentle mist.

"As much as I hate the lightning because of fires, we can always use rain." Tony fell in step with her, and they started toward the parking lot together. "I wish the good outweighed the bad."

"Absolutely." Clio was suddenly aware of his closeness, the feel of him beside her as they walked and the way his hand brushed her side with his gait.

"Would have been better if we had been at my place." With a sideways glance, he gave her his flirting grin, and his eyes gleamed like sapphires. "I'm off of Iron Cliffs, twenty acres of woods."

Clio smiled despite herself, understanding that was the grin he used when he was toying with her. She had witnessed his serious smile and the uncertainty sitting beneath. The afternoon with coffee and pastries, and casual conversation was a nice way to spend her day off, then the storm added another element. The thunder like the pounding of a heart. The lightning like blinding passion. And soft touches from the rain. Its intensity gripped her.

She brushed it off, didn't know what she was doing besides ignoring the existence of Captain Wolt, his secrets, the closeness of Tony, and whatever was happening between them. What was happening between them? Why was Captain Wolt ignoring her one minute and teasing her the next? Clio didn't have the answers, besides knowing he was going to drive her insane. She inhaled and exhaled her anxiety as the light drizzle sent a chill over her skin, the humidity thickened, and a rumble of thunder sounded like it was rolling over the mountains. It wasn't passing. It had called for reinforcements and was getting ready to unleash its wrath.

"I didn't mean to ruin the mood," Tony offered.

"What? Sorry. That much land, it must be beautiful." Clio shoved the questions about Captain Wolt down into a cage and stopped to face him. The gleam in his eyes was bright against the gray sky, his auburn hair held a sheen from the rain, and the shoulders of his T-shirt were darkened. "I enjoyed myself. This was great."

"I hear a but coming." Tony's smile fell as he held her gaze.

"*But* I have a lot going on and if I started something with you, I wouldn't have any time. As it is my cell is connected to the side of my head, and when they call, I have to leave," she explained. Then realized it hadn't made a peep all afternoon.

"I know who you are, Doctor Hyde. It doesn't mean we couldn't see one another. I think the coffee and pastry helped in my cause, and I'm growing on you," Tony countered with a renewed grin.

"Maybe." She started walking toward her car in a valiant effort to hide her smile. When she stood at the driver's door, she found Tony standing several yards from his mid-sized, dark green, lifted 4x4 truck with light bars, big tires, massive grille guard. "Is that your commuter car?"

"Yes, ma'am. You never know when you need to head into the mountains to get away from it all." Tony paused, his thoughts changing his features. "You said maybe. And I meant to rock climbing."

"I did."

"And?"

"Yes, you're growing on me. Maybe, rock climbing," she replied. What the hell was she doing? And why did she feel excited and guilty?

"Another secret. It shall not pass my lips," Tony promised, his low rumble of a laugh gave away his victory, and she liked hearing it. "See you at work, Doctor Hyde."

Clio shook her head, unlocked the door, and got behind the steering wheel. After starting the engine, she watched in the rearview mirror as he walked across the parking lot, his jeans molding to his rear and thighs, *stop staring*, and he got in his truck.

Stop, she warned. Backing out of his parking spot, he made his way to the street and then out of sight. She waited, letting the afternoon, her secrets, and his company filter through her thoughts and what the repercussions were going to be for letting herself think she was capable of having a relationship. If she did go out with him and was called away, maybe he would realize it wasn't going to work. *And if he stuck around and the relationship worked?*

She laughed as she put the crossover in reverse and backing up, the console started beeping, chiming, and transcripts of calls filled the screen. Clio ignored them. She wasn't an enforcer, it was her day off, and if they needed her, they would have called. She drove out from the parking lot to the street, turned in the direction of her townhouse, and started home. Just the thought of seeing Tony on a personal level had her thinking about Captain Wolt. Why did he get to her the way he did? Was she attracted to Tony? It was time to be honest with herself. No, it wasn't like that. From his sapphire eyes, auburn/blond hair, gorgeous smile, muscled chest and thighs, yes, he was handsome, and no doubt would make someone's heart melt as well as their body. Like Liv. But it wasn't her. And why wasn't she attracted to him? Clio groaned with frustration. Because she liked the unattainable Captain Wolt. His dark gaze that held his demons and a life she didn't know about. His strength. The power of his wolf. His damned silence that gave him a bad boy edge. She might as well be sixteen.

An ER doctor, personal physician to Baron and Baroness Kanin, the Kanin family, administrator in charge of the future med room at Foxwood, and this was her personal life. She was an idiot. Turning onto the main highway, an emergency alarm blasted from the console then blinked and shifted to the current call page. Clio glanced at it, saw enforcers had been ordered to Director Kanin's residence, and skimming down tried to read Captain Wolt's orders without hitting the car in front of her. Not wanting to risk anyone's life, she pulled off the highway and into the first parking lot. The transcripts continued scrolling, each one sending a wave of guilt to wash over her, and questions like why didn't they call her trampled a path across her mind. *I'm not an enforcer*, Clio reminded herself for the second time. She took her cell and dialed Captain Wolt, then waited as it rang and rang.

"Come on," Clio pleaded.

"Captain Wolt." Ansel saw the number on the screen, did not want to talk to her, did not want to talk to anyone, he had a job to do, and didn't try to keep the irritation out of voice.

"It's Doctor Hyde. Does Miss Langston need medical?" she asked, the words rushing from her.

"Negative."

She wanted to reach through the phone and choke him. "You can't be serious? Her life was threatened for a second time, does she need Doctor Carrion?" Miss Langston needed someone to talk to; this could set her back.

"Negative. She's refusing medical at this time." Ansel got behind the steering wheel of his truck and sat back, then started counting in an attempt to quell his frustration.

While Jordyn cleaned up from having been in mud churned with blood and body parts, the detectives and sheriff deputies questioned Rutger about the missing witches and accused him of killing Flint. No one touched him. No one moved. But Rutger had motive and reason and was a werewolf so it had to be him. He wasn't going to say anything about the feel of pack magic overriding Flint's evil, if he felt it so did the baron and Rutger. Especially Rutger.

"If she needs me or Doctor Carrion, don't hesitate to call," Clio stated. "I'm serious, Captain Wolt, do not hesitate."

"Copy. I'll relay the message," he replied. "Is that all?" He didn't hang up on her. Bravo for him. He hated the harshness of his voice and the way he was cutting her off, except he needed to end the call and get to communications. The baron ordered him to write a report and send it to homicide, the sheriff's department, and the Organization of Paranormal Investigations, that both Rutger and Jordyn had worked with.

"Affirmative." Clio ended the call before she started yelling at him. "How dare he leave me out? And Doctor Carrion." Miss Langston's care and health came first above all else.

The old feeling of not being worthy poisoned the guilt

saturating her being. And what was she doing; acting like a teenager and giggling with someone she didn't feel threatened by. Clio sunk to an all-time low. Pushing her raging thoughts back, she gained control over herself, and scrolled back through the transcripts. They started the moment Captain Wolt ordered Aydian to respond to Director Kanin's house, then ordered Quinn and Luke to respond as backup. It stated Mr. Platt was with Miss Langston, had taken her into custody, and was in the woods beside the director's house. The transcripts ended when Captain Wolt ordered the enforcers to hold their positions and reported the target was down. There was nothing else. Who took the target down? What did he do to Miss Langston before he was taken down? How was Miss Langston's mental health after facing Mr. Platt? What agency was doing the investigation? The answers to those questions were on a need-to-know basis and Captain Wolt didn't think she needed to know.

Clio sat back in the seat, her hands gripping the steering wheel, causing her knuckles to turn white, and stared at nothing until the buildings in front her grew together to become a giant blur. She jumped when her cell rang, and without checking the number grabbed the ringing apparatus and hit the answer button.

"Doctor Hyde."

"It's your mom."

"Hello, Mom. What's up?" Clio wanted to go home and sulk. She didn't like being on the outside after years of being an enforcer and years of loyalty.

"Your dad and I were wondering if you're free for dinner?"

No. "Of course. What time?" She started the crossover, clicked out of the transcript page, switched her cell to handsfree, and left the parking lot. She needed to go home, remind herself she wasn't going to talk pack politics with her parents, and change out of damp clothes before she went to her parents' house and pretended everything was fine.

"Six. Cocktails at five. How does that sound?"

"Perfect. I'll be there at five," Clio answered. Four sounded better.

"See you then. Love you."

"Love you." Clio ended the call and swore she was going to enjoy the evening and not obsess over Tony, Captain Wolt, his treatment of her, or the fact Mr. Platt hunted Miss Langston down.

Sure, it was going to be easy. No problem. Driving through the city, she watched as the world continued, people walking the glittering streets, having coffee like she had as if nothing had happened. Guilt made a resurgence, and she was out of energy to fight it, so she let it sit on her like a pile of stones.

"Screw this," she mumbled. She hit the screen and called communications.

"How can I help you, Doctor Hyde?" Mandy asked.

"I'm aware of the situation. Does Miss Langston need medical?" Clio asked. Yeah, she called communications from her console in order for it to be recorded.

"Negative."

Clio groaned. What the hell was going on? "Could you explain why a woman who was just assaulted by the person who kidnapped her then tried to sacrifice her to a god, doesn't need medical of some kind?" Her question was met with silence, then seconds began ticking by, and the console screen cleared. *That's new*, Clio thought, and was tempted to hang up.

"Be advised Foxwood and all communications are on

lockdown. This exchange is being encrypted and will be kept in case of an investigation."

"Copy," Clio replied. Lockdown. Encrypted. Worry and fear for Miss Langston and the Kanin family beat back the guilt enough Tony was the last thing on her mind.

"At this time, Miss Langston is refusing medical attention. The Kanin and Langston families have gone black. There will be zero outside communication for seventy-two hours, at which time the threat level will be reassessed. The Paradise County Sheriff's Department is questioning Director Kanin in connection with the disappearances of six witches, people, released from county jail, and the apparent suicide of Mr. Platt. The Highguard's people are currently reviewing the situation and are in conference with Baron Kanin."

They suspected the director of killing the witches and Mr. Platt. "You said apparent suicide. No one killed him?"

"Negative, Doc, and I don't have the details. No one is talking about what happened. Law enforcement is stating the director used magic because he's a lycan. I've explained the situation in the event your services are needed, outside of what I've told you, I can't tell you anything more," Mandy warned.

"Thank you. If you need anything let me know," Clio offered. She hadn't expected that explanation and would have accepted a half ass answer. It would have frustrated her, but she would have understood if Mandy told her she didn't rate a reason, because she wasn't an enforcer. But if she was needed ... It didn't feel right.

The witches concerned her. There was no way Director Kanin would have risked the pack and his life for revenge, right? Although, she would understand if he had, the entire pack and klatch would and would take his side and protect him. Those thoughts led straight to Captain Wolt and her concern he was keeping secrets. Maybe he was and it was the witches, he was protecting the director, and not the people responsible for the attacks ... but he knew about the poison. No, he said it like he was trying to figure it out. He was an enforcer, and his job was to know and anyone who had seen Lado's skin, and the crystals would know the toxin wasn't going to be common. Was she trying to convince herself of his innocence?

"Copy," Mandy's reply broke Clio's inner argument, as she ended the call.

The wipers sank back to the bottom of the windshield as she slowly pulled into the garage, and stopping, she turned the engine off. Behind her the door made its descent, and closing her in it cut the light and left her in darkness. From its place in the cup holder, her cell lit up, and recognizing the number it sent shards of ice down her spine. She wasn't going to answer. Couldn't without guilt creeping up to simmer in her middle. Instead, she sat there watching the screen until it went dark, then a message told her she missed a call and had a voicemail. *Damn.* With Foxwood on lockdown, the Highguard in conference with Baron Kanin, both families going black, and the sheriff's department questioning Director Kanin, she didn't have time to indulge in her personal life. She did, however, owe him an explanation.

If Tony needed an example of what her life was like, he was going to get one. Without listening to the voicemail, she typed out a message ... excuse, leaving out what was happening with the Kanin and Langston families, and explained she had family obligations and had been put on call with the pack. It was a lie, and it wasn't. Clio hit send and waited. Five minutes passed and she figured he wasn't going to respond, and gathering her things headed into the house. She had an hour before she was expected at her parents' place, which gave her time to change her clothes and do something with her rain damp hair.

Out of habit and expectation, Clio checked her cell, didn't see a message from Tony, and hated thinking he might believe she was blowing him off. Like she was, kinda. It didn't change her priorities. The pack came first. As she tossed her purse to the table and made her way to her room, she stripped out of her top. Her mind raced with reasons, excuses, and explanations why she hadn't answered his call or called him back. If she was honest with herself, she would admit to being scared. She had a great time, considered his offer of rocking climbing, and meeting him for coffee. She didn't act like that. It was the exact reason she didn't have relationships. Furthermore, it was proof that when she couldn't answer a call or make time for him, Tony was going to ignore her, and she didn't need the hassle. Clio took her cell, and with her nerves eating her, checked the calls, saw Captain Wolt's number under Tony's, and wanted to throw the thing of frustration across the room. The very person she wanted to talk to and there was no chance in hell he was going to call her.

CHAPTER SEVENTEEN

"Captain Wolt, checking in," Ansel reported. Releasing the button, the radio buzzed with static for a second.

"Copy. The crew was cleared first thing this morning and should have arrived. Director Kanin hasn't confirmed their arrival," Mandy explained.

"Affirmative. They are at his residence and have prepared the house for retrofitting," Ansel replied.

The renovations resembled reconstruction with the windows being removed and replaced with ballistic glass, reinforced steel doors, cameras, palm vein scanners, motion sensors, and license plate reader. Rutger's house would have a military-grade security system linked directly to the communications center where an enforcer monitored the information. The retrofitting also included dozens of floodlights all able to switch between UV, amber, and LED to turn an enemy, like a vampire, to ash, right from Rutger's cell, the baron's cell, or communications.

Ansel sat in his truck at the entrance of Rutger's driveway and watched work trucks and big rigs hauling materials make their way to the property, and after unloading they promptly left. A couple of forklifts and a crane waited to move material while workers broke down the supplies and began taking the house apart.

"Copy. Is Director Kanin there?" Mandy asked.

"Affirmative. Is he needed at Foxwood?"

Starting at six in the morning, Rutger's house had been crawling with people from the pack, construction company, sheriff deputies, homicide detectives, and detectives from the OPI. After learning Flint had been on the property for over a week, then had taken Jordyn with the intention of killing her, the baron ordered the security upgrades on Rutger's house be completed immediately. He also ordered the Purification team placed on standby to wait for the sheriff's department to release the scene so they could clean up the remains of the witches and anything else the investigators didn't take into evidence. It was why, before anyone arrived, Rutger had taken Jordyn to Foxwood where there were enforcers, the baron and baroness' sentinels, and several soldiers posted around the estate. No one would see her or get near her.

On his way back, Rutger stopped at the sheriff's department and handed over the files containing information proving his whereabouts. Jordyn had been interrogated by Detective Cliff and confirmed Rutger had been home with her on the nights in question, then the GPS on his cell and truck verified her statement. When there wasn't mention of others being involved, Ansel was sure Detective Cliff wanted Rutger to be guilty and hadn't believed him or Jordyn and until he concluded his investigation Rutger was going to remain a suspect.

Good luck with that, Ansel thought. Detective Cliff wasn't going to outmaneuver the Highguard, made up of the most powerful magic-born that served as the authority over all magic-born from around the world. He definitely wasn't going to outmaneuver Jordyn. If what his senses told him were any indication of what she was capable of, Detective Cliff would be left with his accusations and nothing else. Thankfully, Rutger and Jordyn had Detective Watt from the OPI on their side, and he was actively trying to clear both of their names.

"Negative. Confirming his location," Mandy replied.

"You have his GPS," Ansel countered. This had to be about the witches and Detective Cliff's accusations.

"Affirmative. Baron Kanin wants physical confirmation."

"Copy." The radio went silent, and Ansel wondered how long Baron Kanin was going to check on Rutger. The baron knew what had been done, hadn't disagreed with their actions, but said they didn't cover their tracks.

Ansel checked his cell, went to his call log to see Dr. Hyde's number and closed the screen. The last thing he needed to do was think about her, his behavior and treatment of her when she was out there. And waiting. She hadn't made a move after attacking and nearly killing Lado, who hadn't been released from Celestial, and it was making Ansel crazy. With the Unseelie court holding him responsible for the attack on Daniel, and Lado's parents questioning the baron's ability, he felt like his world was crumbling. He had to face this was her game and he needed to wait for her to jerk his strings. Sadly, waiting meant someone's life was at risk.

"Captain Wolt." Mandy's voice, with a tinge of stress in it, filled his truck.

"Go ahead," Ansel replied as his heart jumped to his throat.

"Sending Aydian to your location. Baron Kanin ordered two enforcers were to be present at all times."

"Copy." Ansel swiped through the screens until he was looking at the list of active enforcers.

There were the eight, special force, some called the

chosen—the list included Aydian, who had parked across from him, Luke and Quinn, who were at Foxwood, Kai, Kellen, and Cassidy who were doing patrols between Foxwood and Rutger's place while Owen and Luca were supervising the others at Foxwood. Two pairs were there as additional guards, and four other pairs were to respond to calls. Lieutenant Torin Bouldin, head of the soldiers, sent three pairs into Trinity to patrol the streets and question shop owners hoping they would see something, hear about something, anything that would help find her and her team. Not that Lieutenant Bouldin, his soldiers, or the enforcers knew who or what they were looking for, and Ansel hated letting them feel helpless and blind, but it had to be done.

With Flint and the witches dead, it left Bronte the remaining threat. They could concentrate their efforts into finding her or those of the Covey. Which he should be doing, not sitting at Rutger's house to watch construction workers turn his log home into a fortress and Jordyn's home into a prison. It frustrated him. He wanted to be on the streets searching for her, needed to be out searching for the woman obsessed with taking everything he worked for from him.

A beep sounded, the list refreshed, and an enforcer was added. Not active, she kept the console in her vehicle in order for the baron and communications to keep track of her by the GPS. Next to the alert was the name Dr. Clio Hyde. Ansel figured she was heading to work, and to make sure he checked her GPS on the map, and switching screens, he saw she was driving toward Celestial. At least she would be surrounded by guards and witnesses. She was safe. He had to believe it was enough.

"The sheriff's homicide investigators are finishing up. Once they leave the cleanup team can go in. I don't want anything left of Flint," Rutger ordered, his voice thick with exhaustion and irritation.

Ansel met his dark gaze, as he stood beside his truck, Rutger's height causing him to lean down.

"Understood. How are the security upgrades coming?" Ansel asked as he clicked out of the map screen.

"Damn slow. What is Aydian doing here?" Rutger straightened to see Aydian parked across from them on the other side of the driveway entrance. "He should be at Fox-wood where Jo is."

Ansel gave the enforcer a half wave and could see his steely blue gaze narrowed on Rutger. With his background and years of torture it was hard to tell what the man was thinking. "Baron Kanin ordered two enforcers stand duty at all times."

"I'm glad he told the Director of Enforcers about the change," Rutger grumbled under his breath.

"He also is having whoever is here give him physical con-firmation you're here," Ansel explained.

"Placating to the sheriff's department and homicide de-tectives. He would say it was a necessary evil to prove I'm not a murderer." Rutger rested his elbow on the window frame as two patrol cars drove out, followed by a crime scene van and an unmarked car. "It's about damn time they got off my property."

The unmarked car stopped, Detective Cliff glared at them, checked Aydian, then drove off. "You're making friends everywhere."

"I hate thinking I might have ruined the relationship the pack had with law enforcement, but I don't regret killing them," Rutger began. "He tried turning Jo against me."

"He clearly failed," Ansel responded. No, he didn't regret killing them either. The court system failed, and whether it was because the witches were considered human and not magic-born didn't matter. It was the hard truth and the extreme difference between humans and magic-born. The three of them had taken control and eliminated the threat.

Removing his elbow from the door, he faced Ansel. "They have no idea who they're dealing with. She killed him."

"Who?" Ansel sat straighter, not wanting to hear the answer and what it meant.

"Jo. Jo made him confess and then kill himself. If that isn't enough, she faced Detective Cliff and his interrogation like he was nothing and she had lied to law enforcement a million times. She held a cold determination." Rutger looked down at the ground, inhaled and exhaled. "I don't like what I see. She deserved to come home and have a life without hiding who and what she is, and she deserved to keep her innocence. After Flint died and everyone had left the house, the beast had a grip on my wolf, and I demanded she not lie to me, then she told we are the beginning of the dark ages. The baron wants to bring back the old ways."

Old ways. "She knows what we did?"

"Affirmative. Said I knew what revenge tasted like and now she does."

"If anyone finds out what she's capable of, mind manipulation, it'll put the pack in danger," Ansel warned. Like he hadn't put the pack and the klatch's lives in danger by lying. Jordyn was innocent and was forced to defend herself.

"That is the beginning of protecting her," he said, pointing at the house, "because someone already knows ... Shadow Lord."

Flint's body hadn't been cold, and Jordyn hadn't been out of the rain for ten minutes when the Highguard's messengers arrived at Rutger's house and delivered letters, the baron kept with him. Shadow Lord, an old vampire, threatened to take Jordyn from the pack. Further, it stated if the baron didn't comply, he was going to blackmail Rutger with proof he had witnessed the three of them killing the witches and his people had moved the bodies to the tree. The second informed Baron Kanin the Highguard was investigating the actions he had taken to enshrine Jordyn as the soothsayer, and then without authorization from them, made Rutger and Jordyn One-Flesh. The family was taking hits from all sides, compelling them to go black to protect themselves, and the baron kept Foxwood on lockdown. Ansel thought the letters had been exaggerated to scare Baron Kanin, Rutger, and Jordyn into obedience. He had been wrong.

"I don't know what to say. I don't think I understand," Ansel admitted. He had no idea how to make things better, when his lies and his past were going to hurt Rutger and the pack even more. He wasn't a stranger, a witch bent on murder, a member of the Highguard flexing his power, he was one of them, kith and kin, and they trusted him with their lives. A poison among them.

"No one does." Rutger looked in the direction of his house, then back at Ansel. "By the way, all you have to do is call her. Stalking her by her GPS location from your truck is creepy."

"I'm not. It's not ... She would never." It was Ansel's turn to look at the house as embarrassment crawled up his neck to scald his cheeks. "It would never work, she has a career, a family, and will be in charge of Foxwood's med room. She doesn't need someone like me in her life. I don't have anything to offer her." The baron's words drifted through his thoughts as his explanation sounded more like a confession, except it felt good and bad to say it out loud.

"You're a Pureblood and Captain of Enforcers with status in the pack. Besides, she doesn't care about that. She's strong, independent, and driven, the reason why she'll be in charge of the med room. Don't you think you should let her make the decision? What if she's interested in you?" Rutger asked.

Fated mates. He was fooling himself. It wasn't possible. Whatever bond Rutger and Jordyn had together had been cultivated and then rooted itself between them since they were children. It wasn't fate. Anyway, there was no way he deserved loyalty, love, and interest from someone like Dr. Hyde. She would never lie to the baron, the pack, and she wouldn't put innocent lives in danger. She saved lives and helped the defenseless. He absolutely wouldn't pull her in close when it would make her a target.

"It wouldn't work. We have different lives."

"I heard a paramedic, I believe his name is Tony, had coffee with her, and they were seen enjoying the thunderstorm from inside a bakery. If you don't take a chance, how do you know?" Rutger continued.

"First, Flint came back here to kill Jordyn yesterday. Second, you're a suspect in a kidnapping and murder case. You should be thinking about that, not my love life." Damn paramedic. "I don't care." Hearing about Tony the Paramedic set his anger on fire, its flames searing his veins as it coursed through him. His wolf wanted to howl as he claimed Clio as his, yelling it to the world, then he would tear the paramedic apart. Except Dr. Hyde wasn't his, and he had zero claim on someone who would end up being tortured in order for Bronte to bring Ansel to his knees. "I don't care."

"Yeah. Suit yourself." Rutger's gaze proved he didn't believe whatever Ansel was throwing at him.

Clio slid her ID card, then entered the passcode into the keypad and waited as the gate rattled and started across the two lanes into the employee parking lot. Her travel coffee mug sat in the cup holder, filled to the brim and teasing her with caffeine she desperately needed to make it through the day. She hadn't slept, had in fact sat up and watched her cell as if it might give her the answers to her questions. It didn't. When she managed to close her eyes, she saw herself flirting with Tony while in front of her Miss Langston's near kidnapping at the hand of the madman who wanted to kill her played out of her reach. And there was Captain Wolt, stopping her from helping and cutting her off as if she was in a soundless prison. The minutes of rest she did get weren't enough and she felt worse when her alarm clock screamed.

As she went about her routine—having coffee, shower, checking her cell, and more coffee—it had taken most of the morning to shed the emotions from the dream. Guilt, shame, and embarrassment clung to her with each second, then tagging along with every thought; like checking on Lado or going through her schedule. The raging emotions reminded her she had done nothing to help Miss Langston, had been denied for a second time. Clio was a doctor and helping people was what she did, lived for, needed like oxygen.

Determined to banish the thoughts and the emotions, she shoved them into a dark vault. Clio parked the crossover in her designated space, turned the engine off, and gathered her bag, coffee mug, and awkwardly got out of the car. July's morning sun met her with its warmth and clean, crisp, yellow glow, promising a cloudless cerulean sky. A stark difference from the day before when dark clouds rolled over the mountains, like an army marching to war, to curtain the sky, making the temperature drop while it unleashed a deluge of rain. All the while Miss Langston's life was being threatened. *Drop it,* she told herself and shook her head.

Two steps and a nagging feeling pulsed, tried to push through the wall Clio created, and without stopping herself, she turned on the ball of her foot to check the parking lot. Out of the dozens of cars, SUVs, family vans, and trucks, Tony's dark green, lifted 4x4 wasn't there, and it should have been. She hadn't checked her cell and now fumbled with the bag, slung it over her shoulder, switched the coffee mug to her left hand, and took the phone from a side cargo pocket. No calls. No messages. She put her coffee on a ledge and dialed Tony's number. One. Two. Three. A professional version of his voice, missing the grin he flashed her, told her his number and to leave a message. So he wasn't at work and wasn't answering his cell, it didn't mean a damn thing. "*You never know when you need to head into the mountains to get away from it all.*" Maybe. Then why did she picture Lado, the wounds, and crystals riddling his body? Because she was an enforcer. And slightly paranoid after yesterday.

Clio convinced herself she wasn't going to repeat her mistake and make assumptions, to wait a few hours before she went to the paramedic's office and ask why Tony wasn't there. She was torn with the possible reasons why—she hadn't returned his call, he didn't want to continue their friendship and seeing her at work would make things awkward, or he simply took the day off. Sliding her ID card, she entered the passcode, heard the locking mechanism click and opened the door. A wave of stringent cleaning chemicals rode the air as the feel of hundreds of magic-born touched her skin, making her shiver.

On auto she walked the path she had taken for years

while greeting nurses, doctors, Celestial employees, and taking a right, then another she was in the familiar hall lined with doors and stopped in front of hers. Repeating the process, she slid her card, entered the passcode, the locked disengaged, and she entered the quiet of her office. Clio placed her coffee on her desktop, her bag on a chair, and sat down behind the desk and her computer. The black monitor came to life and the symbol for the hospital filled the screen while at the bottom was a black rectangle where she typed in a password. The screen blinked and she faced another rectangle, where she entered another password. If she had a book containing all her passwords and codes, it would rival the longest epic ever written.

Clio clicked to her work email, and watching the files pop up groaned at the sheer number of them. One day. She took one day off. Recognizing most of them as advertisements from requesting information about equipment, instruments, and supplies for the med room, she scrolled down to a couple from doctors, no doubt about the upgrades to Celestial submitted to the board, and then the med room at Foxwood. Farther down the list of new recruits, the kids from the pack who were turning eighteen and getting ready to start their two years. They all needed to go through a medical examination, talk to a counselor, and have a physical fitness test. The girls came to mind as Clio made a note to schedule a meeting with Grayeth, Lieutenant Bouldin's second in command and person in charge of the recruits. Done. She could check it off her list, then she saw there was a reply. She stared at the name and email address and didn't want to open it.

"What's the worst that could happen? He said no?" she asked the empty office. Clicking on the email, it opened and her lips moved as she silently read the letter. "He didn't say no."

It was time to put her plea, statement requesting the authorization to hire a new doctor together for Baron Kanin. She had good reasons for wanting Dr. William Baines, the Esme, superior of the Lapis Lazuli coven's son and witch at Celestial and Foxwood. His experience, knowledge, and status with the coven would be inestimable. Dang, Flint's attack on Miss Langston couldn't have come at a worst time. That was selfish, but still ...

Clio replied to Dr. Baines, she was excited to have him join the team, attached the folder of paperwork he needed to complete, and hit send. Closing the window, she started a new document and told herself Baron Kanin was a reasonable man, who put the pack's needs, and those of the klatch, and the territory first. All she had to do was keep the statement professional and declare her intentions and Dr. Baines' qualifications as a physician, an accomplished witch, and they could use the opportunity as an olive branch, proving the pack didn't hold the coven responsible. Sure thing.

By the time she finished with the document, an hour had slipped away from her, and she hadn't been to check on the emergency room, Dr. Arano, Lado's condition, or with the staff. No one had called her, her cell hadn't made a peep, no one came to her office, and she hoped that was a good sign and it was going to be a slow day. She might get all her paperwork completed. With the document in front of her, Clio sat back, read over the request one more time, didn't think there was anything she would change, and adding it to an email, selected Baron Kanin's address and sent it before she changed her mind. Before she let her insecurities—like she didn't rate making the request—get the better of her.

With her priorities done, Clio stood, deciding it was time she checked the ER, and she wanted to check in with Dr.

Arano to see how Lado was doing. A ding sounded, stopping her, and she saw there was an email. Leaning on the edge of the desk she read the newest file. Dr. Baines had replied and completed the paperwork she sent him.

"That was fast," she mumbled as she sat back down, the chair making a soft squeal as she rolled it forward. Several clicks later and she was reading through the documents, liking the skilled way he detailed his traits, his education, extensive travel and where he studied, and was impressed with his background. It confirmed her need to have him at Celestial.

The witches instantly came to mind and the threats they posed against Miss Langston, the pack, and the klatch. Then there was the attack on Lado, the crystals and toxin, and the attack on Daniel. This was proof she needed to fight fire with fire, and her answer was Dr. Baines and the support of the Lapis Lazuli coven. She had to convince the baron Dr. Baines was talented and would be an incredible asset. Attaching the documents to another email, she typed out her thoughts, and sent it to the baron.

"That's that." All she could was wait for the baron to respond and pray he trusted her judgement. She had her doubts due to the Priority Thirteen she reported concerning Captain Wolt, who clearly hadn't been a threat.

Clio took a deep breath, exhaled her anxiety, worry, and frustration and left her office for something to keep her from thinking about the email and Dr. Baines. Making her way to the ER, she greeted staff and patients and felt her nerves ease as she walked the halls. The feeling of being in the right place and she was doing what she was meant to do filled her with confidence. She might be a Wight, and that insecurity might be her default setting, but it hadn't stopped her from doing what she loved. It did, however, have her believing it was the reason Captain Wolt wasn't interested in her. *Because you're so suave with men*.

Shut up, she told herself. Clio wasn't wasting precious time thinking about him, there was nothing there.

"Doctor Hyde," Cruz greeted as he fell into step with her.

"Good morning," she replied. "What's going on?"

"Wanted to make you aware there was a parent here asking about the priming exanimation and fitness test. Their son is turning eighteen and will start his training, and she doesn't feel it's necessary he serve with the soldiers," he explained. "It's dangerous."

She wanted to roll her eyes. "Why didn't she go to the baron if she has a problem?"

"Foxwood remains on lockdown and I think she was fishing for information." Cruz raised one dark eyebrow. "Her concern has to be about the attacks."

She could have called the enforcers. "Probably. I have three young women trying to beat each other up because they want to make it in the soldiers and a mom worried her son might get hurt. What is his status?" she asked.

"Wight. She is human," Cruz answered. "She's seeing this from a human's point of view."

A Wight, figures. Clio cringed with the thought. She judged them as harshly as she judged herself. "Her point of view isn't based on facts. If you get me her information, I'll have a representative from the pack speak to her. They all think it's about guns and bad guys. The recruits attend college, to start their advanced education, as well as physical training, and weapons training. No one is going to send her son into battle."

"Preaching to the choir, Doc," he said as he raised his hands in the air. "Don't shoot the messenger."

"Sorry. Is there anything else I should know about?" She hoped there wasn't. As it was, she had more paperwork waiting for her than the work of an ER doctor.

"Yeah, you should probably talk to Mrs. Adams. The only reason I know is because your name came up, and I have excellent hearing … you know, that werewolf thing."

"My name? Mrs. Adams, the person in charge of the ambulance drivers—" *Shit. Tony.* "I'll go talk to her." Without waiting for Cruz to reply, she left him standing outside of the ER doors and headed to the paramedic's office.

On the way she took her cell from her side pocket and checked for calls and messages. Nothing. She dialed Tony's number and instantly got his voicemail, the sound of his voice making her heart pound in her chest.

"Doctor Hyde," a paramedic greeted. She was sure his name was Luis. "I was on my way to see you."

"I'm on my way to talk to Mrs. Adams." Clio stopped, her cell clutched in her hand, and her imagination heading into dangerous territory. Tony was never late, and he always showed up for work … damn, he lived for work. She heard herself tell him, "*I was there when you drove breakneck speeds to Foxwood. You live for it like an adrenalin junkie.*" She saw Lado's broken body, dying skin, and the thin spines jutting from his joints. No, there was nothing wrong with Tony, he had headed to the mountains to get away from it all. Maybe he went rock climbing.

"She's busy trying to find someone to take Tony's place. He didn't call in and no one can reach him. Word is, you were the last person to see him," Luis accused.

"Really, Doctor Hyde?" Cara teased.

"It was coffee at his cousin's bakery, and he was already there," she explained to the eyes narrowing on her and the questions they held. And what if she had met him there, or they had driven together? Then what?

"No offense, Doc. No one has heard from him since last night," Luis explained. "That's not like him."

"He called me shortly after we left. I wasn't able to answer but had sent him a message explaining my reason. I didn't get a response." Because her attention was on Miss Langston, the near kidnapping, and was sure he had had enough of her, her schedule, and her commitment to the pack. She was more trouble than she was worth. Clio couldn't stop from thinking he would have understood, he was a Pureblood fox within the Red River fold and served them no different than she served the pack.

"I know about what happened yesterday with Miss Langston, it's all over the news. Is that why you didn't answer his call?" Luis asked.

Damn, she hated the news. "Affirmative." Clio checked her cell out of nervous habit and wanted to see Tony's name and a message from him.

"I told him it was a bad idea to partner with you," Luis was saying. "He wouldn't listen."

She wasn't paying attention to him, her attention focusing on Tony. "If you're worried and there are grounds for the search, I can have his cell tracked, GPS, and it should give us his location."

"Leave it to an enforcer," Cara mumbled, all the teasing drained from her voice. She was a Wight, elf and human, who was part of the Seelie court's lower class, and obviously held a level of resentment where the enforcers were concerned. Right then it was her problem and had nothing to do with Clio.

"If you can do it, then find him. We're not blind, we see the soldiers, enforcers, and patrols roaming the city and the outskirts. Someone is here targeting any magic-born who gets in their way and making a fool of Baron Kanin and his great force," Luis challenged, his indignation plain for her to hear. She knew Luis was an Illuminate, his badge said so, but was unsure who he was loyal to. Obviously, it wasn't Cascade.

"Baron Kanin and his great force have kept you and your factions safe for decades. You've reaped peace, wealth, and a life without censure and prejudice from humans. Remember that. If you think there is something wrong, Cascade will do everything within its power to help, you know this," Clio stated. She tried to conceal her own worry as she pushed as much authority as she possibly could into her words. The feeling it was two against one sharpened her defenses.

Luis looked away from her, then nailed his chocolate gaze on her. "I think there is something wrong. Very wrong. This is not like him."

"That's all I needed." Clio took her cell and entered the number for communications.

"Doctor Hyde," Mandy greeted. At least Clio didn't have to listen to the minute-long spiel saved for the others.

"Tony Reed didn't show up for work and no one has heard from him since yesterday afternoon," Clio explained.

"I'm assuming they've tried contacting him. Have they checked his residence?" Mandy asked. "I have his address and Blix is en route."

"Has anyone gone to his house to check on him?" Clio asked Luis.

"Yes. His truck is there, he isn't."

"Did you see signs of a break in?"

"No. Negative. I searched the inside, and everything is the way it usually is," he answered, his worry making his words weak.

"Did you get that?" Clio asked Mandy.

"Affirmative. As soon as Blix contacts me, I'll contact you."

"Copy. Can you track his cell?"

"Give me a minute. I'll need to request authorization," Mandy replied, and the line went silent.

"She's requesting authorization," Clio explained as she faced Luis. "An enforcer is en route to Tony's residence and he'll confirm if Tony is there or not." She wished she had answered his call, maybe asked him if he wanted to go to her parents' house with her. Hell, she wished she was in her office going over paperwork. She wanted to be anywhere but staring into Luis' worried gaze.

God, she hoped Tony was safe.

CHAPTER EIGHTEEN

Ansel checked the time on the screen, the active enforcers, communications, and decided he was going to rip the door off the truck and run for the hills if he had to sit there for very much longer.

Yes, he knew it was important to watch the house to ensure Rutger's safety, to make sure no one entered the property, and to confirm the workers who had been cleared were the only people there. Then to confirm Rutger was there, in person. It didn't change his need to be out searching for her and making sure she didn't hurt anyone else. Hurting people would grow dreary, the hunt and then torture not enough to satisfy the evil living inside her, her innate instinct, she would need a kill. She would need blood. The force she used to hold herself back weakening under the strain would create a ravenous hunger.

Time was ticking.

He checked the screen again, looking for reports from the patrols and didn't find any. The hours he spent watching the construction were eating him and creating their own anxiety he didn't think his nerves were going to survive. Ansel reached toward the screen to click out of the page when the transcripts reloaded, and he saw Dr. Hyde's name. No. His heart escaped its binds, and rising got stuck in his throat and his eyes blurred, making it impossible to read anything.

Looking away from the console, he breathed deep, calmed himself by believing if something had happened to her, he would have been called. Rutger would have been called to the scene. There would have been an emergency broadcast over the console to every enforcer. It was enough assurance he looked back, grateful his sight refocused, and read the request from Dr. Hyde to have Tony Reed's house searched. The paramedic. He was an innocent, no reason she would have attacked him.

Before he could ask why, new information explained the paramedic hadn't shown up for work and hadn't been seen since the day before. After he had coffee with Dr. Hyde. She was the last person to see him alive. Ansel growled at the idea she was sitting with another man, laughing, giving him her quick retorts, and looking at him with her azure eyes with swirls of honey. Thinking about her gave him the smells of warm brown sugar and cinnamon that lingered on her clothing, and he wondered what her skin smelled like.

Stop. Being locked in his truck for hours had added to his sinking insanity. He left the trail his mind wanted to wander and read the rest of the transcripts. Blix reported no one was there and there was no evidence of forced entry, all the doors and windows had been checked. And the paramedic's truck was parked in the driveway, untouched.

He switched over to live feed as Blix's stern voice reported the details of the paramedic's living room, kitchen, bathrooms, bedrooms, and his uniform was hanging by the washer and dryer. Seconds ticked, Ansel's heart stopped, his lungs froze, and he was sure he was paralyzed. The details echoed in the cab of the truck, and he saw three feathers, one to the left, another to the right, then the third which stood straight, while a sword, hilt down was behind the vertical feather. Blix's words began fade, as if they were leaving Ansel behind, then they were gone and all he heard was her throaty voice lit with an accent in his head as she said his name, Brando.

You belong to me, firebrand.

He did. She was stripping everything from him. Like she was peeling his skin from his body and was going to turn his kith and kin against him. Clio. Once she found out who was responsible for the paramedic's death, she would hate him and any chance of having her would become something he only saw in his dreams. He would have to be happy with watching her from afar, to guard her, and make sure no one hurt her. If he stayed in Trinity. Ansel's heart ached from the loss he was going to endure, if Baron Kanin didn't order his execution for the damage he had done, and to appease the territory.

"Captain Wolt." Mandy's voice traveled through the miles separating him, the past he failed to hide, and the present promising punishment. He didn't want to hear what she had to say, didn't want her asking him anything when he was unable to help them. Unable to protect the pack that had taken him in and made him of their own. "Captain Wolt. Captain Wolt, respond."

Out of habit and on auto he grabbed the mic, pushed the button, and answered, "Copy."

"Someone reported a disturbance at your house," she relayed.

"Who?" he asked, noncommitted. Ansel watched Aydian walk back to his truck and get in, and through two windshields saw his steel gaze. He must have been heading to Ansel's truck to get him to answer the radio.

"They made the report and hung up."

"Did you get a phone number?" Ansel asked, as his mind

desperately tried pulling him from the past and his tormented thoughts, to the present. There was chance she didn't have anything to do with the paramedic if there was someone at his house. The slice of hope sent a ripple effect through him and gave a moment of reprieve. She could be waiting for him.

"Negative. I'm working on it. Advised I'm working with technicians to fix a persistent problem."

The day the office was complete was going to be a good day. "Copy." Ansel went to the screen of active enforcers and went down the list. "Have Quinn relieve me, and I'll head over to my place. No reason for anyone else to bother."

"Copy."

Ansel prepared to leave when Blix's voice sounded from the console. "Guy was a neat freak. Base, I found his cell phone." Seconds turned into minutes that felt like hours when Blix finally reported, "The last call he received was from Doctor Hyde, there are other calls we'll have to check the names, a couple of voicemails, and several messages. He stopped responding around midnight."

"Copy. I'll cancel the request and I'll inform Doctor Hyde. You're positive there's nothing there?" Mandy asked. "Nothing indicating someone had been there? He had been forcibly taken? There was duress? A scent?"

"Negative. It's like the place has been wiped. If he left, he walked out on his own," Blix replied. "I can do surveillance on the house for a while."

"Negative. Return to base," Mandy ordered.

Wiped. Like the area around the tree. "What game are you playing?"

The request to track his cell came from Dr. Hyde. The paramedic missed work and she thought it rated calling the enforcers? Track his cell? His wolf howled as his jealousy took any rational thought from him. She must like the man, potential mate with a future, better than Ansel if she was willing to risk exposing her relationship with him. He probably treated her with the respect she deserved, kindness, showed her he cared for her, and saw a smart, beautiful woman, capable of achieving her goals. He probably enjoyed every time she confronted him. Ansel did. He saw all those things in her, but couldn't allow himself because he belonged to another. Ansel prayed she was at his house to end the game she was playing.

"Leaving Director Kanin's property," Ansel reported.

"Copy, Captain Wolt. Inform me when you can," Mandy replied.

"Copy." Ansel pulled away from the shoulder as Quinn drove behind him, taking his place.

Once on the main road and heading toward his place, his raging emotions, guilt, and jealousy ebbed, his anger draining from him as the scenery changed and he wasn't sitting still with idle hands. He wanted, needed for her to be at his place. His hands ached to be around her neck, to feel the soft skin of her throat and the way it would cave when he squeezed, while his wolf wanted to taste her blood. This time it would be his teeth embedded in her flesh. Freedom would be his when he ended the game. And those he cherished, his kith and kin would be safe from a wrath they didn't deserve. The truck ate the miles and his mind wandered back to Dr. Hyde and her relationship with the paramedic.

"You treated her like her existence didn't matter," Ansel growled as he took a corner. "To protect her." Except she didn't know, it was his little secret like his past and the woman trying to destroy him.

At his driveway he stopped, checked the tree line and

beyond, and finding no one eased the truck up the drive and parked in front of the garage. The house was as he left it, its windows dark, the front door closed, the yard empty save for his truck. Above the trees the dying sun cast spiderweb shadows on the hood of his truck, the ground, and were reflected in the windows. There was no one there. Nothing moved. It had been nothing. With a lifetime of anxiety, fear, and frustration that had built up in matter of minutes, he shoved the truck into park and killed the engine. Thrusting the door open, he stepped out and thin whips of death teased his nose at the same time his senses exploded with a warning. Ansel's wolf rose up, its instincts overriding his weaker human side, and he felt his eyes change to bronze, resembling his Pureblood father as his mother's magic warmed his skin.

He unholstered his weapon, whatever was waiting for him was long dead, he hadn't sensed a heartbeat or a presence, and whoever it was had been a shapeshifter. Checking behind him and the tree line one last time, he headed to the back of the house, his boots smashing wild grass, rocks, twigs, then sinking in rain-softened soil from the day before. He stopped at the corner, leaned out with his pistol at the ready, saw it was clear and continued to the stairs of the deck. The scent of blood, death, and her touch reached out for him as if it knew he was there and needed to feel him. She slithered over his thoughts, she had been there, on his territory, and had brought the dead with her. What would he find? He reached the first step, stopped, and inhaled as guilt's sting sank into old wounds to create new ones laced with her hate. This time he wasn't talking about the abomination that was Bronte, no, it was Clio.

He lost her.

Ansel stood at the foot of the patio table, his pistol holstered, his hands in fists, his body trembling from rage, and his mind trying to tell him what, who he was looking at. The open eyes stained from burst blood vessels stared at nothing, the flesh of his face where his cheekbones had been sank in, making his nose protrude from his skull. His broken arms sagged off the edge of wood, his hands pointed in the wrong direction, and his crooked fingers twisted every which way. There were nails, the same ones used on Lado, sticking out from his joints and surrounded by cracking skin. Where a rainbow of bruises had marred the wounds dark purple almost black from lack of blood and his death took their places. Deep lacerations scarred his naked torso, thighs, calves, and his bare feet were missing toes. Drawing in a slow breath, Ansel felt remorse as he looked at the bare scalp where auburn hair had been, now tuffs stuck out from crimson tarnished wounds, and back at his eyes lacking life but had known fear. Carved into his chest was the Covey's symbol, her badge of pride. Her weapon of choice, a sword was missing, in its place was one of his shortswords from the trunk in his closet. It had been stuck through and pinned him to the table, its blade stuck out underneath.

Taking a deep breath, he clicked the mic. "Base."

"Go ahead," Mandy replied.

"I've found Tony Reed. My address, you'll need to send a coroner," Ansel reported, his voice flat.

"Repeat," Mandy said slowly, "Captain Wolt."

"Tony Reed. My address. Coroner. He's dead. Cautionary unknown weapons used. Kyanite crystals present." Send whoever you have to, he wanted to add, but the words and his ability to say them were lost in the loss of life in front of him. Grabbing his cell, he wanted to call Doctor Hyde and beg for her forgiveness and confess it was all his fault. Except he was a coward and he shoved the cell back in his pocket.

If he wasn't executed or banished from the pack, she would never speak to him, never cast him a hooded gaze containing a challenge. "Damn you, Bronte." Why would she attack an innocent when he had nothing to do with Ansel's life? It took him a couple of seconds, his mind trudging through what was in front of him, the consequences of his lies, to realize it was Dr. Hyde. Ansel didn't have a connection to the paramedic, he did have a connection to Clio, who had a connection to the dead man. Why would she care? He had no idea. And where was he going to be while the enforcers, if they weren't replaced with someone outside of the Cascade pack, investigated the murder? Locked in a cell as a traitor and murderer and waiting for news of Clio's death.

Time ceased to make sense when he heard a truck engine and tires crunching over gravel, the numbness that had held him vanished and was quickly replaced with fear. Then the second and third vehicles arrived, followed by a heavy diesel engine he recognized as the forensics team's new bus. He didn't want to face Rutger at the same time he wanted Rutger to be the one to put him in White 47, the synthetic version of silver, restraints and taken into custody. Where, when construction on the office was in full swing? Celestial. The same cell Rutger had been in. If he clawed at the walls and ripped his nails from his fingers, would they gas him? God, he hoped so.

Ansel raised his head as Rutger came around the corner of the house, his shoulders square, his gait strong, and his eyes glowing gold with his wolf. "I came home to follow up on the call and this is what I found."

"You haven't touched anything?" Rutger asked.

"Negative." He should be confessing, not trying to be

part of the investigation.

Rutger stood beside Ansel, his hand on the butt of his gun, and stared at the body. "Tony Reed," he whispered. "They tortured him."

"Affirmative. The spines are the same as the ones used on Lado, and I don't see any use of a toxin. They beat him to death," Ansel added. He wasn't going to say the torture lasted for hours and she made him beg for death, then denied him, with her usual cruelty. She probably threatened Clio's life and explained in great detail it was Ansel's fault he was being tortured. If Ansel said anything, it would make him look guilty and he needed time to speak to Rutger alone.

"The body was moved here. There's no blood, and there should be. A lot," Rutger stated as Dr. Hyde rounded the corner, her walk quickly turning into a run, then she skidded to a stop at the stairs. "This isn't something you need to be here for."

"I came with forensics as the coroner," Clio replied.

She hadn't taken the time to grab anything from the van, she left it for Dr. Ross, who she met as she forced her way into the vehicle. With her heart hammering in her chest, her pulse in her ears like she was in the midst of a windstorm, she stood at the first stair unable to move. If it was Tony— she wasn't convinced it was—he was someone she had known, she chose to, not because he was pack. He had made her laugh, feel comfortable, and made her feel like she was more than a doctor, a Wight, an enforcer ... he made her feel normal. Like a person. Woman. He couldn't be dead. Then there were Luis and Cara's accusations. She had been the last person to see him alive.

"Doctor Hyde, go back to the bus," Rutger ordered, his eyes softening to pale butterscotch then mahogany.

When Dr. Hyde ignored him, Ansel stepped in. "We know

about your relationship with him. You don't want to see him."

"Don't tell me what I want," she snapped. "I'm here as medical personnel."

"You are not the coroner," Rutger stated. "You have no authorization."

Captain Wolt's gaze hardened for a second, his eyes turning a sharp bronze, and she thought about apologizing. She wouldn't. After the way he treated her, and Tony was dead in his backyard, she owed him zero kindness. Clio couldn't shake the looks of pity in both sets of eyes staring at her as she took the first stair, then the second. The scent of iron and the trace of bitterness made her hesitate as she dared the third and fourth steps. She didn't have to walk farther to see the top of the victim's head and the wounds.

With his striking, thick, auburn with blond hair gone, his sallow scalp gave away how long he had been dead, and she pushed the thought away. She told herself she was there to confirm the victim's identity, collect the body, and take it back to Celestial for an autopsy. Facing the truth and the guilt seeping into her, she felt her determination splintering. Clio walked forward as Director Kanin moved out her way, and taking his place at the foot of the table, she gazed at what was left of the victim. When she couldn't lie to herself any longer and admitted it was Tony, all the blood in her body drained from her, her heart stopped, her lungs refused to give her air, and her mind fought against what she saw. Tony. They destroyed the man, making him unrecognizable.

"I-I-I didn't answer his c-call. I didn't. The p-pack," Clio stammered with her arms hanging loose at her sides, her eyes focused on the sword sticking from his chest, and the carvings. "Yesterday. I didn't. I could have. I didn't. I should have."

"No one could have saved him," Ansel offered softly.

Slowly, as if she was trying to understand what he had said, she turned her head, and met bronze flakes swirling in his cinnamon gaze. "You."

Ansel opened his mouth to defend himself, why he had no idea, she was right. Then he saw the hurt and pain in her usually controlled face. The emotions she kept locked behind an impenetrable wall were leaking through with her sorrow and she was breaking down and it was like a knife in his heart to see her different than the strong Dr. Hyde. Even Baron Kanin's harsh words about her abilities hadn't caused her to lose control over her feelings. As he stared at her, her eyes gleamed with unshed tears in the dying sunlight, the honey blazing from blue, and when she fully faced him, her hands were in fists at her sides.

Taking a hesitant step backwards he warned, "Doctor Hyde ..."

"Don't Doctor Hyde, me," Clio nearly growled. She was losing control, felt the strings around the stress she had been holding weaken, giving the coil room to expand. An inner voice warned her it was a bad idea, hitting Captain Wolt would get her in trouble, maybe fired from the hospital and removed as administrator from the med room at Foxwood. In a flash she saw her fists against his black T-shirt, his muscles straining against each hit, and she didn't care, not anymore, and didn't care if trying to beat the Captain of Enforcers to death was going to land her in a cell at Celestial in the psych ward. He deserved whatever pain she gave him until someone stopped her. Like Director Kanin. "You did this, I know you did. This is your fault." Feeling her fists on his hard chest, she hit harder, faster, until her hands ached, and he groaned from the pain.

Her accusation cut through him, the vehemence in her tone making him lower his hands to take the brunt of Clio's fists to his chest, arms, stomach, and one to his face. Her anger and loss rolled from her in frantic waves, covering him in guilt. She had the strength to seriously injure him but didn't, her hits controlled and measured from years of being around humans. When her eyes were scarlet and tears streamed down her cheeks and her curses turned to mumbled sobs, he held her upper arms. Her heat and energy seeped into his flesh and he fought to give her his strength in an attempt to ease her pain and calm her down. When her muscles softened in his hold and she started to sag, he lifted her and held her to his chest.

Clio didn't want Captain Wolt's arms around her, nor did she want his strength. She wanted to hold onto her hate and use it to hate him, to blame him for the way he made her feel, and she wanted to hurt him. She would have if the adrenalin hadn't drained from her, and as embarrassing as it was going to be afterwards, she wanted to feel him. Ignoring the inner warnings, she buried her face in his T-shirt, his strong arms tightened around her and she smelled him—male, wolf, the woods, and spice. Cinnamon like his eyes. She felt him, his muscles flexing as he began assuring her, his voice a rough grumble in his chest, his words soothing at the same time he was stroking her back. Up. Down. Up. Down. She couldn't stay there forever, and with her mind clear from her rage and guilt, she felt the multiple sets of eyes on her.

With as much dignity as she could pretend to possess, Clio eased away from Captain Wolt, his arms releasing her, his hands slipping down her sides to her hips, and she took a step back. Wiping tears from her heated cheeks, she inhaled a breath of air infused with fresh grass, flowers, the woods, and a tinge of floral from the pond. She may have acted like a damn fool, but she felt better.

"I'm sorry, I didn't mean ... My behavior ... I mean, I'm sorry. I'll get to work."

"Negative, Doctor Hyde. You're going to go wait in the van. Your job here is done," Director Kanin ordered. "Fail to obey and you'll be put on restriction."

"But, sir—" Clio began.

"I'm ordering you. Go. Now," he demanded.

Clio held the director's gaze then looked at Captain Wolt, whose darkened stare made her feel like a scared child who needed a hand to hold. This was not who she was. "Sir." Turning away from both men, she faced the questioning stares of the coroner, the forensics team, and the director's trusted enforcers, Kellen and Cassidy. How could she argue about having been relieved of duty when she fell apart? Like crashed and burned. Clinging to Captain Wolt, like he was her savior. Clio would never live through the humiliation.

With her head as high as she could manage, she left the group and their glares behind, retraced her steps around the house, and heard bits of their conversation. The wind swept through the treetops as it tossed the blades of grass back and forth and the sun started its decline behind the mountain ridge. Above her and oblivious to her pain, wine and honey smeared through the sapphire sky casting a warm hue over everything it touched. Standing beside the passenger side door of the van, she took the bottom of her scrub top, wiped tears and makeup from her face, then stared at Captain Wolt's simple, two-story house. It was clean, well kept, nothing fancy, and sat tucked between clusters of trees. She wanted to see it from the moment he had asked her and then told her about his geese. Would he see her as anything other than a weak Wight?

"I blew it today," she mumbled. The respect she had worked years for had gone up in smoke in matter of seconds. And in front of Director Kanin. She could almost tell herself he knew what she was feeling and understood, then he ordered her back to the van. He expected her to be professional.

When her head was clear and she wasn't on the verge of falling apart, and the world didn't feel unjust and unfair, and she could form a sentence, she was going to the director and tell him her suspicions about Captain Wolt.

Damn him.

CHAPTER NINETEEN

"Removing the sword," Dr. Ross reported. He stood on the body's right side, his hands around the grip, his feet shoulder width apart.

"I have an evidence bag," Dr. Green said. She stood beside Dr. Ross, giving him enough room so he could work.

"The sword is symbolic. Why stab him when they killed him before they moved him?" Rutger asked.

"He wasn't dead. The sword through the heart killed him," Dr. Ross replied.

"He was alive in that condition. Where's the blood?" Rutger countered.

"Underneath him the table is saturated. I'll do a DNA test to confirm, but I'm sure it's the victim's. How they collected it and what they're going to do with it, I have no idea."

Ansel looked at Dr. Ross, the coroner, as he pulled once, then twice, and dislodged the blade from the body and the table.

"You're saying whoever pinned him to the table, cleaned him up, then left?" Rutger questioned, his disbelief plain in his voice.

"Affirmative. There's a film on his skin, could be what they used." Dr. Ross leaned over the body, left a sliver of space, then drew a breath and shook his head as if the smell assaulted him. "I'll test it to confirm, but my guess is it's saliva.

They've tried to disguise the smell with ... cinnamon. Like a breath mint. This is an assumption, and a crazy one, it reminds me of vampires."

Ansel's heart stuck in his throat. He should be telling them everything, explaining they were right, but lost the ability to speak.

"In the middle of the damn day." He made a half circle. "I hate witches and vampires."

"If I'm correct, we'll have their DNA," Dr. Ross offered.

"We're dealing with a sociopath," Rutger growled.

"Have a look at the cross-guard, it has something etched into it." Dr. Green said as she handed it to Rutger.

With a gloved hand, he handed it to Ansel and asked, "It's the same symbol. And it's carved in his chest."

It was over. "Affirmative. It's mine." They were going to hang him.

Rutger's gaze narrowed on him, the swirling gold hardening as he stared, and everyone stopped working. If a feather dropped it would have sounded like a gunshot.

"It was a gift," he continued. "She gave it to me."

"Finish the job, and get out of here," Rutger ordered the group. Grabbing the mic clipped to his BDU top, he said, "Confirm, the deceased is Tony Reed. The scene is being cleared.

"Copy," Mandy replied.

"Kellen, Cassidy, you'll escort the forensics team and the coroner back to Celestial," Rutger ordered. "Make sure Doctor Hyde is secure."

"Copy, sir," they replied in unison.

"You are coming with me." His demand was set in stone, then without waiting for Ansel, Rutger opened the right side of the French doors, and went inside.

It had been late afternoon when he found the paramedic, sunlight evading the thick branches of the trees to cast its glow on the pond, deck, and the body. The sun had begun its descent, its halo touching the ridges of the mountains, a golden hue brightening the azure sky, while a pale violet was creeping through the clouds. Ansel bowed his head, knew what was in store for him, and readied himself for his confession. He met the puzzled gazes of the group, then took one last look at his land, territory, and felt it being ripped from him like she had torn an arm or leg from his body. Walking into his house, he unclasped his thigh holster and belt and set them on the tabletop, then untucked his black T-shirt with Cascade's crest on the back.

Feeling stripped of his worth, he faced Rutger. "I know what this is."

"Do you?" Rutger asked from the kitchen. He placed a bottle of beer on the counter, left it, then removed the top from his and took a drink.

"It's an interrogation," Ansel answered.

"Where did the attacker get the sword?" Rutger asked, ignoring him.

"It was in my room. I can show you," Ansel replied.

"Please do." Rutger set his beer on the counter and waited for Ansel to lead the way.

Hesitating, he watched Rutger for signs of his anger, feelings of disloyalty, and didn't see anything except the same misery he had been living with. After nearly losing himself to the beast and what he had gone through with Jordyn, the witches, killing the witches, and Flint's return, Rutger shutdown his emotions and didn't let anyone see him. He betrayed his friend and brother. With his head hung, Ansel crossed the living room and going upstairs walked down the hallway, not knowing what he was going to see in his room.

She had been in his house. In his room and had touched his belongings. It made his stomach clench knowing she invaded his territory, his house, and left without anyone knowing.

Ansel searched his room for anything out of place and saw nothing had been moved or taken. While it looked like no one had been there, her scent gave her away. Clinging to the air was a mix of sweetness and bitterness, woman and vampire. When he stopped at the closet door his heart pounded.

"The warning."

"What are you talking about?" Rutger asked. There was no patience in his voice or his face.

"The call Mandy received said they saw someone was at my house, it's why I left your place. I came home to check it out and found the paramedic. It was her. She called. If Mandy can confirm her number, it can be traced, we'll have her location," Ansel explained. Was it possible? They might have her DNA and her location.

"I'll have Mandy focus on getting the number," Rutger stated. "The sword."

"Right." Ansel opened the closet door—everything was the same as he had left it—and reaching toward the back brought the trunk out. Rutger backed up as he took it to the bed and opened it as he had before. The second shortsword remained, while in the empty space was a piece of aged paper, with the symbol of the Covey on it. Ansel picked it up, held it in his hand, then held it out for Rutger. "She was here."

"She came in here, took the sword, left a note in its place, and killed Tony?" Rutger questioned. "Then called communications."

"Affirmative. You can't take a blade from someone

without leaving a token." Ansel was sure Rutger didn't believe him. He didn't know if he heard it, if he would have believed him. This was her way, her game. She didn't want to end his life, she wanted to ruin his life, then take her revenge. Rutger didn't respond. In silence, he left Ansel standing beside the bed with the open trunk, the note, and headed downstairs.

When Ansel joined Rutger, their gazes met, his friend and pack brother's gold with his wolf. Hunting and then killing the witches wasn't going to matter, their friendship wasn't going to matter when Rutger was the Second to the Alpha, and served as the pack's legatee, who presided over the punishments the baron ordered. What would the baron order the slayers to do when he found out Ansel was responsible for Daniel, Lado, and Tony Reed? And that's if they stopped there. He knew they were watching and had seen the comfort he gave Dr. Hyde, and the way he held her when she clung to him. She targeted the paramedic for a reason. To see how Ansel would react? To confirm he cared for Clio?

"The interrogation?" Ansel asked.

"Yep, of sorts," Rutger responded casually. He took another swig of beer, leaned against the counter, and watched him.

"I don't think human law enforcement allows their suspects to drink during an interrogation." Like he was going to refuse the beer. Ansel sat in the counter-height chair, took the bottle, and drank.

"Let's call it an interview. And we aren't human." Rutger took his cell from his pocket, moved his fingers over the screen, then placed it on the counter. "I'm Director of Enforcers Rutger Kanin, interviewing Captain of Enforcers Ansel Wolt after the attack on an employee of Celestial, member of the Red River fold under Cascade territory, Tony Reed. Do you, Captain Wolt, understand the interview is being recorded for evidence?"

"Affirmative." Ansel met Rutger's gold gaze.

"You are cooperating voluntarily?" Rutger asked as he set his beer down.

"Affirmative." His confession was patching itself together, the details threading his past into the present.

"Did you have any foreknowledge of the attack?"

"Negative." He wasn't wearing his enforcer's uniform, wasn't armed, and was drinking beer. Ansel didn't know where he stood with Rutger.

"Do you know where the attack occurred?"

"Negative. My location can be confirmed through communications and proved by eyewitnesses and my GPS location," Ansel answered.

"Do you know why they would transport him to your house?"

"To prove their point." Ansel took a deep drink almost emptying the bottle. "To expose my relationship with the Covey."

Taking a folded piece of paper from his BDU pocket and unfolding it, he handed it to Ansel. "Why is this symbol tattooed on your side? Why is it etched in the hilt of the sword used to kill the victim? And what does it mean?"

Ansel stared at the copy of the Covey's symbol and saw his mistakes taking over his life. "I was part of their group. It symbolizes their family."

"Their family. Your family?" Rutger asked, his eyes going completely gold, and hardening like stone, as his body tensed.

"Was. It's in the past. Decades in the past." Guilt reared

its ugly head and Ansel felt her laughing at him and his attempts to save what he had.

"How many decades?"

"Four."

"Is that the point they wanted to remind you of?" Rutger looked at the wall, the fridge, and back to Ansel. When he met Ansel's gaze his face was blank as if emotions weren't part of him. As if his betrayal was an added weapon Rutger needed to protect himself against.

"Affirmative." He had a million things he wanted to say, explain, and couldn't find the words for any of them.

"Are they responsible for the attempted murders of Daniel and Lado?"

"Affirmative."

"How long have you known it was them?" Rutger took another drink, eyeing Ansel over the bottle.

"Daniel." Ansel hated the accusation in Rutger's voice, and the dark look in his eyes, as if their past had burned to ash.

"I asked you if you knew what it was, and you said you didn't. Why did you lie to me?" Rutger demanded, his voice thick.

"I thought I could find them and stop them." Sure he did. He didn't know where to start looking let alone stop them.

"After what happened to Jo, you risked the lives of the pack and the klatch. They tortured and murdered a man. It could have been any one of us."

The hurt in Rutger's eyes nearly killed him. "I never intended to lie. Everyone was dealing with their pain and I didn't want to make it worse. You were healing and dealing with the witches. And Jordyn."

"Bullshit," Rutger roared. "Don't be pathetic. And don't use Jo or me as an excuse to lie to all of us."

Dammit, he wasn't. He really wanted to protect them. How did this turn on him? He needed to fix it. "It's my past, my problem."

"Did you see Daniel? How about Lado and what they did to him? Did you see what they did to Tony Reed? Someone stabbed him through the heart and pinned him to your picnic table," Rutger roared. "It's not your problem anymore. That stopped when they attacked someone from the Unseelie court, one of the pack, and murdered another. It's all of our problem. They have terrorized the territory. It has made the pack look weak. It has made the enforcers look like fools. Like we were protecting you." Rutger finished his beer, and with a forced calm set the bottle on the counter, opened the fridge, and took another one. Waving the bottle at Ansel, he waited.

"Please. Bring two."

Setting two bottles in front of Ansel, Rutger took his position against the counter. "Has anything you've said over the years been true?"

Rutger was genuinely hurt, his heartache swirled around him like a coming hurricane. Rutger trusted him, needed him to be his anchor as his world crashed and Ansel had abandoned him when Rutger needed him most. "I've never lied to you."

He grunted an irritated sound. "You've done nothing but lie. Who are they? Why are they after you?"

Ansel twisted the top off both bottles. "They are the Covey. They're after me because they think I betrayed them. I owe them a blood debt."

Rutger shook his head as if trying to wrap his mind around what he said. "Like a Covey of quail?"

He could hear the disbelief in Rutger's voice. A Covey

capable of killing. "Affirmative. She believed that's what we were, its why there are feathers with the sword."

"Start at the beginning. The very fucking beginning, Ansel."

"Rutger, I didn't lie about my parents. They were killed in a fire and I would have been next if it hadn't been for her. She saved me. I spent weeks healing from burns, then when I was healthier, she offered to take me in. I had nothing. My parents were gone, their house, barn, everything was gone. There was no work for me, back then I wasn't accepted by society, and I'm not talking about being a werewolf." He took swig, swallowed half the bottle, like he was trying to swallow the hate and despair, and continued. "I was alone, I had nothing, not even clothes, and would have done anything ..." He laughed. "I did do anything, and they gave me a family. I didn't know what they were and when I did, I was too far indebted to back out."

Rutger raised his hand to stop him. "What are you talking about, accepted by society?"

"I'm a half Native American and half Italian. My parents were disowned by their families and I didn't belong in either world."

"You are a Pureblood?"

"Affirmative." Ansel didn't go into detail about his parents, why they perished when they could have survived, and what they were. It was automatic to keep it a secret.

"If this prejudice happened it was years ago. How old are you?" Rutger asked.

"One hundred forty years old."

Rutger's eyes widened. "Right. It explains your taste in furniture. The sword is real?"

He thought his furniture was fine. "Very. As is the other one, and the pistols."

"Of course. What are they?"

"Assassins for hire, who specialize in torture. Whether it be the target or their family. If you need information, they'll make sure you get it." The words tasted sour, their tang sticking to his mouth, while the spilled blood of his victims stained his hands.

"You were part of that? You were an assassin? An information collector? A mercenary?" Rutger didn't look at him; he took a drink, and stared at the fridge like it would change what was happening.

"Affirmative. I wear the symbol of the Covey as proof."

"The feathers and sword." Rutger faced him. "I've seen it before."

"Where?" He had Ansel's attention.

"When they took Jo, I researched everything from witches, witchcraft, holidays coinciding with magic-born to crests and symbols. I saw a picture of the sword and feathers and the article said the wearer was part of a secret sec. It didn't explain what kind. Another said it was a mark of a slave. Having seen it on you, I tried to find out and hit a dead end with every search. With Jo missing, my head was somewhere else, and everything that followed, I figured if you wanted me to know you would tell me."

"I should have." Ansel looked at the beer bottle as the word slave mingled with regret and guilt. Rutger had the opportunity to question him, and he let him have his secret.

"Yeah, you should have. Who trained you?"

"She did." Ansel smelled sweet cinnamon and pungent aspen as if it filled the room and its smoke made the air hazy. Her lessons that drew blood and the nights he spent locked up, chained up, or buried attacked him, then he felt her touch when she came to his rescue. Feeling like ice, her arms cradled him as she whispered reasons why she hurt him, and why she saved him. With his need for her acceptance and to please her, she would take his vein, the punctures marking him worse than the tattoo. He shivered with the memory. "I did it well. I became hers."

"She. Her. Now hers. Does she have a name? What do you mean hers?"

There was a reason Rutger was the Director of Enforcers, and not because his father was the alpha of the pack and baron of the territory, he was thorough. His drive to get to the truth would make the interview into a daylong confession. If it did, it might save Ansel's life. "*She* goes by Bronte. It's Greek and means *the sound of thunder.* She thinks very highly of herself. If you survive her tests and training, she gives you a name, and explains your past life is over and a new one has begun. She manipulates the Covey by demeaning them. Tearing them down, building them back up. Humiliating them in front of others. And when the verbal assaults are coming from everyone, and you want to yield, she sweeps in to save you. She explains she's the only person who understands you, you need her, and everyone else is against you."

"She did this to you?" Rutger asked.

"Affirmative. For decades." Ansel scrubbed his face with his hands as humiliation veiled him.

"She punished you?" Rutger's solemn voice held his pity.

"Affirmative. Pain teaches the best lessons."

Rutger paused, took a drink, then asked, "What was your name?"

"Brando. It's Italian and means *firebrand, sword.* She saved me from fire, and I became her sword. I proved my worth, and she rewarded me with her attention and her body. The Covey viewed us as a couple." *And you gave her your throat.* Ansel suddenly felt sick.

"Did you love her?" Rutger asked.

"Negative."

"You said you owe them a blood debt. For what?" Rutger was looking at him again, as if he was categorizing Ansel's confession.

"I left."

"Every fucking detail, Ansel," Rutger ordered.

"In the beginning, strong factions hired the Covey to take care of their undesirables and criminals on the run. It wasn't enough for her, she wanted more and started taking contracts, murder for hire. When the thrill faded, she began killing the innocent ... human and magic-born, it didn't matter. Her hold over me was weakening with the bloodshed and I couldn't do it. I was getting drained from her games, being on the run, living as a rogue, hiding from humans and magic-born, and wanted to stop the killing. I can still hear their begging, their cries in my dreams. Bronte wouldn't let me, said if I tried, I would be hunted and punished. I kept saying I couldn't do it anymore that it was going to kill me before she had the chance. When I touched her, I saw my victims, and heard her praise for finishing the job. I stopped." Ansel inhaled and exhaled as images from the past filled his eyes.

"Her skin repulsed me, her voice grated in my ears, I couldn't touch her, and I refused to let her—"

"Let her do what?"

"Feed. Take my throat." Ansel felt hot shame burn him from the inside out but wasn't going to let it stop him. "For a while we pretended everything was perfect in front of the others, she feared losing control. Then she recruited a therian, male, took an interest in him and he took interest in her.

She cast me out of her bed, then paraded their relationship in front of me, us, making a show of how much they *loved* each other, and how they had the same beliefs. I didn't care. I spent most of my time alone, didn't hang out with the Covey, and didn't participate in their meetings. When I declined to do a couple of assignments, they saw me as a threat and a runner. Pressure from the Covey forced her to make a decision, and she offered me a deal, two kills and I would be free." Ansel's chest felt tight, his shoulders ached from the tension gripping his muscles, and despite his stomach wanting to purge the first beer, he drained the second bottle and took a drink from the third.

"Continue." Rutger's beer sat forgotten and half full on the counter, the sides slick from condensation.

This was about to end. "I was sent out with her boyfriend, Dayton. The target was a political figure in some small town in the middle of nowhere. He was a nobody, and I should have known it was a trap. She had planned the entire thing. We were approaching the staging area when Dayton was stabbed from behind. I didn't have time to react when I saw the tip of the sword sticking through his chest. Bronte stabbed him through the heart, and stared at me as Dayton lay dying, then said I was meant to be hers and hers alone. She wanted to trap me. Standing in the alley, the alarm screaming, and police on their way, I saw the Covey punishing me for killing Dayton, and while they were drawing out the pain, Bronte would save me from them. She would have saved my life as she had every time and she would remind me of the fire. I would stay because I needed her, I was hers, I was marked, and was hers to use as she pleased. I felt her fangs in my flesh, tasted my blood on her lips, and couldn't go back. I couldn't do it anymore, so I ran. And ran. For years. Until I came here." She left enough of a man behind Ansel survived.

"The blood debt is for Dayton's life?"

"Affirmative."

"But she killed him."

"You don't understand the mental and emotional games she plays. Bronte preys on the weak, they want her, need her attention, her praise. She builds them up, then relentlessly tears them down. When they're being trained or punished, they want her to go to them and save them. They weren't going to believe me over her and wasn't going to when she had been sharing her bed with Dayton," Ansel explained. It was brainwashing. A cult. Like the witches.

"How do you think Bronte found you?" Rutger picked the beer up and sipped.

"The news. It's the only way. You know how I live. I don't go out and I don't have relationships. I've never put another's life at risk," Ansel answered. He put two lives in danger and was responsible for another's death. Damn, he was tapped out and ready to serve his punishment, whatever it was going to be.

"Why do think they shot Daniel?"

"To confirm it was me. Lado was a warning they were here and she's coming for me. The paramedic, as sick as it sounds, could be a twin to Dayton, and she killed him the same way, sword through the heart. The torture was for my benefit, to show me my future. I know it's them, they left so many clues it's absurd, and I would have to be stupid to think otherwise. Bronte wants revenge, she sacrificed one of the Covey to trap me, I denied her, and left. Knowing she is coming for me, I would protect my family, if I had one. I don't. I'm alone. There's no one they can take from me."

"You are not alone. Do you think they'll try to attack you?"

Rutger drained his beer and put both empty bottles in the trash.

Ansel ignored the part about not being alone. "Negative." *Lie.* "Since I don't a family or a lover, I think she's trying to dismantle my life. She'll take what I've worked for and what is important to me piece by piece. She's turning the pack against me, Doctor Hyde proved she doubted my ability to do my job. If the Unseelie and the Seelie Court aren't content with the outcome of the investigation and decides I'm to blame, they'll demand the baron do something. She would love to see someone punish me. Add in the Red River fold and if the baron doesn't imprison me or punish me in some way, it'll put a strain on the relationship the pack has with the entire klatch. You said yourself, the pack looks weak. It will make the baron look incompetent, and with everything that's happening, it'll cause the pack to question his ability to remain baron." He drank his beer as his mind raced. "To know I was working with Lado, they have to have been watching me. I'm going to assume she watched everything that happened here today."

"They know Lado is alive and at Celestial," Rutger added. "He knows who they are."

"If she wanted him dead, she would have killed him. Lado knowing who she is gives her power." Ansel thought about what he said. Lado was safe. "My past with her is in the open. You know who she is."

"Do you think they'll target someone else?"

He almost answered no, she was going to come for him. "Fuck. Doctor Hyde."

"What about Doctor Hyde?" Rutger asked with a growl running through his words.

"She killed the paramedic, who was with Doctor Hyde. Bronte is making a point to destroy my loyalty to the pack.

First Doctor Hyde was at Foxwood, and she was close to me, then she was here, I held her, and comforted her. Doctor Hyde touched me. Depending on how long I've been watched, she knows I don't have a mate or a lover. No one touches me. Doctor Hyde did, she was in my arms," Ansel explained, the words rushing from him. He savored her touch. "They'll go after her."

"You're sure?" Rutger took his cell from the counter and stopped the recording.

"Positive. When we were at the hospital." *I treated her like she was the plague.* "Negative. No, it wasn't the hospital. I called her ... it was about setting a time for you to visit Jordyn. I was out on the deck and asked her if she wanted to come over to see the views of the mountains and if she wanted to see my geese."

"You are interested in her. Wait, you have geese? Never mind. Knowing her, I'm going to assume she said no."

"Rejected. It might have saved her life." Ansel finished his beer, placed the empty bottle beside the others, and stood.

"Sit. You aren't going anywhere. You're too close to this and you've been suspended pending a hearing. With the connection made between the three attacks and the possibility of a phone number and DNA, I have a place to start. I will have a transcript made from the recording as evidence in your case, you didn't kill Tony Reed and aren't responsible for his kidnapping, and I'll hand it over to the baron, and he will consult the elders." Rutger raised his hand, stopping Ansel from interrupting. "I understand why you lied about your past and weren't completely forthcoming with the information about the Covey. I wish you would have given me the benefit of the doubt. You're a pack brother. The Captain of Enforcers. I'll repeat myself and tell you, you aren't alone.

Now I'm going to have Quinn and Aydian here."

"Negative. You'll be risking their lives. I won't have their blood on my hands," Ansel argued as he sat down in defeat. If Bronte wanted to take him, let her. "No one else needs to be hurt."

"They're trained. They can hold their own," Rutger insisted.

"Maybe from the Covey, but not her. She's a dhampir, that's why there wasn't any blood, she's dangerous, and can mess with a shapeshifter's senses." Ansel was hesitant about going further. Hell, what did he have to lose? He was suspended from his position with the possibility of losing it and facing time in a cell somewhere. Ansel pointed at the fridge. "Hit me."

Rutger took two bottles out and handed one to Ansel. "Daytime. I thought she was a vampire. Were you going to keep that detail to yourself?"

"She took me, my throat, and pinned me to the ground as she drank my blood. It's not something I want to remember. I don't want to talk about it. I should have said something to Doctor Ross, my mind was elsewhere." Ansel was thankful the mood had shifted and Rutger's tension had eased. The air around them thinned and the buzzing of power was a low roar. It made his second confession less forced. "Unlike most dhampirs, her birth hadn't been an accident, it had been orchestrated by the elders of her sire's clan. Her mother was a mage from one of the most powerful covens and chosen because of her magic."

"Damn witches. Reminds me of Jo," Rutger mumbled. "Why would they purposely create her?"

Ansel paused ... it was like Jordyn or what the baron wanted Jordyn to become. "The clan was trying to increase their territory and needed daywalkers loyal to them able to defend the territory. The magic-born they fed on weren't powerful enough to withstand their training. They took the strongest males from the clans and the strongest female magic-born they could find and created them. She is half vampire and half mage. She has the traits of a vampire and possess strong magic. It explains the kyanite crystals."

And her focus on revenge. "Her first mission had been when she was ten years old. She said it wasn't successful, she had been punished, received concentrated training, and sent back out. Bronte's mission was to eliminate vital leaders of other clans and factions in order for her clan to increase their territory. She did this. With her success, her clan became increasingly wealthy and their territory vast. She didn't have a family, a mother or a sire, she wasn't raised, she was trained like a tool to be used, a weapon set aside until needed. She wasn't a person."

"Her life sucked, no pun intended, but it doesn't explain what's happening now." Rutger's voice was edged with frustration and exhaustion as he pushed his fingers through his hair. "You sound like you're defending her. The bitch treated Lado like a pin cushion. One of your *own*." Rutger stressed the word own. "And tortured an innocent to death."

"Dammit, Rutger, I'm not defending her. She was in my life for a hundred years and I can't erase that. And she can't erase her past, the way her clan treated her, or the over nine hundred years that she's been alive." Ansel wanted to yell with frustration. He took several deep breaths, counted to one hundred or close to, and continued explaining, "At some point the vampire council decided the dhampirs were too dangerous and sent assassins to eliminate them. They sent assassins to kill their assassins. I hate vampires. They wounded her, and believing she was dead, left her. She lived, got her revenge, and left her homeland. Her clan turned her into a killer, used her, betrayed her, and left her for dead. She didn't have anyone, just like me. It's the reason she started the Covey." She saw Ansel like she saw herself. Living in two worlds and belonging to neither. It had been in front of him the entire time and he hadn't recognized it for what it was. When he denied her, then left her, he did the same thing her clan had done, and he took the one thing that made her feel like she was a person and belonged.

"It's a group of assassins, who are gunning for you," Rutger argued. "That isn't a family."

He knew that. Ansel wanted to be left alone with his regrets, his memories, his guilt, and the rest of his beer until she came for him. His mind latched onto reliving his past, when he saw her, how she felt, and was there with her. Maybe he was defending her. Maybe he was defending his life and why he followed her for so damn long and let her own him. Let her use him the way she had been used. If he went back with her, she might leave the pack, Dr. Hyde alone. Was his loyalty that flimsy he would give up the kith and kin prepared to defend him?

"Maybe if I left with her," Ansel mumbled. *Affirmative.*

"Negative. You said she wants revenge. Going anywhere near her is signing your death warrant." Rutger shoved off the edge of the counter, made a lap around the kitchen, and resumed his place. "You are part of Cascade. We protect our own."

"You don't think I'm capable of charming my way out of it?" Ansel asked as he lifted an eyebrow.

"Negative."

"Her vampire half is dominate, forcing her to feed. Bloodlust is a thrill to her, and she lives for it. I've seen her cruelty in person. Have felt it." Ansel drank his beer and tried to ignore Rutger's glare. He felt ashamed for putting his pack brother's life at risk. "She's playing with me. She won't come for me, she'll target someone she thinks is close to me, that I care for, and right now it's Doctor Hyde. She's female and direct competition to Bronte."

"The dhampir will go after Doctor Hyde because she's jealous. Guess you were her one true love. Maybe you could charm her." The sarcasm dripped from every word. "I won't put my enforcers at risk. If you think you're in danger, I want you to call me, or better yet, haul ass to Foxwood. She can't take us all."

"Understood. Does this mean I'm on house arrest?" Ansel asked.

"Affirmative." Rutger finished his beer, threw the bottle away. "If you need anything let me know and I'll have it delivered."

"I need beer." Ansel held his bottle up and pointed at the label.

"Consider it done." Rutger walked out of the kitchen to the living room, then turning enough to meet Ansel's gaze, his eyes rolled gold. "We protect our own and you are part of Cascade. We are your kith and kin. I'm not going to hold your past against you and I'm not going to abandon you."

Ansel didn't know what to say. He should be restrained in White 47 chains and rotting in a cell. Instead, he found himself a true family with no strings attached, no conditions, no working for their approval, no begging for their attention, and they supported him. And he was about to lose it all. "I love you like a brother, Rutger."

"A much better looking, younger brother." Rutger laughed a rough sound threaded with stress. The sad smile didn't reach his eyes, as they softened, letting Ansel see his emotion and the loss in them. Exposing his feelings told Ansel Rutger knew it was his way of saying good-bye. A painful heartbeat later, Rutger walked out of the house.

Ansel stood in his living room looking at the door and listening to the silence as twilight held onto its place for minutes when night pushed it back and took control. The dark house felt alien, lonely, and like a prison. His time with the enforcers was over, he was going to lose his pack, and he would never experience Clio's love or have her to himself. Why that bothered him the way it did scared him more than knowing Bronte was coming for him.

CHAPTER TWENTY

The pale beige walls of her office felt like they were closing in on her while the oxygen was being sucked from the room. Clio shifted in the chair, tried to focus on the computer screen, her report, the details of Tony's death, Dr. Radford's forensics report, Dr. Ross' autopsy report, and the information regarding the kyanite crystals.

Her concentration wasn't on any of it and soon the words blurred. Her concentration was on Captain Wolt, how he knew about her relationship with Tony, and how he held her against his body. Damn him. She made an absolute fool of herself. And now Tony was dead. Clio looked at her cell and phone beside it.

"Don't do it, you'll humiliate yourself even worse. He doesn't want your help, doesn't need your help. Doesn't need you. He thinks you were dating Tony. And let him." She stared at the screen, then without an internal pep talk, chose which apparatus would propel her pride to the trash can, picked up the handset of the phone, entered the number for communications, and waited. She would find out what was happening, have her curiosity taken care of and get back to work.

"You've reached Cascade communications, this is Mandy how may I help you?"

That's odd. "It's Doctor Hyde."

"Doc, what can I do for you?" Mandy inquired.

"Is Captain Wolt there?"

"Negative."

The line went silent, making Clio's nerves hit a new high with her anxiety. Mandy's unusual silence told her volumes. "Can you tell me why?"

"Negative."

All right. "Who is in charge of the investigation?" Anger worked itself into her anxiety. Damn them, she played *go between* when Miss Langston was in the hospital, was on call twenty-four hours a day, was attached to her cell, and they weren't going to tell her what the hell was going on.

"Director Kanin."

"Is he available?" He might explain what was going on and why.

"Negative."

"Can I speak with Baron Kanin?"

"Negative."

"You aren't going to tell me anything?"

"Foxwood remains on lockdown. All construction has ceased. There are no visitors allowed. The pack, klatch, and factions have been informed of the murder of Tony Reed of the Red River fold and the ongoing investigation. Baron Kanin advises everyone not to travel alone. If it isn't a priority, do not go anywhere. The enforcers and soldiers have been put on tactical alert for the safety of the territory. If you have an emergency, you are advised to call Paradise County Sheriff's Department. If you have a medical emergency, you are advised to call Celestial."

Mandy sounded like she was reading from a script. "Why wasn't I informed? I have information regarding the investigation." Clio's anger drained from her and was replaced with fear.

"What? You weren't told what was going on?" Mandy asked, her voice tight.

"Negative," Clio replied with as much sternness as she could muster.

"You should have been called, at the very least sent a text. The computer still has some bugs and communications is overloaded." Mandy cursed.

Clio understood the lockdown. If they were bold enough to attack an enforcer, and allow him to return to Foxwood, then murder another and move the body to an enforcer's house without fear, the baron and baroness' safety were priority. And Miss Langston was staying there. Clio didn't understand why Captain Wolt wasn't there, unless he was busy. That's it, right? Something bad hadn't happen to him. Director Kanin hadn't taken him into custody for the murder? She knew he wasn't because he wasn't at Celestial. The murderers hadn't targeted him, they had been at his house. She wanted to ask, the question was on the tip of her tongue, and didn't. If Captain Wolt had been hurt, he would be at Celestial, and she would know. If he had been killed, his body would have been transferred to Celestial, and she would know.

Focusing, Clio asked, "What should the call or text have told me?"

"You are to stay where you are, and if you need to go anywhere, you're to wait until an enforcer can escort you," Mandy explained. "You'll have soldiers at your house."

"You're kidding me? I'm not being escorted anywhere," Clio protested. "What the hell, Mandy?"

"Doc, listen to me, you were there last night, you had a personal relationship with the victim, and the baron doesn't want you to go anywhere without an escort. An enforcer should have been at the hospital by now. In fact, it should be Kia. Let me check." Clio heard the clicking of keys in the background and soft curses from Mandy. "She is en route. Are the soldiers guarding Lado?"

"Affirmative."

"Well that's something. I'm being honest when I say, I don't know what's going on. What I told you is what they told me, and I give everyone who calls the same speech."

"It's all right. This is crazy," Clio mumbled.

"You have no idea. And it will change the way we are, again."

Clio knew what Mandy meant. The shift from casual pack to military grade discipline put a divide between everyone. It wasn't Clio asking Mandy a question, it was Dr. Hyde asking communications about an enforcer's case and being denied access. There were titles and positions, and on a need-to-know basis and she didn't have a title and didn't need to know. The Enforcer's office with an underground prison and Foxwood's upgraded security was proof of the change and it was going to get worse. A rush of panic burned her insides and she wanted to blame someone and everyone for letting it happen, for making her feel like her world had been jerked out from under her. The trails her mind chased always went back to the baron and his soothsayer, Miss Langston. Was the assassin with the kyanite crystals sending a message to the baron about his soothsayer? Like cease and desist with the dark ages crap. She didn't know.

"I'll let you get back to work," Clio said, wanting to hang up so she could call Captain Wolt.

"It's a direct order from Baron Kanin, do not go anywhere without an escort," Mandy ordered.

"Copy." Clio set the handset on the receiver and sat back.

Picking up her cell—damn her—she called Captain Wolt. One. Two. Three. Four. *Come on.* His low rumble of a voice told her to leave a message. She opened her mouth to obey his request, her brain going completely blank, and she stopped before stuttering noises came out and hit the end button.

She would give it a day, then when she had time, she was going to drive to his house, make sure he was all right, and try to explain why she fell apart. *Good luck.* Once she shed the shroud of embarrassment, she was going to find out what was going on. And if he didn't tell her? Clio didn't know. She hated not knowing.

The night had dragged on and on, and with each passing hour his emotions raged between panic and rage. A slight reprieve was when he thought about Dr. Hyde, her assuring presence, their banter, the way she felt in his arms, then he was reminded he was never going to see her again. That brought instant fury and it lasted for hours.

While he waited for her and her Covey to come through the front door to take him, he paced, and must have marched a hundred miles, he was positive there should have been ruts in his wood flooring and carpeting. At dawn, as the sun crept into the sky, he collapsed on the couch and slept for a couple of hours. His dreams were filled with his confessions, Rutger's deep voice, Bronte's face, her cold touch, and Clio's bloodshot eyes as she cried for Tony. The paramedic. Dr. Hyde, he corrected himself, it would never be Clio. He had become the poison to the pack. And that's when he decided it was time to clean and pack his enforcer gear.

Dressed in civilian clothes of a gray T-shirt, jeans, and

boots, Ansel folded the last T-shirt with Cascade's crest on the back and his name on the front, then placed it in a box beside his tactical belt, holster, gun, and gear. He checked the drawer to make sure it was the last one, then the dresser top for gear, and finding he had gotten everything, folded the sides and tapped it closed. With his enforcer gear packed, his heart ached, his confidence faded, and he pushed the feelings aside.

He had spent the morning cleaning house, making sure there wasn't too much Rutger would have to take care of once Ansel was gone. He set the box against his bedroom wall beside the others, and backing up sat down on his bed. Taking the time to look at his room, he saw it through new eyes and heard Rutger's comment about his choice of furniture. Like the rest of the house, it was basic, stark—the walls were bare, the furniture plain, and there was nothing telling someone he lived there. It looked like it was a house and not a home. He wasted the years by denying himself a home. With frustration and regret darkening his already bad mood, he stood, left his bedroom, and walking down the hall, went downstairs. On the dining table was a bottle of bourbon Rutger had Luke drop off when he delivered the two cases of beer and enough food for a week. If he was going to be on house arrest, Rutger wanted him comfortable. It made Ansel feel worse and the guilt tasted toxic.

After taking a glass from the kitchen and going to the table, he grabbed the bottle and poured. Ansel went to the couch and sat down to watch his cell light up with calls and messages. *Please stop.* It was a reminder of what he was losing. They depended on him, and he was ignoring them. He had been ordered, by the baron, to ignore all calls while under house arrest and while Rutger conducted the investigation. He wasn't sure what they were doing, 'cause no one was talking to him. Rather, he couldn't talk to anyone. He took a long drink, and swallowing the liquor, felt its heat slide down his throat and into his middle where it heated the chill Bronte's pending arrival had created. Another long pull and he set the glass down, grabbed the cell, turned the sound off, and tossed it back to the coffee table like it would bite him. With the next call it vibrated against the oak top, the screen lit up with Dr. Hyde's number. *Fuck me,* he cursed and was never going to say that again. What the hell did she want? Maybe tell him she knew he was guilty of her boyfriend's death. Taking the cell, he turned the vibrate off and placed it screen down on the table. He didn't want to see a reminder of her.

Again, the house amazed him. The plainness of it. The emptiness of it. He didn't own a TV, didn't have time to sit and watch anything, if he knew what to watch. His one purchase, besides household items, guns, ammo, and archery equipment, was a stereo. Ansel stood, grabbed his bourbon, walked over to the console, and hit the button. A smokey, female voice glided into the room, erasing the sharp edge from the thick silence. God he loved the blues. The memory of walking along Beale Street, the aromas of fried catfish, and the moody music drifting from bars to find him, cradled him in a good part of his past. Taking a sip of bourbon, the combination of liquor and music bullied through his manic thoughts and helpless mood.

"I could fight back," he mumbled. "In retaliation she would stalk and target someone else. Doctor Hyde. Rutger."

The song ended, there was a pause, long enough he thought he heard an engine, and another song started. He didn't hear traffic from the road, and if he heard an engine there was someone at his house. It could be Bronte. Sure, she was going to drive up, tell him to hop in, and off they would go. Ansel left his post as a lump formed in his throat on his way to the large picture window. Dammit. What the hell was Dr. Hyde doing at his house? She was making a pending kidnapping by assassins, punishment that was torture, and then killed way harder than it needed to be. Her pearl white luxury crossover crept toward his house and he could see her checking her surroundings. She parked beside his truck, and he wanted to see the vehicle there overnight then gleaming in the rising sun. *Stop*. Like she would leave the city life and townhouse for a plain cabin and a murderer. He was torturing himself.

Dr. Hyde got out of the car wearing a fitted racerback tank top that showed off her sculpted arms, a pair of scrub pants with cargo pockets that emphasized her hips, and if she turned around, he knew the view would be outstanding. Her blonde hair with strawberry highlights was up in a loose ponytail, its end in the center of her back, and stray strands feathering her cheeks. Her lightly tanned skin made the honey streaks in her cobalt eyes standout. Ansel stared taking in her beauty, traits of her wolf, and her confidence as she made her way between his truck and her car, up the stairs and to the door. The soft rapping was enough to make his heart pound. Inhaling and exhaling, he kept the glass, he wasn't going to put it down for fear of grabbing her and holding her to his body and crossed the room. He knew it was from desperation to hold onto his life and not from the need twisting inside him.

Opening the door, he greeted, "Doctor Hyde."

"Captain Wolt. May I?"

"Please." Bad idea, he was waiting for Bronte.

Passing Captain Wolt, Clio walked into the living room and looked around. There was nothing giving the room character. No personal affects. Nothing saying Captain Ansel Wolt lives here. Not even a picture. Clio didn't think it needed it when scents from outside laced the inside and then there was the music. It fit him.

"After yesterday, I was worried." His dark eyes gauged her like he was waiting for her to start crying. "I wanted to check on you."

Worried about him? What did he say to her? *I slept with the person responsible for killing your boyfriend. Right.* "I'm suspended until further notice." It was the truth. He couldn't bring himself to remind her there had been a body found pinned to his picnic table.

"I see." Did they suspect him of murdering Tony? Negative. He wouldn't be home. Clio shifted her eyes to gain the strength she needed, and when she thought she could go on she met his gaze. "I'm here to apologize for losing it yesterday. It was unprofessional, lacked strength, and I put both you and Director Kanin in an awkward situation. I'm sorry."

She was apologizing to him for her behavior. Like she was weak. Clio Hyde was the strongest, smartest, most loyal, passionate woman he knew. "You were in shock. To see someone you care about, someone you're in a relationship with harmed and in that condition ... no one should have seen that." There he said it, and now maybe she would leave.

"In a relationship with? No, we were friends. Coworkers." Clio's mind raced.

"You don't have to explain yourself. I'm sorry for your loss." Ansel held her azure gaze, hoping she continued to deny the paramedic was her boyfriend and hated himself.

"I'm not explaining myself. I'm telling you he wasn't my boyfriend. When do I have the time to date?" Clio insisted, like she had said it a million times. "This isn't about him ...

well, it is, but it's not. I'm sorry. I failed you and the pack yesterday."

Dear god. "Fine, apology accepted." He took a drink of his bourbon and felt time crashing down around him, the seconds ticking off in his head and putting marks on his skull. What the hell was Bronte waiting for? "It's not wise for you to be here. You could get into trouble. I thought the baron had someone watching you." Ansel needed her gone.

She was an idiot. "I'm a big girl," Clio replied, trying to keep her voice from giving away her feelings.

Captain Wolt held his glass with a death grip as he stared at her with cinnamon eyes. He wasn't wearing his uniform, instead he wore a T-shirt that hugged his arms and chest, a pair of worn jeans hung low on his hips, broken in boots, and his dark hair wasn't back but loose, combed through with his fingers, the ends grazing cotton and his muscles. Clio was sorta stunned by the sight of him out of uniform, holding a glass of liquor, and standing in his house. The music and sultry voice made it worse like they were moving between them, the melody making the room smaller, intimate.

"You need to leave." Ansel barely got the words out. Why was she staring at him? Did she see a murderer? A traitor? Or his house was a space and not a home and she felt sorry for him? It didn't matter. He was going to call Rutger and confirm there was an enforcer watching her. Right now, he needed her gone. "Right now, Doctor Hyde. You need to leave."

Clio felt the coldness in the way he said her name. *Damn him*, she thought as she gathered some of her pride, straightened her shoulders, and said, "I realize after my behavior yesterday, and my association with a coworker, and knowing you don't fraternize with the lower class like me, a Wight, you want me gone. I am a medical doctor with an

MD, and it's my responsibility, whether you like it or not, to make sure you're all right. And sorry."

If he wanted her to leave, fine, she would. Clio didn't need the constant rejection and cold front from Captain Good Mood. She glared at him, hoping lasers shot out of her eyes, then turned to the still open door. What the hell was wrong with him? What the hell was wrong with her? MD. God she was stupid. She hated herself for going straight to her default setting and using it as an excuse to tuck tail and run.

Not this time.

She stopped at the door and faced Captain Good Mood and saw he hadn't moved. "A body was found here at your house. Your life could be in danger. I wanted to know you're all right. That I'm not prone to tears, I'm stronger than that, and if there is anything I can do to help, I will." There it was, out in the open. Clio needed him to tell her it was going to be fine. They were going to find who murdered Tony, and the accusations coming from the klatch would be put to rest.

"Why?" It was Ansel's fault. He stormed outside, and stood on the porch, his hand on the rail and the other gripping the glass. "Why, MD, does it matter to you if I'm all right?"

She deserved that. Clio stared at his back, his nearly black hair grazing his shoulder blades, his muscles flexing when he moved, and his shoulders tense from stress. "One of our own is in the hospital and we lost Tony to these murderers. I won't lose another." She paused, waiting for him to react, and when he didn't face her, she admitted, "Maybe I care." Entirely too much.

"You shouldn't, not after yesterday. Why do you think I've been suspended and on house arrest?"

"I don't know," she whispered. She didn't like the tension

in his shoulders and back, like every muscle was straining.

"I have a past with those responsible." He faced her and she narrowed her gaze on him. "That's right, I know them. I'm to blame. Damn house arrest, I should be locked up in a cell for being a murderer. I don't deserve your care or worry. There's your car. Get in it and get out of here." He needed to get her the hell away from him before he took selfishness to a whole new level and gave into his wants. "Leave."

Damn him. "I don't know what you mean."

"My past. This is all part of my past, my life. The things I did. I'm an assassin. A killer. I was part of them. The sword used to kill Tony is mine," he confessed. He wasn't any closer to getting her to leave. "His death was a message to me. Lado was a message— "

"I get it. Your sword," Clio whispered as she studied him. His eyes had always held something darker. A hardness. Sadness. Loneliness. Detachment. Assassin. What had happened to him? "Are you a part of them now?"

"Don't Doctor Hyde. I'm not worth your time." Why wouldn't she leave? Her closeness put him on the edge of telling her how he felt.

"I decide who is or isn't worth my time. Are you a part of them?" She nailed him with narrowed eyes he knew too well.

"Negative."

"Do you know where they are?"

He shook his head. "If I did, they would be dead."

The resistance in his eyes and the darkness in their depths gave away his demons and the damage they were doing. The enforcers and the elders had his life in their hands, his future with the pack, his future as an enforcer. She wasn't going to make it worse. "Exactly. I'm not judging your past when we all have one. Are you going to be all right?" Clio asked as she slid her fingers around his upper arm. She was touching him and felt him tense under her palm as his heat seeped into hers then their hearts beat as one. Like it had when he held her. His past. His relationship with the murderers temporarily put aside, but not forgotten. "Do you feel that?"

Her closeness brought him her scent of cinnamon, spice with a pinch of sweet, which he had hated for years and now couldn't get enough of. Ansel closed his eyes, felt his wolf rise, its need to prove he was strong enough to protect her, his mate. His power seeped into the air carrying his wolf's essence as it took possession of her. Before he lost himself in her feel, in wanting her, he backed away, letting her fingers trail down his arm, regretted the chill, and put distance between them. Ignoring her, he sipped his bourbon.

"Doctor Hyde, I'm fine, will be fine. Rutger will find them, and it'll be over. You really need to leave. It's not safe for you to be here," he said softly.

Clio heard him and didn't hear him, she couldn't get her body to move. Instead, she stared at him. There was something happening to them, between them. Her wolf weaved through her, forcing her to face the truth ... she wanted him. Needed him. Needed to touch him. Was she losing her mind? Was this proof of how lonely she was? Maybe Tony's death had affected her more than she thought. How sad was it that she was pining after the Captain of Enforcers? And willingly taking Captain Good Mood's rejection over and over again. It was simple. She wanted something she couldn't have, and it was a challenge. Nothing more. She needed to smack herself into next week and get over it.

"You're right. I need to leave. Captain Wolt, please accept my apologies for my behavior and barging in on you," she mumbled. Clio stared at her car, his truck, and the woods surrounding them.

Ansel knew what he was losing. His mate. He knew this in his soul. His wolf howled in his ears as Clio left him and took the stairs. He told himself she deserved better and a future, one with a man who wouldn't put her life in danger with his corrupted past. He was a Pureblood without a family, a legacy, a crest of his own. He had been an assassin, a rogue, felt like one right at the moment, and lived in hiding from humans and magic-born alike. He associated himself with Rutger and the other enforcers, living like he was in his thirties, taking on their habits, their language, when really, he was a one-hundred-and-forty-year-old monster. Once she was in her car, she would be out of his life forever. Bronte would make sure the pain from losing Clio would end and a new one would start. He welcomed it knowing when it ended, he would be free.

Clio stood in front of Captain Wolt's truck, the sunlight filtering through the tree limbs, leaves, and casting spiderweb shadows around her. Summer's warm breeze wove between the treetops and caressed her bare skin while the smell of the woods, which she associated with him, filled her nose. Yes, he was a Pureblood who had fought his way to captain, held his place, and solidified his status and worth to the pack. *This, though*, she looked around, *was Ansel ... a silent strength, grounded, secure, straightforward, and unpretentious, while too scared to live.* She desperately wanted to help him heal. Wanted to take the darkness from his past and give him a future. She regretted having turned him down, when she should have driven to his house when he asked. Clio faced him and met a bronze gaze that took the breath from her lungs.

"It's beautiful out here. Peaceful. I understand why you like it."

Like you. Ansel couldn't stop his smile or the pride he felt. She liked his house and his land. Damn, it would have been good. "Not quite like your townhouse in the city."

No, it wasn't. Clio relaxed with his grin and wanted to do anything to keep his demons from destroying him. She didn't want to leave. There at that moment for the first time in her life, she felt like she belonged. And she was going to walk away from him. "Enjoy your evening, Captain Wolt."

"Clio." She stopped when he said her name and faced him, her blue gaze holding him. "Call me Ansel." He needed to hear her say his name one time. Needed a connection to her. "I know there's a new decorum and understand if it makes you feel uncomfortable."

"Ansel it is. Enjoy your evening, Ansel." A warmth flooded her middle. Had she made a crack in Captain Good Mood's protective barricade? God, she hoped so.

Twice. He loved the way she said it, like he was the only person in the world, and she was savoring his name as it left her lips. "Enjoy your evening, MD."

Clio laughed and felt heat spread across her cheeks. Yeah, she was going to enjoy her evening. She was going to lock herself in her city townhouse, pour a cocktail, and gush over Ansel like a sixteen year old whose crush had acknowledged their existence. And after getting it all out of her system, she was going to go over the reports and see if there was anything they missed, and she would help find the murderers. Still laughing, she watched a smile curve his lips and felt his power on the air.

Ansel watched her take a step, his heart was going to explode, when she flinched, mumbled a curse, then palmed the back of her neck. "What is it?" he demanded a little too harsh. *No.*

"Nothing. I think something stung me," Clio answered. In case it was a bee, she gingerly felt around the bite, and felt something in her skin. "What the hell?"

"What?" Ansel used his senses to search the area, knowing if Bronte didn't want him to feel her, he wouldn't. "Talk to me, Clio." This was not happening. He dropped the glass, jumped the stairs, and closed the distance between them, while fear swamped him in a cold wave. "Clio."

His alarm drove into her, causing her hands to shake and making it difficult to keep hold of whatever was in her neck. After pulling it free, she held her hand out to show Ansel. "A crystal?" She knew what it was before he sucked in a breath. The thin kyanite needle glimmered in the sunlight. "It's her." Clio met his bronze gaze and prayed he told her no, desperately wanted him to tell her it wasn't real.

"We need to get you out of here." Ansel's words rushed from him, making Clio's eyes widen with her fear.

"Her. She's here." It was them. The assassins.

She was in trouble. As a sting reached out from the punctures, images of Lado's wounds flooded her eyes, DIC, his skin dying and falling from him, his lips moving around intangible words, his mind feeding him nightmares. A medically-induced coma. Nails in his joints. Tubes and monitors hooked to him. Tony dead and pinned to a table, his body beaten and broken. Clio reached for Ansel as three more needles punctured her shoulder and sides. Twisting from the sting, she lost her balance, fell to her knees, and putting her hands out in front of her tried to save herself. Ansel was in front of her, holding her, talking to her, his lips moving around soundless words. Her pulse was rushing in her ears while her heart was pounding her sternum and felt like it was going to explode. Did he say sorry? She didn't know.

"Fire. There's fire everywhere. My skin." Clio struggled in his hold as pain saturated her, lava coursed in her veins, and her lungs began shrinking.

"Clio, I'll get you help. Stay with me, *tesoro*," Ansel whispered, the name slipping from him heavy with truth and possession. At her suffering, rage and hate flowed from him. She wasn't going to take Clio from him.

Tesoro. She wanted to stay with him. God how she wanted to stay with him. She didn't want to self-combust in his front yard. "Staying with you," she whispered.

Her lips burned, her throat felt tight, and her chest squeezed like metal bands were wrapped around her. She met his bronze gaze as his arms circled her and his feel veiled her in his wolf's essence and strength. Somehow, she felt protected, and knew he would do anything to keep her safe.

"I have you," he whispered. The years being denied a life sat heavy on his shoulders as he gazed at Clio and her strength.

"Ansel." He was hers. With the admission, her magic threaded between them, her wolf claimed him, and she felt him take her into him. A smile tried curving her lips and failed. She couldn't keep her eyes open. *Do not pass out, stay with him.* Lifting her hand, she touched his cheek, and watched him close his eyes. She wanted to stay with him. Clio clenched her teeth when searing pain rushed through her making her body cave in on itself and she curled into a ball, her arms scraping gravel, leaves, and dirt.

"I'm sorry, tesoro. So sorry." Ansel was powerless to stop the convulsions as he watched her writhe, and with pink tears streaming from her eyes, her hands clenched in tight fists.

"While watching you suffer as your life is taken apart and

your pack sees you as the monster you are has been gratifying, I wanted more. My patience has rewarded me." She stalked between Clio's crossover and his truck. "I didn't know you had a thing for the weak, Brando. Really, a Wight? I'll acknowledge she's cute but not worthy of a Pureblood whose legacy comes from a shaman and a priestess. The paramedic was more her type."

Her body relaxed as the convulsions eased and Clio fought to focus on Ansel, his bronze gaze, and she struggled to listen to the woman. Did she say shaman and priestess? Who was Brando? "Ansel," she whispered.

"You've taken your given name. You're lying to yourself as that person no longer exists. Tell the Wight how he died in a fire," she mocked, her accent giving it a sharp edge.

Thick fog moved in, and crowding Clio's mind muddled her thoughts while pain continued its attack and the fire marched over her flesh. She was going into shock. She needed help. Straining to get off the ground, she failed, her muscles going limp, and she couldn't hold her head up. "Ansel," she whispered. Easing backward, Clio saw the sunlight through the trees, the bright green leaves, the azure sky through half closed eyes. She was failing. She wasn't strong enough to stay with him. Her wolf sank deeper and took his feel with it. A tear, she feared was blood, slid down her cheek when the world shrank, turned black, and surrounded her in silence.

"Clio. Tesoro." He gathered her limp body in his arms and held her to his chest. Her head rested against him, her heat sinking into him through his T-shirt.

"For a Wight, she's quite the little fighter. Thought two spines were going to do the job," Bronte mused.

"What have you done to her?" he growled.

"What do you care?" she snapped.

"Tell me." Ansel couldn't get Clio close enough to him, when her muscles went limp and his heart sank.

"A hallucinogen mixed with a depressant with a splash of toxin. There isn't enough of the toxin to kill her, but she'll beg to die, from the pain alone, then there are the nightmares. Whatever she fears will tear her mind apart while despair will crush her. Your Wight's demons will create her own trip to insanity inside that pretty head of hers," Bronte explained proudly. "My own creation."

She said it again. His Wight. Dr. Hyde, Clio, who despite having a giant chip on her shoulder about being a Wight, was confident, poised, self-assured and used her mind as a weapon. While he respected her for that, her self-awareness was scary as hell. The hallucinogen was going to test her mental strength at the same time the depressant tested her emotional capacity. He didn't want to lose her.

"She doesn't have any demons, Bronte."

"Everyone has demons," she hissed.

"Not her." Innocence was the quality that called him to her and drove him away. Ansel forced himself to take his stare off Clio's pale face and the tears turning a darker red to look up at Bronte's white eyes, like pearls with webs of scarlet staining them. "She's innocent. Something you nothing about."

"There's no such thing as innocence," she seethed as she glared at Clio in his arms.

Her jealousy whipped in the air, weakening the grip she had on her fury. Her thick, black lashes framed her livid stare while her red-painted lips were pulled back in a near snarl to expose her white teeth and fangs. Bronte shifted her stance, her onyx hair swayed with her, its ends touching the slim, burgundy blouse tucked into tight fitting jeans, that ended in black-heeled boots. She looked almost human. Almost. The scar running from her right ear to her cheek and the other one circling her neck reminded him of her past, their shared past, and her evil.

He had been defending her when he made his confession to Rutger. He was convinced the years with her had been easier. There was less worry, less pain, all lies, he let himself get caught in the fear and panic of losing his pack and wanted to go back. Back to a life of servitude where he wasn't responsible, wasn't a man, was a thing to be ruled and fed from. Shame oozed from him, turned to disgust, and then fury. He wasn't the boy who had been defenseless on his back as she dominated him to take his throat. A spasm rocked Clio's body, and he held her tighter to his chest, whispered he was going to save her, and when it eased Clio relaxed in his arms. He couldn't believe he had missed Bronte and wanted to go back to her.

"Fitting in was never your way," he taunted. He tilted his head to give her a sideways, you're not worth my time glare.

"These are different times and humans take offense to ... well, everything. Sad, desperate, and hate filled bags of flesh they are. Not the same as the cloak and dagger days of old. I do miss the drama and flare of it all," she mused with a flip of her hand, her red nails catching shards of sun.

Especially the drama. "This has nothing to do with her," Ansel protested, indicating Clio. "She's an innocent."

He cradled her body, feathering his hand up and down her side, and going to her hip, held her for a painful second, then his hand went lower to her thigh, his fingers grazing over a pocket, and he froze. Her cell phone. He wanted to sag in relief, she was never without the thing. Pretending to struggle with her body, acting like he was trying to shift her to a more comfortable position, he took the cell from her pocket. Leaning into her, he whispered, "I'm getting you help."

"Your insistence is admirable. Your Wight, an innocent? I think not," Bronte countered, her voice sounding too sweet. "She was all over the paramedic, batting those baby blues, and he couldn't get enough of her. Her name was on his lips as his last breath left him."

"Stop. She isn't mine. I have no one," Ansel growled. He wanted to yell. "You made sure of it."

"Did I, Brando? No female repeats a male's name when she understands her life is coming to an end. Look at her! Despite understanding you're the reason for her pending death, she seeks solace in your arms. Your Wight loves you." Her eyes gleamed scarlet for a breath, then faded to white.

"I have never been with her. She's my pack mate. Your jealousy has made you delusional and time has rotted your mind." *Good job. Antagonize her so she kills you faster.* "You should seek the truth instead of acting out on your fabricated assumptions. It's made you weak. You've hit a new low."

"You. Don't. Have. A. Pack. This," Bronte sneered as she waved her arms, "is an illusion. You're mine." Her mood swerved back and forth between rage and cool aloofness.

Ansel's didn't. His fury rushed over him, and before he compromised Clio's life, he dismissed Bronte by taking his gaze from her and looking at Clio while he fumbled with the cell. Keeping it between their bodies, he was sure he looked like he was being inappropriate with her, but he had to make sure the sound was off, he didn't care if it was on vibrate. He didn't want Bronte to take it from him. Bringing her closer to his chest, as if he was keeping her from tumbling to the ground from the seizure, he made sure the GPS was activated and communications could find her. After awkwardly putting it back in her pocket, he slid his hand up her side, removed the spines, and letting them fall to the ground, removed another lodged in her shoulder. Whoever responded would find them and know the Covey and Bronte were responsible. His heart hurt a little less with the accomplishment. Inhaling her spice, he tasted it as if he had kissed her, and lingering on his lips he wondered if she really did love him. Was it possible? New pain in the form of loss took hold of him and felt like chains had wrapped around his heart and was dragging him to hell. Whether or not Clio loved him was irrelevant. He was going to die.

His glare shifted to Bronte. "How empty is your life you had to hunt me down, then terrorize innocents?"

"Your tongue needs to be leashed." She knelt by him and he could swear he smelled brimstone, then she moved hair from the side of his face with the tips of her cold fingers and leaning closer left a sliver of space between their lips. "Your taste remains on my tongue, like the feel of your hardened body against mine."

"Don't touch me, ever," Ansel warned with a bronze glare and a growl. The disgust from her closeness made his stomach clench.

"I will do with you what I please. You're in no position to threaten me. Time has sharpened my blade, Brando. You betrayed me, the Covey, we lost one of our own, and for that you owe the Covey a blood debt. We're here to collect," she whispered.

"You murdered Dayton, stuck your blade through his back and ran like a coward. You took the Covey from me because you're jealous and weak," Ansel shot back as he stood.

"Your memories of the past are as skewed as your life is

here," Bronte mused as she stood.

Three men walked out from the woodline as two women rounded the back of his truck. They all wore basic civilian clothing, plain shirts, jeans, boots, nothing to draw attention to them, nothing special to identify them. They drifted through the humans' world doing their job, leaving death in their wake, and were never noticed. Regular people here, ignore the bodies and move along. Cradling Clio in his arms, Ansel gave Bronte his back and started toward the house. She should have had an enforcer watching her, and if she ditched them to come to his house, they would be looking for her. And she had her cell. He had to believe Mandy or one of the enforcers would realize she was missing and find her and take her to Celestial.

"Brando, she comes with us. A hallucinogen isn't any fun if there's no one to watch."

"She's staying here. This isn't about her," Ansel protested without facing Bronte. Blood seeped from her ears as the spasms gained strength and came one after another. Clio's muscles tightened, and her weak moans of pain drilled into him.

"The next spine will tip the scale and the toxin will kill her. All before the fun starts. The Wight is significant to you," Bronte hissed. "Bring her."

Ansel spun around. "Damn straight. Doctor Hyde is important to the pack. She saves lives. They depend on her. You're dead, Bronte, you died a long time ago. You have no worth but to cause others pain. You have no idea what life is."

Shock stole over her face in a flash, then was gone and replaced with eyes blazing scarlet and her fury lashing out at him and taking quick bites as if it had blades on its edges.

"Living here has given you a superiority complex. The Wight will watch you die."

He lost. This was it. He lowered his head to Clio's face, touched her cheek to have blood smear on his, and listened to her faint heartbeat, her frail breaths, and tightened his hold on her. Ansel understood, if on a different level, what Rutger had gone through when he thought he lost Jordyn. He couldn't do it, wasn't strong enough to allow fate to have him, them. He had worked to protect her innocence from his evil and failed. He didn't deserve her. Didn't deserve her love. Didn't deserve her forgiveness. Gazing at her blonde lashes resting on her stained cheeks, he saw her smile when he called her MD. He would never see her smile again, and when she remembered him, it would be in her nightmares. Ansel would leave a lasting impression on Doctor Clio Hyde with his death. It would be a tragic romance and poetic if it wasn't for Bronte.

"You destroy everything you touch," Ansel growled.

"I'm about to touch you, guaranteeing your destruction," Bronte promised.

CHAPTER TWENTY-ONE

Clio fought to crawl out of the haze of her mind, when the seizure released its grip on her taught muscles, the searing pain eased, and exhaustion swept over her. She knew the woman used ghoul toxin. And something else. She couldn't imagine what the something else was and forced herself to remember the toxicology report.

As she fought to stay awake, fog threatened to swallow her and shove her back to its cave of darkness where pain waited. Like flipping through pages of a book, she saw the report on the toxin, it worked at the neuromuscular junction causing muscle paralysis by inhibiting the release of acetyl-choline from presynaptic motor neurons. The crystals prevented the victim from shapeshifting and healing their wounds. She remembered and would have laughed if she was able to move. She couldn't save for the seizures.

The ability to concentrate wavered, her clarity slipping from her, and she focused on the report, then Lado's medical record. He had been shot with the same kind of poisoned kyanite crystals and survived. It had taken over a week for the toxin to weaken, its effects unknown. Treatment consisted of being in a medically-induced coma in order to heal and on a steady routine of fluids, BioThropy, plasma, pain meds, antibiotics, and syn sanguine, and he had been observed for negative responses.

Clio didn't have that option, no one knew where she was, and she had to wait for help and survive until they found her. Simple. Another seizure plunged its claws into her, the fire raged anew, as it tore its way through her insides, and her blood curdled in her thinning veins. She knew her heart stopped, felt its deadness in her chest, and her lungs were collapsing. Fighting through the attack, her hot skin stretched taut, her hands clenched in tight fists, her body ramrod straight, her head back making her neck and spine rigid to the point of snapping. She saw herself breaking in half, her ribs punching through skin, and blood pouring from her eyes, nose, mouth, and ears. She screamed as the pain, like a thousand knives were being driven into her joints and muscles, stole the capacity to think from her. The toxin, the report, her name escaped her. She was left with the harsh sound of her scream as it choked in her throat and blood pushed up to her mouth.

When it started to ease and the vision of her wrecked body faded, she reminded herself to breathe. She was determined to survive. She was going to stay with him. Clio had broken through Ansel's barricade fabricated from ice. With the thought, she let herself drift to her dream where she felt warmth, a hard body next to her, and arms of steel holding her like he was scared she might escape him. By his scent she knew it was Ansel. She wanted to open her eyes and look at him, to see his bronze gaze, and to make sure he was there, and she wasn't imagining it all. Focusing all of her will-power, she tried. And failed. His low rumble of a voice, like a lullaby vibrated his chest and rolling over her, she curled against his warmth.

"Raiden, get the car," Bronte ordered.

Without responding, a man left the group and headed toward the main road. Ansel wondered if their car had been there when Clio arrived at his house and if she noticed it. Or she was focused on what she was going to say to him. *I need to know you're all right*. She disobeyed a direct order from the baron and risked facing his cold front to see him. Risked getting rejected. *I'm a big girl*. He shifted Clio in his arms as another spasm gripped her body but allowed her to move with the pain, while tears fell from her eyes and soft moans left her partially parted lips.

"Looks like the fun is beginning," Bronte mused, eyes gleaming white. "It'll get better, I promise."

He didn't respond, there was nothing he could say to change what was happening. He wasn't going to stop Bronte and he couldn't save Clio or himself. At least, when it was over and he was dead, the pack was going to be safe from Bronte, her twisted mind, and her death.

"Here we are. Get in, Brando," Bronte ordered. She walked to the dented brown van that had clearly seen better days and swung the door open. "It's not up to the Wight's standards, but it gets the job done."

Ansel carried Clio past her luxury crossover, saw a bag, a zip-up hoodie, and purse in the front seat, then he saw the console. After Butte Springs, she had been taken off active rotation, didn't drive a pack vehicle, and was placed on the emergency personnel list. As the doctor for the Kanin family, the baron required her to have a console in her personal vehicle and besides watching her GPS, he was thankful it was there. His heart beat faster with the implications. Clio had her cell on her person, and her car was in his driveway. It was a matter of time before the enforcer in charge of guarding her realized she was gone, and after calling her and not getting an answer would report it to Mandy who would report it as an emergency. Dr. Hyde never ignored a call, she was there for anyone who needed help. A stab of guilt struck through Ansel with the thought. He was taking a vital part of Cascade with him and was going to watch it die.

Clio relaxed, as much as she was able in his arms, and he was just enough of a selfish bastard to cherish holding her. He understood Rutger. Stepping into the windowless van he ducked down and taking three steps to a faux leather seat where yellow foam punched through rips and tears, he sat down. He shifted her in his arms, propping her head on his shoulder, the end of her ponytail on her collarbone, her body turned toward him, her legs resting on his thighs. He was six feet, four inches, making him taller than most, but Clio's five feet, four inches made her a perfect fit.

The Covey talked in murmured voices as they crammed themselves into the beater van, the male behind the steering wheel staring at them in the rearview mirror, his dark eyes changing colors with his thoughts. Magic-born, Illuminate, Bronte would never surround herself with Wights, it was beneath her. When the van settled into a silence thick enough to hack at with an ax, the driver started backing out of Ansel's driveway. He focused on hope, the bitch that never played fair, and mentally went over protocol. With orders from Rutger, Mandy would check Clio's location to find her car was at his house, and they would learn her cell was somewhere else entirely. Rutger, knowing about the Covey, Bronte, and the threat to Clio's life would check Ansel's truck, find it at his house, like his cell, and send enforcers to check on her, them. He was on house arrest, Clio was there, the situation requiring Rutger to send a team. Aydian and Quinn, from his specialized force were heartless and efficient. Ansel estimated how long Clio had been at his house, how long they had been driving, and assumed her disappearance had been reported.

"They'll find you," Ansel whispered, his lips feathering Clio's ear, and he nearly buried his face in the soft skin of her shoulder and neck.

"Do you want to know how I found you?" Bronte asked as she left her seat. When she was in arm's reach, she knelt to one knee.

"Negative." Ansel hoped she felt the ice and hate lacing the one word.

"Brando—"

"Stop the bullshit, Bronte. It's Ansel. My name is Ansel Wolt," he growled. "Always has been, always will be."

"Don't let the years you've spent here fool you into believing you're something that you are not. You aren't the distinguished Captain of Enforcers, the loyal friend to the Second, and you aren't a trusted pack mate," she countered. "You are a rogue. An assassin. A murderer. A lost child. You will never be anything more."

His past punched him in the stomach, and if he hadn't been holding Clio, like she might save his life, he would have doubled over from the hit. The loss, pain, fear, and detachment he felt for decades came roaring back and joining the rage it bombarded him as if trying to pommel him into the seat.

"You can pretend to be one of them, you can lie to yourself, and believe you fit in with them. You don't. You're one of us. You're a Covey," Bronte continued. "Mine to do with what I want."

Ansel laughed. He was going insane and Clio's cries as she fisted his T-shirt and drew her knees to her chest compounded the force of losing his mind. When he stopped to catch his breath and held Clio preventing her from shredding his shirt, he sat back, and made a show of hugging Clio to his chest. "Whatever you have to tell yourself."

"Damn you," Bronte screamed. Everyone bunched their shoulders with her shrieking while refusing to turn to look at her.

Well trained.

"That's why you're here," he mumbled.

Gaining control, she pinned him with a scarlet glare. "It could have been different."

"Enough." Ansel closed his eyes, he wasn't playing her games, and regretted ever letting her manipulate him. As if he had been a dog scrounging for crumbs. When he opened them, he looked over her at a patch of bare metal and listened to the tires on the road. How long had they been driving? Fifteen minutes. Rutger knew they were gone and would track Clio's cell. He guessed they were heading north, they hadn't made any sharp turns, and were heading out of town.

"As you wish," Bronte mocked with her accent in her words and her head slightly bowed. "The Wight isn't what you want ... compliant, reliable, boring. You wanted me, Brando. Me, the passion, and the rush."

The thought of her naked skin against him and her fangs puncturing his skin made his stomach roll. She had taken more than his blood from him. His pride. His humanity. His masculinity. The pack, Rutger, and Clio changed him from a scarred being living like a shadow to a strong man with convictions. They gave him a purpose. Clio and her decency were exactly what he wanted. "Get over yourself."

"Enjoy your Wight while you can," Bronte scoffed.

Her words made Ansel clutch Clio to his chest even tighter, if that was possible, and her warmth, unnatural heat sank into him. She shuddered, mumbled intangible noises, and fisted his T-shirt as crimson tears gleamed on her reddened cheeks. He was watching her fall into the depths of her mind where she may or may not survive. He didn't know what Clio's darkest fears were, what they could be when she was thirty, had a family, friends, and a normal even comfortable life. Maybe she was seeing him and explaining she had a MD, and not to judge her for being a Wight.

With frantic inhales and exhales, Clio raced down the darkened hall, the lights above her blinking off and on, her running shoes squealing on the tile, her name over the intercom of the hospital as screams and yells came from every direction. The hall went on and on, never taking her where she needed to go like a twisted labyrinth with no end. She didn't see anyone, only heard them wailing, while scarlet smears, as if bodies had been thrown against them, discolored the beige walls. Her name blasted above her, ordering her to go to the emergency room. They needed her help. Clio skidded to a stop, looked around as the hospital tilted and swung, and she clasped the sides of head in her hands.

"It's not real," she mumbled. It was the toxin. Screams echoed off her skull. "It's not real."

Opening her eyes, she ran at the wall, part of her hoping she slammed into it and knocked herself out cold, the other part of her wanted to go through it and into a black void where she would disappear, and the pain would stop. Emerging on the other side, the wall disintegrated behind her, and sliding through a puddle of blood she landed on her back. Scarlet covered her hands, the back of her legs, and was soaking into her pants. Someone was crying. She corrected herself, it sounded like the entire hospital was wailing, including the building. As if listening to her thoughts the walls began weeping crimson and bulging out and toward her. She got to her feet as fast as possible and started running when a seizure dropped her to the tiles and her body curled in on itself. The pain gripped her spine, seared her organs, and pulling her through the tile its sharp edges sliced her arms, sides, and legs. She screamed as fire scorched her throat and her chest squeezed the air from her lungs.

"I told you it would get better." Bronte stood, gave him a scarlet glare, then stepped out of the van and into the dying day.

When the tremor ended and her body uncoiled, Ansel gently cradled Clio in his arms, and standing left the van, the smell of burnt motor oil, gasoline, and yellow foam behind him. He was standing in a field, would have noticed the rough ride had he not been holding onto Clio with a death grip as every muscle in her body tensed to rebar and her screams deafened everyone.

"Follow," Bronte ordered, her gait confident as she maneuvered over the ruts, clumps of grass, and saplings in her heeled boots. Like she had done it before.

While the Covey fanned out around him, Ansel obeyed. Why delay the inevitable? Clio was quiet in his arms, her body limp against him, her breathing shallow but constant. Twilight was moving in, taking the brightness of the sun and masking it in deeper tones of gold, garnet, and steel blue. They had twenty minutes, then darkness would shove the sun down and take the night and the stars would witness whatever was going to happen. He recognized the field. *Long Valley*. There was a creek a few hundred yards west of them, an old mining shack, and leftovers from a life long forgotten. He knew it because it was Cascade territory.

"Over here, Brando," Bronte ordered.

Gods, he hated the name, what it meant, the way she said it, and the shame it brought. He wouldn't have to worry about it for long. Ansel carried Clio over to where Bronte was standing, her hands on her hips, a sadistic smile twisting her lips.

"I'm here."

"This is for your Wight." Bronte pointed to a steel stake standing a foot out of the ground with two shackles hanging from it. "Secure her."

"Why? When you've ensured her death with your drugs," Ansel countered.

"I'm not leaving anything to chance. Come on, be a good boy and obey. Or I'll have a Covey do it, and they won't be nearly as gentle with your weakling as you. They might bruise her."

Ansel growled as he knelt to one knee, his weight sinking into the grass, then he gently placed Clio next to the stake. He gazed at her, his mind racing, then taking one of the shackles forced himself to put her right wrist inside. It locked around her, its cold metal on her skin, and he repeated the process with her left wrist. Attached to the stake and three inches apart, the chains allowed her two feet of room. She would be able to sit up, if she could, and rest comfortably like she was, for the moment. Knowing what he was going to face, he couldn't leave her. Ansel didn't know what he was going to do when he leaned over her, his face next to hers, his lips a sliver from hers. Was he going to kiss her? To find out how she tasted, to feel her on his lips. Yes. Not because he needed confirmation she was his fated mate. Damn, it wasn't because he needed her, his mate, his female, the light to his black soul.

If he kissed her and she was his, it was going to make the next couple of hours worse. He was torturing himself.

If they hadn't been about to face death, and had a chance

to live another day, would he bind her to him? Negative. Fated mates be damned. Pain and sorrow raged as he stared at Clio with strands of blonde hair stuck to her flushed, tear-damp cheeks, pale skin, while silently willing her eyes open. He wanted her to see him as the man he had become. Not the shell Bronte was going to leave behind. As if given a miracle, he stared into her blue gaze tinged with honey and scarlet, her slightly parted pink lips, and his whispered name. One touch would tell him if he had in fact lost his mind, and wanted, because Bronte was going to kill him, believe Clio was *his*.

As if his need to have a mate, acceptance, and someone to love him overrode his being put to death. Maybe he needed to be loved just for a moment. Taking her face in his hands, her light tan, a stark contrast to his bronze skin, he leaned in, their lips touched, hers soft and giving into him, while their wolves howled. It hit him like a lightning bolt, and sliding through his chest, his power surged, his wolf demanding he take possession of her, making her his. Clio's essence surrounded him as she moaned against his lips, a purr from deep within her, and kissed him back. Did she understand what was happening between them? Not possible. A second ago she hadn't been conscious. She had been fighting an invisible battle and clawing at him.

"Ansel," Clio whispered.

Oh hell, she knew. "Tesoro, I'm here."

"What was that?" Bronte demanded. "What the hell happened?"

Ansel was not going to tell her the truth, not that it would matter once he was dead. It would add to her enjoyment knowing she was taking his mate from him. "I'm the son of a shaman and a priestess, as you pointed out, I broke through your drug-induced hell and gave her peace."

"Impossible." She looked at him with doubt in her gaze. "Get away from her," Bronte ordered.

"Mine," Ansel growled. He sounded like a madman.

Possession and the need to touch Clio bore down on him, making his wolf's howl turn dark and protective. He held the back of her neck with his left hand while grazing her bottom lip with his thumb. Her eyes fluttered, the bleeding had stopped, then they closed, and he kissed her again, hoping it woke her up and she would look at him. As her lips met his, she tried reaching for him, the chains clinking then stopping her. Ansel kept staring at her as their kiss deepened, creating a fire inside of him he was sure was going to destroy him before Bronte had a chance.

A blazing white light burst through the crimson-stained haze, charcoal walls, screams and shrieks ringing in the hospital, and hit her in the chest as if it had been shot at her. The impact woke her up and she saw Ansel leaning over her, his face a breath from hers, his lips covering hers. Her heartbeat pounded, her pulse deafened her, and her wolf rose up and reached out to him. Their magic blazed between them, intertwining for several precious moments, and she wanted to bathe in its warmth, the security, and the feeling she was loved. She wanted to remain in the clarity it provided, she wanted to remain with Ansel, but then he was gone, the clarity fading with his distance. The hospital which had become her cell and hell on earth opened its doors and swallowed her.

"Get the hell away from me," Ansel demanded as he struggled with the men who had grabbed him and jerked him backward. Clio's head dropped to the ground like she didn't have muscles supporting her, her arms falling to her sides, the chains tugging her toward the stake. His wolf howled with frustration, his skin chilling from her absence, and his mind reeling as it processed the truth. They were fated mates and they were about to die.

"Tsk-tsk, Brando, I think you've fallen for the Wight." Bronte stalked toward him, closing the distance as if she was approaching her prey held in a trap. "It will make this even more divine."

"I have not," Ansel protested. Lied. He fell for her, was in lust and love with her.

"Cute. Chain him up," she ordered the men restraining him.

They jerked him, and Ansel let them. It was time to get it over with. They marched him fifteen feet from Clio to a set of steel stakes, and another set of shackles. When did they set their scene up and why hadn't an enforcer found it? Because Foxwood was chaos. Bronte arrived at the perfect fucking time and she knew it.

"Kneel," the guy on the left ordered him.

Without fighting—there was no reason—Ansel knelt, his knees sinking into freshly churned dirt. Holding his wrists, the men stretched his arms, taking any movement from him, and shackled him to the stakes. He looked at Clio while she writhed, twisted, and coiled into the fetal position as another seizure gripped her. Gods, when was it going to end? When she was dead. Not possible, Rutger was on his way. He knew this. Believed it. Needed it.

When Bronte stood in front of him, she took his chin in her cold fingers, and guided his head and their eyes met. "Brando, you have been found guilty of deserting the Covey and putting their lives in danger. You betrayed one of your own, Dayton, and left his body behind for law enforcement to find, putting the identities of the Covey in danger of being exposed."

"You murdered Dayton, stop blaming me," Ansel mumbled. "You called the cops. Wanted them to find us, me." He didn't know if she was listening, if any of them were listening, and guessed it didn't matter. They were brainwashed, as he had been. "Four decades, Bronte. Four. You should have gotten the hell over it."

"Time is useless to me. Is there anything you would like to say to me?" she asked, letting go of him.

The skin where she held him was cold despite it being July and the sweat rolling down his spine. Ansel craned his neck to look at her and imagined taking her head from her shoulders. "Move so I can see Clio."

Bronte's eyes blazed scarlet and darkening became a deep crimson with her fury. She looked at Clio when she rolled to her side and fought to get up and off the ground. "Your Wight is fighting for nothing."

"She's fighting against you. Clio isn't broken, she isn't weak. She isn't one of us." Ansel laughed a sad sound. With his damaged past, he didn't deserve her, and she still treated him with kindness. "She's good, has compassion, and loves freely. You've grown used to preying on the weak and bullying them. You won't break her."

His words hit their target and he saw the recoil pinch her face, then her scowl returned. "Did I break you, Brando?"

"I denied myself ..." he hesitated, "a life because of it."

Bronte slowly swung her head toward Clio. "You denied yourself the Wight. You love her. Do you love her?" Her steady voice gave away her rage more so than when she yelled.

Ansel didn't know if it was true love. He convinced himself they were fated mates, did it mean he automatically loved her? His death was coming, and it was going to be painful, was he clinging to the belief they were fated mates out of weakness? He didn't know. Clio opened her eyes to stare across feet that might as well have been fathoms.

"Do you love her?" Bronte demanded.

"She's mine. Mine. I love her," Ansel yelled back. With the admission a weight had been lifted off his shoulders. Released from Bronte's influence, he was free to love Clio. "I love you." She smiled at him as she closed her eyes and her body curled into a ball, the chains clinking with her struggle.

"It will be an unrequited love." Bronte laughed. "We'll see how strong she is. Until then, I have something for you, Brando."

Night's threads thickened, taking the sweeping hues of sunset from the sky and staining it in its shadow. Ansel's eyes adjusted to the dark and focused on Clio, her cries, and the way she was pulling on the chains. He ignored Bronte, her threats, and the others until he smelled kerosene and he closed his eyes. The day came back to him and he was watching the firestorm, its flames reaching higher and higher into a smoke-filled sky as its body, like a giant demon, snaked over the land consuming everything in its path. Carried by wind, the heat blistered his face as it swallowed his mother, and once she was ash, it focused its attention on him its hunger demanding to be quenched.

It was going to hurt.

"I saved you from the flames that scorched the land and devoured your family. I'm giving you back, Ansel Wolt. I'm returning you to the blaze's gapping maw," Bronte whispered. "A complete circle."

Ansel tore his eyes from Clio, met her pearl white gaze, watched red tears slide down her pale cheeks, and draw attention to the jagged edge of the scar. Complete circle. "Then do it, Milanka."

She snapped her fingers, and the two women who had stayed out of the way came forward, one carrying a tin can and the other a box. No doubt it was the kerosene and matches. She did like the cloak and dagger of it all. The drama. Clio moaned and rolled to her back, her left arm on the ground, her right arm across her chest and held up by the chain. He stared at her and let his mind play scenes he would never see and emotions he would never feel, and imagined his hands roaming over her curves as he tucked her to his side. He was going to lose it all. Clio would remember him the same way he remembered his parents ... in the throes of pain as he burned to death.

The charred walls of the emergency room buckled, creating a cloud of black dust that fell and sank into the pools of blood on the broken white tile. She raised her hands to see shattered fingers twisted and bleeding, then the man she had been trying save liquefied in front of her, the fluids splashing on her shoes. The bodies of others she had been trying to help melted into their beds, their flesh clinging to the stained sheets as their weight pulled them down. Clio couldn't look away as their bones hit the floor, the skulls cracking, the pieces bouncing, and landing near her. She lost them all. They were all gone. Her instincts pushed her to get out of there, escape from her failure. Sucking in a breath and getting ready to run for her life, she smelled the sharp scent from smoke, saw the scorch marks on the silent equipment, and under her feet the tiles turned to ash and she was falling.

She didn't scream, she didn't think her throat could take it, and fell in silence. She was too tired to fight. Too tired of it all. When she landed, it wasn't the crash she expected, rather she floated then met the ground. If it was a replay, she expected to feel Ansel's warm embrace and his lips on hers.

That had been real? Their wolves, their magic? Not her imagination feeding her lies. She prayed it was real. Hard consciousness weaved in and tangling with her thoughts the images plaguing her served her bites of reality.

Wherever she was, she wasn't in Ansel's warm embrace, and it was cold, and getting colder. The last shards of the nightmare and the hospital fell from her, leaving her shaken, feeling weak, unneeded, and rejected. Clio hated the feelings. Like her damn default. They made her weak. She tried opening her eyes—she wanted to see the real world—failed, and accepted the fact she wasn't going anywhere. She was trapped in her head with her faults and the dead she wasn't able to save. The threats, the reason she was there, the spines they had shot her with all drowned under sadness, pain, and loss. The fog threatened to shroud her mind in its haze when Clio's heart stopped, the fog cleared, and a howl thick with anguish and etched with heartache dug its nails into her.

She knew the voice.

With his weight on his knees, the toes of his boots digging into the dirt, Ansel squeezed his eyes shut and gritted his teeth as Bronte—he wouldn't use her given name again unless he was killing her—touched the metal rod, its tip candy apple red, to the sensitive skin of his under arm. Creating a hole, blood flowed freely, he could smell it and the singed skin, and knew a couple more times and she would push it through his upper arm. His left arm hung loose, his wrist raw and bleeding from struggling, his forearm blackened, the skin peeling back from the muscles beneath, the air drying the moisture seeping up.

"I'm playing with you, darling. Four decades is a long time to embrace revenge as a lover." Bronte placed the metal rod in the fire. "You say you've denied yourself a life because of me. You ripped my life from me when you betrayed me. Left me."

Ansel risked lifting his head, and stared at Clio through the smoke. "You had the choice to let it go." His voice sounded like he was trying to swallow gravel. "Your fault."

"How sensible," Bronte mocked. "I'm ending this."

He didn't care. Hope had failed him, and no one had shown up to save Clio. They were both lost. Complete circle. Job finished.

Bronte took a stick she had been poking the wood with, lifted it out of the flames, and put it next to his cheek. "I've envisioned this moment for a long time. Played it in my head night after night." She tapped him, and Ansel jerked back, his arms screaming in pain. "Do you remember how I found you? Begging the fire to consume you. Scared and covered in blisters. Your clothing charred and burning. Your hair singed."

Ansel recoiled. He felt the loss of his parents, the flames encasing him, the wounds and the days it had taken to recover. The silence ate him, and he needed to see Clio. She had been quiet for too long, and he couldn't tell if she was alive or dead.

Clio inhaled a breath of air, choked on smoke, and got ready to sink back into the burned husk of the hospital and her nightmares. When the horrors didn't take her to their playground, she raised her hand, wanting to move the hair out of her face, except she was stopped short. *What the hell?* She opened her eyes, really opened her eyes, the night sky with its stars stared down at her, and she saw the shackle on her wrist. Wrists. Plural. She jerked her arms, the clinking of chains sounded, and cleared her head. She wished it hadn't as she sat up, then as quickly as she could she searched for

Ansel. When she saw him, she got to her knees.

"Ansel," she whispered. *Please, no.* "Ansel." His arms were stretched out to his sides and chained to posts, his knees deep in dirt, and blood pooling around him. "Ansel," she yelled.

His head jerked up, his blistered cheeks watering, his hair shorter on one side than the other, and his eyes rolled bronze. With manic jerks Clio pulled on the chains, the stop jerking her shoulders making the muscles in her back scream in protest. She tried to call her wolf and the strength it provided and was denied. She couldn't shift. She couldn't help Ansel. The woman with black hair and scarlet eyes nailed her with a glare as she poured liquid over Ansel's shoulders, its thickness glittering in the fire's light. Over the smells of burning wood and smoke, Clio caught another scent. An accelerant. Kerosene. Putting the can down, she took a stick from the fire, a flame dancing on its end, and lowered the torch to Ansel's side.

No. No. No. Ansel's bronze eyes were on her, drilling into her, possessing her as his T-shirt caught fire, the gold and scarlet wave raced over kerosene's path, and patches fell to his jeans and caught fire. Clio felt the warmth from the blaze on her face as her heart broke.

The flames ate their way up Ansel's side, scorching his skin as its white-hot claws reached for his face, the heat scorching his eyelashes and hair, and blistering his lips. He didn't take his eyes off Clio, seeing her gave him the strength to keep from crying out as the fire burrowed deeper into his body. As the inferno progressed, Clio screamed curses, promised to kill them all, and was rewarded with shrieking laughter from Bronte. His head lowered as his hair melted from the side of his skull, and his body without his consent jerked, his arms pulling against the restraints, his knees frantically hitting the ground while the toes of his boots scraped dirt as if trying to escape without him. When his body seized and lurched, the flames spread across his back, their tips licking at his neck, making his heart pound, and felt like it was going to explode. His pulse raced, the rush of the flames over him deafened him, and he watched fragments of his T-shirt float and land on his legs and the ground. The pain and desperation in Clio's voice squeezed him, and forcing his head up, his eyes were on her. With tears streaming down her cheeks, she jerked on the chains, saying his name over and over again. He blinked, or tried to, his eyes burned. Then she was using her left arm, her right hung limp at her side.

Stop. Please stop. He wanted to tell her it was all right and to stop fighting, it was going to be over. The fire had taken its own and he belonged there. The words of his past played like a lullaby through his mind as the blaze's heat took his tears, embers burned him from the inside out, and his body gave up the fight. Too much damage. He wasn't moving anymore, his eyelids had shriveled and felt like sandpaper, and his heart had slowed to nothing. Ansel saw her smiling at him, her azure gaze with streaks of honey gleaming in the sunlight, and her voice, like her laugh was meant for him. And only him. He leaned in, and she met him, their lips touching, skin to skin, and slowly the world went black.

The sickening stench of burning skin made her stomach clench and bile threaten her throat. Clio kept yelling, and jerking her left arm in frantic tugs. Her throat stung from screaming and the smoke, it choked her, and she tasted blood. Not a sound. The fire wrapped him in its flames, ate his flesh, turning it black, the noises of it popping and hissing echoed in her skull, and he didn't make a sound. He stared at her with his wolf's eyes, his handsome face melting before her, as if she was an anchor for him. Holding his gaze, she didn't want to let him go and needed to give him what he demanded. Her attention. When Ansel's eyes rolled back, his head dropped, his body caved in, and his arms went slack, Clio fell back to her butt. Her right arm at her side, her left arm stretched out from the chain, tears soaking her face, and the breaking of her heart making her entire chest ache.

The world went silent. There was nothing left. She lost him. Staring at his limp form, the flames covering him began dying out as if they knew he was gone while the fire beside him gave one last burst and the gold and ruby flames reached into the sky. Clio's eyes followed the dancing waves as they veiled the moon, turning its silver light to crimson. A crimson moon. Its beautiful tragedy forever imbedded in her mind. As shock worked through her, she didn't move when the area, lit only by the fire's flames, coals, and Ansel, turned to daylight and there was a burst of gunfire followed by hard yells and orders.

Enforcers.

About fucking time.

The men and women scattered, like roaches, and running they fell forward, landing face-first in the dirt when hit by the gunshots. *I hope they're dead.* The red-eyed bitch didn't run, she gave Clio a narrowed glare, smiled, then walked casually to the shadows, her black hair acting like a cloak, and disappeared. What was she? Clio didn't care, because as soon as Clio found her, she was going to be dead. There would be no fire, no drama, a simple bullet to the brain as Clio returned the favor and laughed at her. She was still staring forward, her butt planted on the ground, her scrub pants stained and wet, when a face she thought she knew broke her view of Ansel. Dammit, she tried cursing as she leaned to the left to see around him.

"Doctor Hyde, you have a dislocated shoulder," a male voice explained.

No shit. He smelled of antiseptic, soap, antibacterial products, and the hospital. It made her skin crawl. Clio forced the image of the charred walls and dead bodies from her mind.

"I'm going to put it back into place," Dr. Somebody continued.

Yeah. Yeah. She leaned farther and saw someone spraying Ansel down with green goo, and the others, dressed in biohazard suits, readied a gurney, while sharp voices shared the space with the crackling fire, and gunshots. It was a cluster fuck. She should have been paying attention to how they were treating him, what his condition was, no doubt he was in cardiac arrest, shock, organ failure, if he wasn't dead, but couldn't muster enough thought to focus.

"One. Two. Three."

Clio jerked as the man shoved her shoulder back into place. She didn't feel it. She didn't feel anything. Shock or not, a numbness had welcomed her and who was she to say no. She didn't think she could escape it even if she wanted to, it held her in place and all she saw was Ansel, fire, and the moon reflecting the dancing flames.

"Doctor Hyde, look at me," he ordered.

Negative. She watched them release Ansel from the shackles, the sight of his charred skin falling to the ground, and his limp body had her jerking on her own chains.

"Wait. Doctor Hyde."

"Shot me ... kyanite," she rambled. At least she hoped she said it out loud. "Toxin."

They were covering Ansel with a blanket ... no, it was

medicated, she couldn't remember what it was. She was supposed to be an ER doctor, control under stress, diagnosing problems and saving lives, and she couldn't think passed the images of her nightmares and needing to be with Ansel. He had to have burns over his entire upper body, and his legs. No one lived through that, and if they did, they didn't want to. She had to stop thinking or she was going to start crying and she would go full blown hysterical, and it wouldn't end.

"I know. I have an antidote. You're lucky you're alive."

Clio laughed, it sounded insane, and felt fresh tears sting her eyes and their wetness on her cheeks. "I lost him," she mumbled. "To a crimson moon."

"We're going to take care of him," Dr. Somebody assured.

Two enforcers, dressed in black-on-black with face masks, approached—they each had tools—and started working on the shackles. When the clasps opened, her arms fell to her sides and she tried to stand. She needed go to Ansel.

"Whoa, Doctor Hyde."

Director Kanin was in front of her, blocking her from going anywhere, his hands on her upper arms, which she barely felt, his gold eyes gleaming in the dark. "You can't help him in the condition you're in."

"I-I have t-to see h-him," she stammered as she tried to look around him. She fumbled with her right arm, it didn't work, gave up, and tried grabbing him to move him. She didn't budge him. Did he workout every damn day or what? Loose strands of hair drifted in front of her, and she had a hard time lifting her hand to move it out of the way. "Ansel."

"He's alive," Director Kanin stated. "Doctor Kolt, get her out of here."

She looked at Director Kanin, demanded his attention, and met a gold glare. "A crimson moon took him."

"Get her out of here," he ordered.

More hands were on her, she saw the dead grabbing at her, tried jerking out of their reach, at the same time her head pounded, her skull felt like it was splintering, her stomach churned with acid, and her arms felt detached. "Fire. Smoke. I'm going to be sick," she mumbled.

"I hate this," Dr. Kolt growled in response. "Against my better judgment, I'm giving her a sedative. Once she's out, start BioThropy, syn sanguine, and the antidote," he ordered. "What the fuck? We need to get her wrists wrapped. Now. Cruz, I said now."

The gang was all there. Did she have her own chosen? Clio jerked her arm back, staggered forward, felt a bite that made her flinch—damn, she was so close—and was stopped. "Ansel."

"Doctor Hyde."

Her name faded with Ansel and the world blinked out.

CHAPTER TWENTY-TWO

Hands reached out of the broken tile and thick ash, their bony fingers stained with blood, circled her ankle and dragged her into darkness. Screams and cries echoed off walls and her ears as she twisted out of their claws, then ran and ran, her chest tight and her lungs stinging. Ansel stood at the end of the charred hall, his body burning, his flesh falling from him, while the crimson moon hung above her, mocking her attempts of escape.

Clio jerked awake and sat up, her hands aching from the pressure of fisting her comforter, her mind trying to hold off the nightmare while she told herself it wasn't real. None of it was. Lowering back into her pillows, she released her death grip, stared at the ceiling fan, the butter pecan paint, and breathed normally, or tried to.

"Three damn weeks." She covered her face in the bend of her elbow, felt sweat, and inhaled and exhaled. Every night for three weeks she had the same nightmare of hands reaching for her, faces of people she knew dying while she tried to help them, and being chased through the hospital's charred hallways. Ansel's burning body. Every time she woke up covered in sweat, breathing erratically, and scared. It had to stop.

She kicked the sheets from her legs, took the gun from the nightstand, and walked through rooms, confirming she was alone. When she had cleared the house, she replaced the gun, crawled into bed, stopped herself from replaying the dream, and covered her head with the comforter. Lado had been released from Celestial, his broken bones and lacerations healed, and his body free from the poisons and toxins that had crippled him. It took nearly a month for him to make a full recovery, while it had taken her a week. Of course her body hadn't been trying to heal bones and regenerate skin. Still, it had been considered a miraculous recovery.

Why? Bronte's concoction affected magic-born, not humans, and Clio was half human. She would have laughed at the irony of it, her insecurities about being a Wight, to have her human body save her life. If only her mind healed as quickly as her body had. She remembered the nightmares, the scenes from the hellish version of Celestial, the woman setting Ansel's clothing on fire, the crimson moon, but couldn't remember what Ansel had said to her. It was there and out of reach at the same time. Dr. Kolt advised her to not push herself, it was post traumatic amnesia and eventually she would remember. Straightening, she bunched the pillows against the headboard, sat back, and reaching for her cell stared at the empty glass and the gun beside it. She couldn't remember if she had cleared the house before she went to bed. Didn't matter. It sent a vibration of fear through her. Clio snatched the cell and checked her messages. Nothing. No messages. No calls. The silence had been going on for days.

She dreaded reading a message telling her Ansel had gone into cardiac arrest, again, he had taken a turn for the worst, and she feared she was going lose him. Is that what Miss Langston faced? Fear every day? Did she fear she would lose the director? Opening the home screen, she closed her eyes, her nerves racing like electrical currents while guilt and shame clenched her in their painful grip. Inhale. Exhale. The nightmares were proof she wasn't capable of doing it anymore. She wasn't strong enough to face the hospital and wasn't going to put anyone's life in danger because of her incompetence. Clio opened her eyes and checked her email. Nothing. The air in her lungs left her, and a combination of relief and sadness thickened.

Did she want the baron to email her back and tell her he wasn't going to accept her resignation letter? Kinda. Did she want him to email her back to tell her she was terminated and her time at Celestial was over? Kinda. Of all the scenarios she imagined, total silence wasn't one of them. The baron wasn't a man of silence. If he wanted her to continue working and wanted her to head the med room at Foxwood, he would have come at her with full force. He hadn't.

"Because I'm not good enough," Clio confessed to the empty room. When she left her job, she would be leaving her status in the pack and their respect behind. They didn't see Clio the person, they saw Clio the doctor, Clio the problem solver, Clio the go between. Which wasn't necessarily a bad thing. She loved her job, and she loved helping them, but she wanted someone to see her, respect her for her hard work. "I'm an idiot."

Her letter explained her apprehension with returning to work fulltime and her capacity to do her job. Clio looked at her email one more time, then set her cell on the nightstand and sank deeper into the bed and under her thick comforter like it might shelter her from the world. She was going to have to go to Celestial and it made a wave of panic roll over her. Selfish was what she was. Quitting when things get tough. Not soon enough, Clio was going to have to face the staff and patients and see the pity in their eyes. Damn, she knew how Miss Langston felt. Although Clio's situation was different. Where human law enforcement had been in charge of the investigation into Miss Langston's kidnapping and then into the coven of witches, bringing attention to them, the Covey was being taking care of in house. No human law enforcement. No courts.

The crimes and threats to the pack and magic-born garnered the attention of the Highguard and they sent two cavaliers to assist Director Kanin with the investigation into Ansel's conduct, the questioning of the prisoners, and Bronte's identity. The Highguard's people would hand their findings over to their Prosecution Administration and the Council of Elders of the pack. Once Bronte was apprehended, she would face the Highguard's prosecution as well as their Tribunal for the crimes she committed. If they found her. If Clio didn't kill her first.

Ansel's quick thinking, using her cell to pinpoint their location saved their lives. Mandy was able to confirm the anonymous call about Ansel's house was the same number that had called Clio, and reported the werewolf sighting that Lado responded to. The records, Clio didn't know how Mandy got them, described Bronte's movements while she was in Trinity, and the last eight months. The woman was evil incarnate and maybe a torture expert, but she wasn't tech savvy. It gave them a break and proved Ansel's innocence.

When the enforcers found them, Director Kanin moved his people in and killed one female and two males from the Covey and took one female and one male into custody. The Enforcer's office at Foxwood was at least another month away from being completed, forcing Director Kanin to hold the prisoners at a warehouse. They were in cages made of

White 47 and Cobalt 27 and were chained to the concrete floor, or so she heard. Clio didn't want to know where the warehouse was and wasn't going to visit it anytime soon. *Coward.*

Celestial had been built to be a sanctuary of safety and neutral ground. Her life consisted of helping people, saving them, and healing them. Not thinking about killing them. And she was thinking about killing the Covey's leader, Bronte, whatever the hell she was, slowly. She could make it happen, had envisioned it. Her escape sent fury through Clio and she cursed softly to the room. Another example of why she had written her letter of resignation.

Throwing back the covers, because she couldn't pretend to sleep any longer, she swung her legs off the bed and sat in silence. She needed to get dressed and go to the hospital and clean out her office. Once the task was completed, she would schedule a meeting with the baron, she felt she had an obligation to explain herself and she wanted to be put on active duty with the enforcers to help in the search of the Covey's leader. Because Clio was going to kill her.

"Clio Hyde respected doctor quits to become a murderer. Great." She walked to her bathroom, hit the paddle, and watched dark circles appear under her eyes with the light. "Looking good."

It pulled, tightened, and stretched the taut muscles while his bones reformed, and his wolf flooded him, and held him in the ether for painful seconds. A calm swept over him when the magic of being a werewolf took control. Ansel held onto his wolf form for as long as his weakened body would allow, then it drained, his muscles and bones turned to liquid and he melted back into his human form. Exhausted and his muscles feeling like mush, he sank into his thoughts and let his body relax. The first time the forced shift had taken him, he thought it had been a dream and he fought against it, not liking the loss of control. All of his fighting hadn't stopped his wolf from rising and taking him. Afterwards, there was a clarity he prized, and a weakness he hated, leaving him helpless. This time the clearness was sharper and gave him words plunging through the depths, turning them vague and blurred and making his mind feel tired and slow. Following the muddled sounds were images of Clio, her wide eyes reflecting her fear, and the fire crawling over his body.

Gods the flames.

Ansel opened his mouth to scream, hoping to release the pain and anguish swallowing his body, and was denied. His mouth, arms, legs, and torso remained frozen. Was he paralyzed? The flames had washed over him in a second, eating through his clothes, and scorching his flesh. The stringent smell of his body burning choked him, the smoke and soot laced with kerosene invaded his lungs and lined them with black even as he lost the ability to breathe. In that moment he accepted his death. Complete circle. The memory told him he had died but not in the field. If he was dead, he would be in hell, he didn't rate heaven, no forgiveness for him, and he was sure there would be wailing and gnashing of teeth, and he would be the one wailing and gnashing. He didn't think death brought a stillness and ambiguous sounds, words.

Someone was talking.

Rutger. *I'm not dead.* As his mind chugged along, trying to chase a shred of lucidity, it began to gradually tell him where he was and what was happening. He stopped trying to make his body obey his demands, he wasn't going anywhere. He was paralyzed. His skin, which he didn't think he had much left, felt cool, wet, and not tight and charred. They would have taken him to Celestial, to the burn unit. Picturing the room, he figured he was in one of the tanks. It explained the forced shift. He had no idea how the tank worked, the spell to force the shift, and figured he would never have to worry about it. Until now.

Two voices, sounding as if they were being shoved through miles of ocean, resonated around him then a numbness started, his body feeling as if it was floating, and a hazy veil inched toward his mind. *No. No.* He didn't want to sink back into the darkness. He wanted to listen to them, to assure himself he was going to live through whatever the hell was happening to him. Ansel ordered his eyes to open as the veil turned, shroud molded over his brain function and turned the world off. His last thought as he slipped under and began his decent into the void was of Clio and if she was there, somewhere in the hospital watching over him. His tesoro.

"Doctor Morton," Clio greeted as she entered the room.

She had done her makeup, used pressed powder to hide the dark circles under her eyes, and had put on mascara. Dressed in a black scrub top with matching bottoms, a white lab coat with her badge clipped to the pocket, her hair pulled back in a loose ponytail, and a pair of small, gold hoop earrings, she looked professional. Put together. Right. The chill from the room raced over her fabricated confidence seeped into the cracks and threatened to derail her. She sucked in a breath when they both turned to see her, the restoring chamber behind them.

"Director Kanin."

"Doctor Hyde," Director Kanin greeted. He wore the enforcer's uniform and looked put together. She knew better.

His dark hair sitting at his neck looked like he combed through it with his fingers, and his eyes had a dull edge from exhaustion. She held his gaze until Dr. Morton began talking and the director's attention went back to staring at the steel and glass chamber filled with liquid, the thick gel suspending Ansel's body.

"I was explaining to Director Kanin, that because of the quick response and proper resuscitation and wound debridement and closure, the regeneration of his skin and organ functions are under control. With that, he's been taken out of the medically-induced coma and is lightly sedated. I have started calling his wolf, having the shift aid in his healing, and he has the comfort of his wolf. He is able to hold his animal form for thirty seconds before his body weakens and returns to his human form," Dr. Morton explained with pride. His hands were in the pockets of his lab coat, his attention on the tank. "The deeper burns are healing, and the epidermal cells are regenerating. I believe he won't have a scar on him, even his hair has started to grow back. I have to humble myself and admit, I can't take all the credit for his recovery. Being a domineer and Pureblood is helping him, plus his age, he is established in his magic and strength."

During a session with Dr. Carrion, he questioned her about her relationship with Ansel. Clio kept it professional, detached, she didn't know what their relationship was, and stated Captain Wolt had been her partner when she was an active enforcer, was pack, her friend, and nothing else. She didn't think he believed her when he spent several minutes considering her answer, then divulged Ansel's age, parts of his past, and his relationship with Bronte. How did the information make her feel? Hurt. It had taken her a couple of days to wrap her mind around what Dr. Carrion had told her and for understanding to reach her. She wasn't sure she understood.

"Captain Wolt is a strong wolf," Director Kanin added. "With the strength of his pack behind him."

He's a survivor, Clio thought as she listened and didn't listen. A Pureblood from a shaman and a priestess. Hadn't Bronte said those words, or had they been part of the visions from having been drugged? Like the hospital burning down, coming alive to trap her inside of its corroding cavity while in its bowels the dead stalked her. She blamed the drugs. With hesitant steps and the image of him on fire torturing her, she approached the chamber. Ten feet tall, ten feet wide, there were pipes and tubes going in and out, while bags of medicine hung from steel rods above it. The blue-tinted liquid, consisting of synthetic oxygen molecules, pain killers, and hemoglobin acted to restore the function of the circulatory system and regeneration of skin tissue. Ansel had acute burns over eighty percent of his body, his heart had stopped, and he was in active organ failure when the enforcers rescued him. Yeah, Dr. Morton was proud of his work.

"Has he shifted today?" Clio asked. On the side of the chamber a pad with runes and symbols sat dark, the spell waiting to be incited to call Ansel's wolf.

"Yes, and he has been sedated. More for his safety than the healing process." Dr. Morton replied.

"Safety?" she asked.

Before they had sedated her, she saw Ansel's husk of a body, his blackened teeth, like stumps, sticking out from burned lips that were shriveled and pulled back, his sunken cheeks, and fire-singed skull. His face had been unrecognizable, his torso disformed, and his arms resembled charred, broken sticks. Now he lay vertical in a vat of tinted liquid, was naked, and plugged into a dozen beeping machines in the room. His normally bronze skin was pale pink, looked raw and sickly from the tint, the tubes, needles all over his body, and the tubes in his nose didn't help.

Due to the third degree burns he sustained to his face, he spent the first two weeks in a full mask covering his head to keep him breathing, then when his skin was healed enough, it was changed to an endotracheal tube through his mouth and into the airway. Once he upgraded to the nasal tube, it allowed the liquid to cover his face. What she would give to see his arrogant smirk, and hear him call her MD, then invite her over to see his geese and views of the mountains. She remembered that part. At this point, to have him awake and talking, she would step back from him and take his cold front. Her hands started to shake as the night came back and the feeling of helplessness to stop it from happening dug into her.

"If he regains full consciousness and remembers what happened he could become agitated. It would be like being paused then started again. I don't want him fighting the respirator, the IVs, and then damaging the tubes. It's bad enough I have to remove them when he shifts," Dr. Morton explained.

She knew that. Had witnessed it firsthand.

"Doctor Hyde, are you all right?" Dr. Morton asked, his hazel eyes searching her.

"Yeah. Yes. Affirmative." They didn't have to be magic-born to sense her lies. She smiled at them, her gaze skirting over them, and knew it looked fake and curved with fear. It was too soon. She should have stayed home. *Can't clean your office out if you're hiding at home.* "I needed to check on him." She couldn't believe he was alive.

"He's doing fine. Will be fine. How are you doing?"

Director Kanin asked. His mahogany eyes with shavings of gold narrowed on her. He sounded and acted like the baron and like the baron knew she was going to lie.

"Doing well." Yep, lied. "How is Miss Langston? Is she enjoying being home?"

"Affirmative." They stared at each other like the six feet between them was a valley filled with pain and it actively tried to snag them and pull them into its pits. It had been a shitty couple of months.

"If you'll excuse me," Clio mumbled.

Neither man said anything as she took one last look at Ansel, backed up and out of the room, then closing the door behind her, she left the burn unit at a near run. To not attract attention, she slowed her run to a walk and headed back toward her office when the smell of antiseptic, medicines, and various magic-born assaulted her and brought the corrupted images from her dreams to her eyes. *Ansel was better off sedated.* As she traversed the halls, the scenes embedded themselves in the details of reality making them part of her life and turned them into a living nightmare.

Clio kept going and watched the faces of the staff mask their features as they greeted her in passing, but they never met her eyes. With the enforcer's raid and Ansel's condition they heard the same group responsible for the attacks on Daniel, Lado, and the murder of Tony, had targeted Ansel, and she had been in the wrong place at the wrong time. Making that look worse she had been the last person to see Tony alive, having had coffee with him, then was at Ansel's house. Like Tony's body wasn't cold yet and she had found herself another man. It was gross. It was damning. The news and rumors spread like, well, fire, and she hated it.

After they admitted her, she spent a week in recovery, detoxing the toxin and drugs and shifting into her wolf form, and another week in the mental health unit with Dr. Carrion. While she sat in a chair in front of a window listening to Dr. Carrion urge her to talk about her feelings, Ansel, her nightmares—God, she hated being a patient—he insisted she tell him how the drugs had affected her. She couldn't help but picture Miss Langston silently suffering with her demons and the people who gave them to her. Then she thought about Ansel, his wounds, and what happened between him and Bronte. What history did they share that she would find him and burn him alive? If Clio asked, would he tell her the truth? No. She didn't think so. Despite the closeness she convinced herself was real, she feared when he was healed and returned to the enforcers, they would go back to the way they had been. Strangers separated by a fortress of ice.

Clio always thought she understood the meaning of a challenge; she survived her late shapeshifting, the crushed feeling when she became a werewolf, being tagged a Wight, and then there was the enforcers and medical school. She prided herself on her work ethic, determination to succeed, and knew those traits would carry her through the rough times and were strong enough to battle her self-doubt, and default setting. Never did she guess she would be faced with the challenge in front of her and would give up. Failure. Sliding the ID card through the reader, she entered the code, the lock disengaged, and she opened the door to her office.

Inside, and out from under the scrutiny of others, the weight on her shoulders felt a little less. A little. She was there to clean out her office, ending her passion of being a doctor, and start something else. Tracking a woman down to exact her revenge. What happed after that, she didn't know. She had always been in control, thinking about the bigger picture, the future, and assessing the proper direction. This was not her. Pushing it aside, Clio's attention, like it had a personal vendetta against her, focused on Ansel's condition and if he was going to build the wall of ice between them. She didn't know why it hurt her heart. How it had gotten so deep it affected her. Clio felt like she needed him. Wanted to be with him. The moments she spent at his house talking, even if it hadn't been the greatest conversation, had become precious to her.

"Doctor Hyde."

Clio's heart stopped and she spun around. "Baron Kanin."

"Have a seat," he said as he stood and waved his hand at the chair behind the desk. "This is your office."

My office. He didn't respond to her email; no, he came to the hospital. Full force. Taking her seat behind the desk, she asked, "How can I help you?" Like she didn't know.

"I'm refusing your letter of resignation," Baron Kanin stated and sat down, crossed his legs, and smoothed his jeans with his right hand. His rust-colored, button-up shirt was left open at the collar, letting the black edges of his tattoo peek out.

"Sir," Clio tried.

"You've been through a traumatic experience. I understand, healing takes time."

Yes, he of all people would know. "As I stated in my letter, my competence as a doctor is in question. I can't put people's lives at risk," she explained. Saying the words stabbed her heart. She loved what she did.

"I disagree. Did the poison and toxin take your ability from you? Did Bronte take your years of medical school and the years you've spent here as an ER doctor from you?" His dark brown eyes held slivers of gold and his authority. His calmness was like he was holding back a hurricane.

"Negative, sir," she replied weakly and looked at the

desktop.

"Don't trip yourself up with your self-doubt and lack of confidence. You are a skilled physician and what happened cannot change that." He stood, stepped away from the chair, took in the pictures on the walls of her family, the mountains, her certificates, and met her gaze. "You proved your resolve when you worked as an enforcer at the same time you attended medical school. You saved Detective Watt's life, a human who is weaker than us and was as good as dead. You handled what happened to Lado with proficiency. And you were more than accommodating when you worked between the pack and the medical staff of the hospital. Captain Wolt and Director Kanin are comfortable with you and trust you, Mistress Langston trusts you."

"But, sir—" she tried. She wanted to tell him Tony helped her, had been there to support her.

"You handled Elder Macario and his nephew with professionalism. I have read the report concerning Pearl Ashby, the Esme's Second and one of the Circle, and have talked to Commissioner Courter about your conversation with them. You reassured them the relationship between the coven and the pack was secure. If you don't recognize your importance here, or the work and success you have, you'll never be happy with your accomplishments. What kind of validation do you need?"

Validation. Baron Kanin wasn't checking off boxes to pacify her with attention as he listed her successes. No, he cared. They were personal to him. Maybe she was more to the pack than a doctor with a complex and a Wight. They respected her strength and her work.

"Your carefully crafted world has been unraveled and it challenged your determination and resolve. The pieces will never fit together the same way, but it doesn't mean you can't embrace change and move forward."

She suddenly felt like he wasn't talking about her. Baron Kanin stated there were going to be changes.

"I need you here as I need you to head the med room at Foxwood. I'm asking you, before you make the worst mistake of your life and walk away from your passion, take some time and think about your importance to Celestial and the pack." He waited while she stared at him. "I understand who you are, Clio. You'll take some time." He wasn't expecting her to answer when he had given her an order.

"Yes, sir." She stood, didn't know what she was going to do, maybe run around the desk and hug him. She could go for a hug. She had been feeling detached, alone, as if she had lost a part of herself, and scared if she walked away no one would notice. God, how did she let herself believe that? With his kindness and honesty, life slammed into her bringing her back to reality. "Thank you."

"You're welcome. I'm not going to lose my favorite doctor. Having said that, I have reviewed the paperwork concerning Doctor Baines. Do you need him?"

Was this a trick question? She says yes, wrong answer. She says no, it conflicts with what she told Mrs. Ashby. What were her instincts telling her? "Affirmative. He has an extensive background. And after what we just experienced, I believe he'll be an asset."

"I agree, and I'll talk to the Esme. Anything else?"

"Med Two, sir. I want it stationed at Foxwood." Clio's chest ached and she was sure she was going to start crying. "He had planned to apply—" She stopped before tears rushed down her cheeks and she made a fool of herself.

"Granted. Enjoy your afternoon, Doctor Hyde." Baron Kanin smiled, it was warm, confident, and carried an assurance despite everything going on, and she wasn't sure how he managed it.

"You as well, Baron."

He closed the door behind him, leaving her alone in *her* office. It was her office, Celestial was her world, her carefully crafted world, and somewhere she could make a difference. That part would never change. Clio sat down and all the anxiety she had been carrying drained from her. Baron Kanin hadn't questioned her decision. Validation. She never thought she needed someone's validation when she blamed her default setting. Did she want someone to give her validation, their acceptance, or recognition? She guessed she did, or why would she have worked to prove she was just as capable as everyone else? The damn default setting. She would have to learn how to live with pieces that would never fit back together.

Clio had never had a friend murdered, had never been drugged, chained, and forced to watch someone being tortured. Someone she cared about. The pain from losing Tony, then almost losing Ansel, seeing him on fire, and the drugs created a cage and walls of protection guarding her from being hurt again and feeling helpless and exposed. She was prepared to give up taking risks to stay in the dark. Like Ansel had with his fortress of ice, he used to keep everyone out. No, her puzzle was never going to be the same, and change was on the horizon. The baron's presence and his pep talk, silly as it seemed, changed things. Clio needed to get back to living. Taking her cell, she entered the number and listened to it ring.

"Mom."

"I didn't think you were ever going to call," Evelyn replied, her worry and excitement traveling through the phone and reaching Clio. "I understand your reasons, so don't explain, and if you need more time, I understand. We understand. Just know we love you."

Clio closed her eyes and felt tears building. "I know, and I'm sorry. Can I come over?"

"Cocktails and dinner are waiting for you, blossom," Evelyn replied.

Her parents hadn't called her by the endearment since she had taken her place at Celestial. They thought it made her sound like a child. They had been wrong, very wrong ... it made her feel like a part of them, and she belonged.

"I'll be there."

CHAPTER TWENTY-THREE

The distorted mumbles that had become familiar and comforting sank down to tease him with life and a connection to the outside world. He hated drowning in the darkness of his mind when it shrouded him, stole his energy, and the few splinters of life. Ansel didn't know how long he had been there, his internal clock giving up and leaving him with spent time. With his frustration getting worse and eating him, he stopped trying to figure it out. He was awake. They forced him to shift. They put him to sleep.

They couldn't keep him there forever. Right? When his wounds were healed, his strength returned, and he shapeshifted, and held his wolf form, they would let him out of his prison? Right? When he proved he was ready they would let him out of his suspended dungeon? Unless this was his punishment for lying to them, the attacks, the paramedic's death, and Clio, and like a vampire sent to ground, he would be there for years.

His mind reeled, and he refused to believe they were capable of such cruelty. What if they were keeping him drugged and in the burn box because he wasn't healing? What if he never walked again? What if he was blind? What if he lost his arms? She had scored them before pouring kerosene on him. And his skin. Ansel focused on his body. All he felt was numbness. Like he was a ghost. Panic started to wrap him up in its chaos and he was defenseless to fight. He didn't know what he was going to look like when he came out of hibernation, if he came out. He never considered himself good looking, maybe easy on the eyes, but never someone who attracted attention from women. Clio's rejection proved his ineptness with the opposite sex. Clio. Dr. Hyde. The way she said his name, grinned at him, and her eyes glittering as she admired his territory.

Then it changed, terror filled her azure depths, her body went limp in his arms, and she begged him to help her. He failed. Bronte tortured Clio, and the truth of his relationship with her had been exposed. If she never spoke to him, he wouldn't be surprised. *Bronte.* His wolf rose up with his anger, and spreading through him, it teased him with life. If and when he was physically capable, he was going to hunt Bronte down and tear her limb from limb.

Lost in the feel of his anger and his wolf, he heard a firm yet light tone drift through the miles separating him from the world. It wasn't her. It was his imagination. He was going insane from spending an eternity in his mind and needed an anchor to keep him grounded. Ansel released the grip he had on his fury and focused on the voice. Louder. The resonance of Clio strengthened when a haze crept in and numbed his thoughts as his world grew dimmer. *No. Dammit, no. Fuck.* He wanted to yell for them to stop. *Tesoro, talk to me.* Her voice resonated and he felt her presence, her skin on his, he didn't care if it was his imagination, and holding onto her, sank into the void.

"His heartrate increased," Dr. Morton reported as he stared at the monitor, then checked the other equipment.

"Is that normal?" Director Kanin asked.

Clio felt the director's stare on her as she placed her palms flat on the glass. She wasn't going to acknowledge him, rather she watched the muscles in Ansel's body twitch with his fight against the sedatives.

"It can be. By decreasing the sedatives he's more aware. Despite him being in the chamber, he hears us. He doesn't understand because the liquid distorts what we're saying," Dr. Morton explained.

"But he knows we're here? He would know the difference between us, men, and Doctor Hyde, female?" he asked.

"Yes. He might not understand what we're saying but his instincts are intact." Dr. Morton met the director's gaze and then turned to Clio.

"How long are you going to keep him in the chamber?" Clio asked without meeting the men's gazes.

She kept her hands on the cool surface, believing it brought her closer to him. Director Kanin was making a point, and she didn't think she liked where it was heading. He was willing to believe in fated mates, his was at his house and believed the same damn thing. This was her life, and did she believe it was possible? Fated mates. Her heartbeat gave away her thoughts as she stared at Ansel's suspended body. His features were nearly perfect, his skin returning to its natural color, his arms and legs healed, the tattoo of the Covey visible on his side. *What?*

"The tattoo. It wasn't burned?" she asked.

When Dr. Carrion told her about it and its meaning, hoping she gushed about her feelings, she had wished it burned off. As she stared at him, she heard Ansel's deep rumble of a voice beg her to stay with him, he was going to get her help, and then he whispered, "*Tesoro.*" The word slipping through her mind, creating the feel of his lips on hers, making part of her dream real. He said it. Maybe she could put her doubt aside and let herself believe she would have her visit and see his geese.

"It is a wonder how it survived." Dr. Morton answered. "To answer your first question, another week. He's showing great improvements, breathing on his own outside of the tank, shifts easily, holds its form, and his skin has gained its elasticity. We'll continue to ween him off the sedatives, medications, and the feeding tubes."

A wonder. It was a permanent reminder of his past that stirred his demons and haunted his cinnamon eyes. Clio nodded her response, took her hands from the smooth surface of the tank, put them in the pockets of the lab coat, and tuned out Director Kanin and Dr. Morton's conversation. Her focus remained on Ansel, the fractured bits of memory trying to return. And if she remembered everything, what would she see? And how would those memories affect her?

"I understand you've been put on administrative duty?"

Flames from the fire climbed into the sky, veiling the moon with crimson while shadows stalked to her left and right. As if she was back in the field, her knees in dirt, her wrists in shackles and bleeding from struggling, she tasted the harsh sting of smoke as wispy threads weaved in the air. Trailing close behind was Bronte, her insanity, and threats as she held the flame above Ansel. Clio screamed, her throat going raw, her tears warm on her cheeks, and she jerked as hard as she was able against the restraints. The heat from the fire licked at her as she pulled on the chains and his eyes rolling bronze captured her.

"Doctor Hyde." A hand gently rested on her shoulder, and for split second, she believed she would see Ansel.

Slowly turning, she faced Director Kanin's hard gaze as he took his hand back, and Dr. Morton's stare. "Sorry. Lost in thought. What were you saying?"

"Are you all right?" Director Kanin asked. He knew she

wasn't. She knew he was judging her.

"Yes, fine," she replied and shifted her gaze.

"You've been placed on administrative duty?" Dr. Morton asked, staying with the conversation.

"Yes. I requested a leave of absence and it was denied." In fact, both the baron and Dr. Carrion advised her to request leave, stating it would give her time to deal with her nightmares. "Since I'm part of the committee evaluating the upgrades to the hospital and I'm busy with the med room at Foxwood, I couldn't take the time."

"If I may be so bold, who denied it?" Dr. Morton's hazel eyes narrowed as his brows creased, making a fine line in his forehead.

"Baron Kanin." Who had told her *to take some time*, then said she was better off working. "I'll have a stress test and a psychological evaluation in the next couple of weeks," Clio explained.

"Then she'll be back to work," Director Kanin started and looked at her. "Someone has to keep the ER in shape and have Foxwood's medical facility operational."

He sounded like his father. "I guess," she replied half-heartedly. Clio knew what she had to do to get back to work. She wasn't worried about it. She was worried about Ansel. With him getting ready to return to the real world there were going to be consequences for lying about his past and keeping Bronte's identity a secret. She didn't think Director Kanin would tell her, but she had to try. "What's going to happen to Captain Wolt?"

"The Highguard's cavaliers have concluded their investigation and have turned in their files and stated their conclusion to their Prosecution Administration. Once they review the information, they will add their files to mine and

I'll speak to the Council of Elders," Rutger replied.

"Did the prisoners say anything?" she asked, pushing forward.

"I'm not at liberty to say."

Okay. "Do you know what the report states?" Clio asked, her heart in her throat.

Director Kanin regarded her as silence thickened in the room, leaving the beeping monitors and the gurgling of the tank the only noises, and she could do without them. "Negative, Doctor Hyde."

She knew when the conversation was over. "If you'll excuse me, there's a stack of papers on my desk that I've been dodging."

"Doctor Hyde." Director Kanin's voice stopped her. "You've been officially informed you are no longer allowed to visit Captain Wolt. This is the last time you'll see him."

"What? Why?" The words came out shaky and unsure, expressing the surprise she felt in her soul.

"It's a direct order from Baron Kanin and the Highguard's Prosecution Administration. You are not to have any contact with Captain of Enforcers, Ansel Wolt. Do you understand?"

"Until when?" Questioning the director wasn't going to win her anything.

"Further notice," he sternly stated. "Do you understand?"

"Affirmative, sir."

Clio felt betrayed and bombarded by questions she would never receive the answers to and cut off. Until they needed her, of course. Without arguing, it wouldn't do her any good, and might give away her feelings, she turned to see Ansel, his floating form, and left the men and Ansel for the last time. When she was by herself, she stopped and leaning against the wall, struggled to beat back the panic attack threatening her sanity and control over her body.

Her imagination created reasons for the baron's order and fed her fear of losing Ansel. Bronte didn't have to kill him when she stole his life, his kith and kin, and his future with the pack. She stole him from her. They were the victims of two outcomes. The door to Ansel's room started to open, and pushing off the wall, she sucked in a breath and walked away, hoping whoever was leaving didn't see her retreat.

Ansel repeated quotes, song lyrics, his phone number, and codes the enforcers used, as he had for god only knows how long, trying to keep his brain from turning to mush.

When a clearness, he attributed to a decrease in drugs, lasted longer and longer it gave him the hope he was going to make it out of the burn box, one day. Growing tired of his repetitions his mind wondered to Clio, if she had been near him, if it had been a dream, and if she blamed him for what happened to her. He told himself she was all right, she made it out of the field, and Bronte's poison hadn't hurt her. If he wasn't paralyzed, he would have inhaled and exhaled his frustration, maybe cursed Bronte and ever having known her. Except he couldn't move and yelling in his head was getting old. He was sure he had been awake longer than before but wasn't going to have his hope crushed and waited to be dragged back to the nothing he had grown used to, then gravity and fear gripped him.

In minutes his body turned to stone as the ascension from the dark void to the light where his thoughts fought through the jumble to catch up with him. Again, he expected it to last a few minutes, not that he understood time, when his muscles grew heavy, his body became a solid mass of sensations, and its weight crushed him. Slime slid between his legs, around his arms, over his chest, telling him he was naked, its thickness oozing over the bridge of his nose, cheeks, eyes, and ears. Automatically he tried clenching his fists, failed, the thick liquid escaping at the same time a chill settled on his skin, and he struggled to open eyes. His mind raced with what was happening. Was he being freed of the burn box? What did his body look like? Was he going to be able to walk, talk ... hell, leave the hospital? His physical status kept him from thinking about the case, his lies, and losing his kith and kin.

"It's all right, Ansel, everything you're feeling is natural. Relax and breathe," a man said, his voice soft, comforting, like a doctor. "You're free to breathe."

Ansel did his best while his chest felt restricted, making his lungs struggle, his heartbeat was out of control, and his muscles refused his orders. He was going to suffocate.

"You're doing fine. Inhale. Exhale."

He was sure he recognized the voice and the comfort, and it did nothing to ease the feelings of being blind, weak, and struggling to breathe. The voice emanating assurance continued, and Ansel shoved down his natural instincts to shift into his wolf form. Somehow, a part of him knew it would do more harm than good, like get him sedated, and he'd had enough of the void.

"His heart rate is rising," a rougher voice reported.

Baron Kanin. Power flooded the room, familiar, an alpha calling pack, while its electricity landed on his exposed skin like a million needles had entered his nerve endings, to set him on fire. Fire. Flames swept over him, their heat licking his eyes and ears as it ate its way over his skull and down his back. Skin sizzled, melted, turned to ash, and Ansel's back arched as the memory and sensations of having been on fire dominated his mind.

"Sedative, now," the once assured voice demanded.

No. No. No. Ansel wasn't going to the void. Grasping at his shredded control, he told himself it wasn't real, the fire, he was at Celestial, the baron was there, probably to take him into custody for the charges against him. The sobering thought washed over him as if it was water to combat the fire, and he rested on the bed. Bed. The cotton beneath him cradled his body, its cool touch reassuring and solid, and the next second brought a top sheet to veil the contours of his body. Naked body. He would have let embarrassment get the better of him if he cared, if he hadn't just been taken out of the burn box. Opening his eyes, white light blasted through his irises to sear his retinas.

"Turn off the lights," a male voice ordered.

"Ansel, look at me," the assured doctor asked.

Pain was a good teacher, one Bronte drilled into him, then life had given him lesson after lesson, so disobeying the order meant more pain. As the blasts of white lightning lit up the inside of his skull, then faded, Ansel inhaled fresh air for the first in time in a long time, and slowly opened his eyes. It burned like he had gotten soap in them—irritating, not deadly—and he kept them open.

"Excellent." Ansel watched a shadow move from the side to his face. "Look up."

Ansel followed each of the doctor's orders, everything remained as blurred shadows, and the fear he lost his sight crept over him.

"Is it blurry?" he asked.

"Affirmative," Ansel replied, or tried to. He didn't recognize the rough, gravelly sound coming from him and didn't like the feeling of the word clawing its way up his throat.

"The blurriness will last for a couple of days, like the

soreness when you speak. Your body must acclimate. If you have any worries or questions, feel free to ask."

"Who are you?" Ansel whispered. He suddenly felt alone, exposed. It made him tired, his mind fumbling, his muscles wanting to shut down.

"Doctor Morton, I'm in charge of the burn unit. Director Kanin and Baron Kanin are with me. Are you up to talking to them?" Dr. Morton asked.

"Affirmative." He needed to know Clio's condition and what was going to happen to him.

"You have fifteen minutes, then he has to rest," Dr. Morton advised.

"Of course, Doctor," Baron Kanin replied.

Ansel remained flat on his back, staring up at the blurred ceiling through squinted eyes as gel continued to riddle his arms, chest, thighs, making him feel like he couldn't take care of himself, and then there was the feeling he couldn't move his arms and legs.

"How do you feel?" Rutger asked.

"Great," Ansel whispered. Thankfully, he recognized their voices, and despite the panic trying to consume him, his senses were working to give him information. The magic in the room increased saturating the air and warming his slick skin. "How long?"

"Closing in on five weeks. You left in July and have come back in September. You had fourth degree burns penetrating through your skin and tendons to your bones, they covered over eighty percent of your body. You had gone into cardiac arrest and complete organ failure by the time we got there. You were dead," Rutger answered.

Dead. Maybe he wasn't going to walk out of the hospital. He blew a slow breath out, his chest rising and falling, and as encouraging as the responsiveness was, he felt he was losing himself. He had to think about something else. He felt the tears stinging his eyes, and he wasn't going to start crying in front of Rutger and the baron. "Dr. Hyde." He couldn't say anything else, her name, or make a complete sentence without breaking down. He would expose his feelings for her, and his tears would burst from the dam.

"Dislocated shoulder, bruises, abrasions on both wrists. It took her a week to recover from the poison and toxin, but is still having nightmares," Rutger replied bluntly. "She's in counseling with Doctor Carrion for the nightmares and having watched you burn to death."

His heart sank and his wolf howled at her suffering. He did this to her. He put her life and career at risk, and nearly took a daughter from her parents. He was kidding himself if he thought she would speak to him, ever. He didn't deserve her. All the *what-ifs* created exhaustion that crept over him, slowly at first, then digging into him. He closed his eyes. "Is she alright?" he heard himself ask.

"She will be. Time heals," Baron Kanin answered.

"Tesoro," he whispered as shadows lured him to their protective embrace.

Blocking out Rutger and Baron Kanin, and what they had told him, he couldn't stop from feeling her lips on his, her blue eyes drinking him in, and the loss of his mate. He didn't ask them what happened to Bronte, the Covey, if they escaped or were captured, or what was going to happen to him. *It didn't matter.* He fell deeper into the void promising him precious minutes without pain. Their voices were the last thing he heard as he let darkness take him from reality.

"Doctor Hyde," Clio greeted as she answered her cell. She

tucked her legs under her and pulled the blanket tighter around her while her tequila sat on the table, forgotten but not forgotten, and September's early twilight colored the sky with pinks and violets.

"Doctor Morton has taken Captain Wolt out of the restoring chamber," Dr. Carrion said without small talk.

Clio froze, her heart stopped, and her grip on the phone loosened. It wasn't a surprise, she knew it was going to happen, was told it was going to happen, but it meant he would face the Highguard and the Council of Elders. "Good. How is he?" she asked as detached as she could manage. Why was he telling her?

"Doing as expected. How are you?"

"I'm fine, Doctor Carrion, thank for you asking," she replied.

"Did you clear your house this evening?"

Bastard. She never should have told him. "No. I'm sitting and watching a movie." Lie.

"Are you drinking?"

She shook her head. "Poured a shot two hours ago, still have it." Truth.

"Do you feel you're being watched?"

"No." Lie. They were alive. She was coming back.

"How are the nightmares?"

With his question she heard a pen and paper. "Less invasive. I'm sleeping." Truth and lie.

"A little reminder, writing them down might help you."

"I'll think about it," Clio replied. Not in a million years was she going to write them down. As a Deviant, a human with a supernatural gift, Dr. Carrion didn't believe words held power and weight, he thought if you talked about them enough or wrote them down, it would feel like you were discussing the weather instead of a horrific event. Writing down her nightmares would give them power over her, making them real. She wanted to weaken their hold and forget them.

"That's all I can ask," he finally said.

She knew he wasn't pleased, it reminded her of the way he had talked about Miss Langston and her therapy. She wanted to tell him seeing Ansel, touching him, hearing his voice, and making sure he was real would help her. The next step to her recovery would be to call Mandy and drill her for information about the Highguard and the investigation. That was who she was, but she didn't think he would buy it, when neither was going to happen. Baron Kanin did more than order her not to see Ansel, he ordered the enforcers not to talk to her. She was suddenly on the outside and it hurt.

Clio cleared her throat and offered, "Thanks again."

"You're welcome. I thought you should know before it circulated around the hospital and then the entire territory," he explained.

"I appreciate it." She reached for her glass, hesitated, then taking it sipped the warm flavors of vanilla, cinnamon, and tannins, and tried to act like herself.

"Anytime." He hung up, leaving her alone and in the silence of her townhouse.

"Goodnight, Doctor Carrion, it was a pleasure speaking with you," Clio said as she set the cell on the table. She laughed, a small giggle, and shook her head. Some things changed, drastically, and others, they stayed the same. Thankfully.

While Dr. Carrion was treating her like his patient, which she wasn't and hadn't been for a week, he wasn't treating her like a victim, and she respected him more than before. She did appreciate his warning, the looks she was getting at work wavered between she was an alien from another planet, a broken mess of a person, the reason Tony was murdered, and Ansel's secret lover. No one had confronted her, yet, and she knew it was a matter of time that someone, like Tony's friends and family would say something. Baron Kanin did his best to ease the family's pain by promising them justice. The prisoners were the key to finding Bronte and ending her reign of terror, and their punishment would serve as justice for the entire territory.

With Ansel recovering and out of the restoring chamber, he had a limited time to adapt and go through rehabilitation before the enforcers took him into custody. He won't see anyone, like a lawyer. The cavaliers, along with Director Kanin, would perform the interrogation then add his testimony to the files, and hand it over to the Highguard's Prosecution Administration, and the Council of Elders. They'd compare the information of the investigation to his statement. Clio sat back in the couch, sipped her drink, and wondered why no one had questioned her. She had been at his house. Bronte had shot her with crystals coated in poison and ghoul toxin and shackled her to a stake, making sure Clio witnessed her setting him on fire. Bronte wanted her to watch Ansel's death. She was a victim of a crime.

When her cell rang, Clio flinched, her heart jumped to her throat as her hand jerked, making the clear liquor crawl up the side of the glass, then sank back into itself. From the table the screen lit up with an unknown number. The usual internal fight whether to let it go to voicemail or answer took three seconds and she grabbed the cell. "Doctor Hyde."

"Doctor Clio Hyde of the Cascade pack?" a rich voice asked.

"Affirmative." Not recognizing the voice, her tone automatically sharpened, and she didn't like the way it sounded. Perfect. Cultured. Official.

"Cavalier Braddock with the Prosecution Administration. Doctor Hyde, you've been ordered to appear at the Enforcer's office to give your statement," he explained, his authority and arrogance drenching every word. Clearly no one questioned him.

"Affirmative, sir," Clio replied with an edge of contempt in hers.

"You are not to communicate with anyone about this meeting. If I receive evidence you have consulted, contacted, or otherwise conversed with anyone from the Cascade pack, the factions under Baron Kanin's rule, or the Highguard, you will be punished to the full extent of the Highguard's canons. Do you understand?" Cavalier Braddock's rich voice threatened.

"Affirmative, sir." Clio swallowed her contempt when her heart pounded, and she was positive he could hear it and would use it against her in a court of law.

"If I receive evidence you've spoken to Captain Wolt, I will take your medical license. You will never practice medicine again. Am I clear?"

"Crystal. No need to threaten me, Cavalier Braddock," Clio countered.

"Have a goodnight, Doctor Hyde." The smug look of victory she knew he was wearing mocked her.

Clio didn't have to wait for silence to invade the cell to know he had hung up and was mildly surprised he told her goodnight after threatening her. Etiquette of the Highguard. Staring at the cell's screen, she should have known it was a matter of time before it was her turn to face the cavaliers. She downed the rest of the drink, crawled out from under the blanket, and with her lounge pants skimming the carpet, headed to the kitchen, and poured another. Dr. Carrion's questions were an annoying voice at the back of her head as she mulled over having been cut off from the enforcers and now the pack and klatch. They were pack animals, social, a collective that watched out for one another and was always a call or message away.

The Highguard knew this and was using its mental and emotional effects against her. If she distanced herself from the pack, it was her choice. Having them take that choice away made her feel isolated and alone and if she felt this way how did Ansel feel? She assumed the Highguard gave him the same order. Clio hoped there was a strong support group to help him with his physical and emotional recovery. The unknowns she was dealing with made her feel helpless and was giving her a headache. Sipping the liquor, she turned and leaned against the edge of the counter as twilight's colors bowed under night's invasion and the streetlights came on.

In the picture window facing the street, she saw Tony's body, the sword through his chest and table, his sapphire eyes void of life, Ansel's body buckling as the flames consumed his flesh, and his bronze eyes dimming. She almost lost him and didn't know why it scared her. Was she in love with him? She watched him suffer. Had spent days talking to him about the director and Miss Langston. Maybe she missed his cold front, that's what she knew best. Before Bronte shot her, she had made a crack in his wall of ice and felt his cold front melting.

His confession of having had a past with Bronte and her group of assassins didn't deter Clio or her feelings. Why? She had no idea because she thought it should. And the jealousy trailing it like a monster, confused her. Ansel was a hundred and forty, what could his relationship have been with Bronte, and how long did it last? Was that why he had a cold front, he still cared for her? No way. He had done something to the woman for her to find him and then set him on fire. Those were the actions of a woman scorned. *Good,* Clio thought and sipped her drink. She thought herself into a pit of assumptions and it wasn't accomplishing anything besides wishing she could talk to Ansel and making her headache worse.

She left the kitchen and went back to the couch, the blanket, and setting the glass on the table beside her cell, saw it light up with a message. A message that had the potential of ending her career. Sitting down, she picked it up. *What the hell?* She read and reread the it. Cavalier Braddock had someone at communications disable her cell, except he could contact her, then ordered her to report to the Enforcer's office in two weeks. After the questioning, her psych evaluation would take place, he would be present as well as Baron Kanin. Oh, and she was on administrative leave until they evaluated her records. Which meant she wasn't going to work and was unable to work on the med room at Foxwood. At least not at Foxwood, she had the paperwork and her laptop to work from home.

"Great." Clio dropped the cell to the couch and grabbed her glass. She needed to talk to Ansel, hear his low rumble of a voice, and to feel the comfort it offered. The way it had when the drugs were making her crazy and trying to steal her life.

Thinking like that wasn't helping her. She was either going to walk away and resume her normal life, whatever that was going to be, or her career was over. Taking a gulp, the liquor burned her throat, and she felt pressure from tears strengthening. She was not going to cry. Her best effort couldn't stop a warm tear from sliding down her cheek from the absolute mess her life had become. Baron Kanin's words came back to her. *"The pieces are never going to fit back together."* Change. Clio inhaled, refusing to let the threats take root, and told herself stressing over it wasn't going solve her problems. Staying focused, answering their questions, and proving she was qualified to do her job was the solution to getting her life back.

This wasn't the end.

"I can do this," she told the empty living room as another tear escaped.

CHAPTER TWENTY-FOUR

"I can walk," Ansel insisted as he secured the small duffle on his lap. The contents, several miniature plastic bottles of soap and shampoo—he didn't have much hair, about half an inch over his scalp—body wash, and deodorant made dull thuds against each other. The couple of T-shirts, under-clothes, and shorts he had been allowed to wear were shoved to one side with a pair of shower shoes. He should have thrown those away.

"Affirmative," Rutger replied. He didn't stop the wheel-chair.

"I'm an enforcer and being pushed around in this thing is ridiculous," he tried. Around every turn he expected to see Clio, dressed in scrubs, her strawberry blonde hair up, her bright azure eyes with slivers of honey narrowed with her thoughts. He didn't. There were staff, strangers, and sideway glances. "This is humiliating."

"So you've said. Several times."

Ansel sighed his curses, gave up—he was wasting his breath, at least with Rutger—and dwelled on his victory over Dr. Morton. The doctor had wanted Ansel to wear a pale green jumper thing that looked like children's footed PJs out of the hospital. Just thinking about it sent chills racing down his spine. It was bad enough he was being wheeled through the halls, toward the security doors, looking weak, and incapable of taking care of himself, there was no way he was going to make it worse. And the jumper thing, despite Dr. Morton's concern for Ansel's skin, would have made him look like a damn clown.

He nervously shifted his feet, his boots scraping the metal footplates, as people stopped what they were doing to openly gape at him as they passed. Ansel felt the weight of their stares, their questions, accusations, and their hate. At least some of them. Because he had been admitted to Celestial at the end of July with burns over most of his body, spent time in the burn box, then rehab, and seven weeks later it was September. He knew his presence created talk. Ansel shifted in the wheelchair, thankful for the black T-shirt, under a dark blue flannel, jeans, and boots, the normalcy which he'd been lacking gave him a sliver of pride he used to ignore everyone.

When he had been released from the burn box, Dr. Carrion advised him to start counseling. Ansel politely declined by stating he had over a hundred years of experience in accepting shit that happened to him. And the fire was his and his alone. Then there was the sensational news of the two attacks, a murder of one of Celestial's own, his body found at Ansel's house, the abduction of Clio and himself, and he had been set on fire, that made him a spectacle. The acts and mystery surrounding the Covey held the Cascade territory and Celestial's attention. It had for a time overshadowed Flint's attempt to kidnap and murder Jordyn. Except Jordyn was their soothsayer whose powers were increasing by the day and some said she was going to usher them into the dark ages. The idea of leaving their humanized lives behind caused the divide to gain strength.

What the residents of the Cascade territory didn't know was Rutger and the enforcers captured two of the Covey,

Bronte escaped, his affiliation with her had been exposed, Clio Hyde was his mate, he felt her absence like a knife to the heart, and then there was his age and past. All one hundred and forty years of it. The baron placed a gag order on everyone associated with the investigation, leaving zero facts circulating. It meant what people didn't know they speculated, assumed, or made up.

There were rumors the baron was keeping the case private because he was going to protect Ansel from the Highguard and was keeping his enforcers from being questioned about their investigative abilities. None of it was true. The Highguard's cavaliers interrogated the enforcers, soldiers, the staff in communications, the hospital, him and scrutinized his file, and Clio, her employee file and enforcer file. If there were any discrepancies, they would be added to the pending hearing before the Council of Elders.

When they were clear of the main areas of the hospital and entering the back portion free of staff, Ansel relaxed, his thoughts going to Clio. He hadn't seen her since the night Bronte had taken them, and it was driving him insane. During his stay in the burn box, he thought he heard her, felt her near him, and had to accept it had been his imagination and the sedatives. Then Rutger explained the baron ordered her not to have any communication with him while the Highguard was doing their investigation. If he wanted to clear his name and remain with Cascade, and not serve jail time at the Highguard's Crystal Palace, he would do whatever was necessary, and that meant keeping his feelings, and the truth of his relationship with Clio a secret.

Relationship. If an abduction, admission of love midst being set on fire while she was drugged out of her mind constituted a relationship. It didn't matter when he was sure she was oblivious to their connection, even now as he thought about it, he wasn't completely sure any of it had been real. He lost a month of his life and his memory wasn't the best, plus there was no way, with his past and his wrongs, fate would have given him a mate like her. Innocence to his guilt.

"Did you hear me?" Rutger asked as he stopped at the double doors.

"What?" Ansel craned his head to look up at him. "Negative."

"I've gotten word the Highguard has released their findings and is in session with Baron Kanin. Once they come to a conclusion, you'll face the Council of Elders," Rutger explained. "And you can walk now."

Ansel's heart stuck in his chest like a hunk of frozen meat, as every scenario raced through his mind, and the outcomes were not the best. Gripping the duffle, he stood, leaving the wheelchair in the hall, no doubt someone was waiting for them to leave before retrieving it. "Did they give an estimated time?"

"Negative," Rutger replied. He opened the right side door, held it, and waited as Ansel walked through. "I don't think it'll take long, there wasn't much to investigate."

He hoped Rutger right. Or it was his way of saying it was easy for them to find Ansel guilty. When the early afternoon sun caressed his face and skull, he wanted to spend hours in its warmth. He scrubbed his scalp and short ends of his hair with his hand then inhaling fresh air, it brought a million scents floating around him, and his instincts exploded with information. "I miss the outside." It made him feel alive. If he was sent to prison? He wouldn't last. He would die there. Inhaling and exhaling, he shoved the thought down.

"I know the feeling." Rutger let the door close behind him

and started toward his truck. When he stood on the driver's side, he met Ansel's gaze. "You haven't asked about Doctor Hyde."

Ansel stared at him, knew he looked like a deer in the headlights, and struggled to move his mouth. "I'm responsible for a group of assassins attacking and killing on Cascade territory. I'm going before the Council of Elders and the Highguard's cavaliers. I figured I was in too much trouble to ask about her." He had questions, concerns, and words strung into sentences he wanted to spill, but wouldn't take the chance. He didn't need more evidence against him.

Rutger shook his head like a frustrated parent. "Get in the truck."

In silence he obeyed, and sitting back in the seat, couldn't wait to leave Celestial. "Where is the hearing going to take place?"

"Foxwood, the Enforcer's office," Rutger answered. He drove through the gates, the public parking lot, and to the main road.

Ansel watched the scenery, the leaves were starting to turn from brilliant green of July to rust, yellow, tawny browns, while peppered along the side of the road, bare limbs reached out like skeletal arms with thin fingers. There was a second delay when what Rutger said made sense. "The office is complete?"

"Affirmative. About two weeks. Except the med room." Rutger looked straight forward, his eyes skating over the road, then a quick check in the rearview mirror.

Pain had begun to wrap around Ansel's chest, starting when he stepped outside of Celestial, got worse with the change in season, and now squeezed him in its grip. The office was complete. Life moved on without him, had Clio done the same thing? "What about the med room?"

"It isn't complete."

He was in no mood for twenty questions. "Tell me about Clio," he demanded a little too harshly, while trying to cover the worry in his voice. She was put in charge of the med room, and it wasn't complete, it meant there was something wrong.

"Clio?" Rutger gave him a sideways glance.

"Fine. Doctor Hyde," Ansel ground out.

Rutger took his eyes off the road to give him a second glance. "Why don't you tell me why she was at your house when she was supposed to have been at the hospital and have an enforcer with her. It was a direct order from the baron."

It was Ansel's turn to look at the road snaking out in front of them. She disobeyed a direct order, and the day came roaring back to him ... hell, it was always there. "She said she was a big girl and didn't need an escort, then she said she's a doctor and her job was making sure the pack was taken care of, and she needed to know I was all right."

"I have an MD." He nearly smiled recalling her words.

"And?" Rutger's voice lowered, his shoulders tensing.

"I told her to leave. I told her it was my fault, all of it, and told her to go home. I knew I was being watched and I tried to get her to leave. When I thought she was going to go, she stopped and looked at me like she was going to argue and was shot in the back with those damn poisoned crystals," Ansel explained. "It went to shit from there."

"You didn't call her, contact her in any way?"

"Negative. You've checked our cells. Communications would have records of my calls."

Rutger didn't respond, telling Ansel he was right—Ruger had checked the cells and saw Dr. Hyde had called Mandy several times. "She could have been killed. If it wasn't for being a Wight, her recovery would have taken longer."

Dr. Morton told Ansel as much. Clio hated being a Wight, it was the giant chip on her shoulders, and the fact being half human saved her life was funny as hell. He would have paid to see the expression on her face, one he could envision, when the doctor explained that to her. "What has she said?"

"It's Doctor Hyde, she's sticking to the facts. She did go to your house to check on you, nothing else. There are some saying you had Tony Reed killed because of his relationship with her." Rutger gave a gold gaze before looking back at the road.

"I didn't know anything about their relationship, and if I had, I wouldn't have pinned him to *my* table with *my* sword. I would have talked to her, and not destroyed her life with a murder." Why did saying that make his wolf howl? "Outside of trying to get her to leave, and watching Bronte set me on fire, I've had nothing to do with her. If you talked to her, and you have, she would have told you I've treated her with absolute indifference." *Tesoro.* Ansel turned in the seat to see Rutger.

"Affirmative."

"Why hasn't the med room been completed?" Ansel asked for the second time.

"Doctor Hyde is on administrative leave until further notice."

"How long has it been?" The med room was on hold, Clio wasn't working, and he had lost days.

"A week."

"Why? She c-can't be a s-suspect," Ansel stammered. He had the paramedic's blood on his hands and Clio's career.

"Wait, is she all right? The drugs and their effect. Is she having problems?"

"I'm not at liberty to say."

Dammit. "I won't stand in front of the Elders because you're going to drive me insane."

Rutger gave him another quick glance and Ansel thought he saw a smile. The drive continued in silence. Ansel was glad Rutger stopped needling him about Clio, but he could have gone without hearing how he had the paramedic killed because he had been talking to her, and Clio was put on leave. Ansel didn't even know the guy and that made him feel worse. Damn. And treating her with indifference, she knew it, and still she had made sure he was all right. He had been unfair to her. *For good reason*, he argued. Bronte tried killing her because he talked to her. What if he had showed he cared for her? Clio would have been killed. Like the paramedic.

Beeping came from the console, getting Ansel's attention, and alerting them of an incoming call. Rutger looked at him, then the screen, and answered. "Director Kanin."

"Cavalier Braddock. You will have Captain Ansel Wolt escorted to Foxwood at two tomorrow afternoon for the hearing," his deep voice ordered.

"Affirmative, sir," Rutger replied.

Ansel looked at the road and trees as they blurred while his heart threatened to escape his chest. His future rested in the hands of the Elders and the Highguard, it didn't give him any assurance.

"I said *you will* have him escorted. Your presence is required at Foxwood."

"Affirmative, sir." Rutger's voice held onto its casual tone while his eyes, blazing gold, gave away his annoyance. There was an audible click and the screen changed. "They need to leave my territory," he growled.

"It'll be over tomorrow." A chill gripped his spine and spread its ice all the way to his bones.

"You need to wear a suit," Rutger said, ignoring him. "Do you have one?"

"A suit?"

"That's what I asked."

"Affirmative. Did they search my house?" The lack of evidence connecting him to Bronte had to work in his favor.

"Affirmative."

He hated playing twenty questions with Rutger, and hated the man's silence, it meant he was thinking, and that scared him more than anything. "Did they find anything?"

"Spines in the yard, the weapons you showed me and your poor choice in furniture."

"I like my furniture." He didn't, not really. It was there because he lived there, nothing else. Ansel stared at the side of Rutger's face. "Did they find evidence I was in league with Bronte?"

"Negative."

When Rutger didn't go into detail, Ansel let it go. At least they found the spines he pulled from Clio. They would have also found the drink he dropped, and the boxes with his enforcer's uniform, gun, and equipment. Did that make him look guilty? He almost asked Rutger when he decided he would find out tomorrow afternoon and there was no reason to put Rutger in the middle. With the sun's warmth on him, he relaxed, and fatigue threaded through him while his body wanted to rest, his mind raced with what the next day was going to bring.

"The Covey," he mumbled.

"What about it?"

"Bronte escaped. What about the others?" If they told the cavaliers Ansel was one of them and helped with the attacks and murder, he would lose everything and go straight to Crystal Palace.

"There were two taken into custody. The others were killed," Rutger replied.

Good. "Can you tell me what they said?" The investigation was over, he wanted to add.

"Negative."

Rutger slowed down as they approached the entrance to Ansel's house, and making a right, he crept up the driveway. After seven weeks at Celestial, he was happy to be at home, while it lasted.

"When the cavaliers were done investigating, the Purifiers came by," Rutger explained. "Here are your keys."

The spines had been taken, Clio's crossover was gone, the glass he dropped and shattered was gone, the front door was closed, locked, and the table from the deck burned. Any evidence there had been an altercation had been removed.

"Thanks," he replied as he took the keys, and clutched the duffle.

"Are you going to be all right here by yourself?" Rutger asked as he stopped the truck and put it in park. "I can have an enforcer here."

"I'll be ready at one," Ansel answered.

"If you need anything, call me." Rutger's eyes gleamed with shards of gold while his face remained neutral. It wasn't giving Ansel anything to work with. Was he going to be found guilty? Or innocent?

"Thanks again." Ansel opened the door, got out, slung his duffle over his shoulder, and pushed the door closed. When he started toward his house, Rutger backed up, turned around, and left him.

Alone at his house. Alone with his demons. Alone. He hadn't had a chance to think about the hearing, Council of Elders, the cavaliers, or what the outcome might be. He had been focused on Clio, wishing Bronte was dead, the living hell of regenerating skin, and Dr. Morton's torture. At Celestial he was able to block out the flashbacks of having been set on fire, the way the flames crawled over him, and the smell of burning flesh and charred hair. With the memory he rubbed his scalp with his right hand, felt the thickening growth, and was thankful to be alive. Prison or not, Bronte hadn't killed him, and it would drive her insane, and she would come back. She always finished the job. His circle wasn't complete. And the enforcers had killed her Covey. That was another blood debt he owed.

With each step he felt the weight of his life coming down on him. Ansel unlocked the door, entered the house, and when he stood in the middle of his living room, a wall of stale cleaning solution met him. They had cleaned and removed everything, including Clio's scent. Dropping the duffle, he walked to the couch and sat down. His cell phone sat on the side table, where he had left it, its screen dark, and he thought about calling her. And if she treats him the way he treated her? Or blamed him for Bronte and being on administrative leave? He couldn't take it, not now, not after admitting she was his tesoro, his treasure. His mate. Leaning back, he sank into the cushions, closed his eyes, and saw Clio staring up at him as tremors gripped her body.

It had been in the moment of chaos and fear, and he thought he was going to lose everything. It made him an emotional mess and he had been under a lot of stress. The one person who understood was Clio. Plus, she helped him with Rutger and the visits to Celestial and was the only woman he had contact with. It wasn't a surprise he would be drawn to her, or at the very least feel comfortable with her. Seeing her hurt and having his future with the pack threatened, pushed his emotions and created feelings that weren't real. He had dreamt she was his mate, and she wanted him the way he seemed to want ... need her. It was a dream, nothing more.

"Not real," he whispered. Ansel groaned as his muscles melted into the couch, and with exhaustion cradling him, he let his house protect him and drifted.

When Clio received the message from Cavalier Braddock, the single message in over a week, she nearly jumped out of her skin, then she read it, and her heart stopped. Now she sat, alone, in the newly finished Enforcer's building, in an empty office, save for the chair she was using, a desk, and two other matching chairs. It smelled of fresh paint, the white walls were bare, the tile floor sparkled, and was one of four offices that weren't being used. She couldn't see them but knew there were cameras recording her every move ... which she didn't make and resisted the urge to mumble to herself. She also hadn't checked her cell for the time, nor had she made an attempt to look around the room, or fidgeted while they made her wait for what felt like hours.

The handle turned and the door opened with a whisper. "Doctor Clio Hyde."

Clio waited for the man, with a velvet tone in his cultured voice, to walk around the desk where he placed several files and a tablet down before he took his seat. "Sir."

"I'm Cavalier Jean Benoit with the Prosecution Administration. I'm going to ask you a couple of questions," he explained. He wore his onyx hair loose around his face, his silver eyes held droplets of scarlet as if they were tiny jewels, and his olive skin a trace of summer's sun.

It was his eyes making her want to squirm in her seat. She knew what they meant. Dhampir like Bronte. Trinity's population consisted of witches, elves, shapeshifters, fairies, never had there been dhampirs, vampires, demons, or those living among the Cloaked. The hidden magic-born.

Change. Their world was changing.

"I understand," Clio replied and was glad her voice held. If facing Cavalier Jean Benoit was a test, then she was going to pass.

The scarlet beads expanded, swallowed the molten silver, and saturated his eyes. "Be aware, I sense lies as well as truth, as sometimes you might believe what you're saying."

"I understand." She reminded herself she didn't do anything wrong, she had been a victim. It didn't mean he wasn't going to ask about Ansel. Captain Wolt.

"What was the status of your relationship with Mr. Reed at the time of his murder?"

What? "Professional."

"I stated I could sense lies, the truth, and the corrupted version you believe." He opened a file, shifted papers, and met her gaze. "I also have a statement saying you were seen with him at a bakery the day he disappeared."

Her heart sank. "He was there when I got there, his cousin owns the place. We sat together, that is all." She sounded unnerved, weak, and like she was defending herself.

"Records show he called you, it lasted three seconds."

"I didn't answer. It was the same day Mr. Platt had attacked Miss Langston."

"You're no longer an enforcer, what does the attack have to do with you?" He purposely held her gaze as the scarlet and silver ebbed around his pupil and red lines reached out.

Intimidation at its best and it was working. She saw Bronte in front of her, heard the dhampir's laugh as she lit the kerosene drenched T-shirt stuck to Ansel's skin. "I treated Miss Langston after her kidnapping, and I'm the Kanin family's physician. After the second attack, I asked if she needed medical. I was told she refused."

"Did you explain this to Mr. Reed?"

And betray her pack? "Negative. I messaged him stating I had pack obligations."

"Is that when you called Captain Wolt? What did you think you were going to gain?"

"I asked if she needed medical, if she didn't need medical, I asked if she needed Doctor Carrion. He was her therapist, and since she had been attacked by the same man, I thought she might need to talk to him." That was the truth.

"What did he tell you?"

"He said Miss Langston was refusing medical and didn't need to talk to Doctor Carrion." She heard the frustration in his voice at the same time guilt from having spent the afternoon with Tony spread like a poison. The truth she believed, it was a work relationship, and the lie it was, guilt. She didn't have to ask when Cavalier Jean Benoit's eyes gleamed like rubies to know he sensed the conflict twisting her truths into lies. Kiss your career good-bye.

"You disobeyed a direct order and went to Captain Wolt's house the day of the attack. Why?" His voice turned husky, rough, like her lies were a sweet treat.

"He was on house arrest. I went to make sure he was all right, physically and emotionally, there had been a body in his backyard," she answered. *And to put a giant hole in his wall of ice.*

"You were ordered to have an armed escort. Instead, you

put your life at risk, and as you stated, you're the Kanin family's physician. An honor for one of the pack, let alone a Wight. Yet you went to make sure he was all right, a trained enforcer, Captain of Enforcers. Are you a psychologist?" Cavalier Jean Benoit sat back in the chair, making it squeal with his weight.

Her default setting blazed and fed her every doubt she ever had and then some. Clio looked down at her hands clasped in her lap, her black slacks, and black sensible shoes. "Negative, and while I'm not an enforcer, I didn't know what the threat level was," she mumbled. Once the words were out, disguised as a pathetic excuse, she wished she could have taken them back. She knew what was coming.

"Ignorance isn't an excuse for you to ignore an order." Leaning forward, he rested his elbows on the papers. "What is your relationship with Captain Wolt?"

Easy. "Strictly professional."

"Did you know about his affiliation with Milanka Telep?"

The name slid through her mind, causing pain and creating images she didn't want to see.

"You know her by the name Bronte?"

"Negative. Not until I visited Captain Wolt. He told me." She saw herself walking down the stairs, the blues playing behind her, July's warmth on her bare shoulders, and the heady scent of Ansel's bourbon mixing with his wolf.

"Why? Telling you would incriminate him." His molten silver eyes broken by scarlet turned hard as stone.

"He wanted me to leave. Said he wasn't worth my energy, then he told me he knew her, and she had used his sword," Clio confessed. "I didn't leave." Untangle that mess of information, she wanted to say, then tell her what he learned, because she was confused.

"Noticeably. Do you remember anything after being shot?"

Ansel jumped the stairs to get to her, he called her tesoro, then he took her in his arms and tried to get her into the house. Clio met his stare with her own. "He tried to take me into the house and was going to get help. Bronte told him no, and that's it, until we were in the field. I was aware enough to watch her set him on fire."

"How are you dealing with the drug's effects?" he asked. Looking down at the papers, he shuffled two, then started to read another. "It says here you were seeing Doctor Carrion. And you recovered faster because of your human half."

"That's correct. I have nightmares, but those are becoming less and less."

His scarlet gaze locked on her. "And?"

"She's out there. Yes, I take my gun and clear my house," Clio confessed. She was sure Bronte was going to come back and take her revenge.

"You're a werewolf You have heightened senses, instincts. Why use a weapon?"

She looked at her hands as embarrassment scalded her cheeks. "Armed, and then in wolf form," she answered.

"Cavalier Braddock will aid in evaluating your nightmares."

"Sir." Clio's blood turned to ice water.

"As a demon, I can duplicate what you see," Cavalier Braddock started as he rounded the table and sat down. "You'll react to them as you would if you were asleep. This exercise will determine if you're ready to return to Celestial."

Shame slid over her in a heated wave as tears stung her eyes and there was nothing she could do to stop them. There was, but she wasn't going to give them the satisfaction of listening to her as she quit. Meeting the cavaliers' gazes, she mentally prepared to see the horrors she had worked to get over.

CHAPTER TWENTY-FIVE

Ansel stepped out of the truck, adjusted his tie, suit jacket, and slacks as Quinn rounded the front end, met him, and they walked across the parking lot to the baron's house. The office in its ten thousand square foot of state-of-the-art technology stood strong with the mountains as a backdrop, as did the garage and the combination of enforcer and soldier's vehicles. There were three he didn't recognize, all of them black with dark-tinted windows. Highguard. Cavaliers. It made his heart jump to his throat where it lodged itself.

"Captain Wolt," Sousa greeted. "Quinn."

Ansel nodded in return, surprised to have been called captain, and too scared to talk, entered the house. A soft wave of familiar scents greeted him—flowers, cooking, coffee—and the gentleness of the baron and baroness' power as it wove through the air.

"You'll wait in the greeting room," Quinn advised.

He didn't understand why he wasn't in a holding cell, the office was complete, or one of the interrogation rooms. That's what this was really about. His lies, betrayal, and the pain he caused. Taking a left, he was in the formal greeting room, his pulse in his ears, his lungs seizing, and his knees had started to turn to jelly.

"Mistress, I'm sorry, I didn't know you were in here," Quinn quickly apologized.

Jordyn faced them, giving the large window with views of the yard, parking lot, and Enforcer's office her back. Her onyx eyes were lined in black, her hair loose around her shoulders, and she wore a fitted shirt, jeans, and running shoes. She looked like the Pureblood she was and had the power to match. Again, he questioned why he was waiting in the house, with the Second's mate, and the pack's soothsayer instead of a cell.

"It's fine. Captain Wolt, join me," she offered with a weak smile. It didn't touch her eyes, and he saw pain in their haunted depths.

Quinn gave him a sideways glance with his hesitation, then stared when he remained silent and immobile. "M-Mistress, of c-course," he stammered. Ansel closed the distance between them and stopped when he stood beside the petite woman, soothsayer, Rutger's mate.

"Quite an achievement, the office," she said casually as she faced the window.

"Affirmative. I mean yes." He was making a fool of himself. He expected to be treated like a criminal, a traitor, and not left alone with Jordyn, the woman Baron Kanin guarded as if she was the most important thing in the world, a gem. He couldn't guess the reason behind it. He felt the slightest tremor in her magic, it slid over him like a veil of satin. Was she trying to read his mind? Or was this who she had become?

"You didn't attack those people and you didn't kill the paramedic," she assured, her voice thick with emotion. Jordyn inhaled, exhaled, her shoulders caving for a second when she straightened and watched the office.

Letting her words take root and wondering why she would try to reassure him, he watched Rutger exit the office, his square shoulders concealed in the black BDU top, his hand on the butt of his gun holstered at his thigh. He looked in their direction, didn't see Ansel, his gold eyes focused on his mate. It took him a second for a path to clear through his thoughts and he couldn't believe she was trying to make him feel better. Three werewolves had been tortured then murdered, and then one of their own, a young pup named Zachery, before the witches kidnapped her and stopped their killing spree. She felt responsible for their deaths.

"You don't believe that," he whispered. He risked looking at her and saw her flinch.

Her head lowered, then she was gazing at him while onyx and copper swirled around her pupils. "There are moments."

"Captain Wolt, they're ready for you," Quinn announced.

Ansel turned to leave when she grabbed his upper arm, stopping him. "You were there for him. Thank you."

With his head slightly bowed, he replied, "Mistress."

Jordyn's fingers slid from his jacket sleeve as she released him to face the window.

Ansel left the greeting room, Jordyn's words playing in his head, and when he was outside, he took a deep breath and tried to calm his nerves. There wasn't a snowball's chance in hell he was going to calm down. He followed Quinn—he was the prisoner being led to this cell, not an enforcer—and he didn't engage anyone. Not that anyone was going to talk to him. They stopped to stare, there were hushed whispers, and they moved on. Part of him expected them to be happy he was alive, while part of him expected to be treated like a prisoner. Being ignored hurt all the same.

Quinn opened the door to the office, held it while Ansel walked through, and let it close on its own. Stopping, Quinn nearly bumped into him, and he stared at the lobby area, the tile flooring, and overhead lights giving off a warm glow.

Several chairs lined the left side, while on the right a woman sat behind a counter, with two monitors, a phone, and electronic signature pad decorating its top.

"Baron Kanin and Cavalier Braddock are waiting for you in the conference room," the woman explained as she stared at Ansel.

"Thanks, Tabby," Quinn replied.

He stepped around Ansel, walked through the lobby and to a set of steel double doors. Unclipping his badge from his BDU top, he slid it through the security pad, it blinked green, and he entered a number code. The lock disengaged, and Quinn was holding the right side open for Ansel to pass through. He was a step closer to hearing about his betrayal from Cavalier Braddock and Baron Kanin and then his imprisonment. They walked in silence down the brightly lit hallway, while people peeked out of offices, and he heard voices from another room he guessed was an office. Ansel slowed down to look inside, and saw a large TV mounted to the wall with different viewpoints of Foxwood displayed on the screen. There were desks with computers on them, office equipment, and Mandy sitting at the largest desk with three smaller monitors in front of her and wearing a wireless headset. Communications looked like he thought it would, a command center.

"Captain Wolt," Clio greeted as she met him. She didn't know he was going to be there. Trying her best to conceal she had been crying, she wiped her eyes. God, she didn't want him to see her looking broken and weak.

Ansel felt everyone freeze, target their attention on the two of them, at the same time tension and silence wove between them. Would they assume he and Clio were together? Did it matter? It did to him. He looked into her azure eyes, saw red lines staining them, and wanted to kill whoever had brought her to tears. "Doctor Hyde," he greeted, his voice thundering in the silence. He wanted to ask her how she was, if she needed anything, because he would give her anything, but didn't, couldn't. They were being watched, and he was headed to a sentencing to determine his future.

"It's good to see you're doing well." She couldn't stop staring at him.

While his dark auburn hair was short, really short, his skin gained its color, and he was thinner. Over the month he spent at Celestial he had lost most of his muscle mass, but it didn't matter, he looked good in a suit, and it made her heart flutter. That was dumb. Cavalier Braddock forced her to relive the nightmares given to her by Bronte's poison, and she made a fool of herself, had no idea if she would ever work again, and didn't need to be making eyes at Captain Wolt. And they were being watched like they were a sideshow. Sadly, he had repaired the damage done to his wall of ice, and it was up in full force. She felt the sting from the cold.

Ansel wanted to beg her to say his name, the way she had at his house so he could hear it one last time. Clio's strawberry blonde hair, holding a slight curl, ended by her shoulders, her eyes were lined with soft brown, highlighting the honey streaks, and she wore mascara. A black suit jacket covered a lavender bouse that was tucked into black slacks and ended with heels. Professional. Strong. He hated himself … she was beautiful, and he risked her life.

"Thank you." He tried to lessen the harshness of his tone and couldn't, when if he let himself feel, he was going to lose his mind. Words were meaningless, when he wanted to take her in his arms, like he had in his dreams, and find out for sure if she was his mate. How would he know? No idea. To feel her against him.

"Doctor Hyde." The man behind her wearing a black suit, black button-up, sapphire tie, and matching sapphire band around his left arm was a cavalier. His eyes told Ansel he was a shifter, what kind he had no idea.

Clio didn't respond, found it hard to string a sentence together from believing she lost Ansel. Plastering a sad smile on her face, she took a hesitant step. Was this the end? As if in answer, he moved to the side and away from her.

Ansel stayed behind Quinn, as Clio walked by him, and turning he watched her walk away from him. His feelings were tossing him all over the place, and there was nothing he could do about the hurt he caused her.

"Sir, this way," Quinn advised.

When she was out of sight, he followed, and felt the stares on him eating through his sleeves, button-up shirt, to his skin where they burned holes in him. He didn't know how far they had gone when Quinn ushered him into a room. There was a single chair placed in front of a table where Baron Kanin was sitting with another man in a black suit and sapphire band. Cavalier Braddock. Behind Ansel and along the back wall, were rows of seats that looked stacked like theater seating. No doubt that's where the Council of Elders would sit. He didn't know why they weren't present.

"Captain Wolt, please have a seat," Baron Kanin ordered. He didn't wear a suit, like everyone else, instead he wore a gray sweater over a white button-up, the collar undone to leave the edges of his tattoo exposed, a chain with a wolf's head, Cascade's crest, jeans and boots. Why he looked like he was having a casual cocktail party and not a sentencing hearing for his Captain of Enforcers that betrayed his trust, Ansel had no idea. Unless he was flexing his status and wearing civilian clothing separated him from the rigid dress code of the Highguard. Baron Kanin would do it to prove a point. His power.

Ansel sat down, pushed his sweat-damp palms down his slacks, and tried to get control over the panic flooding him. The missing elders unnerved him, his instincts telling him there was more going on. He had no idea what it could be. Then he heard footsteps and figured the elders had arrived. Uncertainty had him making assumptions when he recognized the familiar march, the door closed, and he watched Rutger take a seat at the table beside the baron. He was confused.

"I'm Cavalier Braddock," he introduced himself as he straightened his sapphire tie.

The investigation was over, ended, they made their decision from the interrogation that had taken place while he was at Celestial where he confessed, and the other's statements. They were going to tell him about the charges against him, they didn't need the Council of Elders for that, and take him straight to Crystal Palace, the Highguard's prison. Besides having the worst name, it was also called The Ice Pit of Death, and was in Northern Siberia in the middle of a tundra where winter temperatures dipped to twenty-eight below. Cascade's own below-ground prison was born from the massive concrete prison a mile underground where the most dangerous magic-born, some mystical creatures, were kept locked up without sunlight. He didn't rate the underground treatment. No, they would keep him above ground.

"Captain of Enforcers, Ansel Wolt, you have been charged with obstruction of justice, accessory, accessory after the fact, reckless endangerment, endangerment of the innocent, using your status, authority, and influence to impede the investigations into the attacks on Daniel of the Low Valley of the Unseelie court, Enforcer Lado Reyes of the Seelie court and Cascade pack, and the murder of Tony Reed of the Red River fold, paramedic with Celestial Medical Center."

Murder. The cavalier's voice faded out as he accepted they weren't going to send him to Crystal Palace, it was too good for him, they were going to sentence him to death. Ansel refused to look at Rutger—he couldn't handle seeing the disappointment and betrayal he must be feeling—and kept his gaze on the cavalier while the rush of emotions cascaded through him. He was going to lose the pack. His pack. He was going to lose Clio before he had the chance to have her. Mate or not, he would never know. He would never know what it was like to live freely and without fear. He would die while Bronte was free. *She won the game*. The thought made his heart stop.

"You endangered the lives of magic-born, the Cloaked, and risked exposing their traits to humans," Cavalier Braddock continued. "You endangered the life of Doctor Clio Hyde of Cascade."

With her name, Ansel met the hardened gaze of the cavalier and felt both the baron and Rutger's eyes on him.

"The Prosecution Administration with the Highguard's authority—"

Ansel was listening and not listening, not wanting to know what they were going to do to him. The words sounded far away as if he had been drifting in the opposite direction of the table, the cavalier, the baron, Rutger.

"Expunges the charges stated against Ansel Wolt. You are hereby reinstated as Captain of Enforcers of the Cascade pack, effective immediately," Cavalier Braddock finished.

Rutger stood, a tight smile pulling on the corners of his mouth, and with his hand on the butt of his gun, he walked past Ansel and opened the door. "Please take your seats."

Ansel remained staring forward, the cavalier and the baron blurring as the sounds of multiple people entering the room, their clothing shifting, their soft murmurs, and then their shoes on the tile, and the clicking of heels. His mind hadn't caught up with what was happening. He thought he heard the cavalier say he was reinstated, but he might have made it up, he couldn't trust himself.

"Welcome, ladies and gentlemen of the Council of Elders of the Cascade pack, Chancellor Frost of the Unseelie court, Chancellor Roarke of the Seelie court, Lance of the Red River fold, I'm Cavalier Braddock of the Highguard's Prosecution Administration. I would like to publicly thank—"

Tension twisted Ansel's muscles, and his body went rigid with the presence of those he had put in danger. This was when the ax was going to drop.

"Baron Kanin as he has shown due reverence to the Highguard."

"A pleasure, Cavalier Braddock." Baron Kanin stood to address the audience. "Ladies and gentlemen, the Highguard's Prosecution Administration, in alliance with Cascade's Enforcers, have concluded their investigation. The statement is as follows; upon hearing of the travesty invoking Soothsayer Jordyn Langston and believing the Cascade territory had been weakened by the tragedy, the terrorist group Crimson Moon, led by Milanka Telep, aka Bronte, seized the opportunity to exploit this weakness by threatening those within the Cascade territory and targeting its kith and kin through fear, violence, and intimidation. Milanka Telep, dhampir, and trained assassin, orchestrated to undermine my authority and that of the enforcers to allow the group to eliminate leaders of the factions under Cascade rule. In accordance with the canons of the Highguard, I have dispatched a team to hunt Milanka Telep and bring her to Cascade for expiation."

Crimson Moon. It wasn't real. Ansel's mind replayed every word, latching onto their meaning, and tried to make sense of what the baron was saying. It couldn't be real.

"Please bring in the prisoners," Baron Kanin ordered.

The door opened, and rustling of chains alerted Ansel the prisoners were being escorted into the room. He turned enough to see them. The male with red hair and green eyes glared at him from a bruised face. The female hung her head, her dirty brown hair shielding her face, her thin shoulders caving.

"Levi. Spring. You have been found guilty of terrorism, conspiracy to commit terrorism, possession of a weapon to use against the magic-born, possession of a poison to use against the magic-born, assault and bodily harm to Daniel of the Low Valley, Unseelie court, and Enforcer Lado Reyes of the Seelie Court and Cascade pack, the torture and murder of Tony Reed of the Red River fold, paramedic with Celestial Medical Center. Treason and conspiracy to commit treason against the magic-born, the attempted assassination of Captain of Enforcers, Ansel Wolt, the attempted assassination of Doctor Clio Hyde with Celestial Medical Center, disobeying the canons of the Highguard, trespassing on Cascade territory with the intent to do harm. Being part of terrorist group to do harm against the magic-born through force and fear. The punishment for said crimes is death."

As silence spread through the room, choking the air, Cavalier Braddock stood. "The death sentence will be carried out at Хрустальный дворец, Crystal Palace. Take the prisoners and prepare them for transport," he ordered.

Stunned by the events and the fact no one was taking him into custody, Ansel's guilt for his part burned his insides.

"Lance of the Red River fold, Tony's loss is greatly felt, our hearts are given to you and your kith and kin. Tony Reed's name shall be added to your Sacred Writ with honor and for his loyalty to the Highguard, the Cascade pack, and the Red River fold," Cavalier Braddock stated.

"Thank you for this," Lance replied, his voice thick with his sorrow.

"Tony's name will be echoed in the halls of Celestial Medical Center where his presence served a vital part. Upon the request of Doctor Clio Hyde, Med Two will be stationed at Foxwood. May the territory protect your kith, and may Tony's fox run free in the mountains," Baron Kanin offered.

"Baron Kanin, your compassion and contribution are received with open hearts," Lance replied.

"This concludes the session. You are dismissed," Cavalier Braddock announced.

Ansel sat with his palms flat on his thighs, his eyes staring straight forward, tension racing through him, his mind rebuking what he heard, and eyes stinging from unshed tears. He didn't know if he was going to be able to walk out of the room, out of the building, anywhere.

"Ansel." Baron Kanin stood in front of him.

"Sir. I-I can't. I kn-knew," he stammered. "I don't deserve—"

"It's over. We're your family. Kith and kin. We take care of our own," Baron Kanin began as he placed his hand on Ansel's shoulder and squeezed.

"Crimson Moon, how?" he asked.

"Doctor Hyde stated the fire that nearly consumed you turned the moon crimson. The Highguard recorded Crimson Moon as an assassin group. You've been seceded from

Milanka's association. You are no longer responsible for her actions," Baron Kanin explained. "Rutger is going to take you home."

He felt a hand under his arm urging him to stand. Ansel looked at the baron, his gold gaze, and Rutger. He had become a volcano of emotion and one word was going to make it burst and he was sure his heart was going to explode.

CHAPTER TWENTY-SIX

The first couple of days of her administrative leave Clio had gone to the store, cleaned house, organized her closet, dresser, and kitchen. That was disrupted by periods of shifting into her wolf form to clear the house, then clearing it again while armed, and then sitting in the dark with her glass of tequila. She stopped herself hundreds of times from calling Ansel, the threat of punishment rearing its ugly head. Clio needed to hear him. Needed a connection to him. Damn, she wanted to know what he was thinking. Then she had her interview, psychological evaluation, and saw Ansel for the first in over a month and her motivation stalled.

Clio blew a breath out and shook her head as she sat cross-legged on the couch, a throw over her, and holding her coffee mug, stared out the window passing hour number two. Her nightmares weren't the only things she recalled ... she also remembered what Ansel had said to her, felt his lips on hers, and the helplessness when Bronte was torturing him with the flames. Ice skated down her spine, leaving her chilled despite the hot coffee, thick throw, and the sun coming through the window.

"He didn't say anything to me," she complained to the empty room. "Like he doesn't care. Anymore."

There was a lecture she was going to give herself and it would start with she needed to stop feeling sorry for herself, and think of Ansel's feelings. Hell, he had spent seven weeks in Celestial, and when he was discharged, he faced a sentencing hearing. She couldn't imagine the fear he must have been feeling. Was feeling. She didn't know the outcome. No one would tell her, and she tried, and tried. *Tesoro*. She couldn't get the name out of her head or his voice and the way he had said it, with passion. Or she was fooling herself ... drugs, nightmares, near death, watching someone she cared about, romantic or not, go through hell, would affect one's perception.

Was that what the cavalier was going to prove? She wasn't mentally capable of handling pressure? Clio wanted to slink under the throw, block out the world, and never leave her townhouse in the city ever again. One lesson she did learn—relationships were emotional roller coasters. She laughed a rough sound turned bitter by unshed tears. Relationship. That was a joke.

A buzzing, then her cell bouncing on her table switched her attention. The phone hadn't made a peep since Cavalier Braddock disabled it. She snatched it, excited it might be about her psych eval, and read the message, and her heart sank for a minute. It was a pack wide announcement sent from communications. Then it beat so hard it felt like it hit her sternum. With shaking hands, she reread it, focusing on each word, as if they might change and her imagination was creating what she was reading. Captain Ansel Wolt had been reinstated, the Highguard's cavaliers had taken the prisoners into custody and were transporting them to Northern Siberia where they would be executed at Crystal Palace. The Highguard in partnership with a team from Cascade were actively searching for members of the group Crimson Moon, and the leader, Milanka Telep, for the crimes listed. She stopped reading, she knew what the crimes were, she had been there.

Ansel was cleared of any wrongdoing and able to go back to work. Clio didn't know what she was going to say when she dialed communications.

"Doctor Hyde, good to hear from you," Mandy greeted.

Sure it was. "Is Captain Wolt at work?" she asked. *Please answer.*

"Negative." The line went silent.

Clio checked the screen, making sure Mandy had in fact hung up on her, and seeing the call had ended she carefully set the cell on the table beside her coffee mug. This was her chance to figure out whatever was happening between them. With edgy nervousness, she kicked the throw off her legs and ran to her room.

An hour later she had showered, done her makeup, her hair, was dressed in a fitted black top, zip-up hoodie, jeans, running shoes, and was driving out of the city toward a two-story house with a pond and geese in the backyard. Clio squeezed the steering wheel, turning her knuckles white, while she tried to sing along with the song playing on the radio. Any distraction failed. She couldn't stop from warning herself she was setting herself up for a heartbreak, that is if her heart hadn't taken the hint and left her to her own devices.

When she reached the entrance to the driveway, she slowed, the day in July coming back to her. All she wanted to know was that he was all right. *I don't deserve your worry.* Stubborn. Clio crept up behind Ansel's truck with her heart in her throat and parked her crossover and turned off the engine while telling herself she was an idiot. She had to know. Fuck. It was what drove her. Soldiers. Enforcers. Medical school. Celestial. The med room at Foxwood.

Researching fated mates. She rested her forehead on the steering wheel and considered banging it against the inlaid wood. Had it been staring her in the face the entire time? Her doubt hadn't stopped her from talking to him, thinking about him, wanting to see him, and his cold front hadn't stopped her. It infuriated her but didn't stop her. *What if this is what it feels like, fated mates?* Thoughts like that were going to doom her and damn if she didn't let the idea corrupt her. While she was at home doing nothing but worrying and assuming, she had plenty of time for it to play with her imagination. Clio picked her head up and looked at his truck. Streaks of sunlight broke through nearly bare tree limbs to highlight the silver lifted 4x4, with Cascade's crests on its sides. Silent strength. That's what he was. A storm held in by sheer determination.

She inhaled and got out of the car before she put it in reverse, and tucking tail, got the hell out there. As she walked up to the steps, the scents of the woods, water, and Ansel circled her as if they knew why she was there. Yeah. Her default setting blared, telling her Ansel didn't want a Wight, he wanted a Pureblood, and that was why he hadn't said anything to her. Those weeks in Celestial gave him the chance to think it through, come to his senses, he wasn't facing death and he wasn't watching her suffer. She was an idiot. Turning on the ball of her foot, Clio took one step toward her car ... there was no reason to make things worse.

"Where are you going?" Forgetting he didn't have much hair, Ansel scrubbed his hand over his skull, expecting to run his fingers through his hair. Self-consciousness wormed its way over his confidence, making him wonder what Clio saw.

After the message went out stating he had been reinstated, he received a dozen calls congratulating him, which fed his guilt. He still didn't understand why the baron protected him when it was clear he had been involved. Baron Kanin repeated forty years was a long time, and the past was the past. What it had cost him, Ansel couldn't imagine. Bronte wanted her revenge, and Ansel wasn't responsible for those she hurt. It overwhelmed him with emotions he didn't think he had. He always thought of the pack as his family, but kept them at arm's length because of his past, Bronte, the lies he told, and knowing he wasn't good enough. Bronte set him free. As if he had been purified by fire.

Rutger had called him. The investigation into Bronte's whereabouts was going forward with the help from Mandy and forensics confirming Bronte's DNA, they created a file on the Assembly software, and sent it worldwide. His heart had raced with finally finding her, ending her, and having closure to that part of his life. When he hung up, he heard the car, recognized its sound, and holding his breath waited for her to knock on the damn door. She didn't. Obviously, if he had waited, he would have passed out from lack of oxygen and she would have driven off.

Clio faced him with her pulse in her ears and knew he heard her heart's erratic beating. With the blues playing in the background, he ran his hand over his skull as if reminding himself he didn't have any hair, at least the shoulder-length locks he had before, and it broke her. Then his eyes gleamed bronze, he leaned against the post, his arms crossed over his chest making his biceps bunch, the blue T-shirt hugging his thickening shoulders and his jeans hugging his hips. Bald. Hair. She didn't have any pride and she was in deep.

"I didn't ... I-I mean, I'm bothering you," she stammered.

"I didn't think I would see the day I witnessed Doctor Clio Hyde speechless."

She laughed and couldn't believe he was teasing her. "I don't want to bother you."

"Did you leave your townhouse in the city to tell me that?"

Was he grinning? "No. Yes. No. I don't want to bother you."

"You said that. You're not bothering me," Ansel replied as he straightened. He could tease her all damn day. "Please, come in."

Yes. Yes! "All right. If I'm not bothering you," Clio repeated. She could cringe with the throaty sound of her voice.

"You aren't. I promise." Her azure eyes held him, gauged him, as her thoughts passed over her face, and he worried about what she saw. A man. A monster. A wreak of a person. When she accepted his invitation, the blue darkened, bringing the honey shards forward and his entire body warmed. The fitted shirt showed her curves while her jeans molded to her toned legs. She was going to be in his house. Ansel opened the door and held it for her.

Passing him, his power reached out, and she swore she felt his wolf. She pushed the thought away and looked at the living room. It was the same as before—spotless, orderly, and the furniture plain—unlike her townhouse, which was seemingly cluttered with throws draped on the couch, candles on the side tables, photographs, knickknacks, and personal touches. Ansel didn't need those things when it was his intoxicating scent and presence making the house his. He could have lawn furniture inside, and she wouldn't care. She stopped and turned to face him as he closed the door. His worry and questions were on his face, and she wanted ... needed to tell him he was the man she thought he was. Hers.

"I   saw   the   message   you   were   reinstated.

Congratulations," Clio offered to break the silence.

"Thank you. Although, I don't think I deserve it," he replied. The walls started closing in, and heat crawled over him. Ansel left the door, needing to walk, and crossed the living room.

Clio watched him, his gait, the way his left hand rested on his hip. "If Baron Kanin thought you were guilty, you would be in Crystal Palace."

True. He met her gaze knowing his eyes were the bronze of his wolf and giving away his emotions. "I—"

"What does tesoro mean?" she blurted out, interrupting him. She wanted to talk to him, ease into a conversation, not scare him. The terrified expression on his face told her everything she needed to know. "I'm sorry."

"It's Italian ... my mother was, and I learned a little. It means treasure," he answered and held her gaze. He couldn't believe she remembered.

Treasure. Her heart was suddenly in her throat. "I cling to it when the nightmares get bad," she said like it was a confession. *Good one.*

"Clio. Gods, I am so sorry. I know it's not enough."

"It's not your fault. I didn't come over here for an apology." She took a step toward him and waited to see if he stepped back from her. He didn't. "I came over because ..." The truth sat between them, thick and heavy with their emotions and was getting worse. Something was happening.

Her strength amazed him. Her presence made him want things he wasn't worthy of possessing. "Why did you come here?" he asked with a growl running through his words. The air buzzed with their magic, their wolves, their attraction.

"Am I your treasure?" Clio whispered. *Please say yes.*

"Affirmative." Ansel took a step closer to her. "Mine."

Clio swallowed the pure joy she felt, then wasn't sure

what happened to her heart but was sure it bailed on her.

Ansel hesitated. What was he thinking, doing? He wanted to let himself go. No walls. No protection. No fear. He longed to express his feelings. He had been cleared the day before for a murder and two attempted murders. Clio had a life, one he almost destroyed. A family. A future. Everything he didn't have but wanted. Wasn't that why he fought to stay in Cascade? To keep his family. Her azure eyes turned to sapphire jewels as she watched him. He nearly lost her. He wasn't going to waste any more time.

"Do you think we could be fated mates?" he asked cautiously.

Clio froze. "You're serious?"

"I don't know. Maybe not." Yes, he did. "What I feel for you, I have never felt for anyone. Ever. It's uncontrollable. My wolf recognizes you, wants you. I heard your voice when I was in the burn box. I dreamt about you."

"Restoring chamber," she corrected, her voice sounding cracked. Her knees went to jelly. She was going to crash to floor and make an ass out herself.

This was what she wanted. She wanted Ansel, battled his wall of ice, and now her mind was treating his confession like a disease needing a cure. Default setting. Fated mates. Did her wolf want him? She wanted him, was that the same thing? Were Wights capable of feeling what their wolves wanted? Had she even tried? No. Maybe she didn't believe it was possible. Director Kanin, Miss Langston, they weren't real. Were they? They were Purebloods, it had to make a difference. Maybe this was her way of trying to protect herself. If she admitted what she felt for Ansel, it would make it real, and it could be taken away. He would walk away and construct his wall as he went. Clio closed her eyes, felt a chilled wave coming from him, and opened herself to her wolf's instincts. Battling through her doubt, she found him, his strength, power, and the connection like she had found her mate. It gave her a sense of belonging and love. Unconditional. Unbound. Opening her eyes, she met his bronze gaze and knew she would do anything to keep him.

"I thought I was losing my mind. I feel you like I have a connection to you. Then when we're apart, it's like that connection demands I find you. I need you. I want you. And until I'm with you, I'm not complete. If this need to be near you, to want you, is fated mates, I believe it," she rattled on. Clio believed it, and it set something inside of her free. Like her head had caught up with her heart. Feeling heat slither up her neck to her cheeks, a warmth spread out from her middle, and she wasn't scared.

When she closed her eyes, Ansel knew she was going to tell him to go to hell, he wasn't worth her time, and didn't deserve her after what he had done. He was meant to be alone. Waiting through the silence, the seconds ticking by, he drew in the shame from having exposed himself, and the frozen lump his heart had become started to crack, then she met his gaze, and the walls he spent a lifetime building and protecting came tumbling down. *I need you. I want you.* Without saying a word, his eyes liquid bronze, his wolf rising, he closed the distance between them. Taking her in his arms, he kissed her lips as if his life depended on it, and it did. Her body melted into him, her arms around his neck, while his hands were at her back holding her against him, their bodies together as if they were made for one another.

Kissing him back, Clio let him claim her as he tasted her, then his hands gripped her, and he was lifting her. She wrapped her legs around his waist as a growl escaped him, and going into her, the primal rumble brought her wolf forward. With her left arm linked behind his neck, she held his face with her right then he released her mouth, and nudging her head, left soft kisses up her throat to her jaw where he lightly nibbled.

Ansel drew his tongue along her jaw, tasting her flesh, her wolf, and the spice of Clio as he walked them to couch. When the back of his calves touched the edge, he sat down with her straddling him, her weight pressing on him. She belonged to him, and the truth made his wolf howl in his ears. The days and weeks he had been in the burn box and dreamt about her, held her lush body that softened and molded to his, it had saved his sanity, gave him something to focus on besides his crimes and the flames. Leaning back on the couch, Clio straightened and they stared at each other as if they couldn't believe where they found themselves.

She tried catching her breath then tried swallowing the hot need to strip Ansel out of his T-shirt and jeans, and rip her own clothes off, like she had zero pride. Like he wouldn't judge cool, calm, collected Dr. Hyde. "This. Us. Is it real?" she asked.

"I hope so, tesoro." Ansel's hand worked up and down her sides, then stopped at her hips where he gripped her and pulled her down to him. "I need to make sure you're really here," he whispered. Did he just say that?

"Mmmm, let me help." Clio leaned into him, her hands clutching the cushion behind him. Then, moving down, she held his side, trying to get closer to him and his neck, feeling the tendons tighten and flex as he moved. "You know you're robbing the cradle."

There was one hundred and ten years of difference between them. "Imagine the things I could show you." He was losing himself in her touch and wanted more.

"I'm looking forward to it." Her whisper was throaty, and rough with her desire.

Their lips met, soft at first, then the need they had been holding back burned between them and igniting, its flames covered them in a veil of heat and lust. Ansel's wolf rose, his need to possess Clio pushing his hunger to be with her, inside of her, and have her beneath him. As his magic reached out, he pictured its threads entering her to wrap around her heart and bond them together. He felt her magic match his, and meeting they tangled, power intertwining with power, and creating a fire of their mixed magic it exploded between them. She was his. His wolf had taken possession of her.

"Mine," he growled against her, his hands gripping her, refusing to let her go.

"Mine," she responded with a grin curving her lips. She rocked her hips into him, her jeans scraping on his. "Fate brought us together."

"Fate," he whispered as he slid hands under her top. Groaning a primal sound of possession he savored the feel of her flesh on his palms, and her heat soaking into him. This wasn't meant for him. He wasn't supposed to have what he wanted. He wasn't supposed to be granted his heart's desire. He wasn't worthy of a family. His sins were too great. As if in answer, a cell phone blared in the silence and broke through their passion and heavy breathing.

"Dammit," Clio cursed then rested her forehead against his. Sitting straight, she looked for her cell, which had dropped from her pocket to the floor. She had to leave Ansel, his gaze dark with his wolf and magic, strong body, and her mate. Fated mate.

Clio backed off him, and he wanted to grab her and hold her and break her damn cell but knew her job and her place took priority. Just as his did. As she answered the call, he watched her features, her lips swollen from their kiss, her flushed skin, and the silken curls of strawberry blonde hair he had held in his fingers. When she ended the call, he realized he had been in his head, and hadn't heard a word she said.

She laughed as she shoved the cell in her back pocket. "I stayed up last night wondering when they would call. It figures it would happen right now."

"What are you talking about?" Ansel asked, a low rumble in his voice. He wanted her back on his lap and in his arms.

"My psych evaluation. That was Mandy, I've been ordered to go to Foxwood," she replied.

"Clio, I didn't know. I'm sorry." Ansel stood, unsure of what to do. Did he console her? Give her a hug? The situation was out of his wheelhouse and it made him feel dumb. Inadequate. This was his fault. Administrative leave, a damn psychological evaluation ... His mind raced, and he saw her eyes webbed with red, and Cavalier Braddock. The bastard forced her to relive the day and her nightmares.

"Like I said, I didn't come here for an apology, but thank you." Clio met his gaze troubled with worry and burning with passion and understood he had pieced everything together. "I'm all right. This shouldn't take long." It was going to be good news or really, really bad news.

"I don't know." Ansel stopped himself from saying anything else and making a fool of himself. He would have to admit to not knowing how relationships worked and living like a prisoner because he was hiding from Bronte, and the corruptness of that mess, he hadn't been with a woman in years. And what was going to happen when they told the baron, because they would have to, about being fate mates? He refused to believe in it, then feared it when he saw Rutger and Jordyn, and feared it now. Damn fated mates.

"Me either," Clio said as an awkward silence sat between them. His passion and hunger that had darkened his liquid bronze gaze, tightened his muscles, and fed her own desire, faded under fear. Bronte. Her torture never ended. Clio wasn't letting her win. "I know this is different. We'll do this slow, no rushing. I'm not going to push you. We should get back to our normal lives before jumping into—"

"This."

"Yeah." She looked past Ansel to the French doors leading to the deck and wanted to see the views of the mountains and his geese. Then the image of Tony filtered in and was like cold water over her. "Can I call you after the meeting with Baron Kanin?"

Her strength and perseverance solidified the reasons she shouldn't be with him. "Affirmative."

Clio smiled with his reply, his lips curved in a grin, and her nervous energy felt less like lava in her veins. "Copy, sir." Turning from him, she headed to the door, when he was there opening it for her. "Thanks."

"No. Thank you for giving me this, Clio" Ansel responded. Giving him the chance to have someone to care about. "You believed in me when I didn't. And I've been alone for a long time."

Taken back by his emotion, Clio reached up and touched his cheek, and instantly regretted it—she was in his personal space—then his hand came up and held her wrist. Turning it over, he raised it and kissed the sensitive skin, making her want to moan from the feel of his lips on her. She wanted him, longed to be with him, wanted so much from him. Selfish. He needed to heal—mentally and emotionally—and shoving her life into his wasn't right. Anyway, she had to find out if she still had her career. And if she didn't? She shoved the question down.

"You're not alone anymore. I'm here when you need me," she assured. Her cell went off again, no doubt reminding her she had an appointment with the baron.

"This is going to sound horrible," Ansel started as he let go of her wrist. "I'm not ashamed of what we are, of you, gods know how proud I am of you, but can we keep this secret?"

"I get it, and yes. Things should settle down first." *I don't know if I have a job.* Clio walked outside, relishing the fresh air, the wind through the trees, and her car parked in Ansel's driveway.

"I'll be waiting for you." The words felt foreign coming from him, like he wasn't allowed to say that to anyone.

Stopping at the bottom stair, Clio turned to face him, thinking, *I could totally get used to hearing him say that.* "Yes, dearest."

He cocked his head at her. "Dearest?"

"Trying it on for size."

Her azure gaze held his for a couple of seconds when she walked to her crossover and left him standing by himself, wondering how in the world this was happening to him. When he lost sight of her, he went inside, going straight to the kitchen. After grabbing a beer, he headed out the back-door to the deck. Staring at his land, territory, his heart pounded knowing Clio would be part of it, and she was part of him. When their wolves rose, and they shared their magic, it started the binding that would be finalized when they had sex. After a hundred and twenty years he saw a future, freedom, and love. He would have a mate, and maybe a family. The thought nearly sent him to his knees. Was it possible? Ansel slowed his breathing and his thoughts. The first thing he needed to do was take Clio on a date. He needed to show her he cared for her, like a normal person. He gave the pond, the mountains, and the squawking geese his back, leaned against the edge of the rail, and his heart stopped in his chest.

No. No. No. Leaving his beer behind, he walked, like he was trudging through cooling tar, to the new table. In its center was a photograph. She had been there. The blood drained from him as he took the ivory handle of the dagger, freeing the sepia paper holding him and Bronte. She had been there, at his house, she had been close to him. With shaking hands, from fear and rage, he thought, *she invaded my territory.* Ansel turned it over to see her delicate hand-writing. *Brando.* The name made his stomach roll and nausea swirl. *You love me.*

"I didn't. I don't," he growled, hoping if she was there, she heard the truth in his words. "I'll find you and I will kill you." If her delusion wouldn't let her understand he never loved her, she would understand his promise coming from an as-sassin. "Milanka, as my territory is my witness, I will finish this. Complete circle." There was nothing she could do to him, he had nothing lose. His past had been exposed, his sins had been forgiven, and his pack stood with him.

Nothing to lose. *You have Clio,* his mind threw at him, *and she's everything.*

He felt cold, a chill from fear, his heart heavy, and fury sparked while a numbness started to crawl up his legs. Be-fore it went too far, he knew what he had to do. Marching into the house while cowardice and selfishness nipped at him, he took his cell and entered a number he never thought he would be forced to use.

"Strong Lord of the Fellowship, accept my submission," he pleaded, his voice rough with his grief and anger.

After several gruff words, and a warning that went unheard, the line went dead. His mind raced as he set his cell down, found his gun and shoved the holster onto his belt, grabbed a flannel, his keys, and lastly his cell, he left his house, and the door slammed closed on him and his future.

Clio sat in the baron's office alone, in silence, and surrounded by the baron's life. The massive desk held a flat screen monitor, books that were tomes with broken leather spines, folders, papers, pens, the morning's newspaper, and notes scrawled with a heavy hand. To the side there was an ashtray with the leftovers of a cigar and the fading scent of vanilla. Clio studied the pictures on the walls, the books on the shelves, and the masculine furniture, and saw the personal touches making the office uniquely Baron Kanin's. When the handle of the door moved, she straightened and readied to face the baron and her future.

When it opened, magic skated over her, its touch saturated with aged power, if that was possible, and the feel of the pack. Its intensity sent a chill down her spine. It was not the baron.

"Doctor Hyde."

"Miss Langston," Clio greeted. Her first thought was Miss Langston's magic was increasing, then she corrected herself, the woman was in the baron's house, no reason to conceal it the way she had at Celestial.

"The baron will be with you in a minute," she explained.

"Thank you."

Her onyx hair was up in a messy bun, she wore a gray, zip-up hoodie over a wine-colored shirt, jeans, and running shoes. She had done her makeup, eyeliner accentuating her eye's shape and color, and there were silver studs in the first and second holes in her ears, and black hoops in the third. If Clio hadn't noticed the paleness of her skin, the dark circles under her eyes, or the thinness of her shoulders in her hoodie, Miss Langston appeared to be herself. She wasn't buying it. Miss Langston walked around the desk, and once behind it began sifting through the folders and notes. Clio couldn't believe the baron allowed her to go through his papers or enter his office when she was there to hear the decision they made about her ability to do her job. If they found her incompetent? *Stop.*

"Sorry, I could swear it was here," she mumbled as she searched the desktop.

"It's all right." Like she was going to kick Miss Langston out of the office.

When she found the papers she was looking for, she met Clio's gaze and smiled, what Clio learned was her *I'm perfectly normal* look. Her chocolate stare held weight, power, and there was an otherworldly complexity in their depths. Years. Pain. The past. The pack. Clio had the urge to rub her arms when magic, feeling like a chilled breeze, drifted from Miss Langston. The soothsayer. She had been faced with believing in fated mates, the thought conjuring images of Ansel and the feel of his hands on her, and the possibility Miss Langston was indeed their soothsayer. Whatever she was feeling from the woman—magic, power, her strength—it wasn't the normal buzz of a shapeshifter or magic-born. It was thick, intense, and stronger than anything Clio had ever felt. It scared her.

"I understand Captain Wolt has been reinstated," Miss Langston said casually as if they were friends. Her voice matched the power radiating from her, sure, and again it differed from her physical appearance.

"Yes, thankfully. Hopefully we'll be able to get back to normal." Clio had no idea what to say or why Miss Langston was talking to her.

She seemed to consider Clio, making her want to look at the floor, slide off her chair, and crawl out of the office. After taking a pen and scribbling a quick note, Miss Langston met her gaze. "How are you doing? You've been through a quite an ordeal."

Miss Langston repeated the very words Dr. Carrion had said to her when she was in Celestial. And Clio was pretty sure she had said those words to Miss. Langston. "I'm all right. Healing is a process."

"So it is." She paused then said, "Baron Kanin approaches. Enjoy your afternoon, Doctor Hyde." Miss Langston gave Clio her signature smile as she left the desk and headed toward the door.

Baron Kanin approaches. Clio hadn't felt anything, then again, she wasn't a Pureblood or a soothsayer. Soothsayer being the key. When the door opened, Clio heard the baron's rumble, Miss Langston's multilayered tone, then the baron's presence invaded the office.

"Doctor Hyde, how are you?" he asked as he sat down. Gazing at the papers on his desk, he read the note, took a pen, wrote something, then met her gaze. His mahogany eyes with gold flakes drifting in them held her as his wolf sat below the skin. Wearing a white button-up, the collar left open, jeans, and boots, he looked as casual as possible.

"Doing well, sir, thank you," Clio replied. *Of course I am. I wasn't just at Ansel's house, your Captain of Enforcers, making out with him. We think we're fated mates, and I think your soothsayer knows, and it scares me.* Never mind the nightmares and the changes on the horizon you're preparing for.

"Excellent. Doctor Carrion says you have stopped seeing him," Baron Kanin stated.

"Affirmative. I didn't see a reason to continue." She wasn't positive it had been a question, but she answered anyway.

"I see. I've consulted Cavalier Braddock and discussed his findings. The nightmares from the toxins are severe, and what you were forced to witness was gruesome. One of your own being tortured and you were helpless to stop them." He sat back in the leather chair, making it squeal, and steepled his fingers over his chest, his elbows on the arm rests. Absolutely at ease. Or judging. "But we've discussed that."

"Affirmative, sir. Watching Captain Wolt being set on fire had been a nightmare itself, but he didn't die, and seeing him and knowing he's back at work changes the reality and is reassuring," she rambled. Being in his arms and pressed against his body was reassuring, and she wanted to go back.

"Yes." He paused. "You disregarded a direct order and it nearly got you killed."

Shit. Her heart sank to her feet knowing her time at Celestial was over. "Affirmative, sir."

"You don't have anything to say?" he asked, his eyes flashing gold. "In defense?"

She was in deep. "I have excuses." A million of them. When she opened her mouth, she had no idea what she was going to say, and she didn't want to continue to ramble, she was a doctor for god's sake. *Was.* "I had to see Captain Wolt. The attacks, Tony's death, the construction, and the pack going into full military mode was, is overwhelming. I had to feel a semblance of pack and make sure he was all right. I will go anywhere to make sure the pack is safe and healthy. That's my defense." *My job.*

If there had been a clock, she would have heard the

seconds as if they were being marked by a dozen bells.

"You're a strong person, Doctor Hyde, don't make disobeying a habit."

"Understood," she replied and waited for the rest.

"It's good to have you back. Effective immediately you're cleared for work. And these," he began as he sat forward, "are the approved plans for the med room. The contractor and IT guy are installing the voice-activated security system." He took a file from the stack and handed it to her. "The equipment you requested was purchased and has been delivered. I also took the liberty of telling Commissioner Courter you'll be busy here for at least a week. Having said that, the board of directors has decided to relieve you of your duty as head of the ER. While it might appear to be a demotion, I don't want you to feel that way. I have expressed the need to have you here."

"Sir." Clio sat stunned, file in hand, and was speechless. He talked to the commissioner on her behalf. She was going to be working at Foxwood, with Ansel.

"You'll remain in charge of the recertifications and the recruits. You can do that work from here."

"Understood, sir."

"Doctor Hyde," Baron Kanin said as he stood, "I'll expect you tomorrow and we'll talk about Doctor Baines."

"Sir. Affirmative, sir." Gripping the file, Clio stood on shaky legs, and tried to look like she was thankful for her job, was a professional, a doctor, and the person in charge of a medical facility. She thought she failed; she felt shell shocked.

Baron Kanin was at the door and opening it for her and waited for her to pass. In the hallway, she turned and met the dark and gold gaze and saw years sitting in them. "Thank you, sir."

"You're welcome, Doctor Hyde." He gave her a smile that drew attention and made his handsome face younger than his three hundred years and closed the door.

Clio walked down the hall in a daze, the file in her hand feeling heavy, and her mind racing. She was going to call Ansel and tell him the good news ... hell, great news, and the thought had her smiling.

"Doctor Hyde," Abigail greeted as she opened the door. "Have a nice afternoon."

"Thank you," Clio responded and walked outside.

Crossing the freshly cut grass, that had been planted after construction was completed, and making it to the parking lot of the Enforcer's office, she got in her crossover, and placed the file in the passenger seat. The weight of hopelessness she felt during the weeks she had spent on administrative leave slipped off her shoulders and despair was replaced with motivation. With renewed energy, Clio started the engine, and making sure her cell was hooked up to hands free gazed out at the world of the Cascade pack. They were going about their business, the enforcers and soldiers talking to one another while the mechanics at the garage worked on a variety of vehicles.

She was staring at the office building, the future med room, and was still watching life at Foxwood, when Miss Langston walked in front of the car, and headed in the direction of the office, where Director Kanin exited to meet her. They stood, his height dwarfing her, his body thick with muscles a stark difference compared to her thin, petite frame. It was an illusion, his strength, her weakness. After talking with Miss Langston, Clio would bet money the woman wasn't as frail as she appeared and could kick serious ass if necessary. Her eyes alone made you shudder.

Soothsayer. Fated mates. Those were from the past. A past no one lived in or wanted to bring back. Placing his hands on her shoulders, he leaned down as she leaned in and they kissed.

Ansel.

"Fated mates," Clio mumbled to the car. Her console, dark and soundless for weeks, blazed to life, beeping, dinging, and flashing as it went through its startup process, and it sent a wave of thankfulness through her. She was back in the game. They both were. She would be working on the med room while Ansel would be working with the enforcers.

Director Kanin held the back of Miss Langston's neck, more protective than intimate, as he spoke to her while around them people gave them space. Fated mates. The words filtered through her thoughts as self-awareness and the confidence being a doctor gave her shifted what she believed. She believed in the way she felt about Ansel and their wolves were proof. She didn't believe it was magic. People were attracted to each other. Ansel had said it perfectly when he confessed to having been alone for a long time. Add in an emotionally charged situation of life and death, and yeah, you were going to question your life choices and you were going to get some serious feelings racing through your body. He had been alone. She had been alone. They understood one another without having to explain anything. It wasn't magic.

With her thoughts chasing each other, Clio pulled out of the parking spot, headed down the two-lane drive, and through the wrought iron gate that closed behind her. Outside of Foxwood and on the main road, she debated whether or not to call him. Why wouldn't she? Just because they had been through hell, and they had been in a self-induced single status, didn't mean what was between them wasn't real. Couldn't be real. It was up to them to make it work. It didn't take magic.

To hell with it. Clio touched the screen and hit his number.

"Hey, beautiful," Ansel greeted.

Damn, he made her want to melt. She could hear the grin in his words and couldn't wait to see him. "I just left Foxwood."

"How did it go?" He stood on the shoreline, the water lapping at the toes of his boots, the breeze bringing him the scent of fish and the rumbling of boat engines and a touch of fall. He didn't need to ask; Rutger had called him and told him the med room was going be up and running, then rattled off a list of things they needed to complete, like finding recruits for the enforcers. But this was important to her and she was excited about returning to work. He knew exactly how she felt.

"Hello, I'm Doctor Hyde." She felt a lightness she hadn't in weeks, and it was good. Hearing his voice was good, and hearing him laugh sent her heart skipping.

"That you are," Ansel replied with a grin. "MD." Guilt sank into him as the old Clio returned, her wit, confidence, and strength blazing through her voice. It made what he was going to do that much harder and made his heart ache. He didn't have a choice, not with Bronte on the loose.

"How do you feel about celebrating?" Clio asked.

Suddenly, she feared he might say no. She was excited, and combining that with wanting to see him, she bullied forward. Never mind, she called him like they were a couple, not two people whose only contact had been making out, then she proposed celebrating after promising to give him space. And what, if like her, he used the time to think

M.A. Kastle

through the attraction, and believed there was less magic involved, and it was the situation drawing them together?

"I feel pretty good about it. I can meet you at your swanky townhouse in the city?" Ansel offered. He tried to keep his voice from breaking, his inhale from sounding shaky, and his betrayal from breaking him down. He needed her. Wanted her. Couldn't have her.

"Swanky?" she questioned.

"You don't have a pond."

Clio laughed. "I have a landscaper."

"See, swanky."

"Right. Give me thirty minutes." Her excitement reached a new high as she pictured Ansel relaxed on her couch, the sunset's colors pouring in and over him, a grin curving his lips. Lips she was going to kiss. Her default setting starting barking doubts, she listened for a second, then shoved it down, screw it.

"Anything for you, tesoro," Ansel replied. God, he hated himself.

Clio would never get used to hearing him call her that or feeling the heat it created. "Then I'll see you, sweetheart."

"Sweetheart?" She loved him.

Clio giggled, a purely girly sound, and felt her cheeks heat. "I'll work on it, bye."

"Bye," Ansel barely whispered the word and ended the call.

"Tesoro?"

His treasure. "Don't," Ansel warned. His patience and control over his rage was cracking apart.

Raising his hands, like he meant no offense, he said, "Having you in the Fellowship puts you at a confluence. Are you willing to risk the wrath of Cascade? Your mate's trust when she finds out?" Yellow eyes, the sharp color of the sun, narrowed as lips pulled back in a grin meant to mock him.

"She isn't going to find out." That was a lie. "I don't have a choice," Ansel replied. He hated the Fellowship, and being beholden to them was a death sentence, yet here he was. Except Ansel and Clio had shared their magic, their wolves, and the need to be with one another would never end. Even as he stood there, the lake beside him, a vow on his lips, his body wanted to take Clio and make her his. There was nothing stopping their connection.

"Chivalry isn't dead," he jested.

"What do you want?" Ansel asked, struggling to ignore his jabs.

"You. You are to take your place at the Stone," he demanded. "Your powers have been dormant long enough."

"Fuck you, Griffin," Ansel growled. He knew it was going to cost him, had known what they wanted for years, but wasn't going to hand himself over without putting up some resistance and irritating the Strong Lord of the Fellowship and head of the Stone.

Griffin was a shifter and a griffin, the mystical creature with the half body of a lion and half of an eagle, and one of twenty members of the Fellowship. They were all mystical creatures created from magic whose existence over the centuries had fallen into legends and myths and overtime became nothing more than a figment of someone's imagination. They were real, their power great, and their magic made them born enemies of the magic-born and humans alike. With his lies and Bronte exposed, he thought he had a chance at freedom, a foolish thought. He had to kill Bronte to be free and to guarantee Clio's safety. It was going to take time to find her, time he didn't have. Making a deal with the devil—Griffin—and being part of the Fellowship while Clio was going to be protected, he was chaining himself to more lies and a different master.

"You use their language, how disappointing." Turning his head, he listened to the cries of birds, then met Ansel's gaze. "You can walk away." Griffin's white hair, thick with feathers, glittered in the sun while his mocha skin seemed to drink in its rays. At seven feet, he was taller than Ansel and was over three hundred pounds of solid muscle. "Do you want to go through with this?"

"Affirmative." Ansel needed time to think. "I'm not what you think, you're wasting your time." He was exactly what they thought. "I'll be your minion, but I'm not taking a seat at the Stone."

"I know who and what you are, *Principe*. Royalty, my prince," he cursed. "You will take your place."

Principe. The word sank into him and he heard his mother's voice. The sorrow from her death joined the pain of losing Clio and the weight of his grief was going to crush him. "When she escaped them and mated with my father, they removed her existence from their history, then they searched us out and destroyed her magic and stole mine. I'm nothing, I don't have a crest, a legacy, no one is going to accept me," Ansel countered. Bronte had believed the same story, thinking he was more than he was and she could free the magic locked inside of him. She failed. He was going to fail.

"That was a thousand years ago, Principe. A different time. They aren't the same rigid beings they once were." Griffin gazed at the sun as it started behind the mountain. "The sands of time are not in your favor."

"And if it fails?" Ansel asked. As if he didn't know the answer. If it failed, everything he did would have been for nothing. He would have sacrificed his future, Clio.

"You'll die," Griffin replied easily.

Ansel ignored his answer. "What about her?"

"Her? When you see her, you'll feel her, your desire for her will eat at you, your wolf's demand to possess its mate will drive it mad as your denial to protect her will churn inside of you every minute of the day. If it fails, take comfort in knowing it'll ease the agony of having to watch your fated mate live without you."

Fated mate. Ansel wanted to ask if one like him—ancient, mystical—believed the magic was real. He wouldn't, it would give the griffin ammunition to use against him for the eternity he would be serving the creature. Ansel could feel steel bands constricting around his chest and didn't care about the pain. "Vow."

"So says the covenant." Griffin held out his hand, palm up.

Ansel grabbed the strong hand and fire snaked up his arm, into his shoulder, and spread out, then concentrated in the center of his chest. Flames licked at his flesh, their heat burrowing into him, making his knees weak and his wolf howl from pain, and gave him the nightmare of having been burned alive. Winds rose up around him, the sky darkened, and the terrain fell into an abyss, to be built into cliffs, the ocean, and the crashing of waves. The world shifted, his memories flooded him, he heard her voice, and felt her years raining down on him. When Griffin released him, Ansel inhaled. He was back on the shore of Lake Shasta, the rich cerulean sky with smears of white clouds and the piercing gold of the sun above him. Seconds ticked by and the buzzing in his head faded.

"It's there, Principe," Griffin mused. "Know this, your legacy is blood, and your crest is stained scarlet."

"Is that a warning?" Ansel was going to lose.

"You can't live in two worlds."

"I have been my entire life," Ansel cursed. "It's my business."

"As you wish, Principe." He bowed his head making the feathers wave in the breeze. "It is done." His eyes gleamed crisp yellow almost white as he shifted, his huge body of lion and eagle hanging in the sky then was gone.

Ansel fell to his knees, his weight sinking in the soft sand, and the waves darkened his jeans as tears streamed down his cheeks. He betrayed his mother's last wish. He betrayed Clio. Bronte should have killed him. The fire should have engulfed him and destroyed his magic. He wasn't worthy of the life he had been given.

He knew only one thing now.

Clio was dead to him.

CHAPTER TWENTY-SEVEN

Clio checked herself in the mirror, fixed a rogue curl, added lip gloss, which she never wore and wasn't sure why she put it on, and put it back in the drawer. Taking a tissue from the box, she wiped it off, then looked at her makeup supplies, and groaned.

"Get it together," she mumbled at her reflection. "It's not a first date."

He knew what she looked like, and it wasn't like she hadn't been straddling him in his house as his hands roamed her body a couple of hours earlier. Those thoughts had to stop, or he was going to find her in the fetal position on the floor. Clio left the bathroom, checked the time on her cell, and grabbed her glass from the kitchen, then headed to the living room. Life was getting back too normal. She had Ansel. Fated mates or not, there was something between them. She never felt as comfortable as when she was with him, and the feeling she had known him her entire life made it natural. Like they belonged together.

Her heart jumped, hit her sternum, and fell back in place, with the knock on the door. He was there at her house, her swanky townhouse. Clio inhaled, exhaled, calmly placed her glass on the table before she dropped it, and walked to the door. Maybe she should have kept the lip gloss, she didn't have to look the same all the damn time. What if he liked it?

What if he hated it? Wow. The second round of knocks jerked her back to reality, and grabbing the handle, she pulled it open.

"Clio Hyde?" a man asked. A vase of flowers blocked her from seeing his face.

With quakes cascading down her spine and her nerves trying to recover, she answered, "Yes, that's me."

"These are for you." He lifted the vase, like he was showing her, then handed them over.

"Thank you," she mumbled. Flowers? Did Ansel send them? No, he was headed to her place. Her parents? No, she hadn't told them the news. And orchids, lilies, and jade? All were rare, especially for the area and time of year.

"Clio?"

"Yes," she replied as she met pearl white eyes set in an angular face. Magic-born. His body exuded power, making her take a step back. Bronte. Fear stole her confidence and she prayed Ansel found her.

Matching her, he walked forward as words from another language fell from his lips, like a spell. Clio backed up and watched him lift his hand. "Clio Hyde."

Was that inside her head?

"Listen to me."

"No." She had to get her gun.

"Let me see," he whispered as he blew powder into her face.

"No. What are you doing?" she asked as she continued backing up. She didn't need an answer when magic cloaked her, its power invading her nose, eyes, and mouth. Coughing she choked out a weak plea. "Stop."

Letting go of the flowers, she expected to hear the crystal vase crash to her floor, but there was nothing other than a deafening silence. Clio covered her face with her hands, felt her heated cheeks, and retreated deeper into the house. She needed her cell phone, she needed help. She stumbled, tried to open her eyes, only to see black. *God, I can't see.* Then there was a numbness starting to climb over her, and the echo of the chant in her ears.

No. No. This is poison, toxin, I've felt it before. Bronte. Panic drove through her, knowing she was going to die like Tony. Would she mutilate her body? Would Ansel see what was left? Clio fell, her knees hitting the wood flooring as her mind brought the nightmares to life.

"Tesoro," Ansel whispered. His voice a rumble of wolf and man, and his eyes like bronze jewels, captured her.

Ansel. He picked her up, cradled her in his arms, and carrying her, went to her room where he gently set her on the bed, the thick comforter cushioning her. When he crawled in beside her, she cuddled close to him, her body following the length of his. She reached up, needing to make sure he was real, held his neck and pulled his face close to hers. When their gazes met, a warning boomed in her head at the same time a sense of dread overcame her. This was wrong, so wrong. He was wrong.

No. "Stop."

"Let me see," he whispered.

Pain seared across her mind, leaving a blinding flash in its wake, and she held the sides of her head. *Why?*

"My vow," Ansel roared as his face contorted, shifted, his eyes gleaming white then bronze, and flames surrounded him to take him down into the ash.

Clio screamed, tried crawling from the blackened body only to get tangled in the sheets, her legs twisting, and failing to gain ground. Fighting for her next breath, the world shifted to slow motion, they were back in the field, his bronze eyes were holding her, the flames climbing into the sky, and he drifted into darkened smoke and was gone. Like a ghost. *No.*

"Come back," she begged. She couldn't save him.

Clio jerked awake, her begging still on her lips and sat up. Even alone, she was embarrassed having dreamt about Captain Wolt, begging him to stay with her, and wiped sweat from her forehead. She gathered the covers she kicked off, then straightened her tank top that had been tugged to one side. *Deep breath in.* Exhaling, she slowed her rapid breathing and looked around the dark room, used her senses to check if anyone was in the house, and found she was alone. Except there was an eerie feeling someone was there, and she was being watched.

Despite the nightmare—which was slightly better than seeing the walls of Celestial bleeding and patients dying—she gathered herself enough to reach over, and opening the drawer of the nightstand, took out her enforcer's weapon. She was capable of turning into a two-hundred-pound wolf with teeth, the cavalier had pointed out, but bullet wounds in would-be home invaders were more accepted by human law enforcement. Clio waited to hear a noise, and when nothing happened, silently crawled out of bed. Without turning a light on—she was a werewolf with heightened sight—and wearing a tank top and underwear, went room to room, then the garage, and cleared the house.

"I call bullshit," she mumbled. She wasn't losing her mind. Holding the gun, she went to the window and looking out at the darkened street didn't see anything out of place.

As if needing to add to the dream's weight, she heard Dr. Carrion ask her about the gun, getting up in the middle of the night to clear the house, and her drinking. Guilt and failure touched her throat like bile, and she forced herself to swallow it down. She wasn't that person. Baron Kanin cleared her for work, she was going to Foxwood to work on the med room, was going to officially hire Dr. Baines, and her cell and console had been activated. She was back.

"Sure I am." Clio shook her head, saw the open file and papers spread out on the coffee table, then started toward her bedroom when she paused. She bent down, her knees on the wood flooring, and with her free hand—because she wasn't giving up her gun—picked up a pink petal. "Shit." Standing, she looked around the house; there weren't any flowers, she wasn't a fan. No one was there. No one had been there. After leaving Foxwood, she went straight home, called her parents to tell them the news, declined eating with them explaining she was expected at Foxwood in the morning and had work to do. Then she ate dinner, looked over the files the baron had given her, added notes, checked on equipment, and went to bed.

Why was there a nagging feeling she was missing something? And where the hell did the petal come from? She tossed it in the trash, continued to her room, and after putting the pistol back in the drawer, saw the empty glass. "Whatever." Clio crawled into bed, the soft flannel cuddling with her, pulled the covers up, and settled in. Maybe the petal had stuck to her shoe. *That's it*, she thought as she drifted off. Clio sank into another dream, the faces blurring, the scenes changing from Foxwood, Celestial, and she couldn't stop herself from seeing Captain Wolt's house.

Ansel parked his truck in his designated spot, killed the engine, and nonchalantly searched the parking lot. When he spotted Clio's pearl white, luxury crossover parked on the opposite side, his heart stopped. He knew she was going to be there, thought about it all night as he stared up at his ceiling fan, and told himself it was better this way. It was the only way to keep her safe from Bronte, and his mistakes, and the ones he was continuing to create. Sometime in the night, sleep had taken him and tossed him into Clio's bed, her arms, and for precious moments he felt her against him. He convinced himself the day before and his meeting with Griffin had been a nightmare, a horrible dream, and Clio was his.

Mine.

The illusion hadn't lasted long. Griffin made sure he was reminded by giving him a collar to wear with a gold medallion in the shape of a wolf's head; it had become his crest of scarlet, the legacy of blood he created. Absently he felt it where it sat hidden under his T-shirt and against his skin. The ancients who cursed his mother and destroyed her magic, rendering her powerless, had decided he was worth their time. He had become their prisoner. He had another master. And why did they change their minds after a thousand years? Baron Kanin was trying to bring back the old ways, the dark ages, they thought Ansel possessed old power, and they saw Jordyn as a threat, and the Highguard was sanctioning the baron's decisions. It put Ansel against the pack. And if he wasn't the selfish bastard he was, he would break contact with the pack, saving himself from seeing and feeling Clio, and take a permanent seat at the Stone. The baron, Rutger, and the pack might hate him, but he would have spared them from another one of his mistakes. Not going to happen. Not when Clio was his fated mate. He truly believed he was going to get out of the covenant he made with Griffin and the Fellowship.

"I'm a damn fool," Ansel groaned.

Rutger stepped out of the office, and keeping the door open, saw him, waved, and waited as Ansel got out of his truck and walked over. "Morning."

"Morning. What's up?" Ansel asked and prayed his thoughts didn't betray him. Wearing a black T-shirt with his name and Cascade's crest, dropdown holster, jeans and boots, he looked his part.

"Doctor Hyde is going to give a demonstration." There were dark circles under Rutger's eyes, his hair had been combed through with his fingers, his BDU top was wrinkled like he had slept in it, and he hadn't shaved in days. He looked like hell, and it made Ansel jealous.

"Demonstrate what?" *Act normal.* Act like he didn't care. Like he hadn't had her straddling him the day before. Like he hadn't been pawing her. Act like his wolf hadn't taken possession of her. With the thought, a spark of lust burned through him, then a wave of longing gripped him.

Stepping out, the door closed behind him and a dozen locks engaged. "The voice-activated security system," Rutger explained like Ansel should know. "What the hell is wrong with you?"

He scrubbed his hand over the ends of his hair, hated how it felt, then down to his neck where he tried to work out the knots in his muscles. "Bad night. No sleep. Nightmares."

"I get it. The demonstration will take ten minutes max, then we'll go over the list of soldiers Torin gave me." Rutger froze, his eyes blazing gold as he watched a sporty, red SUV park next to his truck. He inhaled and exhaled, then growled, "She hates training. She hates being here."

"Why is she here?" Ansel asked.

Jordyn hesitated to get out of her SUV, the same car Rutger used to track the witches because it didn't have GPS. They had fucked up lives.

"Baron's orders. I'll meet you at the med room in five," Rutger growled as he started toward Jordyn.

Ansel watched the couple, saw their broken communication, and thought maybe he had done the right thing, and not because Bronte was free. Neither one of them needed the pain. Fate damned them, then evaporated while they were left to navigate rough waters. Taking his badge, he slid it through the slot, entered his code, and heard the locks disengage. Walking through the reception area, Tabby greeted him, and nodding in response, he wasn't going to stop when he felt stares on him, he repeated the process at the double metal doors. On the other side and in the hallway where he was surrounded by enforcers, his nerves eased, and the tension gripping his body relaxed.

He stopped at the door to his office and read the name plate, Captain of Enforcers Ansel Wolt, and the beaten feeling of being a fraud reared its head. He wouldn't do anything to harm the pack, the Kanin family, and anyone under Cascade rule, but his list of wrongs was getting longer by the minute. Ansel slid his badge, entered the code, and opening the door entered his office. It resembled his old one—no pictures on the walls, nothing personal on his desk, a blank space save for the computer, files, printer, filing cabinets that every office had. *It looks like my house,* he thought. With his poor choice in furniture. He would have to invest time to find out who he was and maybe get a plant. Maybe. He might not be able to handle the commitment.

CHAPTER TWENTY-EIGHT

Clio scanned the med room—the crisp white walls, ceiling lights, hidden cameras, stainless steel counters and cabinets containing catheter sets, tubes, scissors, and gloves, then the two refrigerators with medicines and sedatives, and the bank of glass front cabinets containing patient gowns and blankets, and lastly the beds, and varied equipment. Pleased with what she saw, she looked at the clipboard in her hands to make sure she had covered everything. Baron Kanin, along with Director Kanin and Captain Wolt, were going to visit the med room, and she was supposed to give them a demonstration of the security system.

After the night she had and the embarrassing dream where she was naked with Captain Wolt—even thinking about it set her cheeks on fire—it was all she could do to focus on the task at hand. She kept her mind on business as she organized cabinets, checked off supplies, entered the information into the computer system, and updated the MedTech software, but then the dream would inch up on her. While drinking the strongest coffee she could find, she had to remind herself several times she was a doctor ... professional, cool, calm, and collected. Absolutely. Working directly for the baron. A hardass. She had worked her entire life to be recognized. Because she was a Wight. *Stop.* Her cell dinged, getting her attention. Placing the clipboard down, she took her cell from her scrub pocket.

"Doctor Hyde."

"It's Doctor Baines of the Lapis Lazuli coven. I was checking in with you about the position at Celestial," he explained.

She hadn't had contact with him because she was on admin leave and ordered not to talk to anyone. "My apologies, Doctor. Yes, if you would like to meet me at my office, I have a couple of questions."

"I understand. What time would be good for you?" Dr. Baines asked.

What time was good? After the show and tell, she was expected to have a meeting with the baron to discuss the parameters of hiring Dr. Baines. Clio needed him and had expressed her opinion to the baron by detailing his knowledge of the magic-born, poisons, toxins, and having studied plant science and biology. It would be a bonus if he helped research and define the ghoul toxin.

"Doctor Hyde."

"One second, I'm checking my schedule," she replied. If standing and staring into space was considered checking her schedule. "How's four tomorrow afternoon?"

"Just fine. I'll see you then. Have a nice day."

"Thank you, you too," Clio replied and ended the call. That's great. She just made an appointment with a witch doctor in order to hire him.

"Doctor Hyde, good morning," Baron Kanin greeted, his rumble of a voice filling the med room.

"Baron, good morning." She shoved her cell back in her pocket and grabbed the clipboard from the counter.

"Doctor Hyde," Director Kanin greeted.

"Good morning," Ansel greeted. He couldn't say her name.

"Director Kanin, Captain Wolt," Clio returned, her eyes skating over the captain slower than she wanted, and back to the baron before scarlet seared her cheeks.

"You've managed to accomplish a lot of work this morning," Baron Kanin offered. He walked around the room, scanning the equipment, then turning, met her gaze.

"Affirmative. The supplies have been verified and entered into the system, and I have organized most of them. I'm hoping I'll have everything completed by this evening so tomorrow it will be fully functional."

"Excellent. What do you have to show us?" he asked.

Clio switched to her doctor voice and started, "Right now the med room and the computer system are locked. As are the refrigerators, cabinets, the oxygen, as well as the heart monitors and respirators. Basically the equipment." She walked over to a cabinet and clicked the handle, proving what she said was true. "No one entering will have access."

"If someone is hurt, the doors are unlocked, allowing them entrance, but only authorized personnel will have access to the equipment?" Director Kanin asked.

"Affirmative. Once authorization has been verified, the security system will begin recording both video and audio. It works the same way as communications, it'll make a transcript, and can be downloaded to Baron Kanin's computer, yours, or to central control, Mandy." Clio caught Captain Wolt staring at her—like he knew she pictured him naked and begged him to stay with her—and felt heat snake up her neck. "Let me show you." She was thankful her voice held. "Doctor Clio Hyde, authority code One Heka."

Bright LED lights glared down on them at the same time locks disengaged, and panels that had blended into the wall slid open, revealing touch screens.

"Right now, we're being recorded. Admitting Captain

Wolt, enforcer, injuries unknown." Clio's nerves jumped under her skin. She should have used the director or the baron, who were staring at her. "The information has been added to his medical records, and any treatment will be added. Laceration on left bicep. From this point I would explain if it was a defensive wound or accidental, and the weapon used." Walking over to a counter, a monitor came alive and she entered a code. "Here is his record."

His medical history filled the column on the left side, the transcripts continuing down the page, and her heart plummeted. She should not ever, ever have used Captain Wolt as an example. In the middle of the screen a 3D image of a male body appeared, and a second later red highlighted the wounds that had been treated. Red covered the body from head to toe. Her eyes skated over the information and it made tears well in her eyes. Clio inhaled, trying to take a deep breath, failed, felt like she was suffocating, and saw the flames swallowing him, and his body crumpling under the glow.

"I'm s-sorry ... I-I shouldn't have. I didn't m-mean," she stammered. She should have used the director or the baron ... no, she should have used someone who didn't have an extensive medical history.

Ansel watched the body on the screen glow red and listened to Clio stammer from seeing the extent of his wounds. Burns. Destroyed skin, nerves, organs. The screen switched and showed them all his internal injuries. Heart failure. Organ failure. Circulatory system failure. The list went on. He was lucky to be alive. Lucky, he wasn't. The fire should have taken him. "The burn box," he mumbled. Where he spent five weeks.

"Restoring chamber," Clio corrected and faced him. A

sense of déjà vu washed over her, and she saw dark awareness sink into his eyes. She felt horrible for forcing him to relive what had to be his worst nightmare. "My deepest apologies, I didn't mean for you to see this."

"I'm not sure what that means, besides you're a hard man to kill," Rutger said as he took a step closer to Ansel.

"Doctor Hyde, remember what we talked about," Baron Kanin warned.

He's alive and standing in front of you, she told herself. Clio took her gaze from Captain Wolt to meet the baron's. "Yes, sir. Affirmative."

"Good. This information is coming from Celestial. Will information from here be accessible to Celestial?" Baron Kanin asked.

"Negative. Not unless they're given authorization. Any record of treatment is sealed," she replied. The overwhelming sadness and fear eased, giving her time to gather herself.

"Impressive," Baron Kanin stated.

Clio gave the three men her back, and with shaking hands closed the screen, making the glowing red and columns of information disappear. *If only it was that easy.* In its place was Cascade's crest, the Rod of Aesculapius—from Greek mythology, the serpent-entwined rod belonged to the god Asclepius, a deity linked to healing and medicine, and symbolized the link between the med room and Celestial—then lastly her name.

"Doctor Hyde, MD," Ansel read out loud. He wanted to say MD, he longed to take her in his arms to prove he was all right, and to ease her pain. Oh how he needed to ease her pain and prove he was there for her. His skin felt like it was on fire, which wasn't helping him, and his wolf howled. Griffin's warning came back, and Ansel fought every instinct riding him to act normal.

Clio's stared at her name while her heart was beating faster than it should and she didn't know why him saying MD affected her like he had touched her. "Do you have any questions?" she asked to get back on track.

"Since he doesn't have a laceration on his left bicep, how will you correct the information?" Baron Kanin asked.

"It has to be manually adjusted, and requires the signature of two authorized personnel, and your authorization, sir," Clio explained. She wanted show and tell to be over. "Treatment has been terminated. Captain Wolt has been discharged. Shutdown order One Heka. His medical records are sealed. However, the recording continues until personnel signs out."

"Doctor Hyde, you've surpassed anything I could have imagined. Well done." Baron Kanin faced her. "We'll let you get back to work."

"Thank you, sir. It's much appreciated," she responded. Thank god, she wanted to say.

Director Kanin gave her a nod before turning and following the baron, while Captain Wolt stared at her like she was supposed to say something to him. "Can I help you?" Had her voice cracked?

"Negative. Good work, Doctor Hyde."

Ansel held her gaze a moment longer, the urge to take her in arms increasing at the same time he felt his heart turning cold and black. He couldn't allow himself to feel for her, and when he said MD, he almost laughed and had expected her to join him. Mistake. How was he supposed to handle this day in and day out, for how long? Before he made another mistake, like taking her in his arms and tossing her lush body to one of beds like an animal, Ansel left Clio standing by the monitor, her eyes gauging him like he was a stalker.

He hit the hallway leading to the dorm room area at march and met Rutger's glare.

"What the hell was that about?" Rutger asked.

"No idea what you're talking about," Ansel answered. Not his smartest move.

"My office, now," Rutger ordered.

In silence, they marched through the dorm area, kitchen, down the stairs, through the hallways, all of it a blur, and stopped at Rutger's office. Going through the security procedures, he opened the door and swung it wide enough Ansel made it inside and it closed behind him.

"Sit." Ruger walked around his desk, sat down, and nailed Ansel with a gold gaze. "I know I'm not as conflicted as you. I mean, you were set on fire by an ex-girlfriend, who remains at large. And I haven't lived for over a century, and I've never been an assassin, so I don't want to hear I don't know, or I don't understand. But I do have a mate. Fated mate. I've bonded with Jordyn, the pack's soothsayer." He laughed a bitter sound. "I know Doctor Hyde is your mate."

"You don't know—" Ansel began and was shutdown, his confession on his lips.

"I may not have been an assassin, but I am Second to the Alpha, and as werewolves we can sense when a wolf has taken possession of its mate. You've done that, I can smell it on you, and I can sense it in her. Her wolf recognized you." Rutger pushed away from the desk, the chair's wheels scraping tile, and stood. "It's a magic and scent thing, so other males don't make a move on your female."

"I know what it is," he mumbled. He was losing the argument.

"Here's something for you to think about ... if I know, the baron does."

"There isn't proof," Ansel tried.

"I said it's a magic and scent thing, he senses it, he's your alpha. That's the proof." With agitated steps he walked to the filing cabinets and back to his desk. "You don't know the baron. Have you talked to Jo?" Rutger asked.

A strange question. "Negative." Dammit. "Affirmative. Before my hearing."

Rutger smiled, and all the rage and pain of the last months hardened his gaze to stone. "He's known for weeks, and she gave him his confirmation. So, don't fucking lie to me."

The baron planned the meeting with Jordyn. She knew. "I am. I'm not." Ansel sat heavy in the chair, his mind racing with his lies. "You're right. She's my mate. Fated mate. I didn't think it was possible."

Rutger sat down. "I know the feeling. What happened?"

He looked down at his hands, and knew he had to trust Rutger. He needed someone who would protect her. "She came to my house yesterday, to talk, then we were kissing, just kissing, then my wolf took possession, and the next minute our wolves created this magic, and it was between us," Ansel replied and felt like he was rambling. "It wove between us, into us, connecting us."

"It's pretty intense. What happened after that?"

"Our magic bonded us. I feel her. I feel her all the damn time. It's like she's right there and I have to have her." Ansel looked up from his hands and into mahogany eyes. "What?"

"You didn't consummate the relationship?"

"Negative."

"She could have been playing it cool, you two keeping the relationship under wraps until everything settles down, or you don't want your sadistic ex kidnapping your mate, but I don't think so. She stared at you like she had no idea why you were paying attention to her. What did you do?" Rutger demanded.

Damn, sometimes he hated the man. "I called in a favor, and they erased her memory," he blurted out. He had no intention of saying anything about the Fellowship.

"What? Before I get into who, what, or what kind of magic that is, you took her right to choose away from her. Doctor Clio Hyde. The woman who survived Bronte's drugs, and is single handedly putting a state-of-the-art med facility together?" Rutger leaned forward with his elbows on the desk. "Smart. Independent. She isn't going to appreciate your precaution."

"You're one to talk," Ansel countered.

"I'm reminded everyday of what I have. Damn, that sounded bad. It's not like that ... hell, it doesn't matter. You're a dead man when she finds out." Rutger's eyes looked haunted. "And I won't save you from her."

"Not funny," Ansel shot back. He was a dead man anyway. "I didn't take anything away from her. Bronte is out there, she left this at my place. It was stuck to my new table with a dagger." Unfolding the photo, he handed it to Rutger, and saw light break through the blade-size cut.

Rutger looked at the photo for a second, then turned it over, and after reading the back lifted his eyes to Ansel. "She's sick. We'll have to step up our patrols. Her note proves she doesn't have any plans to leave Trinity. She has to be here." Rutger handed Ansel the photo like it might bite him. "Do you want to install cameras at your place?"

"Negative. If she does anything, she'll expose herself." He made cluster fuck out of his life.

"Who erased Doctor Hyde's memories?" He nailed Ansel with the narrowed gold gaze of his wolf, and waves of frustration.

"A vampire," Ansel answered, and prayed Rutger believed him.

"You know a vampire?" The gold paled as a ghost moved behind his eyes. Rutger had his own secrets.

"Affirmative. I've been alive a long time." Not a lie.

"What do you owe this vampire?" Rutger asked, his disbelief plain in his voice.

Nope, didn't believe him, but he was going to let Ansel have his lie. "A favor."

"Elaborate."

"Information about the pack. Some think the Highguard is using their authority to infiltrate factions and then align themselves with those they believe are powerful. The baron rules over a territory, an expanding territory, and has been open about Jordyn, and bringing back old traditions. The Highguard favors old traditions and power." Not a lie. He convinced himself he was giving Rutger a warning about the Fellowship. Ansel suspected the reason Griffin met with him was because he wanted information about Jordyn and the baron's relationship with the Highguard. It was also a low blow when Ansel was using Jordyn against Rutger.

Rutger sat back and considered him, the seconds turning into minutes. "The shadows have found spies. We can use your *vampire* to spread bad intel."

Ansel didn't like the emphasis on vampire or the confirmation there were spies. And what else wasn't Rutger telling him? "Affirmative."

CHAPTER TWENTY-NINE

Clio walked the hall, skirting enforcers and soldiers, her bag over her shoulder, and her thoughts focused on Captain Wolt. Why the hell did he get under skin? Because she couldn't have him. Same song, different day. Despite being reminded of his injuries and the fire, his voice and the way he said MD made her smile, one she quickly stopped. She didn't need Baron Kanin thinking she was incompetent, a lovesick puppy waiting for Captain Good Mood to give her a little attention. She should be taking pride in the fact she was ahead of schedule for the med room and that meant it was time to choose her staff. Approved staff.

"Hey, you weren't going to stop and say hi?" Mandy hollered.

Clio stopped, took a couple of steps backwards, and leaned into the communication center. She blew a breath out at the sight. Any military would be envious of the equipment. Then she saw Mandy behind a desk with three monitors and wearing a headset. "You look like something from a spy movie."

"I know, and it's not trendy." Mandy pushed a button, changing the screen. "Did you get the med room up and going?"

"Affirmative. Hopefully we never need it," Clio replied.

"Did you call Captain Wolt after I talked to you?" Mandy's

violet-tinted eyes held a level of humor.

Clio wanted to roll her eyes. "Negative." She didn't think so.

"Since he wasn't at work, did you go to his house?" The sliver of humor turned straight comical.

"Absolutely not. And if I had, it was to make sure he was all right," Clio said in defense.

"Sure, Doc." Mandy laughed. "No one is going to blame you for thinking he's hot. Poor choice of word, but you get it."

Yeah, she got it. "I don't think he's hot. He's the Captain of Enforcers." His bronze eyes. Lies. Lies. "Is Baron Kanin available? I have to talk to him." She had to get out of there. She didn't need anyone asking her about Captain Good Mood.

"One second." Mandy's fingers danced over the keyboard, and the corner of the left screen changed to messages. "Affirmative. He'll see you now."

Creepy. "Thanks."

"No problem," Mandy replied. "Clio, it's good to have you back."

"Thanks, it's good to be back."

Clio left Mandy in her command center, pushed through the double metal doors, walked into the reception area, then out of the office. She stopped and looked at Med Two parked in front, the silhouette of a fox head on its side, and smiled. Tony would be on every call. The baron gave her that. *The baron.* Clio hadn't finished everything on her list, and wasn't worried, she needed to talk to the baron about staff, and was glad she stopped early.

The sun sat high in the cloudless, cerulean sky while a chill held the air, promising fall was closing in. As she left the sidewalk and started toward the mansion, she slowed then stopped. The intense feeling she was being watched had her turning around, her breath caught, her heart hammered, and her lungs begged for her to breathe. Not only hot, but a damn presence.

Captain Wolt stood beside his truck, his hand on the butt of his gun, and his molten bronze stare locked on her, and it sent heat sweeping over her skin that pooled in her middle. His black T-shirt was tucked into dark jeans that hugged his hips and thighs and ended in black boots. She felt there was more than her physical response to him, which was embarrassing enough. There was something on a personal level. It sat inside of her, like she should remember but was out of reach. Damn amnesia. It was taking what it wanted, then teasing her with shreds of her memory.

Was it amnesia? She didn't remember calling Mandy, and it happened the day before. And she never would have gone over to Captain Wolt's house when she had already faced disciplinary action from disobeying a direct order from the baron. Still, it was like they had been together. Her dream came back to burn her cheeks, another round of déjà vu, only way worse. How many times had he let her get close then shut her out? Too damn many for her pride to admit to. Damn him. She wanted to scream at him. If he was going to be nice, then fine, but if he was going to keep her on the other side of the wall of ice, he needed to leave her the hell alone. Maybe that's exactly what she should do. With whatever it was sitting in her head like an itch she couldn't scratch, Clio hitched the strap of her bag on her shoulder and started in his direction. She was ending this.

Ansel would have jumped in his truck and burned most of the rubber off his tires driving away if he thought it would do any good. She was angry. No, pissed off. He could feel it coming off her in waves.

"Doctor Hyde," he greeted. *Act natural.*

"Captain Wolt. What are you doing?" she demanded. She had one hand on the strap of her bag, one on her hip, and her sapphire glare looked like it had been cut from ice.

"Standing beside my truck," he answered, stoking the fire. He needed to get away from her before he did something he regretted, like confess. "I work here." Lifting a file, he showed her.

Was he mocking her? She didn't care, nor did she care how he felt. "I'm sorry about bringing up your medical records, it was uncalled for and inappropriate. Having said that, do you have a problem with me?" Staring at him conjured images, feelings, and Clio lost her direction and had no idea what she was doing.

Always the professional. "Negative." Ansel scanned the parking lot for witnesses and didn't see anyone who stopped to watch. The others might suspect but no one would say anything to him. Like Rutger had.

"I doubt that," she mumbled.

"You're a valuable asset to the pack." To his life. She was his soul and made him think he could have a mate, a family, and a future. He needed to touch her, feel her against him, have her tucked in his arms. This was going to kill him.

Something in the way he was staring at her made her comfortable. *She's a glutton for punishment.* She watched a woman set him on fire, and for a moment he was a man. Not Captain of Enforcers, a man she would give her life to protect. The truth was not setting her free, but it did take the wind out of her sails. "I'm sorry." She needed to leave. "I'm always saying that to you. I'm glad you're back at work."

He was sorry. "You too, Doc." He watched her thoughts

battle for their place and her emotions sweep her into their chaos. Smart. Too damn smart.

Clio turned to walk away, her shoulders slumped, deciding a dysfunctional relationship—he was an enforcer, she was a doctor, they were going to see each other—was better than nothing. And she couldn't bring herself to tell him to go to hell. With her step, Mandy's words filtered through her mind, her memories like tumbling blocks fell into the fathoms of an abyss she couldn't see into.

He was going to think she was losing her mind. Clio faced him and asked, "Did I call you yesterday?" The confused expression on his face confirmed it, she was losing her mind.

"Negative. I would remember that," Ansel answered. She was trying to put the pieces together. Rutger's warning screamed in his head. She was going to hate him when she found out what he had done. He wasn't entirely sure what had been done.

"Did I go to your house?" she asked as her pride went up in flames.

"Negative." He was going to call Griffin. "You like the townhouse in the city, and I'm more of a cabin in the woods guy."

Swanky. Where had she heard that? She didn't know. Clio admitted she had a rough night, and this was the result. Hell, she cleared her house for the millionth time. It didn't stop the thread from teasing her with the shard of information sitting out of her reach. If she wasn't at Foxwood and about to see the baron, she would have roared in frustration.

"Sorry." Clio smiled—it felt fake and like the one Miss Langston always gave her—and leaving Captain Good Mood with his truck, started back toward the mansion.

"Fate damned us, my Tesoro," he whispered to her back. Ansel watched his mate walk away from him with hurt and confusion riddling her. The pain he felt for doing this to her was going to destroy him.

Don't push it, she told herself. Dr. Carrion had warned her battling the missing pieces was going to make it worse, and it would frustrate her, and slow the natural progression. Clio met the border of asphalt and grass, the shift from Enforcer territory to the baron's house, and stopped. In slow motion she saw the pieces trying to fit together, the mass putting her in her car. She had called him, and heard his voice. Swanky. It was him.

Making a slow turn, she faced him and closed the distance. No one else needed to hear her make a fool of herself. "Captain Good Mood."

What did she call me? "What?" He met her azure and honey gaze holding a challenge he desperately wanted to accept.

"Captain Good Mood. Do you think my place is swanky?" she asked.

That was not a term of endearment. Ansel swallowed the lump in his throat to answer. "It could be I guess."

He was going to call the psych ward on her. Maybe it wasn't him. Had it been Tony? She was confusing two men, she should slap herself. She had one more question, and if he didn't know ... "What does Tesoro mean?" *Dig yourself a deeper hole*, she thought as her narrowed gaze softened with her doubt.

Ansel stopped breathing. He was going to kill Griffin. "Never heard it before. It is English?" He hated himself. He was punishing her for his wrongs.

She was losing it. Blame the amnesia. Was this the result of her carefully crafted world coming unraveled? She needed to embrace change and stop trying to fit what her life had been into the present. Shaking her head, she met his worried, no fearful gaze and smiled. "I'm sorry. It could be the amnesia or the fact I had a rough night. Not that you need to know that. I'll leave you be." She couldn't believe she told him.

Humiliation dressed her in its shroud of shame as she, for the third time, left Captain Good Mood—she couldn't believe she called him that—by his truck. Clio needed to accept defeat that her battle against his wall of ice failed and burned to ash. He wasn't going to pay attention to a woman who was clearly losing her mind and falling apart. Clutching the strap of her bag, she gathered what pride she had left and prepared to face Baron Kanin. She had a witch to hire.

Ansel wished he had amnesia to take the guilt of doing this to her and making her think she was confused and had lost her memories. He felt her confidence weaken as she walked away from him, heard his wolf howl in pain, felt his heart dying, and was going to call Griffin. He knew he made the situation worse, but it had been a close call, and it couldn't be repeated. He hated himself.

When she entered the house and his hands had stopped shaking, he opened the file Blix had given him on the property where Bronte had stalked Elder Macario and then shot Daniel. He knew magic-born owned the land, he felt its presence, and figured since it sat across from the elder, the info might come in handy in the future. Taking the first page, he began reading about the current owner, saw the sanctions to keep the land from being developed, then flipping to the second page looked at the company name and logo. His blood pressure dropped, and he was sure his body turned into a sieve and he was bleeding out.

Griffin Enterprises.

The embossed griffin could belong to anyone, but he

doubted it. Ansel believed Griffin answered his call because he wanted him in the Fellowship and wanted intel on Cascade. What if it was about Bronte? He knew. He knew she had been there. The entire Fellowship had. Had she been part of their plan? Did they use her to get to him? Ansel gazed at the office, the house, but didn't see any of it, as his thoughts raced with almost losing the pack, his kith and kin, and feeling betrayed. Tricked. Was the Fellowship hiding her? He was going to find out. Closing the file, he looked at the house where he could walk inside and touch her, Clio, his mate, and was denied.

"I'm taking back what's mine," Ansel swore.

THE END